The Little
Orchard on
the Lane

BOOKS BY TILLY TENNANT

The Summer of Secrets
The Summer Getaway
The Christmas Wish
The Mill on Magnolia Lane
Hattie's Home for Broken Hearts
The Garden on Sparrow Street
The Break Up
The Waffle House on the Pier
Worth Waiting For
Cathy's Christmas Kitchen
Once Upon a Winter
The Summer of Second Chances
The Time of My Life

AN UNFORGETTABLE CHRISTMAS SERIES
A Very Vintage Christmas
A Cosy Candlelit Christmas

FROM ITALY WITH LOVE SERIES
Rome Is Where the Heart Is
A Wedding in Italy

HONEYBOURNE SERIES
The Little Village Bakery
Christmas at the Little Village Bakery

TILLY TENNANT

The Little Orchard on the Lane

Bookouture

Published by Bookouture in 2021

An imprint of Storyfire Ltd.
Carmelite House
50 Victoria Embankment
London EC4Y 0DZ

www.bookouture.com

ISBN: 978-1-80019-344-4
eBook ISBN: 978-1-80019-343-7

To Kath, thank you for the walks

Chapter One

The rendering of Oleander House glowed cream in the afternoon sun. Posy counted four high sash windows across the top floor and three across the bottom, framing an entrance porch hugged by rambling honeysuckle. There were also two windows sitting in the roof that must have shone light into attic rooms. Posy had spent the last two weeks dreaming of what this impossibly romantic-sounding place might look like in real life. She'd spent hours poring over their website, but seeing it in photos was hardly the same. It was like looking at the moon in the reflection of a street puddle – you knew it was beautiful, but you got only the diluted emotional effect.

Oleander House was bigger than it had looked in the photos too. Much, much bigger. In fact, Posy had never seen a house with so much space that hadn't belonged to a Russian oligarch or Saudi prince. But then, she had spent her life living in London and you needed a lot of money to buy space in London. Her family weren't poor by any standards, but they certainly weren't rich enough to buy a place like this where they lived.

She took a breath in. The air was heavy with the scent of the giant rhododendrons that bordered the gleaming gravel path to the house, boughs laden with purple and fuchsia blooms. She couldn't remember ever smelling anything so sweet and intoxicating. She must have, of course, because it wasn't like flowers didn't grow in London, but she couldn't remember it right now at all.

An immense, iridescent dragonfly crossed her vision, sapphire and emerald scales glinting in the sun – its presence must mean there was water close by, though Posy couldn't see it. Perhaps the grounds of Oleander House had a pond, or even a lake. She hadn't seen that on the official website but perhaps that was private, just for the family. The thought was exciting, but the idea of such grandeur was also a little daunting.

They'd parked some metres away, on the road, leaving the car out of sight of the house. Somehow, even though they'd been invited, to be here felt like trespassing. And Posy, hard though it was for her to admit, secretly wanted some kind of get-out clause. If the occupants of the house didn't see them arrive, they could always make a quick getaway if her courage failed her.

She turned to her mum now, who had a hand to her forehead, shielding her eyes against the sun as she gazed up at the house too, the same look of wonder and trepidation on her face.

'This is definitely the right place?'

Carmel – Posy's mum – nodded uncertainly. 'I followed the directions to the letter. But it's…'

'Massive!' Posy breathed. 'They must be loaded!'

'I don't know about that. We're judging prices here by London standards. It might be a lot more affordable to have a house of this size in Somerset.'

'Even so, it's a fair pad and not too shabby a location either. It must have cost more than your average house.'

Nerves showed through the thin veneer of Posy's laughter. The only way she could deal with this was to make light of it, but the fact remained that she was about to meet her blood relatives for the first time – two uncles who, until very recently, had been blissfully unaware of her existence, as she had been theirs.

Their relationship would doubtless prove to be complicated too. From what Posy had managed to glean, her biological mother, Angelica, had done something dreadful that had led to her leaving their family home – Oleander House – as a young woman and cutting herself off from them for many years. She'd later died, but not before she'd given birth to Posy and in the same breath given her up for adoption.

Angelica's brothers – Giles and Asa, both younger than her – hadn't been in contact with her and hadn't even known she'd had a baby. The only person who had known was Philomena – their mother and Posy's biological grandmother – who had since died from cancer but had left the bombshell secret she'd kept for the past twenty-odd years to be revealed in her will.

It was like something out of a midweek TV drama, and Posy could scarcely believe this melodrama was her beginning. The life she'd been given with her adopted parents, Carmel and Anthony, was so ordinary and secure, so far removed from such tidal waves of upheaval, that it felt as if all that was someone else's origin story, not hers.

She'd asked herself many times since the start of the year, when she'd first been contacted by a solicitor, how she felt about it all, whether there was any sadness for a mother who had been marked by such tragedy, for a grandmother who had seemingly done very little to help her, keeping Posy's existence a secret from everyone else. Eventually she'd had to conclude that because it all felt so utterly removed, and as if it was happening to someone else, there was no sadness, only curiosity, a thirst to discover the truth of who she really was.

Carmel had told her that was a good, sensible attitude to have, and that she ought to keep her guard up because she honestly wondered if this new family would prove to be a little toxic, and Posy had been forced to agree on that point.

For a start there was her grandmother, Philomena. Regardless of what had gone on before, what kind of woman refused to help a daughter in need, and what kind of woman kept a granddaughter secret, never acknowledging her to another soul until her dying day? Who had she thought to protect – Posy? The family reputation?

Posy was bursting with questions – who else might have known, did anyone suspect, why hadn't anyone ever gone in search of Angelica after she'd left, why had Angelica given Posy up? Would her new uncles, Giles and Asa, have any answers? Even if they did, would they want to give them? And if their mother, Philomena, was as hideous as Posy imagined she must have been, would they be just as bad? Would Posy regret making this trip to meet them in just a few short minutes?

At least, she mused as she took in the view, she'd got a nice weekend away out of it all. If the house was breath-taking, the backdrop was even more so: a patchwork of fields, greens, golds, yellow and lavender, stretching for miles to frame the house with vibrant colour.

'It is gorgeous,' Carmel agreed. 'You could get used to a view like this.'

Posy shook herself. 'Just because they've invited us to talk about the will, it doesn't mean Giles and Asa want us as a permanent fixture in their lives.'

'It seems like a friendly enough invitation though. They didn't have to reach out personally; they could have done all this through solicitors and never had to meet you. They could have chosen not to contact you at all, but they did.'

Posy nodded, her eyes still fixed on the house. 'I suppose that makes them good people at least,' she said, doubting her words even as she uttered them. 'Nice people… But it still doesn't mean we'll ever see them again after today.'

'You underestimate how easily people fall in love with you.' Carmel smiled and looped her hand around the crook of Posy's arm, pulling her close. 'So… on a scale of one to ten, how nervous are you right now?'

'Twelve. I'd swear like a trooper if it was anyone but you standing next to me right now.'

Carmel laughed. 'Feel free to let rip if it makes you feel better.'

Posy gave a quick grin that instantly faded. 'I feel sick – absolutely horrendous now that I'm here.'

Carmel slid her hand down her daughter's arm to take her hand and give it a squeeze. 'I know it's your big deal and not mine, but I feel a bit sick too. It's a scary moment.'

'You're perfectly entitled to feel scared too. It's a whole new family for both of us – of course you're nervous; I wouldn't expect anything else.'

'Nervous for you more than me. I couldn't bear it if they were horrible to you.'

'They won't be,' Posy said, though she didn't sound certain of that at all.

'Posy…' Carmel began slowly, 'we don't have to go in. Nobody would blame you if you turned around right now and we never came back. We could go back to life as it was, forget all this and nothing would have to change… I can only imagine what it took for you to even come this far.'

Posy let out a long sigh, turning her gaze back to the house. 'I wish Dad could have come with us.'

'I'm sure he would have done if he could.'

'I know. It's silly to need him – I'm a grown woman and it's not as if I'm not used to having to do things without him; he is, after all, away from home more than he's there. You'd think I'd be more than capable of talking to some people for the first time.'

'Not *some* people,' Carmel reminded her. '*Family*. Family you've never met and who didn't even know you existed until a few weeks ago.'

'I suppose it's going to be strange for them too,' Posy replied thoughtfully. 'I just hope they don't see me as a threat.'

'Nobody could see you like that.'

'But they don't know me from Adam—'

'True. But you've decided not to take anything from the estate and so I don't see what other kind of threat you could pose.'

Posy had said from the start she was going to tell Giles and Asa that she didn't want anything from Philomena's estate, which had apparently stipulated that she ought to receive a sum equivalent to what would have been Angelica's share, had she been alive. But it was a lot of money and would they take her statement at face value?

To Posy it felt like cursed money. Taking it might make her enemies where she wanted friends – it would certainly cause resentment and bad feeling and risk breaking up a family she'd only just discovered she had. She only wanted to meet them (and at times had admitted to Carmel that she didn't understand fully why it mattered that she did), but would they believe that either? Would they trust there was no other agenda?

There had been a brief discussion on the phone with Giles – older than his brother Asa by six years – and he had seemed friendly and welcoming, but it was hard to tell from a quick phone call what he really thought about any of it.

Judging by the size of the house in front of them, Giles and Asa had a lot to lose if Posy did decide to pursue a share in the estate. There was the house, but there was also a sizeable parcel of land containing orchards, sheds for commercially produced cider, outbuildings and gardens as well. If the tables had been turned, would Posy and Carmel trust two strangers who could easily walk off with a chunk of their livelihood?

Posy glanced at her mother and her other frequent and nagging doubt occurred to her again – would today's meeting change things between them too?

That was a question much harder to answer.

Chapter Two

As Posy and Carmel arrived at the gates, three people – two men and a woman – were already walking down the path to greet them. Clearly the occupants of Oleander House had been anticipating the meeting as keenly as they had.

There was an obvious family resemblance between the two men. Posy assumed this was Giles and Asa, though she was disappointed that she didn't recognise much in either man's features that was like what she saw so often in the mirror. Perhaps she looked a lot more like her unknown father than she did her mother. She didn't know who the woman was, but she did know that Giles was married to a woman named Sandra while Asa was single. So was this lady Sandra?

Posy's heart was thumping in her chest so hard she thought it would burst free. If she felt like this, God only knew how her poor mum was feeling. Carmel would be plagued by her own fears, and Posy had to admire her guts for coming here at all. Posy had reassured her adopted mum that she'd always be the most important person in her life, and Carmel had taken that in good faith, but she wouldn't have been human if she didn't have doubts.

She glanced across to see Carmel wearing a frozen smile, fixed in place not by pleasure but by fear. Posy wanted to make a good impression, but it was hard to make charming, easy small talk when you felt like you could hurl yourself inside out.

The trio approaching them now looked far more relaxed and were all wearing smiles (which was a promising start), but then, perhaps it was natural that they would be more relaxed. This was, after all, their turf, and – as far as Posy could see – they held all the aces.

The men were both tallish – around five ten, five eleven – with mid-brown hair. One was thinning a little at the temples. The younger-looking brother – Posy guessed this was Asa – was stylishly dressed in dark denim and a fitted dove-grey sweater, while the older had on baggy corduroy trousers a little worn at the knees and a well-loved flannelette shirt. The woman reached for the hand of the older man, a gesture that seemed so natural and unconscious that she probably didn't even realise she'd done it. She was a bit on the tall side too – certainly a few feet taller than Posy and her mum – her blonde hair cut into shoulder-length layers, with dark roots just poking through to suggest that she wasn't a natural blonde and didn't make root touch-ups a priority. She had on a full-length denim skirt and a sleeveless cotton shirt. She was hardly skinny, but she looked toned and fit.

It was the woman who spoke first. She opened the gate and looked at Posy with a warm smile.

'Posy?'

'Yes.' She put her hand out.

'Oh, nonsense!' the woman said. Instead of shaking her hand, she pulled Posy closer and kissed her lightly on both cheeks. She then turned to Posy's mum and welcomed her in the same way. 'So you must be Carmel? We've been looking out for you. Did you find us easily enough?'

'Yes…' Carmel said, though she looked vaguely shell-shocked, as if she might well have said yes to anything at this point.

'The directions were brilliant,' Posy said.

'I'm Sandra. Married to Giles – for my sins.'

One of the brothers stepped forward and offered his hand, rather than the less formal cheek-kiss they'd had from Sandra.

'I'm Giles,' he said, shaking with Posy and Carmel in turn. 'And this is my brother, Asa.'

Asa also offered his hand to shake. Posy noted that his grip was a lot less certain than that of Giles.

'Pleased to meet you,' Posy said. Asa gave a brisk nod in return.

Posy studied both men, trying to read them. While Sandra was very open, the two brothers were less so. They were friendly enough on the surface, but something about them suggested they were scrutinising Posy and Carmel as much as Posy was scrutinising them now. It was hardly surprising, she had to conclude, given the circumstances of this meeting. It wasn't every day you discovered you had family that, up until a few weeks ago, you had no clue existed.

'How was the traffic?' Giles asked.

'Once we left the motorway not bad at all,' Carmel said.

'Good…' He plunged his hands into his pockets and nodded slowly, as if giving the information as much thought as he might had he just been presented with the secret to the meaning of life. 'Good…' he repeated.

'You must be parched,' Sandra said. 'I put the kettle on as soon as Giles saw you approaching; I should imagine it's boiled by now. You drink tea? Or would you prefer coffee? I can do a cold drink if you'd prefer of course…'

'Tea would be lovely,' Carmel said. She glanced uncertainly at Posy, who wondered if her mum was thinking of making a run for it. Posy wouldn't have blamed her at all – the thought had crossed her mind too. Perhaps it would be less awkward once they settled down to tea.

'So…' Sandra placed a tray on the mosaic-tiled table that graced the broad patio. The space was shaded by a wide trellis with what looked like some kind of vine woven into it, paved with dark slates and furnished with the table and chairs, a swinging seat and two rattan armchairs. She poured tea from a fine bone china pot into matching cups and saucers. Like everything they'd seen of Oleander House so far, they looked old but well loved and very traditional, decorated in a classic blue and white willow pattern.

Posy, Carmel, Giles and Asa sat around the table after Sandra insisted she could manage the tea-making by herself and that the brothers needed to be with Posy because they had so much to talk about.

Sandra cut in as their polite chat grew silent. 'Who'd like a slice of cake with their tea? We've got apple sponge – made with apples grown here, of course.'

'Not from the orchard, though,' Giles added. 'We use a different kind of apples for our cider-making. We have a couple of trees in the garden for cooking apples.'

'I'd love one,' Posy said. She couldn't remember the last time she'd eaten home-made cake. Carmel was no baker and neither was she. In fact, she didn't know anyone who had time for baking, let alone the inclination. It was yet another way that life here in Somerset seemed impossibly romantic compared to her own in London, like she'd just stepped into the pages of an H.E Bates novel. She half expected Ma Larkin to appear from inside the house with a towering tray of scones and clotted cream she'd made from milk produced from a cow only hours earlier.

Sandra poured the tea while Giles cut slices from a generously layered sponge decorated with white icing. He handed one to Posy who wasted no time sinking her fork into it.

'My God!' she exclaimed as the tanginess of the apple chunks hit first, followed by a balancing hint of vanilla and sugary icing. 'That's divine!'

Carmel took a mouthful of her slice and nodded enthusiastic agreement. 'You're a baking genius,' she said warmly.

'Actually, Giles baked it,' Sandra said mildly.

Posy smiled at him. 'Wow!'

'I know I don't look like much of a baker,' he replied, almost apologetically.

'What's a baker supposed to look like?' Sandra asked as she settled with her own plate.

'Big poofy hat and a white tunic,' Posy said, instantly wondering whether she'd misjudged the joke and wishing she hadn't made it.

'Oh, he saves those for his private time,' Asa said in such a deadpan tone that it took Posy a full second to realise he was joking too.

'That's true,' Sandra said. 'I can't get him out of that poofy hat. Morning, noon and night – he'd wear it to bed if lying down didn't flatten it.'

Carmel laughed lightly. Posy had heard that laugh many times before – it was reserved and polite and meant she still didn't know these people well enough to show them what her real laughter was like. But it was still warm, as was Sandra's answering smile. Carmel and Posy didn't know them yet, but Giles, Sandra and Asa seemed easy to get along with, free of airs and graces, and it gave Posy real hope that she would be able to build a meaningful relationship with her new-found family.

Posy had been raised as the only child of two only children, and their family group had been tight-knit but necessarily small. Growing up, she'd always envied friends with big, noisy, chaotic homes full of siblings or other extended family. Her own had always seemed far too quiet and dull in comparison, even though Carmel did her best to make life for Posy as interesting as she could and had always explained that only adopting her had been a financial decision – with one child they could comfortably give her what she needed without worrying about money. Having discovered Giles, Asa and Sandra certainly expanded Posy's family exponentially.

Now that Posy thought of it, Giles and Sandra hadn't mentioned having any children and neither had Asa. Did that mean there were none? Was that why they seemed unduly relaxed about their farm – because they had no kids to pass it to? Most people introducing themselves as long-lost family would mention children as part of that deal fairly early on, and now that Posy thought about it, she hadn't seen any signs of children around the place – no discarded toys or textbooks, no brightly coloured trainers kicked into a corner or photos and school certificates on the fridge.

Sandra topped up Posy's cup. 'Why don't you tell us a little about yourself.'

'There's not much to tell,' Posy said, lifting the freshly filled teacup to her lips. 'Not much that's very exciting anyway.'

'There must be something. Surely living in London is very exciting all the time?'

Posy gave a light laugh, a little like the one Carmel had given only a few moments before. 'Well, there's always plenty going on, but when you've grown up there you sort of take it all for granted. I suppose that's a shame, isn't it? I mean, I do appreciate that there's lots to do but sometimes I wish a little bit that it could be quieter.'

'Well, there's plenty of quiet here,' Asa said. 'So much that I often wish for some disaster just to liven things up.'

Posy's smile slipped and she looked to see if Sandra and Giles were shocked at Asa's statement, but they both remained serene. Perhaps it was the sort of thing he said a lot but didn't mean. For Posy, not knowing him meant it was hard to know how to take him.

'So you must be… twenty-seven now?' Giles asked.

Sandra laughed. 'You know you don't ask a lady that! Have I managed to teach you nothing in all our years of marriage?'

'Oh, I'm sure Posy's young enough not to care about questions like that yet,' Giles replied breezily, reaching for his cup.

'I don't mind,' Posy said. 'Yes, I'm twenty-seven. Only just – couple of weeks ago.'

'Oh, happy belated birthday,' Sandra said.

'Posy's an interior designer,' Carmel said with a fond glance at her daughter. 'A very good one too.'

'Oh, you have to say that.' Posy smiled at her mum. 'I wish my boss at the agency could be as enthusiastic about my work as you are.' She looked at Giles again. 'I don't have my own consultancy or anything yet. I'm really still finding my feet in the industry. I work for a design agency. We do a lot of commercial interiors. I'd like to have my own business one day, of course. I'd love to design private homes and things like that rather than corporate places.'

'That sounds very exciting.' Sandra looked at Asa. 'You said you wanted to redesign your place, didn't you? Looks like we've found your woman.'

'As long as you're cheap,' Asa said to Posy. 'We're hardly made of money around here.'

It was yet another statement Posy just didn't know how to take. Was he warning her that if she and Carmel were after a fast buck they wouldn't find it at Oleander House?

'I could always take a look,' she said, choosing not to take offence. 'I'd be happy to make some suggestions and I wouldn't expect you to pay for that.'

'That would be very kind,' Sandra said. 'Wouldn't it, Asa?'

'Very kind,' Asa repeated before hiding his face behind his teacup as he took a sip. Out of the three of them, Asa gave Posy the most cause for wariness because it was becoming clear that he was the one who trusted her least. That wasn't to say he wasn't trying as hard as Giles and Sandra were – Posy believed that he was – but maybe for him a natural instinct to trust was just that bit harder to find.

'Do you all work in the family business?' Carmel asked.

'Yes,' Giles said. 'We employ some people too. I expect you'll meet a few of them if you come back on a weekday.'

Carmel exchanged a brief glance with Posy. They might well have been thinking the same thing – Giles mentioning them returning here was a good sign that he at least wanted them to.

'Are you planning to drive all the way back to London today?' Sandra asked Carmel. 'It's such a long way.'

Carmel shook her head. 'We've booked a room at a little guest house. We'll leave tomorrow – we thought we might as well use the opportunity of coming here to explore the countryside. After all, it seems a shame to come all this way and not see any of it.'

'That sounds lovely. Is your guest house close?'

'I think so. At least, it looked close on the map. Sunnyfields? Do you know it?'

'Oh, yes, that's Karen's place. Not too far at all. She'll treat you like royalty – you'll have a lovely stay there.'

'She does have very good reviews online,' Carmel agreed. 'Now I know it's nice I'm beginning to wish we'd booked for longer.'

'Well,' Sandra said, smiling, 'you can always come back. Somerset is beautiful at any time of the year.'

Giles very deliberately set down his cup and saucer and looked around the table. His expression had hardened, barely perceptibly, but to Posy it looked as if they were finally going to get down to the real business. Because while the meeting had been pleasant so far, everyone knew that the reason Posy and Carmel had come to Oleander House was to address something a little more thorny than whether the guest house they'd chosen to stay in that night was nice or not.

'Perhaps we ought to tackle that great big elephant we've been trying so hard to ignore. Not that the conversation hasn't been delightful of course, but I think now's the time to be serious for a moment.'

'I don't want anything from you,' Posy said firmly. 'I haven't changed my mind on that. I know Philomena left instructions that I ought to be provided for, but I really don't need it and I don't feel it's due to me.'

Asa looked faintly disbelieving while Giles and Sandra maintained expressions of calm neutrality.

'I don't feel I'm owed anything and I don't want it,' Posy insisted. 'I only wanted to meet you because… I can't explain it; not really. I just needed answers, I suppose.'

'We wanted to meet you too,' Sandra said. 'But surely—'

Posy gave her head a firm shake. 'I don't want anything else.' She glanced at Carmel, who gave a nod of encouragement. 'I'm already happy enough with my lot, and even though everyone could do with a little more cash I don't want to get it like this – it doesn't feel right.'

Sandra gave a slight smile. 'You've obviously given this a lot of thought.'

'I've thought of little else but meeting you since I first found out about you,' Posy said. 'But it took two seconds to decide that I'd rather have more family than money. I don't want to be the cause of a rift before we've even begun, and if you having to give me a share of my grandmother's estate means it affects your home and your business by making you sell bits off then…' She shrugged, uncertain how to finish her sentence but hoping they would understand.

'A lot of people would feel they owed us no loyalty,' Giles said. 'In fact, many would feel just the opposite. And Mother said—'

'I know all that,' Posy replied. 'It makes no difference to my decision. I'm not going to change my mind either, in case that's something you're worrying about.'

Sandra glanced at Giles, sombre and silent for a moment, and then they both looked at Asa, who was just as serious.

'Well,' Asa said finally. 'I think it's safe to say you've thrown us a curveball. We were expecting some kind of fight – at least a heated negotiation. Instead, we find ourselves practically begging you to take some of our inheritance.'

'I said all along I wasn't going to do that,' Posy reiterated.

'I can't say I'm not a little bit disappointed actually,' Asa replied. 'I was quite looking forward to a *Dynasty*-type showdown.'

'It's very noble and generous of you,' Sandra said. 'What Asa means to say is that we were all a little bit worried, despite what you'd told the solicitor. This place is our life – Giles and Asa especially have never known anything else. The orchard is in their blood… the thought of having to sell bits off or break up the property in any way to pay someone a portion of the estate was scary. And Philomena left no actual cash; everything is tied up in this place.'

She paused for a moment, exchanged a brief look with Giles, and then turned to Posy again. 'If it's not too delicate a question, would you be prepared to sign something to that effect? Not that I doubt your intentions for one second, it's just…'

Her sentence tailed off, but if she'd been afraid of offending Posy she needn't have been.

'I'd be asking the same thing,' she replied. 'I wouldn't be able to relax for a moment with something like that hanging over me. I could easily be the sort of person who changes their mind like the weather.'

'Thank you for being so understanding,' Giles said. 'You have no idea just how much of a relief something like that would be to us. I wish we could somehow return the favour, but I feel there's no way that would ever be possible.'

'Inviting me here is enough,' Posy said.

'If you'd like…' he began tentatively, continuing after a brief smile of encouragement from Sandra, 'perhaps we can fill in some blanks for you. It wouldn't be much, I know, but perhaps there are things you'd like to know about your mother? I'm not sure what you do already know, but—'

'Why did she give me up?' Posy asked, hardly missing a beat.

'Ah...'

Giles looked uneasily at Asa now before turning back to Posy.

'That's one question we don't have the answer to,' Asa said.

Giles nodded. 'We only found out a couple of weeks before you did that Angelica had even had a child of her own. Apparently our mother had known for some time and also knew that you'd been given up for adoption, but she'd never made us aware and forbade us to ask.'

'She could be strange like that,' Sandra said. 'She often didn't share her reasons for keeping things to herself either.'

'So,' Giles continued, 'Mum had already passed by the time we learned of you, and even though she'd left details of your existence for the solicitor to pass on to us, she'd never actually spoken about you while she was alive... I'm so sorry; I know that's not what you wanted to hear...'

Giles looked genuinely pained to deliver such crushing news, and in that moment Posy felt desperately sorry for him.

'Why did Philomena and Angelica fall out so badly?' Posy asked. 'I can't imagine what would make me stop all contact with my family – it must have been bad.'

'Mother always blamed her for Father's death,' Asa said. 'They just couldn't get past it.'

'Was it her fault?' Posy asked, wide-eyed.

'I suppose you could say the events that led to it were her fault,' Giles said.

Posy waited for him to elaborate, but he didn't. Then Asa spoke.

'You can't tell her that and not expect her to need detail, Giles.'

Giles paused, and then nodded.

'Angelica was having an affair with someone in the village – she'd always been a little wayward like that. The guy was twice her age and should have known better. She asked him to leave his wife; he wouldn't. Things got messy when the wife found out and came to have it out with her. Dad – your grandfather – stepped in to break them up. In the fracas he fell backward and hit his head…'

Posy stared at him as a strange, loaded silence settled over them.

'He never woke up,' Sandra said briskly.

'Was I…' Posy's mouth was dry. 'Was I… you know… from the affair?'

Sandra gave a brief nod. 'We think so – at least the timing would suggest so. But as you were born after she'd cut ties with everyone here at Oleander it's only guesswork.'

'Who is he?' Posy asked.

Giles glanced uneasily at Sandra.

'You mean your father?' Sandra asked Posy, who nodded.

'If we're right, then it's a man named John Palmer. We don't think he knew about you either. He and his wife left the village shortly after Angelica, and we heard, I'm sorry to tell you, that he died about five years ago.'

'Oh…' Posy said faintly. What was she supposed to make of that? She'd got more answers today than she could have hoped for, but they'd only created more questions. 'What was he like?'

'We, um… we didn't really have much to do with him after Angelica left,' Giles said. 'As you can imagine it was a little bit awkward.'

'He means John and his wife avoided us like the plague,' Asa cut in. 'Hardly surprising really, given the circumstances.'

Posy held back a frown. 'But you must know a little about him.'

Sandra gave a slight shrug. 'I married Giles long after this had all happened...' she turned to him. 'You were only sixteen at the time, weren't you, darling?'

Giles nodded. 'I was really too young to take much notice before all the trouble, but from what I remember he was always pleasant and polite whenever we bumped into him... that was before Angelica and he...'

His sentence tailed off but Posy didn't need the rest to know what he meant. 'What did he do? Did he farm?'

'Oh, no,' Giles said. 'Commuted for work. I think he was an investment banker or pension-fund manager or something.'

Posy was silent for a moment as she absorbed this new information. 'Why didn't Angelica stay in touch with anyone here?'

'She and Mother couldn't get past what happened with Father. I suspect Angelica must have felt we blamed her for it too – Asa and I – but we didn't. She just left one day and fell off the face of the earth. I'd heard of her popping up here and there. I think there were some mental health issues, or maybe falling in with the wrong people, and I even tried to contact her a few times, but she never seemed to stay in one place long enough to be found.'

Posy wasn't sure they were telling her the whole story and she vowed to get more when she knew them better. 'What do you think people will make of me if they learn who my parents are?'

'Don't worry – I don't think you'll be judged for it,' Giles said.

'There'll be curiosity for sure,' Asa put in. 'But if it makes you feel easier we can keep it all low profile and it might stop folks asking questions.'

'I suppose it's more or less what I expected,' Posy said. 'I had hoped I might find out more about my biological dad...'

'Is there anything else?' Sandra asked gently. 'We could tell you other things… what Angelica was like…'

'That would be nice,' Posy began slowly, 'but if you don't mind perhaps we'll save those stories for another time. It's not that I don't want to know; it's just—'

'I quite understand,' Sandra cut in with a pained smile. 'I'm sure I'd feel the same way in your position. I imagine it's going to take some time to get used to all this.'

'I never even knew her name until a few weeks ago,' Posy said.

Sandra looked desperate to scoop her up and hug her, but instead, she reached for the teapot to top up Carmel's cup.

Silence enveloped the table again. Nobody knew what to say next and it was only the sound of a jaunty ringtone that saved them from a very long and awkward pause.

Asa pulled his phone from a pocket and frowned at it. The action prompted a silent question from Giles, but Asa simply shook his head and rejected the call before stowing the phone back in his pocket.

Though Posy was intrigued – clearly something significant had happened – it was hardly the time or place to give it any more thought, and as Asa quickly dismissed the incident, it was evidently something he was hoping would pass without too much notice. Besides, they had more important issues to address right now, though it was proving hard to tackle them.

'Will you stay for dinner?' Sandra said into the silence. She gave what was obviously a forced smile to Carmel and Posy. Posy looked at her mum.

'Oh, we couldn't…' she began, wondering whether Carmel was feeling a little threatened right now. Maybe it was best they had time together alone to process what had happened here and what it meant for them as mother and daughter.

'It wouldn't be a bit of bother,' Sandra said. 'I always make too much and it would be lovely to get to know you a bit better. I'm sure there's lots to talk about.'

'It's very kind of you,' Carmel said with a small smile, 'but we're tired and I think it would be better to head to our guest house before it gets too late.'

'You could always stay here if it gets too late to go on,' Sandra insisted. 'Couldn't they, Giles?'

Her husband looked less certain about this suggestion but he nodded anyway.

'We'd be an imposition,' Carmel said firmly.

'Perhaps next time?' Posy added, stepping in to support her mum. 'I'm honestly exhausted and I'd be terrible company.'

'Then at least pop back to see us before you leave for London tomorrow.' Sandra poured some more tea into Posy's cup now, even though Posy still had half a cup left.

Posy looked at Carmel. She felt it might be a good idea for them to do that – if nothing else a good night's sleep might make them fresher and less emotional.

'We'd like that,' Posy said finally, glancing at Carmel who nodded encouragement.

'Wonderful!' Sandra said. 'For now, why don't we have another slice of cake?'

Chapter Three

Sunnyfields Guest House wasn't hard to find, and the fact it was only a few minutes away by car meant it probably wasn't much of a walk for anyone who chose to wander up to the orchard from there. Posy thought she might suggest it to her mum when they went back to Oleander House again, as they'd agreed to, the following day before they started back for London. They could pack the car up and perhaps the landlady, Karen, wouldn't mind them leaving it there for a while after they'd checked out of their room. Judging by the car park as they pulled in now, it looked as if she had the space.

'Oh, this is lovely!' Carmel gazed up at the exterior of the building with a broad smile as they got out of the car.

'It's certainly in keeping with everything else around here,' Posy replied. 'I feel as if we've wandered into a fairy-tale land; everything is just so quaint and adorable.'

They stood side by side to take in the view for a moment. The exterior of the building was similar to that of Oleander House, only a little smaller – but it was built from the same buff stone with a smart slate roof. In addition there were original sash windows dressed in soft floral drapes, vibrant pink clematis garlanding the entrance, neat green lawns that stretched the width of the house dotted with flower beds and the odd garden statue. Along to the left of the garden was an old iron street lamp and next to that a gleaming red telephone box, no longer home to a public telephone but stuffed with books. The sun was working its way down the sky as the afternoon aged, and in the rose-gold light, clouds of gnats played over the grass.

The front door opened and a woman came out. She was perhaps around Carmel's age, hair piled up on her head, fastened in place with a crocodile clip, long, full white dress swooshing around her, the odd flash of gold from some very blingy sandals visible as she walked. She had a ring for every finger and three or four gold chains around her neck.

'Hello there!' she called as she hastened towards them. 'Are you here for a reservation?'

'Yes… Dashwood?'

The woman stuck out her hand for Carmel to shake, and then did the same for Posy.

'Smashing. I'm Karen. I saw your car pull in and I wondered if it might be you. I've just this minute finished getting your room ready. Do you have much luggage? I've got a trolley inside if you need it.'

'Don't worry, we travel light,' Carmel said. 'We should manage perfectly well.'

'Wonderful. Well, when you're ready I'll be waiting inside at the reception desk with your paperwork.'

With a bright smile and a flurry of white cotton she turned and hurried back to the house.

'She seems nice,' Posy said as Karen disappeared inside.

'She does. And the hotel looks delightful too. If it's as pretty on the inside as it is on the outside I'll be very happy.'

*

'This is you…' Karen opened the door to reveal a room with a large window dressed in the sumptuous floral drapes they'd seen from outside. The curtains were a heavy plum silk, pulled wide to let in maximum light, and a window seat was built into the space below, upholstered in the same fabric, cushions scattered over it in complementary colours. The wallpaper was shades of pink in a swirling oriental flower motif, the floor dressed in Eastern rugs and fringed lamps atop mirrored furniture. It might have been too much, but it managed to stay just on the right side of cosy and bohemian and seemed to reflect what they'd seen so far of Karen perfectly.

Posy would have been ostracised by her boss for producing a design like this for any of their clients, but, on a personal level, she was already in love with the place. It felt like somewhere that didn't care who you were or what you did, only that you were happy and comfortable and completely yourself. She glanced at Carmel – who had made the booking and so must have already seen the hotel on the website – and could see that she wasn't a bit disappointed. This was exactly the sort of place that would appeal to her mother's artistic sensibilities too.

'There are maps of the local area and information on days out in the reception if you need them,' Karen said. 'I've put plenty of tea and coffee and biscuits out for you, and the kettle is just there on the dresser,' she added. 'But if you'd rather come and take tea in the day room you'd be more than welcome. We've got a full house, but most of the other guests tend to spend their days out so it will probably be just me down there today and I'd be happy to have the company.'

'Aren't we a bit late for afternoon tea?' Posy asked.

'We've an hour or so before dinner but really we don't have any rules around here – if you want tea and cake at midnight in the day room then I don't mind at all. It's your trip, after all, and you must do what makes it enjoyable.'

'That's very kind of you,' Carmel said, but Posy guessed that she still wasn't quite herself and might prefer a reflective hour in her room before dinner to collect her thoughts and mull over what had happened at Oleander House. In a strange way, the day had probably been more stressful for Carmel than for Posy herself.

Posy had decided very early on that nothing she learned would change her relationship with her adopted mother, and yet, despite Posy saying so, Carmel must have felt she was suddenly faced with competition. Angelica was dead – from an alcohol-related illness, Posy had later found out from Asa – but that didn't make her any less Posy's mother. Carmel must have worried that things would change now that Posy had met her biological family, and Posy just didn't know how to articulate, in a way that could leave Carmel with no lingering doubts, that they wouldn't.

Depending on how Carmel felt about it and whether she'd prefer that quiet hour to be alone or in company, Posy thought she might have a little snoop around Sunnyfields Guest House. If the rest of it was as cute as what she'd seen so far, it would go a long way to nourish her creative soul in a way that it rarely did professionally these days. At work there was always a brief, always constraints, often designs that she didn't personally love or even like. As a student she'd never imagined that the art she was so passionate about would become such a chore at times, but she'd never really factored in that she wouldn't be able to do as she pleased when she produced art for other people. It wasn't until she'd started to work that reality had hit her with enough force to make her question – if only for the first months, but question nonetheless – her career choices.

As a self-employed potter Carmel had a little more creative freedom, but even she often found she had to rein in a design in order to sell it. It was something they'd discussed often when Posy had started to work, something that Posy's father, Anthony, really didn't understand. To him, work was work. You were given a project and you delivered it, and that was all there was to it; it didn't matter how you felt personally about it. And even though Posy could see a certain beauty and grace to the vast, towering wind turbines that he helped to install, at the end of the day they were functional, above all else, and she could see why he looked at his job that way.

'Well, I'll let you get settled in,' Karen said. 'I'm just downstairs if you need me – or you can dial for reception on the phone and I'll be able to answer wherever I am.'

'Thank you,' Carmel said.

As Karen left them and closed the door softly behind her, Carmel dropped into a squishy armchair in the corner of the room and closed her eyes with a long sigh.

'Tough day?' Posy asked, glancing briefly at the twin beds and deciding to claim the one nearest to her by stretching out on it.

'I should be asking you that.'

'Oh…' Posy waved an airy hand, just to show she was fine. 'Shall I make us a cup of tea?'

Carmel opened her eyes and smiled across at Posy, who was still flat on her back. Despite her offer, it looked as if she had no intentions of moving any time soon.

'You're sure that wouldn't be too much effort for you?'

Posy pushed herself up with a grin. 'Early starts don't agree with me – you know that.'

'That's true. No – don't worry about me. I'm just going to sit here for a while… maybe phone your dad – he'll be wondering how it's gone today.'

'In that case I might go and explore. Do you want to come?'

'You want to explore? Are you… well, are you OK? I mean, with all that's happened so far today?'

Posy nodded. 'I just need time to process everything, but I think I'm almost more OK about it than you are. It honestly doesn't change anything for me, you know. You and Dad are still my family – my number-one family, the people who really matter. I'd like to get to know Giles and Asa better, but they're never going to be more important than you and Dad. You know that – right?'

Carmel pushed a smile across her face, and Posy wasn't fooled for a moment. But she also knew that it would take time for her mother to feel better about it.

'Of course. You go ahead and explore and I'll meet you downstairs for dinner.'

Posy grabbed her phone, slotted it into the pocket of her cotton jacket and headed for the door. She kissed her mum briefly. 'Tell Dad I said hello and I'll speak to him later.'

'Of course. See you later.'

'See you later—'

'And, Posy…'

She stopped and turned back to her mum.

'Thank you,' Carmel said with a tired smile.

'I should be thanking you,' Posy said, returning the smile with one of her own. Nobody meant more to Posy than the parents who had brought her up, and nobody ever would.

*

After a wander around the gardens, which were split between the neat and structured beds and lawns at the front of the house and a wilder more rambling section at the back characterised by wildflowers and shrubs, a little pond, a greenhouse containing tomato and cucumber plants, a guest terrace with iron furniture, some free-roaming white ducks and a pen inhabited by a miniature pig, Posy investigated the books in the telephone box. A sign was stuck to the inside of the door and it seemed the stock was to be enjoyed by the guests, who could take a book away with them if they liked as long as they left another in its place, or returned the book once they were done with it.

There wasn't anything Posy really wanted to read that she hadn't already read and, besides, she was here for only a night so she wouldn't really have time anyway. Perusing the shelves was really more for something to do than anything else.

Once she'd done that, and spent another ten minutes taking photos of areas of interest around the house, she decided to go back inside to see if Karen was in the day room. She wasn't, but then, hearing voices from another room, Posy went to investigate and in the process discovered the location of the dining room. Karen was in there with another woman who was setting the tables. The woman looked perhaps Posy's own age, or maybe early thirties, and was dressed in a very practical but shapeless shift dress, her dark hair scraped into a high ponytail; she wore very little make-up and her only jewellery was a pair of large gold hoop earrings. None of this, however, could take away from the fact that she was very attractive. If she looked like this dressed for work, she would have been a real femme fatale dressed for a night out.

Posy was about to duck out when Karen looked up.

'Everything alright? You need something? Perhaps that cup of tea?'

'Oh no… you're busy… I'll just…'

'It's no bother. Ray's got everything under control in the kitchen and Pavla only thinks I'm more of a hindrance than a help when I try to set the tables with her, don't you, Pavla?'

The other woman grinned at Posy. 'True enough. Please take her out of my way – I'll be much quicker on my own.'

'Honestly,' Posy said. 'I was just exploring… that's OK, isn't it? Only my mum is having a lie-down so I was making myself scarce for a bit.'

'Oh, she's not unwell, is she?' Karen said, making her way over.

'No… it's just been a long day – early start, you know?'

'Every day's a long day here, let me tell you,' Karen said cheerfully. 'Starts with sun up and ends with sun down. Not that I'd have it any other way – I love running this place.'

'It's yours?' Posy asked. 'I mean, you don't run it for anyone else?'

'All mine,' Karen said. 'Well, I suppose it's a little bit my husband's too.'

'Does he work here too?'

'Ray's your chef for tonight,' Karen said. 'And tomorrow morning for breakfast. In fact, he's your chef whenever you eat. I do the hospitality and he does the food – if it was the other way around we'd have gone bankrupt as soon as we opened because I can't cook and he has no social skills whatsoever.'

Posy smiled politely but Karen found her own joke so funny that she erupted into a loud chuckle.

'So… can I get you anything before dinner?' Karen asked. 'Tea, coffee…? Perhaps an alcoholic drink? You're welcome to take it from the bar and sit anywhere you like.'

'You know what?' Posy said. 'A gin does sound nice round about now.'

'Gin it is,' Karen replied with a smile. 'I've got all sorts – in fact, I have a very nice orange and lime-flower one that's brand new to me. I haven't tried it yet but the guests who have say it's lovely.'

'That does sound amazing,' Posy said. 'I'll give that one a go.'

'No problem,' Karen said. 'Right this way.'

Posy followed her out of the room and down a narrow corridor which opened up into a bar area. It was every bit as cosy as Posy would have imagined – dark wood panelling and varnished floor, heavy silk drapes that kept out a little more light here than they did in the bedrooms, the upholstery on the chairs a matching oriental print. It was very much in keeping with the rest of the house, the only difference being it was slightly more restrained and functional down here than in the bedrooms and the lounge, where Karen had really indulged her inner hippy.

'So…' Karen began as she poured a measure of gin into a glass behind the bar while Posy took a seat on a high stool at the other side to wait. 'Did you drive straight here today or have you been visiting first? You said you'd got up early?'

'We went somewhere first,' Posy said, taking the drink from Karen. 'Could you charge it to our room?'

'Of course,' Karen said.

'Oleander House… do you know it?' Posy asked, recalling now that Sandra had known Karen. She took a sip of her drink and spared a fleeting moment to appreciate that it was very good, just as Karen had promised.

'Oh, yes!' Karen said, her attention wandering to a spot on the bar top. She pulled a cloth from beneath the counter and rubbed at it for a moment before turning back to Posy. 'I know them well – we get our cider from them of course. Have to keep things local, don't you? Always have a natter with Giles or Sandra when they come to deliver. I didn't know they'd started doing tours for the public.'

'They haven't – we were visiting… They're family.'

Posy took another appreciative sip of her drink and pondered for a moment how strange that sentence sounded. Family. That's exactly what they were, but she wasn't sure she'd ever get used to thinking of them that way.

'Oh!' Karen looked keenly at Posy now. 'I didn't know they had people in London; they've never mentioned it before and you'd have thought they would, me being an ex-cockney and all.'

'I thought I recognised an accent,' Posy said, seizing the opportunity to steer the conversation in a new direction. While there was nothing to hide, she wasn't ready to have the conversation just yet. It was a long and complicated story and she was still very much processing it herself without sharing with a complete stranger. 'Have you been here a long time?'

'Oh yes, about thirty years now. Ray and I visited Glastonbury and we loved it so much we knew we had to live close by one day. This place came up for sale and it seemed like fate, so we sold everything we owned in London and moved here. It was tough getting going in the early days, I can tell you, but we wouldn't be anywhere else now.'

'Thirty years?' Posy asked.

Karen smiled. 'Makes me sound very old, doesn't it?'

'Not at all,' Posy said. 'So if you've been here that long you'll know someone who lived here… John Palmer?'

Karen's appraising look was keener than ever now. 'The Palmers left a long time ago. Friends of yours?'

'Not really. I just wondered if you knew them.'

'Not terribly well,' Karen said. 'Kept themselves to themselves after—'

She stopped mid-sentence and stared at Posy for a moment before shaking herself. Posy felt a hot kind of panic suddenly burn through her and wondered if her innocent question had given away more than she'd wanted to. Could it be that her landlady had figured everything out? She was being paranoid, surely?

'What did you do before you moved here?' Posy asked hastily, changing the subject and hoping that the one she'd chosen would put the idea of affairs and secret love children out of Karen's mind.

'Sculpted. Not much money in it, though – at least, there wasn't for me, but it might just be that I'm not very good.'

'So you trained in art?'

'Saint Martins.'

'Wow! They wouldn't have me,' Posy added with a small laugh, relieved that they seemed to have moved on from the subject of John Palmer. 'Not for the fine art course I wanted to do, so I opted for interior design instead. I do love it now even though it was my second choice.'

'A fellow creative? It's a shame you're not staying longer. It would have been lovely to chat art into the night.'

'Mum's a potter – works for herself, has a studio and everything. She does OK but you're right, it's hardly a stable income.'

'All creative industries are sadly undervalued,' Karen said sagely. 'I dabble a little here but the guest house keeps me too busy to do much and I can't complain about that, because it enables me to live in this beautiful house in the most heavenly place on earth. Have you been into Astercombe yet?'

'Where's that?'

'The village. It's not very big but it is very pretty. It has a couple of darling little art and craft shops and a very good bakery.'

'Perhaps we'll have a look tomorrow,' Posy said.

'If you were staying longer I'd be able to give you lots of leaflets and ideas for tours and day trips. So you've been to Somerset before then?'

'No – this is our first time.'

'Oh, but I thought—'

Karen seemed to think better of finishing what she'd started to say and Posy guessed that she'd been about to come out with something about them visiting Oleander House, particularly as Posy had told her they were relatives.

'It is lovely, though,' Posy said. 'I mean, what we've managed to see of it is gorgeous. We'll definitely come back.'

'Well, you'll find plenty to see when you do.' Karen glanced up at the clock and made an apologetic face. 'I'm sorry – you don't mind if I get on, do you? Dinner is fast approaching and I want to make sure everything is ready.'

'Oh, God, of course not! Don't mind me; I'll just finish my drink and go see if my mum is ready to come down.'

'Take it with you if you don't want to sit in the bar alone,' Karen said as she made her way out. 'I can always collect the glass when I clean your room tomorrow. And if your mum is very tired we can always arrange to bring your dinner for you to have in your room – it's no bother.'

Posy couldn't deny it was a tempting offer. She was quite tired herself now and it would be far easier to hide in her room. But they'd come all this way and it would be a shame to waste the opportunity to make the most of their visit – which included making the most of Karen's lovely guest house.

'Thank you,' she said, 'but I think Mum would rather come down.'

'It'll be fine either way. I'll see you shortly unless I hear otherwise.'

Posy watched her leave the bar and, as the space then suddenly became unbearably silent, she decided that she would take her drink upstairs after all.

Chapter Four

There was no ham, no cheese, no croissants, no smashed avocado or *huevos rancheros*… breakfast at Sunnyfields Guest House was decidedly no-frills and very full English, but delicious nonetheless. Posy couldn't remember the last time she'd eaten so well in a morning. Usually there was time for a slice of toast on the run if she was lucky; some days she'd reach for a banana and stuff it into her bag to eat mid-morning and sometimes it was literally eating dry muesli from her hand as she strode to the Tube station. If it was up to her, she'd go without, but Carmel would never let her.

So Posy pushed her plate away this morning absolutely stuffed and a little stunned that she'd faced a plate containing two Lincolnshire sausages, locally sourced bacon and eggs, tomatoes, beans and hash browns and had managed to conquer it very convincingly. All there was to show the plate had contained a breakfast at all was a thin sliver of bacon rind pushed to the edge.

Posy's best friend, Marella, would have been utterly horrified to see it. Her idea of breakfast was taking a peek through the window of Pret a Manger as she ran past for work. Carmel said that was why she was so thin, but Marella was someone who could never sit still and had to be doing everything at a thousand miles an hour, and Posy thought that was more likely the reason she didn't put on weight. Posy said Marella was lucky because, although perfectly slim and healthy, she didn't have to watch what she ate to stay that way. But Marella said that Posy was fortunate because at least she could produce a decent cleavage with the right bra, while Marella had a couple of pimples that didn't even deserve a bra. And so they agreed to disagree on who was the luckiest.

Dinner the previous evening had been in a similar vein. There had been a choice of beef and ale pie, roast chicken with seasonal veg or butternut squash and sage bake. Hearty fare meant to fill bellies and soothe souls, not to bedazzle and confuse with odd flavour combinations and pretentious little piles of nothing. Not that Posy had anything against a bit of experimental cuisine, but what Ray and Karen served to them in the dining room of Sunnyfields seemed very apt and perfectly suited to where they were. Dessert had consisted of locally grown strawberries and ice cream, chocolate cake or gooseberry tart.

Posy and Carmel had planned to check out at 10 a.m. and then head over to Oleander House, but Karen had told them she wasn't in any rush to get them out as nobody had the room booked for a day or so and suggested they might want to delay their checkout and use the extra time to take a wander around the local area.

Posy had been keen on this idea, if only to get a feel for the place that had already become so significant to the story of her beginnings. But Carmel occasionally suffered with a touch of arthritis and this morning she hadn't been sure she'd be able to accompany Posy on her exploration. Posy had reassured her that she was fine going alone, and Karen had chipped in that if they fancied something more relaxing still, she had time to do an Indian head massage. Posy had been quite tempted by this too, having never had one before, but ultimately felt a bit silly at the thought of someone rubbing at her head and declined the offer.

Carmel, on the other hand, had been all for it. So, as soon as breakfast was cleared away and Karen had a spare hour, she arranged to see Carmel in her private sitting room and Posy decided to take a walk to explore the place her biological parents had once called home.

Even by 10.30 a.m. the sun was high and hot, far too hot for spring. Posy stepped out onto a lane bordered by high grass and dense hedgerows, the sounds of bees and crickets coming from them. Occasionally the odd car would make its way down the narrow track, but always respectfully slowing as it passed Posy, giving her as much room as possible. Despite the heat shimmer on the tarmac, visibility was good and the traffic was light, and she didn't feel at all worried that she was walking on the road.

After only a few minutes the rooftops of Oleander House could be seen. She'd had no idea their guest house was so close. As they were heading there later to see the family before they went back to London, at a fork in the road where one direction led to Oleander and the other somewhere totally unknown, she decided to take the path that would surprise her.

A little further on an old wooden signpost pointed to the village of Astercombe, which Posy recalled Karen telling her about the evening before. It did sound very quaint and appealing, and even though it said the distance was three miles, if Posy walked quickly enough she might be able to take a quick look and still get back in plenty of time for their afternoon meeting with Giles, Sandra and Asa.

Another ten minutes took her to a second fork in the road, but this time there was no signposting and she had no clue which way she was supposed to go to reach the village. She pulled out her phone to see if she could use the map function but was frustrated to find that the signal was so bad she couldn't get directions on there either. After a moment of indecision, she heaved a sigh and took a wild guess, deciding to follow the path on the left.

The further she went down this way, the taller the roadside shrubs got, until they became trees that threw a cooling shadow over her. And then, as she peered into the gaps between them, beginning to worry that she'd made the wrong choice, the unusual geography of the land beyond caught her eye. She stopped to get a closer look and could see now that the trees also hid a wooden fence, the type you saw on farmland, so low and flimsy that Posy couldn't really see the point of it. As far as she could tell, the trees themselves offered far more protection from the road than this fence did. Unless, of course, it was meant to mark a boundary of some kind.

Posy found a gap in the trees large enough to fit into and stepped onto the bottom rung of the fence to appraise the fields beyond. She could have taken an extra big stride and been over it in a heartbeat, and she was sorely tempted, just for the hell of it. The wild meadowland, strewn with fire-red poppies, daisies and cornflowers, their colours shimmering in the sunlight, was like something out of a Monet painting and she longed to walk through it, hands brushing lazily against every flower as she went. The only obstacle between her and that hazy dream sequence was a rickety old fence that was hardly keeping anyone in or out and, shaded by the trees as it was, she felt sure nobody would be able to see her get past it anyway.

She paused, shielding her eyes with her hand to look further. In the distance the land seemed to dip away into some kind of gully – at least, she couldn't see what came immediately after the meadowland and before a hill that was marked out by neat lines running through rows of green. A vineyard? Posy had no idea whether grapes grew in this part of England – though she'd heard that they did grow in parts of the south – but she couldn't think what else they could be. They certainly looked like vines to her.

Before she could fully process any of these thoughts, she'd hopped over the fence and landed lightly on the other side. Perhaps she wasn't meant to be here but she hadn't seen any signs to warn against trespassing, and she wanted to get a closer look. All thoughts of finding the village were suddenly and inexplicably forgotten.

The stiff, dry grasses brushed against her denim-clad legs, and while she was glad of the protection from the odd thistle or bug bite, the sun was so hot as it burned into the back of her neck that she was beginning to wish she'd settled on something cooler to wear. A cute pair of denim shorts and a bikini vest would be her usual choice on a day like this but, not having anticipated such freedom as a glorious walk in a sun-drenched meadow, she hadn't packed anything like that to bring with her.

Once she'd reached the furthest point of the meadow she'd been able to see from the fence, she was gratified to note that she'd been right about what lay beyond. There was more meadowland, starred with flowers of scarlet, blue, white and yellow, running downhill into a sort of valley, and from down there she thought she saw the glint of sunlight on water, though it was still too far away to tell. If she was very lucky, it would be a crystal-clear, ice-cold stream where she could take a moment to dip her toes and cool down.

The promise of that was enough to get her walking again. It smelled so sweet here in this meadow in the sunshine, like the scents of every perfume shop she'd ever been in all mingled and messed up together in one place – fresh and sweet and spicy. Half the flowers growing in this riot of colour she didn't even recognise.

A white butterfly with orange-tipped wings settled on something tall close by that might have been a foxglove, and she watched it until it flew away again, delighted by its beauty. She rarely saw butterflies at all in London – the odd cabbage white or peacock in their tiny backyard but certainly never one like this. Grass in London never smelled like this though, and the air never felt so clean and the horizon never looked so vibrant and vast. A kind of peace like she'd never known stole over her as she walked alone, completely dazzled by her surroundings, and at that moment, if someone had asked her to forsake every one of her worldly possessions to come and live here as nature intended, she might well have said yes.

The grasses rustled and brushed against her arms and legs as she continued down the slope. Somewhere in the back of her mind was a tiny voice wondering if she ought to be here at all. Maybe she ought to have stopped at the fence, content to look but go no further. But the feeling of freedom that being here now was giving her silenced that voice. She hadn't seen another living soul and she doubted she would: even if she did and they told her she oughtn't to be there, she'd just pretend to be lost.

A little further still the grasses gave way to lusher greenery and reeds, and now Posy could see that there was water down there – a small pool that had been almost hidden by the vegetation. The water lapped invitingly against a battered wooden jetty, indicating it was clearly used from time to time – perhaps for fishing or something. Posy was sweating now, and though it was hard to see how clean the water was from this distance, if it didn't look too bad on closer inspection maybe she could sit on that jetty and dangle her feet in it for a while.

So she quickened her step, eager to do just that, sending up butterflies and bees and even a dragonfly from where they'd been quietly minding their own businesses and causing grasshoppers to chirrup their indignation.

The closer she got, the more stable the wood of the jetty looked and the more inviting the water looked too.

She was perhaps feet from her objective when she noticed ripples forming on the surface of the pool, as if something was moving the water. A bird, perhaps, though she couldn't see it. Perhaps there was something behind the tall reeds that obscured part of the pool. Maybe she ought to be certain of what it was before she got closer – not that she imagined for a minute it would be anything more dangerous than a mildly annoyed duck.

Even as she thought this, something appeared from behind the vegetation. Posy stopped dead and dropped to the ground, heart beating madly. A man was swimming towards the jetty. It was then that she noticed the neatly folded towel on the bank. The man hadn't seen her yet, but if she made a move to run for it he surely would. But if she stayed where she was, he'd probably see her then too.

There was no time to do anything, however, because a second later he'd hauled himself out of the water and onto the jetty and unfurled to stand, dripping wet and completely naked.

It took him about that long to realise that he wasn't alone, but in that time Posy had been able to look for long enough to be absolutely mortified, and yet shamefully appreciative of the fact that if Greek gods really did exist, one of them might just be standing in front of her right now. His torso was impossibly sculpted, his arms firm and taut, his chin strong and square, and a head of black curls framed dark eyes. Then she let out a squeak of shock and averted her gaze, only for his own exclamation of shock to cause her to involuntarily look back for another eyeful.

'What the hell!' he yelled, grabbing for his towel and wrapping it hastily round his waist, his thick Scots accent the only clue that he wasn't actually a Greek god at all, only a very angry mortal.

'I'm so sorry,' Posy said faintly, not knowing whether to laugh or cry as she scrambled to her feet, dimly aware of the fact that her face was burning like it had never burned before. She didn't know whether that was embarrassment or the sun or a perfect combination of both.

'What are you doing here?' he demanded.

'I was lost—'

'No you weren't!'

'I was out walking… I can walk, can't I? It's a free country!' Posy fired back, now taking offence at his tone. What if she had genuinely been lost? That was no way to talk to anyone. Yes, maybe the manner of this meeting was embarrassing for both of them, and maybe it was excruciatingly awkward now, but there was no need to be so rude.

'You shouldn't be here – this is private land.'

'How do you know? There are no signs to say so!'

'Because it's my land!' he roared, and for a sickening moment Posy wondered whether he was going to start chasing her off it.

'Oh,' she said, not knowing what else to say.

He took a long breath and seemed to gather in his anger. 'Kindly leave,' he said now in a more even tone, though it was firm enough to leave no mistaking that he meant it, and that he meant for her to leave instantly.

Posy hesitated, torn between an impulse to go as he'd asked or to apologise again and try to explain herself – after all, it was what she'd been brought up to do in these situations and she did feel bad about it, even if he was rude. But he gave her no further time to think about it.

'Now!' he growled.

Posy blinked, considered once more having some kind of last word, but then thought better of it. Instead, she turned and began to march back up the hill as fast as the grass and the oppressive heat would let her.

Chapter Five

'Darling!'

Carmel smiled broadly as Posy found her and Karen sitting in the garden chatting over a pot of tea. It looked as if they were already forming a very good friendship, even after only a day. 'Did you enjoy Astercombe?'

'I didn't get that far,' Posy said, feeling sticky and flustered and wishing she had time to go back to their room for a cold shower. 'I got a bit lost.'

'Well, I'm glad you didn't stay lost,' Carmel said with a light laugh.

'That's a shame,' Karen said. 'Perhaps you can try again if I give you directions.'

'We probably don't have time now,' Posy replied, glancing at Carmel, who shook her head.

'Not really,' she said. 'Perhaps next time.'

'Tea?' Karen asked, holding up the pot.

Posy took a seat at the table. She'd rather have an ice-cold gin and tonic, but Karen looked so comfortable sitting with her mum that she didn't want to disturb her. 'That would be lovely.'

'So where did you get to?' Karen asked as she poured some into a third cup that suggested they'd expected Posy to join them at some point.

'I'm not sure. Some country lanes and some fields. Wherever it was, it was nice.'

She smiled stiffly as she took the teacup from Karen. It *had* been nice, right up until the angry naked man had appeared.

'How was your head massage?' she asked Carmel, swiftly deciding it was safest to change the subject. For all she knew, the angry naked man was a good friend of Karen's and she really didn't want to get into that now.

'Oh, it was wonderful!' Carmel gushed. 'It was like every bit of stress I've ever had in my life just got pulled up through Karen's fingers and out into the air. I can't believe I've never had one before! As soon as we get home I must find the number of someone who does it so I can have another.'

'You do look relaxed,' Posy agreed as she sipped her tea.

'I could do one for you,' Karen said, looking pleased with the praise. 'It doesn't have to take a long time.'

There was no amount of massage, relaxation or meditation that was going to undo the knots of stress in Posy's body right now, and she was so hot and bothered already that she really didn't think she could stand any type of contact. All she wanted was time to cool down, and if she could stop thinking about the angry naked man long enough for her face to stop burning then that would be a welcome bonus.

'That's so kind of you,' she said, 'but I still have to put the last of my things in a bag and we need to get to Oleander House soon, don't we, Mum?'

'I suppose we do have to get going soon,' Carmel admitted, looking faintly regretful at the idea of having to move at all.

'Don't forget to leave me your contact details before you go,' Karen said to Carmel. 'Next time I'm in London – if I ever get time, that is, which isn't very often running this place – I'd love to take up your offer to see your studio.'

'I'd love that too,' Carmel said. 'I'd be more than happy to give you a pottery lesson or two. And if you think about taking it up from here, I'd be more than happy to give you any advice you need.'

Posy looked from her mum to Karen and then back again. It wasn't often that Carmel extended an invitation to anyone to spend time in her studio. The house, that was fair game and open and welcome to anyone, but the studio where she worked was a far more private space. Most people they knew weren't that interested in it either; even Posy's dad didn't venture in unless he really had to.

'I'll let you have my email address before we leave,' Carmel added.

Karen straightened up in her seat with a smile before downing the last of her tea. Looking about as reluctant to move as Carmel, she stood up. 'Well, I'd better get on, and I'd better let you two get on if you've got to be at Oleander House. I'll see you when you check out, I expect.'

'You will,' Carmel said warmly. 'Thanks for the massage and the tea. I don't think I've ever been so relaxed in my life!'

'Glad to have helped,' Karen replied. 'If you need anything before you leave, come and find me – I don't expect I'll be far away.'

Posy looked at her mum as Karen went inside. 'I see you've made a new friend,' she said.

'She's lovely, don't you think? We've got along so well this morning I feel as if I've known her for years. And she has such a lovely life here – she's been telling me all about it.'

'Is it making you think about moving to Somerset?'

'Oh, no.' Carmel laughed lightly. 'Come on,' she added, tipping back her cup to drink the last, as Karen had done moments before.

'We'd better get the car loaded up if we're going to be at Oleander House in time.'

An hour later, having bid goodbye to Karen with promises to visit again when they could, Posy and Carmel were sitting on the patio of Oleander House once again. Cold drinks and plates of finger food littered the table. This time it was already a far more relaxed affair than the day before, and conversation had turned to what Posy and Carmel had been doing with themselves during the previous twenty-four hours. They'd told them how much they'd enjoyed staying at Sunnyfields and how much they liked Karen. Sandra had said she liked Karen too, but Ray was so reclusive and antisocial that she felt she barely knew him at all, despite the years they'd been practically neighbours. Then Carmel happened to mention her head massage and how amazing it had been, and then Posy had been forced to tell them that she hadn't had one because she'd been exploring.

'Oh,' Asa said with mild interest, taking so much care to pour a glass of home-made lemonade from a pitcher that Posy half expected him to produce a ruler and measure the exact distance between the contents and the lip of the glass. 'Where did you go?'

Posy was beginning to wish people would stop asking her that.

'I'm not really sure,' she said. 'Just some fields.'

'I'll bet you found that thrilling,' he replied, putting the pitcher down.

'They were lovely,' Posy replied.

'I'm sure they're not very exciting by London standards, though,' Giles put in. 'We're used to living in a sleepy place like this, but we must seem very backward to you.'

'Not at all!' Posy said with feeling. 'I think it must be lovely living here! I don't think I'd miss London at all if I moved here!'

'I wouldn't be so sure of that,' Asa said dryly. He settled back in his chair and took a sip of his drink.

'It's alright here if you're over forty,' Giles agreed. 'We love it but a lot of the youngsters tend to move away and head for where the action is.'

'I'm hardly a youngster,' Posy said. 'I'm twenty-seven.'

'That's a toddler in my eyes,' Sandra said. Giles nodded.

'Mine too. Asa's a bit closer to your age but even he's got ten years' head start on you.'

'Hey – I'm thirty!' Asa said indignantly and Sandra burst out laughing.

'You keep telling everyone that,' Giles said, 'but we all know your birth certificate says thirty-eight on it.'

'Judas,' Asa said, wearing the most comically offended expression.

Even though she'd only just met these people and didn't really have the hang of their tone yet, Posy did want to laugh.

'Honestly, give my secret away to any Tom, Dick or Harry, would you?'

'Except Posy and Carmel aren't any Tom, Dick or Harry now,' Sandra said as she flashed them both a warm smile.

'Well, no…' Asa agreed. 'I know you love to burst my bubble at every opportunity, but at least let me keep my mystique just a little bit longer. It's bad enough being this close to forty, but you could at least let me carry on pretending.'

'There's no bubble and no mystique,' Giles said, laughing. 'You work on an orchard and live in a shack in the back garden of the house.'

'Insults again!' Asa cried with a look of deepest indignation that only made his brother laugh harder.

'Somebody has to keep your feet on the ground,' Sandra said with the sort of fond look a mother would give a favourite but rather wayward child.

Before Asa could form a reply, Giles turned to Posy and Carmel. 'So you didn't make it into Astercombe this morning after all?'

'No,' Posy said.

'That seems a pity. I could run you in this afternoon if you'd like to spend some time there... It's understandable you'd want to take a look around.'

Posy glanced at her mum but then gave her head a slight shake. 'That would have been nice but I think we'll probably head off in the next hour or so. We don't want to get back too late.'

'That's a shame,' Sandra said. 'Perhaps next time?'

'Maybe,' Carmel replied.

'If not a run into the village then is there anything else you'd like to see?' Giles asked.

'I'm not really sure,' Posy said doubtfully. 'Do you know... my mum... is she buried nearby?'

Giles seemed to pale slightly. 'I'm afraid not. She was buried in Argentina where she died – we didn't get to hear about her death for a month or so after it had happened, so the people she'd been staying with had already organised it. They don't leave it long there, you know.'

'I'm sorry,' Sandra said. 'I suppose you were hoping to visit the grave?'

'I don't know...' Posy said. 'I suppose so, yes. How long ago was this?'

'Around eight years now.'

Posy nodded slowly. Her mother must have been forty when she'd died, and it seemed so cruel to go so young. She felt as if she ought to somehow mourn her, but when she asked herself how she felt about it, she had to admit that she felt very little. Angelica was a woman she'd never known and it was hard to feel anything but the sort of pity she'd feel had she seen her death reported on the news – she could acknowledge it was sad but not really experience that sadness in any meaningful way.

'What about John Palmer?' she asked.

'We don't know where he was living before he died,' Giles said. 'We could try to find out if it helps?'

Posy shook her head. She didn't even know for sure the man she was asking about was her father – though he seemed the best candidate. Was it worth asking them to do that? What would it achieve for her to visit the grave of a man who might or might not be something to her? Most of all, was she ready? Perhaps she'd try to find him, but it might be best to give it some time first.

'I suppose it would be nice to see your orchards,' she said in a bid to put Giles, Asa and Sandra at ease again. She didn't want to think of them tense and stressed around her, worried about what new and difficult questions she was going to ask every time she was with them. She'd ask, of course, and eventually they'd feel comfortable giving her what information they knew, but for now she decided all that could wait.

Sandra looked at Giles with a relieved smile. 'Why don't you give them a quick tour of the orchards and the barns and I'll clear up here?'

'I'll tag along,' Asa said. 'It's always fun to see your dull old home through someone else's eyes – makes it seem all new.'

Giles beckoned them as he made for some large gates at the bottom of the garden. Posy and Carmel followed, with Asa bringing up the rear. Posy couldn't imagine she'd ever find Asa's home dull, not for one second. Everything was so delightfully chocolate-box cute here that she couldn't imagine anyone thinking this place was boring, no matter how long they'd lived here. But having just met Asa it was still hard to know when he was displaying the dry, cutting wit that she was beginning to recognise as one of his most prominent characteristics, or if he actually meant what he said. Giles and Sandra already seemed easier to read; when they said something, generally they were being completely straight about it.

In fact, as they made their way through two more gates and emerged at the entrance to the orchards, Giles tried his best to be informative about the varieties of apples they grew, what each one was good for and why they'd chosen to grow them, and many other facts besides, but he kept getting interrupted by Asa, who was more interested in London life. He wanted to know about restaurants or clubs someone had told him about, and Posy felt very boring and disappointing admitting that she had personal experience of very few of the ones he'd named. She and her friends had regular haunts that they tended to favour, and these were often in the less glamorous parts of the city. They went back to those places again and again because they felt comfortable there, content with familiar faces and rules and etiquettes they understood. You never quite knew what sort of crowd you were going to find when you ventured elsewhere, and when they'd been tempted to try, they'd often all agreed that they preferred their regular places.

Of course, that was back in the days when going out every weekend had been a must. That didn't happen so much these days. Friends were busy or tired or bored or settling down. Half the time even the singletons with nothing better to do struggled to muster any enthusiasm for a night stuck to a bar trying to shout over music that they didn't really care about and would never listen to at home, being hit on, felt up by drunken men old enough to know better, queuing for toilets and dodging the drug dealers plying their trade in shady corners. The gloss had certainly worn off for Posy long before now, and on the occasions she did bother, she'd arrive home at the end of the night wondering why she had.

'It's still very early for the apples,' Giles said apologetically. 'I'm afraid they don't look that impressive at the moment.'

They were certainly small, intense green and bullet-hard, but the sight of branches groaning with fruit and foliage despite it being early in the season was still beautiful. Posy looked up, a ray of sunlight piercing the canopy and making the leaves glow. If she tried to picture heaven, it might look a lot like this.

'There are so many,' Carmel said. 'I never imagined the orchard was this big.'

'Oh, this is only a section of it,' Giles said. 'We've got other varieties further on. We tend to use blends for our cider – single-variety ciders are difficult to perfect but if you blend them it's much easier to get the perfect taste. You could look if you want.'

'But it's only more of the same,' Asa cut in. 'Once you've seen one apple tree you've seen them all. I'd say the cider house is much more interesting.'

'We'll take a look at that now,' Giles said. 'If we haven't bored you enough already?'

'I'd like to see it,' Carmel said.

Posy agreed. She'd never really thought about how any alcohol was made, only interested in where it ended up (in her tummy on a night out), but she was always open to new experiences.

They followed Giles, who led them into the barn where they made their product. It looked a lot more ramshackle than Posy had imagined it, with rough whitewashed walls and a concrete floor. It was much colder in here, with very little natural light, and monstrous machines stood silently at one end, while at the other there was a faint hum from a lot of tanks.

'All the pulping is done as soon as the apples are picked in the autumn,' Giles explained as he patted one of the silent machines. 'We do that in these, then' – he moved along to another – 'we press the pulp here to extract the juice. We do various bits and pieces to purify it, and then it goes into the tanks down there to ferment. Last autumn's juice is in there now, doing its thing.'

'And then it's cider?' Carmel asked.

'We do a bit more to it but basically it's a cycle – that lot will be out of there and ready to go by the time this harvest is ready to go in. There's not much room for manoeuvre – it all has to go like clockwork, but we've got it down to a fine art after all these years.'

'I'm sure that's enough of our boring processes,' Asa said.

'It's not boring at all,' Carmel said. 'I've never really thought about it before; it's a shame we can't be here to see it all in action.'

'Maybe this autumn…' Giles said, smiling. 'We'd be happy to have you over – we may even rope you in.'

'I'd like that,' Posy said with a smile of her own and a warm feeling. When she'd come to find her family, to be accepted like this was exactly what she'd hoped for.

It had all been perfectly delightful, but as they were walking back across the courtyard from the cider house, a smaller building, shaded by a beech tree, caught Posy's attention. The bricks were worn into shades of red, orange and white, while the wooden windows were framed by pink clematis and the door was a sturdy blue.

'That's so pretty,' she said, pointing to it. 'Is that your part of the house, Asa?'

'Oh, no,' he said, looking suddenly apprehensive as he shot a brief, loaded glance Giles's way. 'That's Mother's old place.'

'We built her a granny flat,' Giles said. 'After Dad died and she got a bit older and a bit less patient she couldn't stand all the hustle and bustle at the house with workers going back and forth and such. We had two old buildings out of use, so we took out a loan and had them converted; one for her and one for Asa...'

'Just to give me some privacy,' Asa put in, 'and for Giles and Sandra to have some privacy in the main house – not because I was annoyed with the workers or anything.'

They all stopped and gazed at the house. Then Giles broke the silence.

'Would you like to take a look inside?' he asked.

Posy nodded uncertainly but Asa looked sharply at his brother.

'Perhaps you'd be more interested in the main house...' he began, but the argument quickly tailed off. It was hard to know who he was trying to protect – maybe all of them. Perhaps he was trying to protect the seedlings of a new relationship, ever so fragile, just poking through the soil, and perhaps he felt that Posy seeing the place where her unforgiving biological grandmother – the woman who'd pretended not to know Posy even existed – had lived out her final days wouldn't help at all.

'No... I'd like to see...' Posy said, straightening up. 'I think I ought to.'

'I can unlock it for you and let you go in… I understand you might want to see this alone and it's absolutely no problem… Asa and I could just as easily wait outside for you.'

'I'd like that very much,' Posy said, though she sounded even less certain than she had moments before.

'We'll be right here when you're done,' Giles said, striding over to unlock the building for them.

'Do you want me to come with you?' Carmel asked.

Posy nodded and then opened the door.

The first thing that hit her was the smell. Like violets and talc and dust. It had the beginnings of dampness from being shuttered up for many months, though it hadn't quite taken hold yet. Carmel closed the door softly and Posy wanted to tell her to open it again. She didn't like it being closed. It felt as if they shouldn't be there and that closing the door was blocking off their escape. The house felt sort of haunted; not by ghosts, but by lives and loves that never were, as if Posy's mother Angelica had been ghosted out of existence in this space and Posy herself being here was the rudest paradox.

There was a beat of silence during which Posy could just make out Carmel's shadow in the now darkened hallway and hear only her gentle breaths.

'Mum…?' she said.

'Don't worry; I'm here,' Carmel said quietly. 'Are you alright? You want to carry on? We can leave—'

'I never knew her,' Posy said. 'I knew nothing of her – of the person she was, of her likes and dislikes. I don't know what her favourite colour was, what she liked to eat, how she sounded when she laughed… I don't even know if this smell on the air is what she smelled like.' She let out a sigh. 'But I might find some clues to all of that here.'

'Would it change anything to know all that?' Carmel asked.

'Not between us,' Posy said firmly. 'You'll always be my mum, but it's about knowing where you came from; your DNA, who made you. I never felt that was important until I had the opportunity to find out, and now it does seem to matter, as if that piece of the puzzle had been missing but I just hadn't allowed myself to notice.'

'Well, there's no harm in finding that out if it doesn't hurt you.'

'It's always going to hurt me, but that doesn't mean it's not important. And sometimes the pain is a good pain. Like saltwater on a wound. It stings for a while but ultimately it helps the healing.'

Despite this, Posy felt uncomfortably like she was trespassing and half wished they could go back out into the sunshine. But she pushed on down the tiny hallway and into the drawing room beyond.

'I wonder if Giles and Asa will worry we're looking for hidden jewels or something,' she joked. Not because she thought it was funny, but because she desperately wanted this to feel like less of an ordeal than it did.

'I suppose this is all as nerve-wracking for them as it is for you,' Carmel reminded her. 'They've been so lovely since we first met them; I feel they're trying very hard to make something up to you.'

'They really needn't. They had no idea about me and it was hardly their fault anyway.'

'I can understand why they'd feel guilty. They had everything you didn't.'

'I've had a happy life regardless – there's nothing for them to feel guilty about. They're really nice, aren't they?'

'Yes. I think that's a good sign.'

'Of what?'

'That your mother was a good person.'

'It doesn't sound like it from what we've been told. If nothing else, she sounds a bit wild. I'm not sure she wasn't just the bad apple – and I know I just made a pun!' Posy smiled briefly. 'But meeting Giles and Asa, I can't imagine she was much like them at all. They're both so stable and responsible and my mother sounds nothing like that.'

Carmel smiled. 'Well, we can't really say how Angelica was. I suppose the events of her life might have made her act in the ways she did…'

Posy nodded. 'I find it hard to believe Philomena was good or lovely even if she wasn't wild. I've had a good life with you and Dad but she wasn't to know that. I could have been shoved from home to home, desperate or destitute; I could have needed help she was equipped to give but she never bothered to find out…'

'Does it upset you?' Carmel asked.

'No, but it tells me a lot about what kind of person she was.'

'Maybe a little bit. But don't forget life isn't always that black and white. There may have been reasons that we don't understand yet.'

Posy was thoughtful for a moment as she contemplated the room. The biscuit-coloured sofa was well worn but clean, with those little squares of fabric that kept the headrest new in a darker beige and brown floral. There was a footstool in the same pattern as the sofa and cream curtains depicting a faux Regency pastoral scene. This was the kind of room that would have given Posy's design lecturer nightmares. Other than the odd bits of furniture and decor, there was very little to give any kind of clue about the kind of woman who'd lived there – no photos on the walls, no prints, not a single ornament.

'I wonder if Giles and Asa cleared away her stuff,' Posy said.

'Maybe,' Carmel agreed.

But then Posy noted that the cream walls were perfectly blemish-free. If anything had hung on the walls for any length of time then surely removing them would have left a mark of some kind? They could have decorated afterwards, of course, but as nobody was using the building now she didn't see what the point would have been, and there certainly wouldn't have been any rush for it. Maybe there never had been photos and prints. Maybe Philomena just hadn't been the sentimental type. It would certainly fit the picture she was beginning to build of her biological grandmother.

Without words, Carmel and Posy simultaneously agreed that there wasn't much to see here and they moved into an equally dull kitchen, complete with a tiny dining table and two chairs. There was a conservatory/lean-to sort of arrangement at the side of the house, a small bathroom and a box room full of – unsurprisingly – boxes. It looked like years' worth of bits and bobs had been thrown in here when there had been nowhere else to put them.

There was a full-sized master bedroom. Well, perhaps not full-sized compared to what they might have in the main house, but clearly the biggest room in this building. The bed had been stripped so that the mattress was bare, but other than that it looked fairly untouched. They had never actually asked whether Philomena had died in this bed, but the thought of it made Posy shudder slightly. Other than the stripped-back bed, the room looked as if it had remained largely untouched since then and certainly more personalised than the rest of what they'd seen so far.

There were photos here – just a handful on a dresser. On brief inspection Posy was disappointed, though unsurprised, to see that they were photos of Asa and Giles as children, plus a wedding photo of what must have been Philomena and her late husband, but nothing to acknowledge a life before then.

Posy picked one up to take a closer look. It was a group photo, but there was no sign of anyone who might be Angelica. Not that she'd know who to look for, even if she had ever seen a photo of her.

'Posy…'

She looked up at her mum, face screwed into a question as she put the frame down again.

'Why don't you ask Asa and Giles if they have photos of her?' Carmel said. 'They did offer to tell you more and I'm sure they'd have some.'

'I suppose I could,' Posy said doubtfully.

She went to the wardrobe. A handful of very practical clothes hung there – neutral blouses, slacks, a couple of sensibly cut dresses…

Posy closed it again.

'All my life I've wondered about my biological family. Not because I thought I might prefer them,' she added quickly, 'just curious. Now that I'm here looking at this lonely house I feel a bit underwhelmed. From what I can see here my grandmother was… well, I hate to say it, but a bit dull.'

Carmel gave a fleeting smile. 'What did you expect to find?'

Posy sighed. 'I don't know… something more… just more.'

'Maybe we just arrived a few decades too late to see anything more exciting,' Carmel said. 'Maybe your gran had been more once but then she just got old and settled down. Maybe we'll find out more from Giles and Asa about that too – I'm sure they wouldn't mind you asking.'

'Yes, I could. I probably ought to. If nothing else I might find out if there are any funny habits coming my way when I get old.'

Carmel smiled at her daughter. 'There you go – that's the Posy I know. You're stronger and braver than you give yourself credit for.'

Posy closed the wardrobe doors.

'Come on,' she said, a new briskness to her tone, 'I think we've seen all we need to see here. I don't know about you, but I feel I'd rather see more of the grounds in this lovely weather than spend any more time in a house filled with a dead woman's belongings.'

Giles and Asa were waiting in the courtyard when Posy and Carmel came back out, conversing in hushed tones with Sandra, who'd joined them. Their expressions were all tight, a little anxious, but they relaxed as they turned to see Carmel and Posy looking relatively calm. Posy had to wonder if they'd been discussing the likelihood of her having some sort of breakdown in there, faced with the physical evidence of her birth mother's existence. All this must have been as weird for them as it was for her and on first impression they seemed like nice people, the sort of people who'd care.

'Everything OK?' Sandra asked with obviously forced brightness.

'Yes,' Posy replied, the lie as obvious in her tone as in Sandra's. It was clear both women were overcompensating for nerves around a subject too thorny for anyone to dare address first.

'That's my humble abode,' Asa said as they began to walk back across the courtyard towards the main house. He waved a hand carelessly at the frontage of another converted barn or stable, set even further back than the annexe that had belonged to Philomena. 'I'm sure it's very dull and you don't want to be bothered with that right now.'

Which Posy took to mean that he didn't want them poking around in his house and there was no reason not to respect that.

Chapter Six

'But you're coming to the nineties bash – right?' Marella frowned as she dragged a hand through the lengths of her dark hair.

Maybe this Skype call hadn't been the best idea after all. It had been a long day, a long drive home, and Posy was tired. It had been a strange one too, full of new and uncertain situations. Giles and Asa had been only too happy to give Posy some photos of her mother – though they had nothing later than her aged twenty, which was when she'd left home – and Posy had spent a full hour staring at the likeness, marvelling at how much of that woman she now recognised in the mirror, and mulling over the details of what they'd told her.

Her mother was slimmer at twenty than Posy now at twenty-seven, though it looked like the kind of delicateness that came from constant agitation. She had the face of someone who was never settled, and Posy felt she looked far more content. But they shared the same soft, pert features, the same long eyelashes, hair somewhere between blonde and brown – though Angelica's fell much longer and thicker around her shoulders.

And for some strange reason that wasn't the only thing still playing on Posy's mind. As much as anything else, she kept going back to the excruciating run-in with the angry naked man at the lake. Whatever the reason, whenever she thought of it her face burned with indignation and embarrassment, and – much as she tried not to – she seemed to think of it often. He'd been so rude and offensive about what had really been an easy mistake to make that it was hard not to. She supposed she could understand him being a little embarrassed – after all, she'd caught him stark bollock-naked – but what did he expect if he insisted on swimming in lakes in the nip? It might well have been private property but it was hardly hidden from view. Hadn't he heard of swimming trunks? Decency laws? Public right of way? Private property indeed! If it had been somewhere she wasn't allowed to walk then surely someone would have warned her.

'Posy!'

Marella clicked her fingers to bring her back. 'Where did you go?'

'You don't want to know,' Posy said quickly, hoping the heat in her cheeks wouldn't show too much on the screen at Marella's end.

'So are you coming or not?'

'I don't know—'

'But you said you would and I've organised for Vince to meet us there now!'

Vincenzo… Posy tried not to curl a lip. Marella was somehow convinced he was a good match for Posy, no matter how many times Posy tried to tell her he wasn't. On paper he was perfect – there was no doubt of that. Italian parents, hot, toned, good job in the City. Great teeth… very expensive teeth. He'd make a great boyfriend for someone if only he had the capacity to love a woman half as much as he seemed to love his own reflection.

Marella said he had hidden depths and that he was really far more humble when you got to know him, and maybe that was true. But if he did have these hidden depths then, as far as Posy could see, they were so well hidden that it would take an archaeological dig to find them. Certainly a better and more patient woman than her.

'I'm sure he's not going to be heartbroken if I don't go,' Posy said. 'It's not like there won't be any other women there for him to have a crack at.'

'I know but he really likes you.'

'He really likes his biceps. I've seen him admiring them in his window reflection when he thinks nobody is looking.'

'That's harsh.'

'But just a little bit true. Even you've got to admit he's hardly the most modest man you've ever met.'

'He can't help it.'

'How so?'

'It's in his blood.'

'I'm sure it's not.'

'You say that but have you ever met a modest Italian?'

Posy laughed. 'How many Italians do you know? Isn't it just Vince?'

'I know... well, I've seen them on TV.'

Posy's laughter was louder now. 'I'm sorry,' she said once it had calmed down. 'I'm just not into him. I know he's Cain's best mate and all, and you're trying to get off with Cain, and you have this little daydream where we date them at the same time so we can do double dates, but it just isn't going to work. Not for me anyway. Sorry.'

'You couldn't at least give him a chance? You might surprise yourself and have a good time. You do remember what a good time is, don't you?'

'Ha ha, very funny.'

'I'm being serious. I hate to say it but I'm not the only one – these days it feels as if it doesn't happen all that often.'

'Everyone's saying I'm miserable? Great! Couldn't you have told me this before?'

'Of course everyone isn't saying that. All I meant is people have commented that you don't come out as much as you used to.'

'I don't know…' Posy twisted a loose thread on a nearby cushion. 'I suppose I'm getting a bit bored of the same places and faces…'

'Wow, thanks. Now I'm offended.'

'Not you,' Posy said with a half-smile. 'Never you.'

'I should think not. So it's a no to the party?'

'I'm not sure – I just don't think I can muster the enthusiasm. Say you'll forgive me… go on, say it.'

Marella sighed. 'Of course I do. But don't think I won't try to persuade you again before Saturday.'

'You can try, but it doesn't mean you'll succeed.'

'So… the weekend in the countryside was good?'

'It was. Surprisingly good; I actually really enjoyed it, and I think Mum did too.'

'Really? I thought you were terrified to meet these people?'

'I was. But they're lovely and it's so beautiful where they live… If you could see it.'

'I did – you sent me photos. Lots of photos. It looked very nice… green… You know… countryside-y.'

'It is. You'd hate it.'

'With a passion. The countryside is weird – that's why cities were built.'

'So weird…' Posy agreed with a wry smile. 'All that clean air, no car fumes, miles and miles of grass and trees and flowers and pretty houses and not a graffitied tower block in sight. Nobody slamming into you rushing to get somewhere or angry drivers trying to mow you down because you're crossing the road too slowly for them. A lovely cooling breeze blowing through the apple trees instead of sticky, grimy summer heat and the sound of birdsong instead of honking car horns. You're right – it is weird. I can't imagine why anyone would choose to live there.'

'You have just summarised all my problems in one paragraph,' Marella said, grinning. 'Sounds just like some Sunday night drama – you know, the ones where the most thrilling thing that happens is old Farmer Smith's pig gets piles. I'm sure it's utterly charming to look at but it would get boring very quickly. You're a city girl, Posy – you need to remember that. You're about as urban as it gets.'

'I know, but I'm just so bored right now.'

'Boredom is no reason to live in the countryside. If you're bored come to the party with me on Saturday.'

'Not that kind of bored. You're going to laugh, I know, but these days I feel as if I just want something else. I'm sick of bars and night-clubs and constantly checking I'm still cool enough.'

'I'm sure you wouldn't have to worry about that in Somerset. They'd think you were an absolute radical there, an *enfant terrible* with your fancy city ways.'

'It's not *that* backward! Sure it's a slower pace of life but they're hardly living in the Dark Ages. The lady who owns the guest house we stayed at moved there from London and she loves it.'

'Oh God! Please don't tell me this woman has persuaded you to do that! Are you going to write some horrible book like *A Year in Provence* following your escapades after you escape the rat race, find love with some country bumpkin and spend the rest of your fertile years pregnant?'

Posy couldn't help but laugh, even if Marella's appraisal of the average Somerset resident was far from complimentary. 'Don't worry –

if the desire ever comes over me I won't expect you to read my horrible book and I certainly won't expect you to babysit my massive brood.'

'Hmm.' Marella stifled a yawn. 'I'm sure it was very lovely, and I'd probably like it for a day or so but that would be my absolute limit. Anyway, I suppose you'll be seeing these people again?'

'They are my family, weird as that sounds. And I think they're really making an effort.'

Marella's taunting grin faded now, and she was serious. 'Are you really alright? I suppose it was strange. I suppose they must feel terribly guilty about everything.'

'A little,' Posy replied. 'I think they feel responsible for what happened, even though they couldn't possibly be. When my mother ran away from home she was twenty, but Giles was younger at sixteen and Asa was only ten. It's hard to understand these things at that age, let alone do anything about them. I think, over the years, they tried to persuade Philomena to make amends with my mother but she just wouldn't. From what Giles tells me, I think my mother would have been just as stubborn. I think she just didn't want to have any part of that life once she'd left.'

'And you still don't know where she ended up?'

'When they heard about her death, she'd been living in Argentina. She'd been working as a fruit picker, which is ironic when you think about it. But I don't think she ever settled down in one place for long and I don't think she had a proper job or a family.'

'She sounds like a free spirit.'

'I know, I'm very boring in comparison – if she'd met me I'm sure I'd have been disappointing. I feel as if I have far more in common with Giles and Asa already than I ever would have had with Angelica.'

'I can't imagine how I would feel about any of it. It would be horrible knowing my mother didn't want to keep me.'

'I thought it would bother me, but it doesn't. She probably wouldn't have been half the mum my own lovely mummy is. I think, on balance, I've had a much better life here than I would have done with her.'

'And your dad is the guy she was supposed to be having an affair with in the village?'

'I think so. Apparently he moved away with his wife not long after the affair became public and Angelica's father died.'

'And he's dead too?' Marella asked, going over information that Posy had briefly communicated via text but hadn't explained in much detail. 'It's all a bit tragic, isn't it?'

'Yes. Giles and Asa say they don't know where he went to live when he left the village and they said they could find out more for me, but I felt like it was all a bit awkward and not something they really wanted to do.'

'So you're going to leave it at that?'

'When things are settled a bit and I feel that we're all comfortable enough with each other, maybe I'll take them up on the offer, but not yet. I mean, he might be my biological father but it's hard to feel one way or another about him when he means nothing to me except for that. I don't even know whether he knew about me, but I'm assuming that he didn't as he never tried to find me. Perhaps I can be content with the family I have found who do want to know me.'

'It sounds messy.'

'It does a bit,' Posy agreed.

'Well, I know you're getting to know them and I think that's very important for you, but from a totally selfish perspective I hope you're not going to be missing every weekend – you have to come to some of these parties with me.'

'I will,' Posy said. 'Just as long as Vincenzo isn't there.'

'So, are we doing lunch tomorrow then, or are you going to stand me up for that too?'

'Don't be like that,' Posy chided.

'I'm not being like anything, but lately there's no telling with you. Will I be blessed by an appearance at the restaurant or not?'

'Of course,' Posy said. 'I wouldn't miss that.'

'Good, because I've already made a reservation.'

'Of course you have,' Posy said, laughing. 'Don't worry, I'll be there.'

Chapter Seven

She'd been away from London before, of course, lots of times. But never had her return felt so strange and off. Posy was happy enough to get back to work knowing that an exciting new project to design the interior of a swanky café-bar had just come in, and new projects were always fun. She was pleased that things had gone well in Somerset too, but despite all the reasons she had to be content, she was still gripped by a vague sense of melancholy as she boarded the overground train to travel into the office, a strange, unshakeable, low-level sort of… she could only describe it as dread.

Colleagues – older and more jaded, only working to pay the bills – had often described the 'Sunday Night Dreads', that sense of the weekend ebbing away to bring another unwelcome Monday, but Posy had never felt like that herself. And anyway, it was currently Monday morning. If it was the Sunday Night Dreads, why were they so inexcusably tardy? Why couldn't they have shown up the night before, on time and easily banished by a stiff drink?

She caught her connection to find the Tube as busy as the over-ground. It was always busy, of course, but even by Posy's standards this was hot and cramped and almost insufferable. Usually, a busy Tube journey was a minor irritation she'd shrug off, a necessary price to pay for living in the city, but today it only added to the distinct feeling that she just wanted to be somewhere else.

Anywhere else.

Well, perhaps not *anywhere*.

Somewhere like Somerset.

Actually… just Somerset.

Taking a breath and doing her best to shake the strange mood that had settled over her, she pulled out her mobile to check her emails. If there was anything urgent waiting for her at work she might as well know about it in advance. No matter how horrible it might be, at least if she was aware of it she'd be ready.

There was something about post-work drinks on Friday, a reply to a request for paint samples, lots of general housekeeping stuff about training and fire doors and people leaving dirty dishes in the communal kitchen, but nothing to worry about.

But then, even though she ought to have been relieved, that fact alone was vaguely disappointing and unsettling. What the hell was wrong with her?

To take her mind off things she clicked onto her Instagram feed. There was the usual parade of photos: nights out on the town, babies, pets, successful bakes, screenshots of jogging routes and finishing times… and then there was a photo of Oleander House.

Posy's breath caught in her throat. She wouldn't have imagined she'd react like this, but somehow it had caught her off guard. Carmel had posted it and captioned it 'Lovely weekend at this beautiful house' though she hadn't given any more specific details than that. Posy half wondered if Giles and Asa would be OK with their house being on Instagram, but perhaps they wouldn't care; after all, the business they ran from there had an extensive social-media presence and a website with many photos of the house and apple presses that anyone could see.

Relaxing a little, she looked more closely at the photograph. Carmel had dabbled in photography when she was younger and she certainly hadn't forgotten how to frame a subject. The place looked stunning, caught in the rosy light of the golden hour, the branches of a cypress tree dripping into the foreground. Her mother had probably done a little editing to heighten the colours; the scene was vibrant and almost hyperreal.

Even though Posy had visited and met her new family there, it was still strangely alien to her that real people lived in a house like this; normal, down-to-earth people just like her. By their own admission, they'd been fortunate to inherit Oleander House and privileged to grow up there, but it still seemed incredible to Posy, like the sort of thing you saw only on films or TV.

Whatever Carmel had done with the photo, Oleander House looked achingly beautiful and Posy felt a strange tug. All she wanted right now was to be back there, roaming the orchard or the meadows with the sun on her back, crickets in the grass and birds singing in the trees. Already the weekend felt like a distant dream, a tantalising taste of a different life.

She closed the page and opened her camera roll, scrolling through her own photos of Oleander House, Karen's guest house, of fields and trees and flowers and orchards.

Mentally shaking herself, she locked her phone. *It's just the Monday blues*, she told herself sternly.

The train halted and Posy looked up to see yet more people cramming into the already packed carriage. If Einstein had been there, he'd have been taking notes to rethink everything the world knew about physics because, despite appearances to the contrary, they all eventually found somewhere to stand and the train started off again.

Posy tried not to make eye contact with a woman who had her knees pressed against her; any closer and she'd have been sitting on Posy's lap. She let out a deep sigh, drew in a damp breath, and once again wished she was in the wide, sunny meadows around Oleander House instead of sitting in a sardine can of sweat and disgruntlement.

It was strange just how profound an effect visiting Somerset – and more specifically Oleander House – had had on Posy. While she'd often felt bored or dissatisfied with her life as it was now – and she realised that in many ways she had no right to be – she'd never actively desired to change it.

Was that what was happening now? Was this some kind of tipping point? A crossroads in her life? And if it was, why now? Why at all? She had it good in London, didn't she? The perfect life, the envy of so many, and yet something was missing. She'd always known, deep down, that something was missing, but while previously it had been hidden, the noise and bustle of her existence muffling the voice that wanted to tell her so, over the weekend it had suddenly become loud enough to be heard. It didn't want to be ignored any longer and Posy wasn't sure she wanted to ignore it anyway.

Which was all very well, but what was she supposed to do about any of it?

'So, you're back amongst the living then?'

Marella reached for the carafe and poured herself a glass of iced lemon water. The restaurant was busy, as it always was on any weekday lunchtime, other workers sitting virtually shoulder to shoulder at the long trestle tables that ran the length of the room, all making the most of a fleeting burst of freedom. Posy had never liked the seating arrangements here, having to sit on benches with a dozen or so other people as if she was in a school hall or prison canteen, but Marella was obsessed with the food and so Posy often acceded to a request to make this their lunch venue. Today was no different and, if anything, Posy had even less inclination or energy to argue. She hadn't managed to shake the strange, melancholic feeling of dissatisfaction that had plagued her on the Tube that morning, despite having been so busy at work that she'd barely had time to spare another thought to any possible explanation.

She looked up briefly from where she was trying to get her chopsticks to tackle a particularly troublesome gyoza from the plate they were sharing.

'You do know London isn't actually the centre of the universe, don't you?'

'Try growing up in Sheffield and you'll soon realise it ought to be.'

Posy raised her eyebrows. 'Don't let your parents hear you say that. I'm sure they think Sheffield is perfectly lovely.'

'It's alright for you – growing up here you take it for granted. As soon as I could spell London I knew I'd move here one day. I was desperate to get here, but I'm beginning to wonder if you're desperate to get out. Which, in my humble opinion, is complete madness. Why would you want to leave a place where you have absolutely everything you could ever need? You know the grass isn't greener anywhere else…'

'It's definitely, empirically, incontrovertibly greener in Somerset,' Posy said with a smile. 'You can't deny that – it's scientific fact.'

'Yes, it's picture-postcard lovely. The gazillion photos you sent me told me that. It might look nice but you'd be bored inside a month if you lived there.'

'Maybe…' Posy replied slowly. It wasn't what she was thinking but perhaps Marella had a point. The idea of life there was impossibly romantic but she was viewing it as just that – a romantic ideal. The reality was probably bugs and slurry and patchy phone signals. Oleander House and the surrounding area looked beautiful in the sunshine but perhaps it wasn't quite so appealing mired in a freezing grey sleet in January. Like going on holiday to Greece and daydreaming you lived there, just for a while as you wandered the beach. The reality would be very different, but the dream was nice to indulge in. Perhaps she wasn't appreciating enough just what she had here in London?

'It sounds as if your meeting went well, though,' Marella said.

'I actually can't believe how well it went,' Posy said. 'They were so welcoming. '

'There you go then – you'll be seeing plenty of Somerset from now on; the best of both worlds.'

'Sometimes things are so busy here… I honestly don't know how much time we'd have to go.'

'Nice to have the choice at least.' Marella slurped an extra-long noodle into her mouth and licked a blob of sauce from her chin. There were no airs and graces with Marella. She often said you could take the girl out of Sheffield but you couldn't take Sheffield out of the girl. Not that Posy would ever want to.

They'd met on the first day of art college. Actually, they'd both made friends with other people on the first day of art college, quickly realised how boring those other people were, and, by the first lunch break of that first day, had managed to 'ditch the dodos' (as Marella had called it) and snuck off to the pub together without them. They'd collaborated on art projects, fallen asleep at bus stops together after heavy student nights, holidayed together and eventually graduated together. They'd even – on occasion – dated the same boys, though not at the same time.

Eventually the time had come to part, but only because they hadn't both managed to get jobs at the same design agency and had to settle for work at rival companies. No matter where life intersected or where it pulled them away from each other, they'd never been anything other than the most loyal, devoted friends since that first day at art school.

'Actually, one of my uncles… God, it's weird to call someone that!' Posy sipped her iced water. 'Asa asked me if I'd give him some design tips for his house.'

'The whole huge shebang?' Marella's eyes widened and Posy laughed lightly.

'God no! Just his annexe…'

'Annexe? How big?'

'Sort of barn-sized.'

'I hope he's going to pay you well. I thought you said these people were broke?'

'Not broke, they just have a lot of their money tied up in the business. Anyway, I'm not sure I'd be allowed to do it for money. If work found out they might not like it much.'

'They wouldn't have to know.'

'I suppose they wouldn't, but still… Though I could give Asa a few pointers; that couldn't hurt and I don't see how anyone could complain about that.'

'It would get you brownie points too, I expect. Though I'd be tempted to use the opportunity to springboard into a freelance career. You've talked about it enough – maybe now's the time to do it.'

'I'm not sure if I'm ready yet. It's a leap.'

'Sometimes you need to leap.'

'Easy for you to say; have you met me?'

'I know you're not the world's biggest risk-taker,' Marella said, laughing. 'But you're still in a good place to take a risk – no mortgage, no kids, nobody relying on you. If you want that dream you have to gamble, and I'd say now's the time, when you have a lot less to lose.'

'I'd rather not leap blindly though – these things need time spent thinking about them.'

'You'd think forever and a day. How about a push instead of a leap?'

Posy smiled. 'A push could work. But I don't see that happening any time soon. And depending on what sort of push it might be, perhaps I ought to hope it never happens. If I'm going to do it, I'd like to do it on my own terms.'

'Fair enough,' Marella said. 'Are you eating that last dumpling?'

Posy nudged the plate towards her, accidentally knocking elbows with the young man sitting next to her. She offered a brief and vague apology, expecting the same, but instead he stared at her and then smiled, and inwardly she groaned as she detected the first signs of flirtation. He wasn't her type, but even if he had been she wasn't interested. Most of the men she'd dated over the years had proven to be shallow or self-absorbed or spineless or needy or selfish or boring and, in some very unfortunate cases, all of those things at once.

She didn't think she was overly fussy or demanding and she'd give love a fair crack of the whip, but Cupid hadn't done her any favours so far. She wasn't even sure she could be bothered with the chase these days. If Mr Right found her then great, but she was fast losing faith that he existed at all and losing the will to care even more quickly. She had her career, her family, her wonderful friends and a brilliant life – what else did she need? She didn't need a man to define her and she didn't need one to complete her.

Ignoring the young man's attempts to engage in any kind of conversation, Posy turned very deliberately back to Marella and reached for her hand, saying in a loud voice: 'Darling… we should probably get home soon. Little Max will be desperate for his walk before we go to bed… and you know it's date night tonight, don't you? So we won't be going to bed late…'

Marella giggled. They'd played this scene before and it had become an effective way to shake unwanted male attention for one or the other of them – sometimes both on a very busy night out.

'Oh yes…' Marella replied in a husky voice. 'How could I forget date night?'

Posy chanced a glance and saw that the man was now looking very deliberately at his phone. She turned back to find her friend still grinning.

'You're terrible, Muriel,' she said, a reference to one of their favourite films.

Posy returned the grin and watched as Marella popped the last gyoza into her mouth.

'We probably ought to pay the bill anyway,' she said. 'I've got a ton of emails waiting at work and if I don't start going through them soon I'll be stuck in the office till midnight.'

'We could have rescheduled lunch if you were that busy,' Marella said airily as she munched. 'You should have said.'

'No, I wanted to come. It's done me good – I was in a foul mood this morning.'

'And now?'

'Much better now,' Posy said.

'See, that's the Marella effect.'

'It really is,' Posy agreed as she searched her bag for her bank card. 'You ought to bottle yourself for general sale.'

'Hmm,' Marella said, thoughtful for a moment. 'I wonder how that would go down on *Dragons' Den*…'

Chapter Eight

Sometimes Posy found it frustrating and annoying that she still lived with her mum at her age. She'd say she lived with both parents, but her dad was away working on the offshore wind power projects he helped to set up around the country so often that she barely considered him to live with them at all. She knew her mum missed him all the time, and when Posy found herself frustrated and annoyed with her situation she had only to remember how lonely Carmel might be if Posy wasn't there to feel a lot less annoyed about it all. One day she'd have to go, of course, and there had been many late-night discussions about it prompted by this or that minor incident but, for the most part, both Posy and Carmel were perhaps a little too content with the current arrangement to do much about it.

Though that might all be about to change.

Carmel had just cleared away the remains of a supper Posy had cooked. Nothing fancy, just a quick spinach omelette and a salad. While Carmel stacked the dishwasher, Posy stretched out on the sofa in their conservatory, listening to the rain drum on the glass, blanket over her knees as the sky began to darken. Her mind was in Somerset again. She couldn't say why the place had taken hold of her imagination in such a sudden and violent way, but something about it had lodged in there. Whenever she thought of it, she wanted to be there.

'Penny for them…'

Carmel came back in with two glasses of gin and tonic, poured over mountains of ice and topped with a lemon wedge.

'Though,' she continued, 'judging by the look on your face, perhaps I ought to up the offer. Ten pounds for your thoughts?'

Posy pushed herself to sit, crossing her legs and pulling the blanket up round her lap before taking one of the glasses from her mum. Carmel settled on the opposite sofa.

'Want to talk about it?'

Posy smiled. 'I'm alright – just tired.'

'OK,' Carmel said slowly. 'It's just that I'm aware we haven't really discussed at any length what happened at the weekend.'

'Oh, that… Well, there's not that much to discuss that we haven't already been over.'

'Not even how it's made you feel? Whether it's changed anything for you?'

'Nothing's changed.'

Carmel raised her eyebrows. 'Honestly?'

'Honestly, it changes nothing – between us at least. I was more worried that you might feel differently… you might worry that you wouldn't be so important to me now, but you absolutely are and will always be, no matter how many birth families I might find.'

'See – typical you.' Carmel smiled. 'Always thinking of everyone else when you ought to be thinking of yourself.'

Posy sipped at her drink. 'Do you think they meant it?'

'Meant what?'

'Giles and Asa and Sandra… do you think they really want us to stay in touch? Or do you think they were just being polite? Maybe they feel guilty about everything and are trying not to look like the bad guys, but maybe they'd secretly be happier if they never saw us again.'

'They're not really the bad guys, are they? They certainly shouldn't feel guilty about things they had no control over.'

'But I bet they do. I would.'

Carmel was silent for a moment, her gaze turned to the garden beyond the conservatory windows. More of a yard, really – a long strip of paved land strewn with pots containing trees and plants and shrubs of all shapes and sizes and, just at the end, almost in darkness, was the tiny brick pottery studio where she worked during the day.

'Perhaps I would too,' she said finally. 'I think the offer was extended in a genuine spirit of friendship.'

Posy nodded. 'Me too. I just wasn't sure I was reading the signs right.'

'I'd love the excuse to stay at Sunnyside again if nothing else – Karen was a hoot.'

'She was. Nuts, but in the best way. We don't need any excuse to stay with her – we can just go anyway if we want to.'

'True.'

'What a life she has there. She must be deliriously happy every morning when she wakes up to start a new day.'

'What a lovely thought, eh? To love your life that much.'

'We love ours, don't we?'

Carmel smiled. 'Of course we do. Sometimes I'd be happy if it slowed down a little, but I suspect I'm just getting grouchy in my old age.'

'You're not getting old – I refuse to accept it!'

'I'm not as young as I once was either.'

'Young at heart – that's what counts.'

'Isn't that what you youngsters tell us oldies to make us feel better about being old?'

'Maybe. Does it work?'

'Not really. One day you'll see what I mean.'

Posy grinned as she took another sip of her drink.

'Actually, Karen emailed me this morning,' Carmel said.

'Did she? I didn't break anything, I swear.'

Carmel laughed. 'Nothing like that. She thanked us for coming to stay and said she hoped we would visit again next time we went to Astercombe even if we ended up staying at Oleander House overnight. She also asked if either of us had been to the vineyard while we were there… apparently the owner of the vineyard that borders Oleander's orchards has been complaining about someone trespassing. He went straight to Karen, assuming it was one of her guests. Know anything about that? You *did* take that walk by yourself, and you did seem a little flustered when you got back…'

'I didn't even think it was worth mentioning,' Posy said, aghast. 'Oh, God, I hope Karen didn't get into a lot of trouble – he seems like a horrible man. It was an accident; I didn't mean to wander onto his stupid land. If he doesn't want people on there he ought to build proper fences – there was nothing… well, nothing worth mentioning. How was I meant to know it was private land?'

Posy wondered whether to add the small detail of how naked the man had been when he'd caught her wandering his land but decided against it. Partly because the memory made her blush still – and not just from embarrassment – and because she'd rather liked what she'd seen and felt naughty about the thoughts suddenly racing through her mind. Instead, she clamped her lips around the rim of her glass and took a long drink.

'Ah,' Carmel said with a slight grin, which made Posy wonder just how much she – and Karen – knew about the details of Posy's transgression.

'Did Karen sound very annoyed?'

'Oh, I don't think she was annoyed at all. She says he's an absolute pain and found it all quite amusing.'

'I should imagine people wind up on his land all the time. It's not very well marked out, you know. I mean, if it had been the vineyards I'd have known not to walk there but it just looked like wild fields to me.'

'Perhaps, but Karen didn't say anything about that being the case.'

'Oh.'

Somehow it was vaguely disappointing to hear that Karen wasn't keen on her neighbour either. For some reason that Posy couldn't explain she'd half hoped she'd been wrong about the man and that perhaps their misunderstanding was the only thing that had got them off on the wrong foot. But if Karen didn't much care for him either then he probably wasn't very nice, which was a shame.

Why was it a shame, though?

Posy chased the question around her head for a moment, until it escaped and disappeared off into the distance. Pesky thing. But no good could come of answering it anyway and it hardly mattered – it wasn't like she was going to be seeing angry naked man again any time soon. Or even at all. Ever. She didn't even know his name, although she did now know that he owned the vineyard she'd spotted that day.

Carmel's phone rang. Posy watched her pick it up from the table.

'Anthony…' she said, smiling broadly as she answered.

'Tell Dad I said hi!' Posy mouthed.

'You can tell him yourself in a minute,' Carmel replied. 'No, not you, Anthony. I was just saying to Posy I'll put her on in a minute. First of all, how's everything in Lincolnshire…?'

Carmel began to chat and Posy settled into the sofa to wait, cradling her gin and tonic as she watched the rain grow heavier outside.

Posy met the delivery driver halfway up their front path as she left for work the following morning.

'Dashwood?' he asked with a sniff.

'Yes, but I—'

'Wait there…'

Posy glanced at the time on her phone and wondered whether she ought to go and get her mum to deal with this, but before she'd come to a decision the driver had returned from his van, staggering towards her with a box. It didn't seem oversized but it was clearly heavy, judging by the way he grunted as he carried it.

'Where do you want this?'

'What is it?'

'How should I know?'

'Oh… of course… I'll take it.'

Posy held out her arms and he dropped it into them, and even though she'd expected it to be a bit heavy, she almost fell backward under the unexpected strain.

'Do I have to sign for it?' she puffed, but the driver was already down the path and getting into his van.

'I guess that's a no then,' she said.

A moment later the van was gone in a cloud of blue smoke that suggested at least one engine in the capital wasn't going to pass any imminent emissions testing. Posy took the box and set it on the doorstep while she got her keys out. Luckily, Carmel had heard the exchange and appeared, ready to give Posy a hand bringing the box in.

'What on earth could it be?' she asked. 'I haven't ordered anything – have you?'

'Not that I can recall,' Posy said. 'Better open it and find out – it might have come to the wrong address.'

'Lord, I hope not; that's one distraction I can do without today. I've got that Kew Garden commission to finish before the weekend and I'm nowhere near.'

'Well, it's not our job to send it on anyway,' Posy said, though, in reality, she knew from experience that Carmel would feel responsible for that task whether it was hers or not. She wouldn't be able to relax until she was sure it had reached its rightful destination.

Carmel went to the drawer and returned with a kitchen knife. Quickly she slit the tape sealing the box and opened it up to reveal about a dozen bottle tops. Posy lifted one out to look at the label.

'It's cider from the orchard!' she gasped. She looked up to see Carmel smiling broadly.

'Oh how lovely!'

Carmel pulled a card out from down the side of the box. '"*You never got to sample the new variety*",' she read out. '"*We thought you might like a crate to enjoy at your leisure at home. We hope you like it. Please don't be a stranger to Oleander House. Lots of love, Giles, Asa and Sandra.*" Isn't that the loveliest thing?' Carmel looked up, and Posy fought to keep tears from her eyes. This meant a lot to both of them;

more than a kind gesture of friendship, it was acceptance of Carmel and Posy into their lives.

'Oh, and there are cider cocktail recipes!' Carmel added, pulling out a slim booklet and flicking through it. 'These look wonderful – we'll have to try some. We must email them to say thank you!' She began to search for the phone she often left lying around only to forget exactly where just moments later.

'I'd better go, Mum,' Posy said, suddenly remembering that she was supposed to be on her way to work by now. 'I'll message them later.'

'Oh, yes, of course, darling.' Carmel slipped over to kiss her lightly on the cheek. 'I'll see you in time for supper tonight? It's my turn to cook. I thought we might have those Thai fishcakes you like.'

'You will,' Posy said. 'And I'm guessing we might have a nice bottle of scrumpy to go with that?'

'Absolutely!' Carmel said.

Posy turned to leave the house a second time, a beaming smile on her face and thoughts of Somerset once more in her head. It seemed that Oleander House just wasn't going to leave her alone.

She'd already resigned herself to the fact that she was late, but her boss, Joanna, wasn't usually a stickler for time in that way. As long as Posy got her work done, if she started a little later or finished a little earlier from time to time then that was OK. All Joanna cared about was a steady stream of happy clients, and how they got to that state of nirvana was open to interpretation, so Posy wasn't unduly worried as she walked into the glass-walled central London office of Torsten Design.

That quickly changed. Every one of her colleagues was huddled around a single desk, deep in conversation.

'What's going on?'

Everyone turned sharply at Posy's question. Some looked guilty, some worried, and at least two looked downright terrified. Every one of her colleagues was there apart from her boss, who was nowhere to be seen.

'Trouble at mill,' Brendan said – his well-used Monty Python quote that was often trotted out so casually taking on a far more sombre quality this time.

'What kind of trouble?' Posy said. 'Not the Spanish Inquisition?'

She started to smile, but clearly she hadn't read the room well enough. Even as she'd fired the reply that would usually have Brendan grinning in recognition, she realised that this was no time to joke. The smile died before it had bloomed.

'The company's in trouble,' Shania, who sat at the desk next to Posy's, said. She could be melodramatic sometimes but, even knowing that, Posy was starting to realise that she ought to be getting worried. Something had everyone seriously rattled. There were workplace dramas all the time, but they didn't ever leave the room feeling quite so charged as it did right now.

Posy slowly shrugged off her jacket, her eyes still searching the faces of people who were more than colleagues; they were friends too. 'When you say trouble…'

'Money,' Shania said.

'Or a lack of it,' Adele, one of the more senior designers, put in. Adele had been with the company since its founding – fifteen years now. She was Joanna's go-to for big clients and contracts. She looked worried, and perhaps, if she looked this worried, it was time for Posy to start being worried too.

'Surely it can't be all that serious?' Posy asked. She was struggling to understand just what was going on. 'Who told you this? What did they say, exactly?'

'Joanna's in with Cameron now,' Shania said. 'Hardeep overheard them. They mentioned redundancies, reduced hours…'

Posy vaguely wondered how long Hardeep had been listening in and whether he really ought to have been at all, but she let the thought drift for now. She also wondered how she hadn't heard whispers of any of this before. In most workforces as tight-knit as theirs someone would have heard some rumour or other about belt-tightening or cashflow problems, but, unless that person had kept it very securely to themselves, nobody had as far as she knew.

She glanced around and wondered which of her colleagues might already be aware of this and who would have kept it to themselves if they had, but she just couldn't imagine who might do that. Perhaps it didn't really matter in the end – even if she had heard anything like that, what could she have done about it? Would she have taken it seriously or just put it down to gossip? Maybe it was a question for later – right now there were more pressing concerns.

Adele folded her arms. 'I, for one, can't afford to reduce my hours and I certainly can't take redundancy. I've just bought a ridiculously large house…' she let out a sigh. 'I should have known it would be a risk… Just my bloody luck.'

So, Adele had clearly been as much in the dark as Posy. That ruled one of her colleagues out of the secret-keeping.

'I'm on a temporary contract so I suppose I'll go first,' Shania said glumly.

'You've been on that contract for about three years now and they keep renewing it.' Posy tried to sound encouraging. 'You were only supposed to be here for six months, weren't you? They must think you're really good. You'll probably be OK.'

'I'm the same as Shania,' Hardeep said. 'I don't think whether they appreciate our talents or not has anything to do with it this time. I wonder if they've seen this coming for a long time and that's why they never offered us a permanent contract, just kept extending me and Shania. Who was the last person to be taken on permanently?'

'I think that would be me,' Posy said, and as she glanced around a few people nodded agreement. 'So if it's last in first out then I would have to take the redundancy.'

'We don't know any of this is going to happen for certain,' Brendan said. 'Maybe we're all jumping the gun a bit offering to fall on our swords… if that isn't too many metaphors in one sentence there…'

'I certainly haven't offered to fall on anyone's sword,' Adele said, turning sharply to him. 'What part of bigger mortgage don't you understand? I can't afford to lose my position here.'

'I don't suppose any of us can,' Posy said.

'I could offer to resign,' a young girl with short orange hair said. Posy scrabbled for her name. She'd just joined them a couple of weeks before and Posy hadn't had much time to chat to her. Adele jumped in to put Posy out of her misery.

'Becky, you're the intern – we don't pay you anyway!'

'Oh… of course… Well, you do pay me a little… I suppose it's not really enough to make a difference…'

Becky blushed, her gaze going to the ground.

'She's just trying to help,' Posy said. She realised that Adele was stressed and scared but still she felt that her admonishment had been a little harsh. She tried to give Becky an encouraging smile, but Becky didn't look up long enough to catch it.

A cacophony of faint pings echoed in the brief silence that filled the room: messages going to every computer, all at the same time.

'Aye, aye,' Brendan said grimly, his native Yorkshire burr the strongest Posy had ever heard it in all the time she'd worked with him. She wondered if times of extreme drama brought it out – because this was a time of extreme drama in anyone's book. He strode to his desk and opened up his message.

'We've got a full staff meeting this afternoon.'

'I've got the same email,' Adele said, calling over from her desk. 'I think we're all cc'd in.'

'Brace yourselves,' Brendan said, looking round the room. 'Things are about to get interesting.'

Chapter Nine

Posy could barely believe it. By the end of the month she'd be unemployed for the first time since she'd graduated from university. In fact, even then she hadn't been unemployed because she'd plugged the gap between graduation and her first design job (this design job, as it happened) with part-time work at a pizzeria – the same one she'd worked at all through university. Perhaps that was why she felt strangely calm about it all – it hadn't really sunk in yet, and perhaps when it finally did she'd become the proverbial headless chicken, firing out panicked applications for any dead-end job that would have her.

'You've got your savings at least,' Carmel said soothingly. 'And you can stay here with me as long as you like – you know that. Your forever home if you want it.'

Posy clasped the glass containing a crisp and ice-cold sample of the cider that had arrived only that morning – an event that was now so utterly eclipsed by everything else that had happened since it felt like a lifetime ago. She'd been so positive and so happy as she'd left the house for work – how different the end of a day could be to the way in which it had begun.

'That money was supposed to be for my own place. I know I have a forever home here but it's not what people do, is it? I have to move out sooner or later.'

'And I'm sure you'll get a job sooner rather than later too. Chances are you won't need to use much of your savings at all.'

'Hmm. Only there's three of us chasing every design job in London and two of us are a lot more experienced. I'm about the least qualified of everyone being let go at Torsten.'

'Experience isn't everything. You're young, fresh, full of fire… creative industries love that. It might give you more of an advantage than you think.'

While Posy appreciated her mum's optimism she wasn't quite as convinced. But she smiled bravely and tried to share it.

'At least I'll have some time on my hands to do some things for me – until I get another job anyway.'

'You could help me in the pottery.'

Posy raised her eyebrows slightly. 'You don't need me in the pottery – there's just about enough work coming in to keep you busy. And I don't have the delicate touch you have. If your clients want house bricks then maybe I'm your girl, but anything daintier than that I'm afraid is just not in my skill set.'

'It's only a matter of practice,' Carmel said. 'You'd be as good as me in no time if you were making it every day – probably better.'

'I suppose a change is as good as a rest,' Posy said doubtfully, attempting to convince herself as she spoke, trying to picture herself at her mum's wheel, confidently throwing an elegant vase or bespoke soup tureen. 'And it would be nice to spend time in the studio with you.'

'If you decide you fancy giving it a go we could trial it. You're not a total novice, after all. I don't think it would take you long to hone your skills and we could chase more commissions with two of us working. In fact, I think the idea is rather exciting. Your redundancy might prove to be a blessing in disguise.'

'The last time I threw a pot was at uni,' Posy reminded her. 'I might not be a total novice but I won't be far off – and I wasn't exactly skilled back then. I think it might take more training than you imagine.'

'A bit of rust always polishes off,' Carmel said. 'I don't think it would take you long.'

Posy smiled ruefully. 'Well, I've got four weeks yet so I suppose I can get some practice in before I join you properly – that's assuming I do. I haven't decided what I'm doing yet. I love that you want me to join you but I think it's a good idea to look for a job anyway. It's hardly a long-term solution, even if it does work out.'

'It won't work out if you've already decided it won't. And what about all those times you've talked about starting out on your own?'

'Working in the studio with you isn't exactly on my own, is it? Besides, that was supposed to be once I'd got my own place and money behind me – that's years off yet.'

'Not necessarily.'

'The time just isn't right, Mum.'

'Sometimes you have to accept that the time will never be right. Sometimes you have to take a leap of faith regardless.'

'I thought you were supposed to be the sensible one,' Posy said with a wry smile. 'Not encouraging me to be reckless.'

'I'm not, I'm just helping you to explore your options. You're at a crossroads and it seems to be the perfect time to do that. And look at it this way – perhaps now is exactly the right time because you have precisely zero to lose. You don't have a mortgage or rent to pay, you don't have a partner who might be relying on you as the breadwinner, or children to put through school. Money in the bank or not, it might be the time to take the gamble because you have support in the form of your dad and I if it doesn't pay off, and you're still young enough to go back into the workplace and continue where you left off in your career if you have to. I'd never have pushed you, but I've been able to see for some time you've been itching to put on those wings and see what the sun is like from close up.'

'Don't forget Icarus fell to his death,' Posy said.

'I know, because his dad let him go too high and wasn't there to catch him. That's the difference – your dad and I would always catch you.'

'It's not that I don't appreciate that, but, as I said before, if I worked in the pottery I'd be working for you – I wouldn't be on my own at all.'

'Then do something else. Design, paint... you're good at those things. The opportunities are out there if you figure out where to look. Or if you tried potting and took to it I could make you a partner and we could expand, fifty–fifty equals.'

'Working with you does sound lovely, Mum, if only because I think it would be super chilled, but maybe it would be too chilled and I'd get complacent. I need to be pushed. I'm sorry, and please don't be offended, but I think I need to find my own thing.'

'I'm not in the least offended. I'm glad we're able to have this discussion if it helps to give you some food for thought. You know that whatever you decide I'll be here to support you.'

'I know.' Posy gave her a fond smile. 'I'm so lucky to have you.'

'Not as lucky as I am to have you.' Carmel raised her glass. 'To the lucky Dashwood girls!'

'Absolutely!' Posy lifted her own glass with a laugh. She took a long draught of her cider and smacked her lips. 'This really is incredibly good stuff,' she said, gazing into the amber depths of the glass. 'I've never been a cider drinker but I could get used to this.'

'So could I,' Carmel agreed. 'A glass of this on a sunny terrace overlooking the fields…'

'So not in the conservatory with the rain beating on the roof overlooking our cramped garden?'

'I suppose I could still enjoy it that way in the absence of any better option,' Carmel said with a light laugh.

'Do you ever think about leaving London?' Posy asked after a short silence.

'What brought that on?'

'I don't know… As you get older do you think you might like to live somewhere quieter?'

'Sometimes,' Carmel said.

'You could work from anywhere and so can Dad. What's stopping you?'

'I don't know. It's a lot of hassle, I suppose. And better the devil you know and all that. I don't really know where I'd like to be instead. I don't feel that pull to a specific place as so many others who decide to up sticks and change their lives do.'

'Like Karen at the guest house?'

'Exactly. I envy Karen. She knew at once where she wanted to be but I've never really felt that. I've never had to think about it either. My life was in London as a youngster, and then as you grew up you built your life here too.'

'So I'm the reason you're staying now?'

'Of course not, but it's a factor. The idea of moving to the country is lovely but the reality isn't always like that, I'm sure. There are plenty of good things about living in the city that I think I'd miss. You never get bored for a start – there's always something happening.'

'True,' Posy agreed. 'Although, sometimes even I feel I could do with an excuse to slow down.'

Carmel raised her eyebrows in disbelief. 'What kind of statement is that at your age?'

Posy laughed. 'I know. Secretly, deep down, I think I'm just a boring person who likes simple things. I keep up appearances and try to fit in with the cool crowd, but I'm beginning to wonder whether I wouldn't be happier on a farm somewhere bumbling around picking apples or something.'

'Could this be the after-effects of our visit to Astercombe? We all know a brief idyllic visit is very different from the realities of living somewhere.'

'But couldn't you see yourself doing what Karen did one day?'

'Throwing my life here into the air to run a guest house? God no! That's far too much socialising for me. I'm happiest locked in my studio.'

'Not the hotel, but living in the countryside…'

Carmel paused for a moment, her eyes on the windows. 'Perhaps one day,' she began slowly. 'It's not as simple as all that.'

'Isn't it? Surely you just go if you want to?'

'If it were that easy everyone would be doing it.'

'Lots of people do. You know what you said to me about making the leap. Don't you envy Giles and Sandra and Asa their lives, just a little?'

'It wouldn't be like that for us and we certainly wouldn't be living in a glorious place like Oleander House.' Carmel studied her daughter for a moment. 'You really have been thinking about this, haven't you? Anyone would think you wanted me to go.'

'I don't unless you want to…'

'And you'd come with me?'

'I suppose I might…' Posy gave her a lopsided smile. 'I suppose it might be an adventure… don't you think?'

'I think you might find the opposite is true and you'd be pining for the bright lights of home after a month of "adventurous" country living.'

'It might be fun to try, though. You must think that.'

'Decisions like that aren't made because they'll be fun. Decisions like that can alter the course of a life and they have to be thought through. If you get it wrong—'

'But you don't know until you try. Nobody does, even when they feel certain. Don't you think?'

Carmel smiled slowly. 'I think you're in a strange mood. You've just had earth-shattering news on top of earth-shattering news and you're trying to process it. I think you should give yourself a couple of days to do that and then talk to me again about whether it's a good idea to throw our life into the air and see where it lands.'

Posy grinned. 'But I thought you said this was the time to try something new…'

'Did I? That was rather silly of me, now that I think of it. And if I did, I meant something new career-wise. Life somewhere like Astercombe would be charming, I'm sure, but I don't know what kind of career you could build there. Let's face it, the opportunities – or the majority of them – are in London.'

'Are they? Maybe twenty years ago that was true but we have technology now that means I could potentially work from anywhere.'

'Yes, but why there?'

'Why not there? Why not anywhere else? I'm not even saying there, I'm just hypothesising. Why do we have to stay in London?'

'You really want to leave?'

'No… I don't know. I only wonder if a change of scenery might do me good and this seems like the time to do it, if I'm ever going to. I mean, I have a reason, a link to Astercombe now, don't I? Just like Karen had. It all feels like a sign. And please don't think for a minute that this changes anything I said to you about you and Dad always being the most important people in my life. But…'

Carmel was silent for a moment. Posy took another sip of her crisp and tart cider; she could almost taste every apple in Oleander's orchard.

'Perhaps you ought to talk to Asa,' Carmel said finally.

'Asa?'

'He was keen to have you help with his annexe redesign, wasn't he? He said there was no pay, of course, but I'm sure they'd put you up and feed you. And they did seem keen to see a lot more of you.'

'Of *us*, Mum…'

'Of *you*. It would give you the chance to see what life is like somewhere else if you're so keen on it.'

'But when they said they'd like to see more of us I'm not sure they meant *that* much!'

'Perhaps not,' Carmel admitted. 'I suppose it might be a bit forward – it was just an idea.'

'To be honest,' Posy continued thoughtfully, 'I had thought about offering to help Asa, but it was more along the lines of having a look and perhaps drawing up something that I could email to him later on. I suppose that would mean going to have a look in person. So it would be a good reason to visit, if nothing else.'

'And perhaps a good excuse for me to come with you?' Carmel said with a sly smile.

Posy grinned. 'Another weekend away? I'm not going to complain about that.'

'Neither am I.' Carmel raised her glass again. 'Perhaps we can pick up some more of this fabulous cider too. I've never been a cider drinker either, but I think this might have changed my mind.'

'Want me to find out if Karen has any availability?' Posy asked. 'Then I can message Asa to see about meeting up to have a look at his place.'

'That sounds like a very good plan to me,' Carmel said.

Posy was inclined to agree. It sounded like a very good plan indeed.

Chapter Ten

They were driving up the track that led to Oleander House when he caught Posy's eye – fully clothed this time but still an unmistakeable figure; once seen, hard to forget. Every inch of him seemed to be taut, tense, muscles straining and visible even beneath his denim shirt. He eyed the car as he rolled up his sleeves, his stride never faltering as he looked right inside and connected with Posy, who was sitting in the passenger seat. She turned instantly away, blushing and feeling strangely guilty about nothing in particular.

'Someone got out of the wrong side of the bed this morning,' Carmel said mildly.

Posy turned to her. 'Hmm?'

'That man. He looks as if he thinks the world is out to get him.'

'Oh…' Posy hesitated, and then thought, what the hell. Even she didn't understand why she was so reluctant to share their meeting with her mum. 'I think that might be my fault. That's the neighbour Karen was telling you about. The one whose land I trespassed on.'

'Oh!' Carmel laughed lightly. 'You naughty girl! You're going to have to try harder not to upset the locals if you're going to be spending more time here.'

'Don't I know it!' Posy didn't think she'd ever uttered a sentence with more heartfelt sincerity. She most certainly didn't want a repeat of anything like that day by the lake. Despite this, and despite the fact that the charged moment that had begun this confession had now passed and the neighbour was already far behind them, she was also strangely and vaguely disappointed by that. He was handsome – the type of handsome that would turn heads even in London, where the handsome-guy-per-square-metre quota was far higher than everywhere else, because every hot actor, musician and model naturally congregated there to find work. Although a higher proportion were often dickheads too. This guy was obviously a miserable pig, but perhaps he wasn't a dickhead. Then again, she thought, perhaps he was. He'd certainly behaved like one when she'd stumbled across him swimming in the lake.

Naked...

For a moment she was lost in the memory until her mum spoke again.

'It looks as beautiful this time as the first time we saw it.'

Oleander House rose up ahead of them and Carmel was right. If anything, it was more beautiful than the first time they'd seen it, because now they knew what they were heading into and could appreciate the house and the welcome that lay within.

'We'll drive right up this time, eh?' Carmel continued. 'It's much nicer knowing you're definitely welcome than being quite terrified of what awaits.'

'I was just thinking the same thing,' Posy said warmly. 'Much nicer!'

*

As before, Sandra, Giles and Asa came out to meet them.

'We saw you pull in,' Giles said. 'Well, when I say we, I mean that Sandra sent the shout up. She's been like a cat on a hot tin roof all morning, racing around to get everything ready.'

'I wanted to make sure everything was straight – that's all,' Sandra said with a slight frown at her husband.

'You didn't need to make any special arrangements for us,' Posy said as she accepted Sandra's kiss on the cheek.

Carmel nodded agreement. 'Once you've seen the inside of my pottery studio you'll realise we can live in any kind of chaos quite happily.'

'I can vouch for that,' Posy said, smiling at Giles and Asa in turn before Sandra reached to give Carmel a welcome kiss too.

'It's so lovely to see you both again,' she said.

'It's good to be back,' Carmel replied. 'We were just saying how Oleander House looks even more beautiful than we remembered it.'

'Probably because you're not worried about visiting this time,' Sandra said, echoing the thoughts that both Posy and Carmel had had independently. 'I think we were all stressed that day but it's going to be much more fun this time.'

'I'm sure if it has anything to do with you it will be,' Asa said. He turned to Posy. 'How are you? It's good of you to bring a bit of London glamour back to dreary old Somerset again.'

'If you'd ever walked past the pubs in Soho at throwing-out time you wouldn't think it was glamorous at all,' Posy said with a light laugh.

'Come on through to the patio,' Sandra said. 'I'll fix us drinks while Giles puts the finishing touches to lunch and you can get me up to speed about what's been happening since we last saw you.'

*

Lunch was pork and pear salad, followed by tarte aux pommes and cream. All the fruit had been grown on their land and the pork had come from a farm just beyond the far boundaries of Astercombe. They finished with coffee which had come from a little further afield – a few more thousand miles further afield, Asa said with a grin – and then later, when they'd all got their second wind, they continued with cheese that had been matured in the caves of Wookey Hole and a crisp sparkling wine.

'Wow, this is good,' Carmel said. She reached for the bottle to take a closer look at the label. 'Made locally too? Is it made here?'

'Oh no, we wouldn't have the first clue about grapes,' Sandra said. 'It's made by one of our neighbours.'

'Oh,' Posy said, exchanging a look with her mum. There was no need to ask which neighbour – there couldn't be many vineyards in the area.

'Do you swap produce with him then?' Carmel asked. 'He sends you wine and you send him cider?'

'Oh goodness, nothing like that,' Sandra replied with a faint smile. 'I got it in the village shop. It looked nice and I like to buy local where I can. Besides, if rumours are to be believed he needs all the pennies he can make.'

'He doesn't do well? I thought there was a real market for British wines these days?'

'I believe so,' Giles said. 'But like many businesses there are lots of variables and success can be fickle. Just because one does well doesn't necessarily follow that another will.'

'Do you speak to him much?' Posy asked. 'Is he a friend of yours?'

'He's very private,' Giles put in. 'We speak to him when we have to but it's usually strictly business.'

'More's the pity,' Asa added. 'Trust us to get a misanthropic neighbour. Good, interesting company is scarce enough round here, and when the only people who move in are miserable hermits it hardly helps.'

Posy resisted the urge to raise her eyebrows at the remark. It was a little quiet in these parts, she'd imagine, but everyone (mostly) that she'd met was perfectly sociable and very interesting. She was sure they must have events and get-togethers through the year.

'How long has the vineyard been there?' Carmel asked. 'I would have thought it's far easier to grow something native like you do.'

'Oh, years,' Sandra said.

'There was a vineyard on that site or somewhere close by mentioned in the Domesday Book,' Giles said. 'In fact, I think there was a vineyard there until the Middle Ages. It disappears from the records – or so Nigel told me – around then, probably due to the mini ice age making Britain too cold to grow grapes.'

'Nigel?' Posy asked. 'Is that the man who owns it now?'

'Nigel is the previous owner,' Sandra said. 'He replanted the vines in the nineties when viticulture became fashionable in the UK again, but Lachlan has only owned the vineyard for the past couple of years or so. It had become a bit neglected but he's working hard to turn it around. And you can grow some very nice grape varieties here, so I believe, if you know what you're doing.'

'It was neglected by the previous owner then?' Posy asked.

'Not neglected exactly,' Sandra said. 'It was more that he just didn't manage to get it right. He tinkered about with various crops but he couldn't seem to hit on the right one and he never really broke even.

Lachlan arrived a couple of years ago to try his hand. I think he got it for a good price as Nigel was desperate to offload, but he hasn't been much more successful in making it turn a decent profit.'

'He's doing a bit better than Nigel was,' Giles said.

'A run of bad luck didn't help poor Nigel,' Sandra said. 'Bad summers and pest problems – it just wasn't going to happen for him. I think he got very disillusioned with it all. The years before Lachlan came and took over he hardly produced anything at all.'

'So Lachlan is the man who owns it now?' Posy asked.

'Aye, lassie…' Asa growled in his best, gruffest Scots accent, which was so surprising to hear from a man who was so softly spoken that it set Posy giggling. 'What do ye mean, there's nay such thing as the Loch Ness Monster!'

'Asa!' Sandra chided, even though she was trying not to laugh too. He grinned.

'I'm not saying it's not an attractive accent,' he said in his own voice again. 'It's just a bit in your face. Especially when it's coming from his miserable face. It sounds very incongruous amongst all our Worzel Gummidge accents.'

'I would imagine it makes him stand out,' Carmel agreed.

'Oh, he'd do that anyway,' Asa replied with a sudden wicked look. 'He might be as miserable as sin with a heart as black to match, but there's no denying he's a damn fine-looking man. And an airline pilot, I'm led to believe – at least he was in a previous life – which makes him even more attractive as far as I'm concerned.'

'It also explains why he doesn't have the first clue how to run a vineyard,' Giles said.

'I think he runs it OK,' Asa replied carelessly. 'It's just the making-money bit he seems to have an issue with.'

'Perhaps he'd do better if he didn't upset the few staff that are willing to work for him,' Giles said.

Posy got the impression that Giles didn't think much of Lachlan's business prowess, but she supposed she didn't know much about it.

'How does he upset them?' she asked.

'I think he's just his usual sunny self.'

'So he's not very nice to anyone – not even the people who work on his land?'

'These days it's just him,' Sandra said, 'so he doesn't have to worry too much about that.'

'How does that work?' Carmel asked. 'Surely it's too much for him alone?'

'I should imagine it keeps him busy,' Giles agreed. 'Acreage-wise the vineyard isn't huge – more of a second career type of business. Nigel and his wife and two daughters managed it so it's probably doable for Lachlan with the odd bit of seasonal help – although I must say I wouldn't want to take that workload on.'

'You'd almost certainly need help around harvest time,' Sandra reminded him.

'Oh, undoubtedly.'

'So what does he do then?' Posy asked.

'I've no idea what he plans to do this year,' Giles said. 'He had half a dozen or so helpers last harvest, but by all accounts he struggled to pay them and it left him very short. I suppose he could do the day-to-day work at a push, but I don't imagine it leaves much time for anything like a social life.'

'I don't think he knows what one of those is anyway,' Asa said. 'I don't think he's ever had one. I don't think he even has a past.'

Sandra chuckled. 'Of course he has a past. Everyone has a past – he didn't just fall from the sky fully formed.'

'Well,' Asa replied, 'there's not the faintest whiff of gossip to be had about him except that he's single.'

'We hear things about the vineyard,' Sandra said.

'That's not gossip; that's business reporting,' Asa replied. 'Who cares about that? If he had any kind of past it must have been terribly bland.'

'As you might have guessed,' Sandra said with a wry smile at Posy and Carmel, 'Asa is hopelessly in love with him.'

Asa looked at his sister-in-law archly. 'You're telling me you're not?'

'I am not! I'm very happily married to your brother!'

'Yes, I can see why Giles would give William Wallace a run for his money,' Asa said blithely.

'Thank you for that.' Giles reached for the wine to top up his glass. 'Don't forget we share the same genes.'

'Yes, but have you seen the man?' Asa continued. 'He's like a Greek god! I'm not even sure how he can be real!'

Posy suddenly felt very hot, and it wasn't because of the wine or the afternoon sun that was now finding ways to burn through the greenery woven into the trellis they sat beneath. She'd seen his Greek god physique herself, up close and extremely personal – certainly more personal than it was polite for two complete strangers to be – and Asa's words brought the occasion very forcefully back to her now. She could definitely vouch for its effects, but perhaps now, in polite company, wasn't the time for her to be reminded of that.

Then, as if to compound her mortification, Asa turned to her.

'What do you think? You met him, didn't you? So Karen says.'

'I did bump into him…' Posy began uncertainly. How much could she say here? Would they disapprove of her trespassing on Lachlan's land? Was there some kind of unwritten, unspoken law around here that to trespass, even unintentionally, on anyone's land just wasn't cricket? Did they find it supremely annoying if anyone ever wandered into their orchards, even if it was a lost tourist stumbling around?

'Trespassed on his land, so I heard,' Asa said, relieving her of the dilemma. So they knew about that bit at least and didn't seem too disapproving. In fact, Asa was grinning again. 'Did he threaten to release the hounds?'

'I wandered on there by accident,' Posy said. 'I must admit he didn't seem very happy about it, but I didn't do any harm; I was only walking.'

'He's rarely happy about anything,' Asa said. 'I wouldn't take it personally.'

'I've certainly never seen him smile,' Sandra agreed.

'All that work to turn the vineyard around and still struggling to make ends meet – I'm not surprised he doesn't smile,' Giles said. 'I doubt he has time for such luxuries as smiling.'

'It looks like a lot of work,' Posy said. 'And he lives there completely alone?'

'No wife living there, that I do know,' Asa said, and sounded quite pleased about it. Posy had to agree – something about that news pleased her too, though God knew why. Lachlan might be undeniably good-looking but he was just about the rudest, coldest, most miserable man she'd ever met. How could the news that he was single possibly give her any kind of satisfaction?

'More wine?' Giles held the bottle up to Posy.

'No thanks – not just now. I probably ought to take a look at Asa's project first.'

Giles nodded. 'Asa, why don't you go and show Posy what you want?' He turned to Carmel. 'You could tag along while Sandra and I clear up.'

'I'll help you if it's all the same,' Carmel replied. 'I'd like to make myself useful and I'm sure Posy and Asa will get more done if I leave them to it.'

Sandra smiled. 'In that case, your help would be most welcome.'

Asa looked expectantly at Posy. 'Come on then, unexpected but very useful niece of mine, let's get on with it!'

Asa's house was a long, open space, the interior characterised by exposed brick walls and heavy beams criss-crossing vaulted ceilings. Large windows ran along the south-facing aspect, fronted by a long patio to make the most of the sun, and three doors off the main space contained a master bedroom, Asa's study/spare room and a bathroom. The floors were grey slate, worn from years of footfall during the building's former life as a barn. As far as Posy could see, it looked open and contemporary and quite pleasant enough already – far more modern than the main house where Giles and Sandra lived and the second barn that had been converted for Philomena.

Despite this, and all its mod cons and modern sensibilities, it wasn't nearly trendy enough for Asa, who apologised almost constantly that it must be such an eyesore to Posy's trained eye, even though she told him many times that it was anything but.

'I just can't seem to get the look quite right,' he complained. 'I see the thing in my head but it doesn't translate to the room. And I feel certain the space as a whole could be utilised better.'

Posy smiled but thought that he'd probably watched too many episodes of Grand Designs. Her working life would be a lot easier if people didn't watch these television programmes and think that they could achieve the same in a day or so, and on any spare bit of change they had left over from the shopping that week. As for Asa's house, there was a good deal of space here working perfectly well as it was. There was really no need to worry about effective utilisation. But, she supposed, there was always room for improvement, even if it was only a little improvement. He'd asked for her help and she was happy to give it.

'There are a few things I could suggest,' she said. 'I'd have to take some measurements and work them out before I could say for certain.'

'Right… so do you make drawings? Take photos or something?'

'It might honestly be easier if you tell me what you want first. Have you seen a scheme you like? Any ideas on themes or aesthetics?'

'Some.'

'So, do you have photos or anything you can show me, just to give me somewhere to start?'

'I'm afraid I don't…'

'Oh. It would be helpful as a first port of call. I could spend hours designing something that in no way matches your needs or your tastes. It'd be good to get an idea of your tastes before I start, what you want to use each bit of the house for, how you use it day to day now, what features are important to keep and so on. Then I could draw up recommendations from there.'

'You must think me so silly,' Asa said ruefully.

'Of course not – why would you think that?'

'Here's me asking you to come and wave a wand over the place…'

'I wish I could,' Posy said with a smile. 'It would make my job a lot easier. People have no idea how many times a design can go back and forth before it's agreed on, and even then clients can change their mind – sometimes even as it's all being installed. I've had some absolute nightmares... but I'm sure you won't be one of them.'

'I'll try very hard not to be.'

'That's all I can ask for. But I absolutely don't want you to stay silent if I give you anything you don't like or think won't work for you. Better to get it right at the planning stage than be stuck with something worse than you already have. Deal?'

'Deal,' Asa said. 'I bet it's a fabulous career, isn't it, though? Especially when you get to see your designs in the flesh, as it were?'

'It's rarely a solo effort and clients are often heavily involved, so it's hard to take all the credit. I like to think of myself as a facilitator for their own ideas. But yes... it is a good feeling to see people happy when it's done.'

'Right. Tell me what we need to do to achieve this aesthetic nirvana and I'll do it!'

Posy had to laugh. Asa, she was beginning to discover, had such an unexpected way with words that it was hard not to laugh, even when he might not have meant to be funny. And contrary to the more subdued first impression he'd given her, she was beginning to enjoy spending time with him very much too now that he was opening up. She'd never had an uncle and she'd never really considered what one might be like, but if this was the sort of relationship she could have had with one, then she'd clearly missed out.

'Do you have any magazines?' she asked. 'House decor pull-outs from the newspaper... anything like that you might have picked up and saved for reference?'

'I'm afraid not. I really am bad at this, aren't I?'

'How about a Pinterest board or an Instagram account you like?'

'I don't, but if it's important I'm sure I could do some research and find some.'

'It was just a thought to start us off. Why don't I send you a few links to useful design inspiration sites and you can spend time looking at them before we do anything else? When you've got some ideas of what you like then we can look at them together and I can start to figure out what might work and what definitely won't. Sound OK?'

A broad grin spread across his face. 'Oooh, you're good, aren't you? I can tell you've done this a few times before!'

'You could say that.'

But then his face fell and he looked vaguely pained. 'I'm ever so sorry I can't pay you much.'

'I wasn't expecting to be paid at all. You did say last time there was no spare money—'

'Yes, I was being facetious there, wasn't I? It will be my undoing one day. I realised afterwards how rude it must have sounded. Sometimes my mouth runs off on its own when it absolutely needs my brain to chaperone it.'

'It's really OK. To be honest, I won't have much else to do anyway for a while. If it's alright with you, when you're finished doing your refurb, if you do use my designs I'd love to come back and take some photos for my professional portfolio. I could do with a testimonial if you're willing too.'

'Oh, of course, take as many photos as you need and then take them all over again! But why don't you have much to do?'

'I'm about to be unemployed.'

Asa frowned and Posy gave a slight shrug.

'The company I work for needed to lay people off and I volunteered.'

'Why on earth would you do that? Is there a big redundancy pay-off?'

'There isn't one of those at all. But out of everyone who works there I probably had the least to lose having to leave and find another job. Besides, I was one of the last to start working there – it seemed only fair and decent in the end to take the fall and leave the jobs they did have for the others with families and mortgages.'

'Well, I hope these people appreciate what you're doing for them – it's very generous. What are you going to do? I expect you'll snap up another job quickly, won't you?'

'I'm not so sure about that but I hope it won't take too long. Mum and I have discussed it and she thinks I ought to work with her in the studio.'

Asa looked doubtful. 'Making pottery?'

Posy nodded. She couldn't help a small smile at his confusion, because she felt doubtful about such an arrangement with her mum too. It might have suited them both and it might have been the easy option for her, but it didn't feel right. Posy was supposed to be out in the world on her own – she was getting too old to rely on her mum, and taking up Carmel's offer felt very much like relying on her mum, even if it might prove advantageous to them both in the end.

'Let me see if I've guessed this correctly… You don't fancy it but you don't know how to tell her?'

'I honestly don't know what to do,' Posy said. The admission surprised even herself, considering how short a time she'd known Asa. 'Mum keeps saying I'm at a crossroads and this is the time to make changes, and I know she's right. I just don't know what those changes ought to be.'

'I never wanted to work here in the family business,' Asa said, suddenly solemn. This time, Posy was surprised by his frank admission rather than her own.

'Then why did you?'

He shrugged. 'Because I didn't know how to tell my mother – after Father died and Angelica left I suppose Giles and I felt more pressure to be the good children, so that we wouldn't cause Mother more stress. And then later after Mother died I didn't know how to tell Giles, and by the time I plucked up any sort of courage I'd got so used to working here that I thought I might as well carry on. It's not such a terrible life – sometimes it's quite idyllic – just not what I'd ever seen myself doing when, as a young man, I'd imagine the rest of my life.'

'Not exciting enough for you?' Posy smiled at his wry expression.

'I'm an open book, aren't I?'

'From where I am your life looks wonderful. Like a novel.'

'Maybe we ought to swap lives.' Asa grinned. After a moment, he shook himself. 'Come on,' he said briskly. 'Let's carry on into the bedroom so I can get your take on my feng shui. I don't know what I'm doing wrong, but I'm quite certain I'm doing something wrong because it hasn't made me a success yet!'

Posy followed him, deep in thought. She felt, finally, that Asa was letting his guard down and she was beginning to see clearly who he was. He was someone who felt a sense of duty but also felt trapped in a life he wouldn't have chosen, one he'd only settled for to spare the feelings of the people he cared about. She had to admire that and she liked him a lot for it.

From what she'd heard and seen so far, she also had to surmise that he was single. Was that down to his sacrifices too or had something else happened? Had there ever been a significant other in his life? She had a feeling that being single wasn't a state that suited him and she wondered if it was lonely for him at Oleander House, especially having to see his brother happily married, spending every day in domestic bliss.

The sound of Asa's voice brought her back into the moment, and as he smiled at her she felt almost guilty for the prying nature of her thoughts.

'Well… it's not huge but could we do something with it?' he asked, sweeping a hand towards the room. Posy noted immediately a king-sized bed and two double wardrobes. Either Asa had one hell of a lot of clothes or she was missing something far more important, but they were taking up a lot of space somewhere she felt they needn't have been at all. Then she noted two bedside cabinets. Par for the course in most bedrooms, but still she felt there was something more to it than that.

'It's quite…'

'Woody,' Asa said with a chuckle. 'Full of the stuff.'

'It's nice furniture, though,' Posy said. 'Looks like good quality. Don't you want to keep it?'

'It cost an arm and a leg and Giles says it ought to last for decades. He says I'd be mad to get rid of it.'

'But you want to?'

'I haven't completely decided yet whether I can bear to keep living with it. It's dark and really quite ugly. But perhaps I will…'

Posy glanced across to see Asa regarding the wardrobes, deep in thought, but with a sudden melancholy in his eyes.

'Do you use them both?' she asked, thrown by the change in mood and not knowing what else to say.

'Not now.'

'So one of them is empty? Could you perhaps just keep one?'

'But they're a pair, and it doesn't seem right to separate them.'

That sounded like an odd thing to Posy too. If he only used one, and he wasn't even sure he liked them (and it sounded like he didn't), what did it matter if they were separated? What did it matter if he kept either of them?

'It's something to consider later, maybe…' she said uncertainly. 'We'll talk about it as we draw up designs.'

'That would be good,' Asa said, snapping out of his reverie as quickly as he'd fallen into it and looking at her brightly again. 'You really are a godsend, and I don't know what I did to deserve you, but I have a feeling you'll have me sorted out and back on track in no time!'

And even that innocuous statement seemed to have a hidden implication that Posy just couldn't see for now, though she had a feeling that she might soon enough.

Chapter Eleven

'How lovely to see you again!' Karen smiled broadly as Posy and Carmel walked through the entrance doors of Sunnyfields Guest House. She was standing behind the reception desk, her hair tied back by a vibrant silk scarf. 'And so soon after your last visit too! You just can't stay away, can you?'

'Lucky for us you had that cancellation or I don't know what we would have done,' Carmel said. 'We couldn't possibly stay anywhere else after you spoiled us so utterly last time we were here – it wouldn't be the same at all.'

Karen's beaming smile stretched wider still. 'I'm usually fully booked for most of the summer so it must be fate, mustn't it? You were meant to come to me again.'

'It must be,' Carmel said, smiling too.

'Do you need some help getting your things to your room?' Karen looked at their overnight bags. 'I'm afraid you're right at the top of the house this time so it's a bit more of a walk. We have the lifts of course, but still…'

'I think we'll be fine.' Carmel glanced at Posy, who nodded. She was more than capable of taking her own bags anywhere she might want them to go, and she'd dragged far bigger suitcases up to the top floor of much higher hotels before now.

'If you're sure…'

Carmel nodded. 'Quite sure. I'm sure you have lots to do and we're quite capable.'

'Well, there's your key…' Karen handed it over to Carmel. 'Shall I see you both for dinner?'

'I wouldn't miss one of Ray's dinners for anything!' Posy said warmly.

'Oh, he'll be pleased to hear that,' Karen said. 'He takes his cooking very seriously – too seriously sometimes, I'd say.'

'It shows,' Carmel said. 'His food is as good as anything I've tasted in Michelin-starred restaurants.'

If Karen could have smiled any more widely she might have been forced to build an extension onto the reception area just to contain it.

'When you're ready you can come down to the bar if you fancy it,' she said. 'I've had a delivery from Oleander Orchard and their new coolers are to die for.'

'Oh, we tried one!' Posy said. 'They're amazing! I could definitely drink one of those before dinner!'

'Fabulous,' Karen said. 'I'll see you shortly then.'

It was as Posy and Carmel were making their way to the lifts that they heard a man's voice. Posy turned sharply, blood rushing to her face. She'd heard that voice before and she'd never forget it, but even if the voice hadn't been so memorable, the accent would have made it unmistakeable.

'Why give out an email address if you don't plan to respond to anything?' he demanded in a gruff voice that instantly reminded Posy of Asa's uncanny impersonation. She wished it wouldn't, because now she had a bizarre and completely inappropriate compulsion to laugh on top of the excruciating and desperate need to escape.

The fact that she whipped around to face him had been completely instinctive too, and as soon as she had she wished she'd been better able to control that impulse. As their gazes met, his lip curled. Slight, but unmissable. He definitely remembered who she was, and Posy didn't quite know how to feel about that.

'Guests of yours?' he asked Karen, angling his head in their direction.

'Yes, and if you don't mind changing your tone…' Karen replied with surprising mildness. The hackles were rising for Posy and she had to admire the fact that Karen appeared to be taking it all in her stride. Perhaps she was very used to dealing with Lachlan.

'I'll take whatever tone I want to,' he said brusquely. 'If you don't want me to use it then perhaps you might want to inform your guests that some land about here is not for them to wander as they please.'

Carmel looked over now, seeming to realise that he was referring to them. She was set to say something when Karen beat her to it, and the previous mild tone was suddenly gone. For the first time since Posy had met her, she detected annoyance instead. She glared at the man.

'Lachlan… if you've got something to say I'd appreciate you following me to the office where we can discuss it in private.'

With a last glower at Posy and Carmel, Lachlan seemed to decide Karen might be right and followed as she beckoned him behind the reception counter.

The space was suddenly empty and silent as they closed the door to a room off the main area. For a moment, all Posy and Carmel could do was stare after them.

'Wow!' Carmel said finally.

'My thoughts exactly,' Posy agreed. 'Someone needs a term at charm school.'

'Or some anger management classes,' Carmel said. 'It's his problem. Although, I do feel sorry for his neck muscles – being so tense and angry all the time must give him permanent neck ache.'

Posy was inclined to agree. 'I suppose, if what we've heard from Giles and Sandra today is true, it's no wonder he's tense all the time.'

'We all have money worries but it doesn't give us the right to go around offending everyone we meet.'

'I guess not,' Posy said. 'But it does go some way to explaining it.'

'So now I've finally met the neighbour of legend,' Carmel continued with a wry smile as she pressed the button to call the lift. 'And I'm quite gratified to see he's every bit as disagreeable as everyone says he is. Often what's promised by these stories is not quite the truth; it's good to see something live up to the hype!'

By the time Posy and Carmel had arrived in the bar for their pre-dinner drink, Karen was nowhere to be seen. In fact, the bar was empty. They wondered if perhaps it was just a little too early for most people and Carmel joked that they must be a pair of desperate lushes, and then they wandered into the day room to see if she was in there but didn't find her there either. Instead, they found Pavla, Karen's assistant, who informed them that Karen had been forced to go out to undertake a brief errand but would be back shortly, and that she could get drinks for them as she'd almost finished setting up for dinner.

'That's very kind of you,' Carmel said as they followed her back to the bar.

'Not a problem,' Pavla said, and Posy detected an accent that she couldn't quite place but sounded vaguely Eastern European. She wondered if Pavla was here to work over the summer or whether she'd settled locally. Maybe the story would unfold in conversation. Posy hoped so, because she loved real-life stories, especially ones about people who'd uprooted for new lives, how they'd come to be where they were and what had prompted them to make the move.

The story didn't come, however. Pavla served them quickly, making small talk but nothing more, and then, satisfied they had everything they wanted and telling them to look for her in the dining room if they needed anything else, she left them to it, all Posy's questions still trapped in her head.

'Here's to another lovely visit!' Carmel said, raising her glass.

'We'd better not get used to it,' Posy replied. 'Neither of us will want to go home and it would cost a fortune to live here with Karen.'

'I bet she'd let us though,' Carmel said with a chuckle. 'I wonder if she's still busy with that awful man? Perhaps her errand is something to do with his visit – she didn't mention having to go out when she offered to meet us in here earlier so something must have come up.'

'For her sake I hope not,' Posy said.

'Hello, you two!'

They both turned to see Karen at the doorway and Posy wondered if her mum was feeling as shifty as she was, having just been gossiping about their host. Well, not gossiping exactly, though depending on what Karen had caught it might have sounded that way. Still, she didn't look too troubled and she was smiling at them now.

'I see you managed to get your drinks already. I expect Pavla sorted them out, did she?'

'Yes,' Carmel said. 'Thank you.'

'I'm sorry I wasn't here – something came up.'

'Pavla told us,' Posy said. 'Nothing too serious, I hope.'

'Oh, nothing I couldn't handle,' Karen said cheerily. 'Although I could do with a stiff drink myself about now.'

Without waiting for a reply she went to the bar and poured herself a measure of brandy, taking a large, neat mouthful as soon as she had. They'd never noticed any evidence of a drink problem before, but the way she went at this one now had Posy wondering.

'Right,' Karen announced briskly as she knocked back the remaining alcohol and dumped the glass in a sink behind the bar. 'I'd better go and check Ray's OK with dinner. Come through when you're ready, ladies!'

Posy and Carmel smiled brightly and watched her leave. Then Posy turned to her mum.

'Do you think she's alright?' she asked in a low voice.

'Oh, I think so,' Carmel said. 'From what I've seen of her she's equipped to deal with any situation.'

'I suppose so,' Posy said, but she couldn't help wondering where Karen had been so unexpectedly and whether it had been anything to do with the appearance of angry naked man… Lachlan – that was it. She hoped it wasn't anything to do with the fact that he'd seen her staying here. More to the point, she hoped she wasn't going to keep running into him, because if she lived to be a hundred years old the memory of their first ever meeting was never going to be anything other than utterly mortifying.

Dinner was pork cutlet with roasted seasonal vegetables and was every bit as good as the one they'd enjoyed during their first visit to Sunnyfields. Carmel said she had a mind to go into the kitchen and give Ray a round of applause, but Karen just laughed and said that would be enough to send her painfully shy husband running for Cheddar Caves, never to return to polite society. So Carmel resisted the urge to visit the kitchens and, instead, she and Posy went back into the bar for a nightcap to take out into the garden where they could make the most of a sun that was setting gloriously over the distant hills.

Also on the terrace, seated at neighbouring tables, were an elderly couple who sounded American and two middle-aged women who had accents from the north of England. Posy and Carmel exchanged polite small talk on the way through with both couples about the lovely grounds, delicious meal and perfect sunset, and then they took their seats and their conversations became private again.

'I love it here,' Carmel said, eyes on the glowing horizon.

'Me too,' Posy said. 'It feels like a home I never knew I had feelings for until I knew it existed. Not that I don't love my home with you…' she added quickly.

'I know,' Carmel said in a soothing voice that told Posy she understood. 'But it is so lovely; if I was rich I'd be here all the time, every spare moment.'

'It's a shame we're not then. I bet you could get a fantastic second home here.'

'It's nice to dream, though, isn't it?'

Karen came out onto the patio and bid her guests good evening. She was like a queen, moving amongst her people to grace them with her presence. It was obvious to anyone that the socialising at Sunnyfields was more important to Karen than the income she got from it. Of course, without the income she wouldn't be able to survive, but Posy guessed she wouldn't last long without the social contact either. She loved to chat and she loved getting to know new people, and although Posy herself loved those things too, Karen was definitely more successful at it.

After exchanging pleasantries with the people at the other tables she came to Posy and Carmel.

'I told Ray how much you enjoyed dinner,' she said. 'I think you made his night.'

'Oh, we did,' Carmel said. 'I'm absolutely stuffed now because I couldn't stop eating even when I was full.'

'It's a good job we don't live here,' Posy agreed. 'I'd be like a whale after a few months.'

'We do eat well,' Karen said. 'Believe it or not I was a size eight when we first moved here. I can assure you I'm much bigger than that now. Ray didn't have as much time to cook when we were in London as he does now, and it shows!'

'Not much,' Posy said, but then wondered whether she'd actually managed to insult her host with that well-meaning but clunky platitude. She immediately decided not to elaborate for fear of making it worse, though Karen didn't seem bothered by the assertion that it had been noted she was bigger than a size eight.

'I must apologise for earlier, by the way,' Karen said. 'I know I offered to meet you in the bar before dinner but something came up and I'm afraid it couldn't wait.'

'Oh, the grumpy-looking neighbour?' Carmel said airily. 'We saw him earlier today as we were driving to Oleander House and he didn't look any happier on that occasion either.'

'Lachlan. Hmm, he did say something about trespassers on his land again today,' Karen said with a wry smile as Posy's face began to heat up in the way it did every time she thought of him. 'He seems quite put out about it – kept going on and on.'

Posy hoped that Karen wasn't going to bring the whole incident up again – even worse go into whatever details Lachlan had given her about it. Carmel knew the story by now, of course, and thankfully had enough tact to realise that Posy probably didn't want to go over it in front of Karen, no matter how tempting it might be to tease her.

'He owns the vineyard,' Karen said instead. 'I bet you saw it as you were driving here – it's quite hard to miss.'

'We did,' Carmel said. She gave an impish smile and Posy knew exactly what she was thinking. If she dared air it, Posy was going to have serious words with her later. 'He seems to have a reputation that precedes him. Is he always that charismatic and charming?'

Karen laughed. 'Absolutely! He's one of your Mr Rochester, tortured-soul types.' She put on a mock posh voice that made her sound like a film character from a gothic story. 'Very handsome but a haughtiness that hides a terrible secret that tears him apart.'

Carmel leaned forward eagerly. 'Is he now? Do tell!'

'Oh, I don't really know much about it,' Karen said, with an expression that suggested she did know something about it but had now decided that she might have given too much away and it wasn't her business to tell. 'Nobody does. He's very secretive and quite aloof. I mean, perfectly courteous and respectful, but he doesn't socialise and only says anything to anyone if he really needs to. Mostly complaining about something.'

'Sandra told me he doesn't have any family at the vineyard with him,' Carmel said.

'That's right. Pavla worked for him for a few weeks when she first arrived in England; she thinks he has some great tragedy in his past but even she doesn't know what it is.'

'Pavla who works here now?' Posy asked. 'She used to work for him?'

'Yes. As you can probably tell, he's not the easiest man to get along with and I think he upset her a few times. When he had to let her go because money was tight she came asking if I had a vacancy. I didn't at the time, but the poor woman was so desperate that I found one for her. To tell the truth, that's the best thing I ever did – she's absolutely amazing and makes life ten times easier for me. Lives on site too, which means she's always here when I need her. Not that I'd take advantage, of course, but it certainly makes me feel easier to know I'd have her help at a pinch.'

'Pavla doesn't live in Astercombe with family then?' Posy asked.

'No. I think she has rather a large family in Poland. She visits them when she can but I think she's come to like living here now. I don't think she'd go back in a hurry.'

'I don't blame her,' Posy said. 'It's so beautiful here.'

'It is,' Karen agreed, her satisfied gaze sweeping the gardens. 'I couldn't imagine living anywhere else now.'

'So the vineyard struggles?' Carmel asked. 'Sandra said Lachlan took it over fairly recently and money is tight… It's not something you associate with England, is it? Growing grapes, I mean.'

'He's got a lot of catching up to do because it wasn't going all that well for his predecessor. I'm not sure if it wasn't a great-uncle of his or something. I heard someone say something like that in the village. I think the debts and the work got too much for him and Lachlan bought him out. I can see he's making inroads turning the place around and he's producing some very nice wine now. But whether he's making a profit…' Karen shrugged. 'I suppose it's early days; he's only been there for a couple of years and it probably takes a good many harvests to turn things around – not that I'm any expert, of course.'

'Giles says the vineyard is more like a second career type of business,' Posy said.

'I wouldn't say that to Lachlan,' Karen returned with a smile. 'It's very much his first career – though I can see why Giles might say that; I'm sure it looks very tinpot to him compared to the orchard. And I'm sure Giles would admit that the orchard is no business behemoth either.'

'It's at times like this I wish I was a writer,' Carmel said. 'I'm sure there's a tale to be told in the history of that vineyard. Giles also said there was a vineyard there in the Middle Ages.'

Karen nodded. 'And even before that, I think… There's such a long history of growing in this area there were probably lots more dotted around too.'

'So Lachlan runs the vineyard absolutely alone?' Posy asked. 'Giles says so and he says it's not so big as to be impossible, but I find it so hard to believe; it doesn't seem feasible. He must have someone other than his staff, some kind of family on hand?'

'There's no family,' Karen said. 'Staff come and go; he can never afford to keep them. Even if he could, they'd have to have the patience of Job to work with him.'

'Perhaps he has a mad wife in the attic,' Carmel said, and Karen chuckled.

'Imagine that. I'll ask Pavla if she's ever seen a white-clad woman shrieking along the corridors in the dead of night.'

'I wouldn't be surprised,' Posy said. 'I think he's a bit scary.'

'Well, you would,' Carmel fired back impishly. Karen raised questioning eyebrows at Posy.

Time to come clean. It wasn't like it was a big deal and Posy didn't even know why she was making it one.

'It *was* me he caught on his land,' Posy said, heat rising to her face that had nothing to do with the evening sun. 'I suppose you already guessed that, or he told you. I'm sorry if it caused problems for you.'

'He might have mentioned it but I don't know why you're apologising to me.' Karen wafted a dismissive hand. 'And if the silly man won't secure his property then he can expect people to wander onto it. I've told him, if he wants to keep things private round here he needs fifty-foot fences, searchlights and guard dogs, because tourists end up in all sorts of places where they oughtn't through no fault of their own. You weren't to know that field was out of bounds. Anyway, he can't really complain with any conviction because what he doesn't like to be reminded of is that a public right of way runs through that land. Just because people don't tend to use it, doesn't mean they're not allowed.'

'Really?' Posy asked, going from embarrassed to now quite vindicated and not a little indignant too. How dare that man shout at her for being on his land when all along she'd been allowed to walk there? And what a stupid thing to do – swim butt-naked in a lake that was perfectly accessible to passers-by. Maybe he didn't get many, but he ought to at least expect that one day he'd get caught out – assuming that he did that sort of thing on a regular basis. Judging by his physique he was no stranger to physical exercise; whether that was swimming or other things…

Posy had to banish the graphic image of Lachlan's very fine and very naked physique from her mind and focus as Karen was talking again. She'd missed the first part – it could have been anything – and that was remiss of her, but it would be downright rude to miss all of it.

'Can I get you a refill too, Posy?'

'Oh… right…' Posy looked down at her glass. She couldn't recall emptying it, but another ice-cold drink would be very welcome. For some reason she was melting. Perhaps she was coming down with some kind of fever. 'The same would be lovely, thank you.'

Karen got up and took their empties inside.

'I *love* her,' Carmel said as they watched her go. 'It's such a shame she lives so far from us because I'm sure we'd become best friends if she lived in London.'

'Well, it doesn't sound like that's likely to change any time soon,' Posy said.

'Yes, more's the pity.'

'You'll just have to visit Astercombe a lot more often,' Posy added. 'Which I'm sure will be a terrible hardship for you.'

'Oh dear…' Carmel sank back into her chair, closing her eyes as she turned her face to the setting sun. 'I'm sure it would be, but I'd do my best to bear it.'

Chapter Twelve

No matter how old she got or how used she was to her dad being away from home, the excitement of him coming back for a few days never lessened for Posy. If absence made the heart grow fonder then Anthony Dashwood had run up one hell of a stockpile during the course of his professional life. Since discovering the truth about her maybe biological father, her love for the man who'd adopted her was greater and deeper than ever. Here was a man she'd always be able to rely on, a father who would always be there for her, would always care and always have her back, and she'd never been more grateful to know that.

In readiness for his trip home Posy had made an effort to tidy around the house, while Carmel had been to have her hair cut and coloured. Now the curls that were normally threaded with the odd (pretty, Posy thought) grey strand were instead a rich chocolate brown, and she was wearing the long mint-green floral dress she'd picked up that week in the sales that showed off the green of her eyes. Even though she'd looked in the mirror after all that effort and declared she was mutton pretending to be lamb and no amount of titivating would make her young again, Posy had told her she looked beautiful. She really meant it too.

Anthony arrived precisely one week on from Posy and Carmel's second trip to Astercombe, fully prepared to dip into the supply of fondness he'd built up and spend some quality time with his wife and daughter. He'd barely walked through the door when Posy flung her arms around his neck.

'Dad!'

'Steady on!' He laughed as he gave her a whiskery kiss on the cheek. 'I'm getting to be an old man now; you'll knock me over!'

'You'll never be old to me,' Posy said, though even as she did she detected a few more lines since she'd last seen him in the flesh, another outcrop of grey hair.

'Me neither,' Carmel said, stepping forward to give him a rather more passionate kiss. 'It's good to see you, Anthony.'

'Good to see you too,' he said. 'Even better to hold you…'

'Ahem…!' Posy squeaked, but she was smiling indulgently at the both of them. 'Maybe you'd like to keep that for later – difficult as I realise it might be.'

Anthony grinned and Posy grinned back, and for a split second a casual observer might have thought they were blood related, so similar did they look.

'I've booked a table for seven at the Italian,' Carmel said to her husband as he took off his jacket and hung it on the hook by the front door. Posy often felt that row of hooks looked somehow incomplete unless her dad's coat was hanging up alongside those of her and her mum. To see it there now filled her with a deep and happy contentment.

He glanced at his watch. 'Sounds perfect; it'll give me time to get cleaned up and have a quick snooze.'

'You will not snooze when I haven't seen you for two months!' Carmel admonished, and he laughed.

'But I've travelled from Lincolnshire!'

'I don't care. Sleep later – that's what night-time is for. Right now we demand your company.'

'Now you've reminded me why it is I spend so much time away from home,' he grumbled with a pretend sulk. 'You're so bossy.'

Carmel only laughed.

'Come through to the kitchen and I'll fix you a drink and a snack to tide you over until dinner.'

Anthony's favourite Italian restaurant wasn't his favourite because it was swanky or because it was trendy or even because the food was the best. It was his favourite merely because the owner, Enzo, had been at school with him and had once intervened in a fight over a punctured bicycle tyre that would have ended with Anthony getting a good beating from an older boy. Anthony had never forgotten it and they'd remained friends ever since.

They also supported the same football team, and, as far as Anthony was concerned, if ever there was a reason to be friends with someone, if not for the tyre incident, that was it. Especially if that team lost more games than they won, which had been the case pretty much every season for the past fifty years. If Anthony went out for dinner with Carmel on his visits home, it was Enzo's place he'd want to go to more often than not.

Enzo welcomed Anthony, Carmel and Posy warmly as they walked in at seven on the dot.

'You are looking well, my friend!' he exclaimed.

'That's a big lie,' Anthony said, 'I'm looking old. But thanks anyway. You're not looking too bad yourself.'

'I'm looking fat,' Enzo said with a rich chuckle. 'Too fond of tasting my own food.'

'It's harder to keep the waistline trim at our age, isn't it?' Anthony said.

'Sadly, yes,' Enzo replied. 'Your table is this way…' he added, gesturing for them to follow him. 'Average season,' he added as they walked through the restaurant. 'Not too bad, not too good.'

'At least they won't get relegated,' Anthony replied.

Enzo laughed. 'We hope. The season is almost over but there's time and, with that team, any dismal outcome is possible.'

'Even they couldn't get relegated from the middle of the table with two games to go,' Anthony said with a laugh.

Posy caught her mum's eye and grinned. Enzo would be too busy to spend much time at their table talking about football so they could indulge a few minutes now. Any longer than that and Carmel's eyes would start to glaze over anyway, and Anthony recognised the signs of that well enough after all these years.

'I'll bring some olives and bread,' Enzo said. 'On the house while you look at the menu.' He pulled out a chair to seat Carmel, and then did the same for Posy. 'What can I get you to drink?'

'We'll take a bottle of whatever wine you have that's good – I trust your judgement,' Carmel said. 'And perhaps some water for the table so that my husband can pace himself.'

Anthony laughed lightly as he sat down. 'Make that two bottles – I'm almost certain we'll get through the first before we've finished the starter. What?' he added as Carmel frowned at him. 'There are three of us drinking it!'

'I think Dad has a point,' Posy said.

'On your head,' Carmel said to Anthony. 'You'll be fit for nothing later.'

'And we don't need to hear any more about that,' Posy cut in, laughing.

Enzo went to get their olives, bread and wine and Posy got comfortable, letting the ambience of the restaurant – the warm smells of herby Mediterranean cuisine, the gentle hum of conversation, the clinking of glasses and cutlery on china, the soft lighting – chase away the stresses of the week. She'd done the first quarter of her notice period at work, and knowing that she was leaving hadn't made her job any easier. There were still deadlines to meet and clients to please, and on top of all that she had to make sure nothing was left hanging. All ends had to be tied up and all instructions had to be fulfilled or passed on to a colleague so they could do the work in her stead.

Along with all that, she'd spent the evenings working on Asa's designs, job-hunting and trying to fend off Marella's repeated nagging that she ought to go with her to another themed party because it was going to be the party of the year – this time it was a Star Wars fancy dress party. Posy couldn't think of a single thing she'd rather do less than go to a Star Wars fancy dress party, which sounded even worse than the nineties-themed party that Marella had tried to get her to before, although Marella was very excited about dressing up as Princess Leia. Even Posy pointing out that almost all the women would dress as Princess Leia didn't dampen her enthusiasm.

There were other friends Marella could take who would love it, and Marella agreed that was true, but it wouldn't be the same without her very best friend. At least this weekend Posy's dad had given her a perfect excuse to avoid any kind of unwanted social event.

'I'm glad to see Enzo's keeping busy,' Anthony said, looking around. Every table was occupied – though it was only a small restaurant by most standards. It had a reputation locally, though, which was why it had remained popular throughout the years it had been open.

'I'm sure Enzo is too,' Carmel said.

'I've missed you both so much,' he said.

'We've missed you. One day, we might even persuade you to take a job that lets you stay at home for more than three weeks a year.'

'I'm sure you'd be begging them to take me back again if I spent that much time at home.'

'We're used to you being away,' Carmel said, smiling. 'But it doesn't mean we have to like it.'

'I suppose I ought to be glad you don't like it; means you like me.'

Posy laughed. 'Steady on, Dad. Let's not get ahead of ourselves!'

Anthony grinned. Enzo returned with their nibbles and wine.

'Enjoy!' he said, leaving them with a flourish.

'Oh, we will,' Anthony said, reaching for an olive. 'I've been waiting months for my Enzo fix – I'm going to enjoy every moment of it!'

They were well into their second bottle of wine when the conversation turned back to Posy's future. They'd briefly touched on the subject earlier at home and Anthony knew most of the particulars from phone and Skype calls with Posy and her mum, but they still hadn't really got to the crux of the matter – or at least Anthony didn't seem to think they had. Which was what, exactly, Posy was going to do next. Her father seemed to be of a similar opinion to Carmel in that he thought it was a good time to change direction, but Posy was finding it harder to agree.

'I've got to work, Dad,' Posy said.

'We'd have your back for a while if you didn't,' he replied.

'That's what I said,' Carmel put in.

Posy reached for her glass and shook her head slowly. 'I'm not living off you. I'm far too old to be doing that and it doesn't seem fair to place that burden on you.'

'You wouldn't have to live off us. We'd just be giving you some support while you get things off the ground – it's not the same at all.' Anthony looked to Carmel for agreement and she nodded.

'I said that too, but you know what Miss Independent is like. I said she could even work in the pottery with me.'

'I can't see that lasting long,' he replied doubtfully.

'Thank you!' Posy exclaimed. 'That's what I've been saying! I love that you've offered, Mum, but I just don't think making pottery is me. I'd perhaps do it for a few weeks or even months but I couldn't do it forever.'

'It's too boring?' Carmel raised her eyebrows as she sipped at her wine.

'Of course not! I just don't think I have the patience for it. And like I said, I don't have the deftness of touch you have either.'

'I can teach you—'

'I know you can but I still wouldn't be as good as you and I'd worry all the time that I was ruining your reputation by turning out sub-standard ware. It's better if I stay away from it – at least, in the long term. Maybe I could haul buckets of slip around, fill the kiln, sweep up… but that would be about my limit really.'

'And that's no long-term solution for someone of your talent,' Anthony said. He turned to Carmel. 'I have to agree with Posy on this one. What about the people in Somerset? Didn't you say Asa was going to give Posy some work?'

'Largely unpaid,' Posy replied for her. 'He doesn't have much money to spare – it's more of a favour than anything else.'

'Could it be a springboard to your own consultancy?'

Posy gave a slight shrug. 'I've wondered that myself. Possibly… but I think I'd need more than just that to get going. The way I see it, the problem is it has to be all or nothing. I have to give up the job search and go for it, or I have to get a job and forfeit having the time to set up anything for myself.'

'Does it have to be that way?'

'I think to do it effectively it does.'

'Hmm…'

Anthony was pensive for a moment. Carmel and Posy waited patiently; it was clear he was working something through.

'What if we loaned you the money to set yourself up?' he asked finally.

'Absolutely not,' Posy said.

'Why not?'

'I'm not taking anything from you. I do this myself or not at all.'

'There's no shame in accepting a little help,' Carmel said. 'I've told you that already.'

'I know, and you already help me enough. I live with you for a lot less than I'd pay to live in a flat of my own. It's the reason I have any savings to fall back on at all.'

'Then use your savings,' Anthony said.

'I can't – they're for a deposit on my own place.'

'Don't you think it's worth putting that off for a bit to do something that might put you exactly where you want to be for the rest of your life? Surely, to wait for a while to get your flat and set up in business instead makes more sense long term?'

'But I can't continue to live with you and Mum until I'm an old lady.'

'I'm sure it won't be that long,' Carmel said patiently. 'Anyway, I like having you there; you're company when your dad is away, so it's no hardship for me.'

'I know…' Posy gave her a small smile. She knew her mum loved having her there and, the truth was, she loved being there, but it wasn't the way things were supposed to be. You didn't spend your adult life living with your parents – you marched out into the world on your own. She was very aware she was already running late in that regard, and if she didn't move out in the next couple of years it was going to start looking a bit ridiculous.

She was spared the necessity of a reply by the return of Enzo.

'I think you need more wine,' he said playfully as he removed the empty bottle and regarded the remaining one that was less than half full.

'If you can roll us all into a taxi at the end of the night we'll happily order another,' Anthony said.

'No problem!' Enzo cried, laughing. 'For you, anything!'

'To sell me more wine you mean…'

'That too!' Enzo agreed, his laughter louder still. 'I'll get you one more and I bet you have no problem drinking it.'

'That's the problem right there,' Anthony said wryly, 'we'd have no issue drinking it whatsoever.'

Posy smiled politely, but maybe she'd leave the getting drunk to her parents. She had no problem with getting drunk, per se, but the renewed debate about her future had put her in a sober mood, and her sober mood needed a sober mind to work it through.

The more she thought about it, the more she realised her mum and dad might be right. Carmel had said it, and Posy had given it a little consideration, but her dad saying it too inclined her to make those thoughts more serious. Perhaps it was time to take that leap. She still didn't know how to do it – or even where to start – but perhaps just acknowledging it was the first step.

Chapter Thirteen

Posy was giggling. She'd spent the last twenty minutes, on and off, giggling. She ought to have been offended at some of the judgements Asa had passed on her design suggestions, but it was hard not to find it all funny when those judgements were delivered with such wit.

'So no to leather,' she said once she'd managed to control herself again. She put down the mood board she'd been holding up to her webcam and rifled through her pile for something that she knew was completely different from the New York-businessman's-penthouse sort of style she'd put together. From the look on Asa's face, she'd obviously got that one very wrong.

'Unless it's gracing a bulging codpiece then no.'

'I've got something softer,' she said. 'Still quite sleek and a bit manly but lighter woods – a bit more Scandinavian.'

Asa folded his arms. 'Are you just going to show me the IKEA catalogue now?'

'No!' Posy giggled again. She held up another mood board, characterised by clean lines, light colours and lots of natural woods.

'We're going in the right direction,' Asa said thoughtfully. 'I could see that working in my little den. Why didn't you show me this one first – it would have saved a lot of time and my eyeballs a lot of offence.'

'It's the complete opposite of what you have now, that's why,' Posy said. 'It was more of a last-minute backup if I'm honest. And it didn't seem to fit the brief as well as the other schemes.'

'There you go – my brief was terrible then. The problem is, I know I want change; I'm just not very good at working out what that is and how to get it. I want things to be different, but I keep going back to the old things I know. It's honestly quite infuriating.'

'That sounds familiar,' Posy said with a wry smile.

'I'm stuck in my ways, that's the problem. Too many years in the old routine has made me lazy and a bit scared.'

'Scared of what?'

Asa paused, for the briefest second, and then shook his head. 'I have absolutely no idea!'

He started to laugh, but Posy couldn't banish the notion that he'd been about to open up to her, reveal something personal and painful, and now he was laughing just to fend it off. She almost wished he wouldn't because she couldn't help but feel it might do him good to share it.

'Well, how about I work with this aesthetic and do something a bit more detailed for you. Is there anything on this board that's an absolute no?'

'Perhaps you can make it a little more manly?'

Posy frowned. 'You mean manly like in all those other schemes that you hated?'

Asa smiled. 'OK, fair point. You know what, do what you feel and present it to me and, when you do, make me go with it. Perhaps that's just what I need – someone to give me change and make me like it.'

'I couldn't do that, and I wouldn't because you might end up hating it down the line and then you've spent all that money on it. I'll draw up some things and we'll go through them together, and then you can go away and take some time to try and picture your house that way. Then, when you're confident one way or another, we'll go from there. Could that work for you?'

'You really are good at this, aren't you? I can't imagine what your boss will do without you when you're gone.'

'I'm sure she'll get on just fine,' Posy said with a small smile. 'She's got a great team there, but I will miss them.'

'I'm sure you will. I'm sorry.'

'For what? It's not your fault.'

'I know, but I'm sorry anyway. It's hard to lose something you thought would be your life.'

'Oh, I never thought it would be my life, though I did think I'd be there for a lot longer. Perhaps until I'd found a bloke and had kids and they'd grown up or something.'

'That is a long time,' Asa said.

Posy raised her eyebrows and he laughed.

'Not that I think for a minute it would take you a long time to find a man! I meant the other bit.'

'Actually, the man bit is proving tricky too.'

'You and me both,' Asa said. 'Why can't you find one? You're young and pretty and clever.'

'I'm also too fussy for my own good.'

'I'm not. I'd have anyone but I'm still single. What does that say about me?'

Posy laughed. 'I'm sure that's not true!'

'It is – I'm desperate! I'm on Tinder every night swiping right like my finger's in spasm, but nobody wants to come to deepest darkest Somerset to meet up with a country bumpkin like me.'

'I'm sure that's not true either,' Posy said with a smile. 'And you're handsome and funny, so I'm sure someone would be willing to make the sacrifice – even if it was a sacrifice, which it's not.'

'Perhaps when we've finished our remodelling I can post photos of my lovely home to tempt someone to join me here,' he said. 'If I can't sell myself, perhaps my house can sell me.'

'You can sell yourself just fine, Asa. We both can – we just have to be patient, I suppose.'

'Easy for you to say – you have time on your side.'

'You're not exactly ancient.'

'Oh, I feel it some mornings, my love. These days my arse takes a whole minute longer to get out of bed than the rest of me.'

'Honestly!' Posy smiled, but it made her sad that he felt that way. Her uncle was funny, stylish and good-looking. But something had knocked him sideways. Perhaps one of these days, as she got to know him better, she'd find out what it was and she'd be able to help him through it.

'Going back to the design, I'm going to ask you for another favour,' he said, 'and I know you've done so many for me already that it's probably an outrageous imposition, but would you project manage for me?'

Posy smoothed out a frown. 'Oversee the work? It'd be quite hard to do from here.'

'I realise that. Which is why I was going to suggest that you come and stay with us for a while. I mean, you said you were going to have time on your hands when you finish your notice period, and I realise that you have to find another job, but perhaps you could search from here rather than London and pop over on the train if you get an interview? Would that be too difficult and expensive? Perhaps if I helped with the travelling expenses? It'd help me, and it would be a wonderful excuse for us to spend more time together. Now that I've found I have a very lovely niece, I'd like to get to know her a bit better.'

Posy smiled, warmth spreading through her at his words. 'I couldn't take that from you, and I'm sure I could manage the odd train fare; I just don't know how practical it would be regardless of cost. How long do you think I'd be staying for?'

'Well, how long do you think you'd need to stay for?'

'I'm not sure. I suppose it would depend on what designs you choose and how complicated they are to implement.'

'In that case, I might be tempted to choose the one that takes a very long time,' Asa said with a smile. 'You're the most fun I've had in ages and you'd certainly brighten the place up. In fact, you ought to be the design feature I install. Can you clone yourself and let me have the copy?'

'I'd like to oblige but I'm pretty sure I'd struggle. And you should be careful what you wish for – my friend Marella thinks I'm quite boring of late, and if I was very honest I'd be inclined to agree with her. What would Giles and Sandra think about it? Surely they'd have something to say?'

'If you stay in my house that's my choice, not theirs. They had no problem with…' He paused, seemingly about to say something that he then decided it was better to keep to himself. 'It's my house and I can decide who stays with me.'

'Yes, but I'm not just anyone. I'm the niece you hardly know and a constant reminder that your mum and your sister didn't exactly see eye to eye.'

'That doesn't bother me one bit.'

'But it might bother Giles to see me around so often.'

'I don't think it will bother him one bit – he likes you as much as I do. But if you don't want to do it…?' There was an awkward pause. 'Pretend I never asked – I should have known it was too much.'

'Not at all,' Posy said. 'If anything I feel it's too much for me to ask of you. I'd be getting the far better deal, spending so much time at Oleander House.'

'Perhaps we ought to do a house swap,' Asa said.

'You would not want to live in my tiny home. I think your bathroom might be bigger than my entire house!'

'But you get all the excitement.'

'I'm sure there's more excitement to be had in Astercombe than you might think. You're too used to it, that's all; you take it all for granted. I suppose I do too, come to think of it.'

'When you say there's excitement, could you be referring to your run-in with a certain Scottish vintner?'

'Angry Naked Man?' Posy said and instantly clapped a hand to her mouth and blushed right down to her toes. She'd never revealed to anyone the exact circumstances of their meeting – at least not deliberately – but it looked as if she'd just told Asa whether she'd intended to or not.

His eyes turned into saucers.

'I've kind of seen his bits,' she replied sheepishly.

'Oh my God! You saw him as God intended?'

'Stark bollock-naked,' Posy said, blushing harder still despite laughing.

Asa gave the broadest, wickedest grin. 'That's the most brilliant thing I've heard all year! How on earth did this happen?'

'It's a long story.'

'I don't care,' he said, getting comfortable in his chair, 'I've got all night!'

*

'You look amazing!' Marella squeaked as she ran to meet Posy outside the block of flats where the party was being held.

'No I don't, I look like a turnip,' Posy said, laughing as she looked down at herself. 'And I'm only doing this for you, and because I'm going to be away for a while and you made me feel all guilty about it. So just remember that next time you complain that I never go anywhere with you and I'm no fun anymore. You'll pull your face and I'll remind you of the sacrifices I made.'

'It's fun!'

'Easy for you to say in your gold bikini. The only outfit I could get at the last minute was this and it's far from glamorous.'

'You look adorable.'

'I look like an old carpet.'

'Everyone loves the Ewoks – you'll be the star of the show.'

'Nobody fancied the Ewoks though, did they?'

'I expect other Ewoks did. Besides, you said you didn't want to hook up with anyone because all the men in London are so tiresome and boring, so you won't care, will you?'

'Just because you don't want to get with someone, doesn't mean you don't want them to want to get with you.'

Marella tossed her hair back and turned to the building. 'Come on, I think we're late enough to be just about fashionable.'

'Yes,' Posy agreed. 'And we should get you inside before you get arrested for indecent exposure... which is something you definitely couldn't say for me.'

*

Five minutes later they were in a living room smaller than Posy's bathroom at home, squashed onto a sofa with a stormtrooper who'd already given up his helmet due to overheating and some kind of alien that Posy couldn't even recognise. Not that she'd recognise anything but the most popular characters from the Star Wars franchise – the last film she'd watched was with her dad when she was about twelve and she'd never seen any of the new ones. She knew all the obvious, of course, the things that were ingrained in the cultural landscape, but she was hardly what you'd call a fan. That alone made her feel like a bit of a fraud being here dressed up, as well as feeling a bit stupid. And the party wasn't exactly what you'd call swinging so far, which didn't help. Darth Vader handed her a cocktail. She didn't ask what it was but it looked nice enough. Then he handed one to Marella.

'Oooh, thank you,' Marella said. 'Love your costume, by the way.'

'I love yours too,' Darth Vader said, but in a voice with a distinct accent that was more Birmingham than Tatooine.

'Is it hot in there?' Posy asked, more for something to say than anything else.

'Ridiculous,' Darth Vader replied. 'I'll probably slip some ice cubes into my leggings in a bit. It usually helps.'

What did one say to that? Posy certainly didn't know and so she gave a lame smile and put her cocktail to her lips so that she wouldn't have to say anything at all. Besides, she was hot already too and she might have to see if she could steal some ice cubes for her own costume before the night was out. Assuming she lasted the night of course, because she was already itching to leave. She really wished she hadn't agreed to this stupid party, and it was only because she loved Marella so much that she had.

'I bet you're nice and cool in yours,' Darth Vader said to Marella. Which, of course, she was, because she was practically naked.

'Oh yes,' Marella said.

There was a moment of awkward silence as the conversation petered out. It was no more than a second or two but it felt so long Posy was convinced she could have read War and Peace by the time Darth Vader spoke again.

'Help yourself to snacks and drinks from the kitchen,' he said. 'I'll catch you later – off to mingle.'

Posy gave a disbelieving glance around the room as he glided away, cloak billowing behind him.

'Who's he mingling with?' Posy whispered to Marella. 'There's nobody to mingle with but us!'

'That's what I thought,' the stormtrooper said, and Posy whipped round, flustered and guilty that her whisper had carried further than was polite. 'Hopefully it'll fill up later and make it worth our while. I paid twenty quid to hire this suit – I could have got a round in at the Hope and Anchor and had a better time than I have so far.'

'I expect it'll fill up soon,' Marella said. 'I'm Marella, by the way.'

'Jackson,' he said, putting out his hand to give her a fist bump. Posy resisted the urge to roll her eyes, and then was mortified that he did the same to her. How old did she look? Who over the age of twelve gave fist bumps when they met people?

'Like Pollock?' Marella said.

'Pardon?'

'Like the artist? Jackson Pollock?'

'Oh, yeah… I guess so.' He looked at Posy. 'Your outfit is cute.'

Posy pulled down the furry hood that was supposed to be her Ewok head (she'd refused to put the nose and teeth in) and ran a hand through her hair. 'I'm beginning to regret it already.'

'Yeah, it's roasting in here, isn't it? My helmet came off pretty much the minute I got here.'

'Everything was already off when I got here!' Marella purred, and Posy could see that she fancied Jackson. She gave an inward groan. She couldn't deny that he was good-looking – young, blond, a bit skater boy – but even so. This was going to be another one of those parties where Marella got off with someone and disappeared into another room, leaving Posy to fend off someone else who was infinitely less attractive but was labouring under the impression that if two women arrived at a party together it meant that one had to do whatever the other was doing. She braced herself for the onslaught.

While she'd been thinking this, another four guests had arrived: a Luke Skywalker, a Han Solo, another Princess Leia but with the white dress and the buns, and – of course – a Chewbacca. Poor soul, Posy thought. *If I think it's hot in here, he's going to be a puddle by the end of the night.* The Brummie Darth Vader rushed to welcome them.

'So…' Marella turned to Jackson and gave him a flirty look that Posy knew only too well. The charm offensive was well under way and Posy wasn't keen to be a gooseberry for anyone, even the best friend she adored. Time to get out of Dodge.

With that in mind, she downed the rest of her cocktail.

'Don't mind me,' she said, getting up from the sofa. 'I'm just off to get another drink from the kitchen. 'Anybody want anything?'

'No thanks,' Marella said.

'I'm—' Jackson began, but Posy was already on her way, certain he wasn't talking to her anyway and not really bothered if he was. When she'd asked if anyone had wanted a drink she'd actually meant Marella, and if he had anything about him he'd know that.

In the kitchen – which was barely wide enough to let two people pass, let alone when one of them was dressed as an Ewok and one as Obi-Wan Kenobi – Posy located a jug of what was likely punch. She took a sniff and it smelled potent enough – probably worth a punt. Obi-Wan Kenobi came up behind her with a glass as she poured herself some.

'I wouldn't mind some of that when you're done,' he said.

'Oh, sure…' Posy filled his glass for him with a vague smile.

'Me too…'

She looked round to see Jackson standing behind her.

'Oh… Where's your glass?'

'I left it in the other room. Maybe I should get a clean one…'

As Obi-Wan moved aside to let him at a tray stacked with tumblers, Jackson reached across Posy, so close she could smell whatever cologne he'd spritzed before he'd put on his stormtrooper suit. It wasn't half bad. And there was something quite engaging about him, now that she looked again.

'Mind if I hang around here for a bit?' Jackson asked. 'With you, I mean? It's getting a bit crowded in there.'

'There are literally about six people in there,' Posy said.

'Yes, but have you seen the size of that room? That's five too many, even by the standards of a very generous estate-agent listing.'

Posy had to laugh, even though finding herself having to laugh annoyed her too. Was he trying to make her laugh, butter her up?

'I didn't get your name before,' he continued.

'That's because I didn't tell you.'

'Hmm. Would you tell me now? I don't want to be referring to you as that fit Ewok because that's some weird oxymoron right there.'

Posy laughed again. 'I think the idea that you might have to refer to me like that is funny. I'd certainly be entertained.'

'That's because you are the fit Ewok in question. Come on, you know mine…'

'Alright. It's Posy. And don't laugh, or say it's cute, or ask if that's really my name.'

'I wasn't going to do any of those things. I do like it, though. So, Posy… why haven't I seen you at one of Marshall's parties before?'

'Who's Marshall?'

He grinned. 'Well, I suppose that explains why I've never seen you at one of them. Marshall is currently swishing around in a black cape and putting on the lamest impression of Darth Vader you've ever heard.'

'So if he's so lame how do you know him?'

'I didn't say *he* was lame. Just his impression. I was at uni with him; he's a good guy.'

'Oh, that's like me and Marella.'

'The best friends you'll ever make,' he said.

'That's the truth.'

'So, where do you normally go if you don't come to Marshall's parties?'

'Why do you need to know?'

'I don't…' He gave her a steamy smile and she took another good swig of her punch; it was beginning to feel like a potent combination. He dropped his voice and made it huskier. 'But I'd like to.'

Wasn't he meant to be in an advanced state of flirting with Marella right now? Why was he here, flirting with her? There was no doubt he was flirting with her.

She handed him the jug, feeling more than a little thrown by this sudden turn of events.

'Thanks. How about I top you up as well?'

Posy looked down at her cup and saw that she'd drunk half already, though she couldn't remember doing it.

'I suppose that wouldn't be so bad.'

He held her gaze as he filled her glass.

'Whoa!' she said, glancing down to see her tumbler was almost overflowing.

He laughed. 'Sorry. It's just... I never noticed in the light in the other room... your eyes... they're green.'

'Murky green – like pondwater,' she said. 'In most lights they look brown.'

'They're... I like them. They're not like pondwater... they're sort of stunning.'

'Thank you.' Posy looked away, embarrassment, pleasure and a new spark of lust fighting for control of her brain. If this was his come-on technique, he was doing a good job of getting through defences that she'd thought she'd toughened up significantly since the last time some chancer had got through them. Whether it would turn out to be another disaster or something far nicer there was no way to tell, but she couldn't deny she was enjoying the attention.

'Marella...' she managed to mumble. 'She's on her own...'

'She's talking to Luke Skywalker,' he said. 'I made sure she had someone to chat with while I came to get a drink.'

'And is she expecting you back?'

'Well, I did say I might be some time... and she did ask if I was coming to see you... and I said I might be, and she said, go get her, tiger...'

He gave her a sheepish grin.

Posy laughed. 'She never misses a trick. Thank you for making sure she was OK... *tiger...*'

It was his turn to laugh. It was an easy, relaxed kind of laugh and Posy liked it. Maybe this party wouldn't be so bad after all.

Carmel had commented that Jackson was keen. Posy supposed that he was, but she didn't mind. He'd called her the day after the party to see if she fancied going out again. It hadn't taken her long to decide that her answer was an emphatic yes, and as she'd got dressed that morning to spend the day with him, she wondered if he'd be as much fun as that first night. Most people would be a more fun version of themselves at a party because it was easier to be witty and interesting with a ready supply of booze and a heady atmosphere. Today it was just the two of them, stone-cold sober and in broad daylight – a very different prospect.

They met on the South Bank in a square shaded by trees. A short walk away stood the squat, concrete blocks of the Tate. Jackson complimented her dress, kissed her lightly on the cheek and checked his watch.

'We've got time before we go in,' he said. 'Want to get something to eat first?'

'It's a bit early for me,' Posy said. 'But it's roasting and I wouldn't say no to an ice lolly.'

She nodded towards a gleaming silver refreshment truck parked at the far end of the square overlooking the Thames. It was one of those retro fifties-styled converted motor homes, colourful awning shading it from the glare of the sun.

'Sounds good to me,' Jackson said. 'Come on, my treat.'

'So,' Posy said as they walked over to it, 'have you brought me to an art exhibition because I told you I was an interior designer and you thought I might do art exhibitions all the time?'

He laughed. 'I'm that transparent?'

'Yes, but I like the train of thought. It shows that you were listening when I told you about myself.'

He grinned as he ordered their lollies and then handed one to Posy. She unwrapped it and began to suck, a burst of chemically enhanced, ice-cold orange hitting her tongue and making her smile. Eating an ice lolly always made her feel like a kid and this was no exception. It was a much appreciated refreshment too, considering it was the hottest day of the year so far, the heat burning up through the soles of her shoes and the sun glittering on the surface of the water as the pleasure boats ploughed up and down the river.

'I mean,' Posy continued as they began to head for the shade of a loose clump of trees, 'I'd have been down for a pizza and the new Marvel film.'

'I wish you'd said that before I tried to be all sophisticated for you.'

'I'm glad I didn't.'

'So I get brownie points?'

'Absolutely. Tons of them.'

He grinned, then bit the end from his ice pop and winced as the cold burned through his front teeth.

'Serves you right,' Posy said, laughing lightly at him.

'I never did have any patience,' he said ruefully. 'My mum always says it will be my undoing but I didn't realise she meant death by ice lolly.'

'I'm actually looking forward to seeing this exhibit,' Posy said. 'I haven't been to one in ages.'

'No?'

'Too busy. Last time I came there was some world photography my mum wanted to see. That must have been about three years ago.

I feel a bit ashamed actually, being in my line of work and not taking a bit of interest in current art.'

'I suppose it's a bit like a busman's holiday for you.' Jackson bit the last of his lolly off and then dropped the stick in the bin. Posy resisted the urge to tease him about how fast he'd eaten it.

'I suppose you could see it like that,' she said. 'My boss would call it professional development. Maybe that's why she never promoted me – didn't think I was dedicated enough.'

'Well, you'll be able to do what you want soon, won't you?'

'I wish!' Posy said with a wry smile. 'I'm not planning on being unemployed for long if I can help it… although I am going to enjoy the change of scenery in Somerset for as long as I can get away with.'

'Tell me again who it is you're going to stay with?'

'My uncles.'

'It's weird that they live together like that.'

'Not really. It's the family home, handed down to them, and it's also where the business runs from. And they don't live together as such – Giles and Sandra have the big house and Asa has a little building to himself on the grounds.'

'It's like an ancestral seat? Does that make you a posho?'

Posy laughed. 'Oh yeah. So posh! No… not posh at all. I mean, their house is pretty big but it's hardly a stately home.'

She finished her lolly too and dropped the stick into the same bin that Jackson had used. He smiled down at her and shyly reached for her hand.

'Want to go in now?'

'Sounds good to me.'

*

Before going to the visiting exhibit, they took a tour of the permanent installations too. Posy had seen a lot of it on previous trips, but she wanted to make the most of the visit and her time with Jackson. And it was nice to wander the portraits, landscapes and sculptures and just gaze at them as an interested admirer, rather than working to fathom meaning as she would have done as a student.

It was even nicer to listen to Jackson poke gentle fun at each one and not have her artistic sensibilities offended, as they would have been a few years before too. She'd taken it all very seriously back in the days when she'd been studying art, whereas Marella had always got the balance right. Marella always knew when something they were looking at was utterly ridiculous but she would often find something meaningful to say about it when questioned by a tutor. Blagging was what she called it, but Posy had to be impressed. Marella usually said it was down to her northern roots, which meant she always had her bullshit radar switched to high. She had a constant conflict raging inside her –appreciation of art and culture battling the practical sense handed down from her parents, who would have looked at almost any modern art installation and announced it to be twaddle.

Jackson halted at a blank canvas.

'Is there supposed to be something on here?' he asked.

'It represents the fullness of a void,' Posy said, looking intently at it.

'You can tell that by looking at it?'

'No.' She pointed to an information card next to the artwork. 'It says so right there.'

'I think someone saw the gallery owner coming,' Jackson said. 'Looks like money for old rope to me.'

'It's not even that,' Posy said patiently. 'But when you've studied as much as I have nothing that's meant to possess artistic merit surprises you anymore.'

They moved on.

'What's going on here then?' Jackson asked. He'd stopped at another white canvas, this one scored across the middle with a knife. 'Did someone have an accident and hoped nobody would notice until they'd picked the pay cheque up?'

Posy smiled. 'Possibly.'

'I don't mind admitting these ones make no sense to me.'

'But I like that you're trying.'

'How many more floors of this do we have to go?'

'It's pretty big in here…'

Posy paused. Jackson was still looking at the canvas but she could tell he wasn't impressed. She'd been able to tell that he hadn't been impressed with much he'd seen so far, but he'd been doing his best.

'You know what?' she continued. 'I've seen a lot of this before. How about we head straight up to the visiting exhibition and then we get that pizza and film after all?'

He turned to her. 'You really don't mind?'

'No. It was sweet of you to bring me here but I can tell you're not really feeling it, and it doesn't seem fair to subject you to hours and hours of it.'

'You'd be here for hours?'

She smiled. 'Easily. In the old days, give me a rainy day with nothing to do and I'd spend it here. And it's not like I can't come any time I like. Let's cut this bit short, head to the top floor, check out what we came to see and then go from there.'

'You know what,' he said with a grin.

'What?'

'I think you might be bona fide girlfriend material.'

Posy raised her eyebrows and then grinned in return. 'I think I'm supposed to take that as a compliment, right?'

Chapter Fourteen

'You certainly picked a fine time to get yourself a new boyfriend,' Asa said as he negotiated the winding roads towards Astercombe and Oleander House, eyes fixed firmly on the route ahead, hands solid on the steering wheel. 'Will you miss him terribly?'

'I've only just started to see him so I shouldn't think so,' Posy said. 'It's nothing serious.'

'But you like him? You must because when I asked what you'd been up to on our way out of the train station that was the first thing out of your mouth.'

'I like him; he's nice. At least he seems it, but as I keep telling you, it's probably too early to tell.'

'Now I feel guilty for dragging you away from London. You won't see him for ages.'

'I can go back for the odd day and if things got really desperate Jackson could come here. It's not that far away and I'm sure we can manage anyway. We're hardly getting married or anything – it was just one party and one follow-up date, that's all.'

Posy looked out of the window onto a sun-drenched landscape, golden fields, green meadows, towering trees and flower-filled hedgerows flashing by. It was good to be back in Somerset, even though she did secretly think she was going to miss Jackson a little. Asa was right – it was a hell of a time to get a new boyfriend.

But, she reasoned, she wasn't going to be in Somerset forever and what she'd said to Asa was absolutely right – it wasn't like she was going into outer space. A couple of hours on the train would see them easily able to meet up if they wanted to. If he really liked her – and she thought he might – then he'd make the effort. She was certainly happy to.

'Well, I can't pretend I'm not jealous.'

Posy turned to him. 'Still no luck on Tinder?'

'Oh, I've deleted the blasted app. It's full of posers and weirdos.'

Posy laughed. 'It's not.'

'Says the woman who goes to a party dressed as an outer-space teddy bear and still pulls.'

'Since you put it like that, it does seem very unlikely. I can see why you might find it annoying. I can assure you, romance was the last thing on my mind. I only went so Marella could go.'

'And was it worth her while?'

'She had a good time but she didn't pull, if that's what you mean.'

'And she had the bikini on – that must have been galling for her.'

'She was very gracious about it,' Posy said, laughing again. 'I think she'll get over it eventually.'

'And now you're a free woman too.'

'Free?'

'You have no job to tie you down.'

'Oh… so you mean *unemployed*…? Not so glamorous when you put it like that.'

'Well, no. I only meant you don't have to worry while you're here. Treat it like a huge holiday.'

'I'll have to leave as soon as I'm done,' Posy warned.

'I know.'

'And I'll still have to job-hunt, so it's not going to be exactly like a holiday.'

'Yes, of course. But you have nothing to rush back for.'

'Apart from my actual real life?'

'You know what I mean,' Asa said, and if Posy didn't know him better she'd have thought it sounded a bit sour. But then, she didn't know him – not really. She felt as if she did, but, when all was said and done, she'd been acquainted with him less than two months and during that time had seen him in the flesh on only three occasions. They'd chatted endlessly over Skype but that wasn't the same, and mostly it was about house designs. Perhaps she didn't know the real Asa at all.

'So,' he began, 'do you have a photo of this Jackson character?'

'No. But he does have an Instagram account and there are some on there.'

'You'll have to show me when we get back to the house and I'll tell you if your uncle Asa approves or not.'

'That's still weird,' Posy said with a small smile, turning her gaze to the windows again. In a distant field cows were lying in the grass. Maybe they were soaking up the sun – Posy herself was certainly looking forward to doing that later.

'Having an uncle?' he asked.

She turned to him and nodded.

'Imagine me suddenly getting a niece then. I somehow feel terribly responsible for this person I hardly know.'

'You don't have to feel like that.'

'Isn't that what uncles do?'

'I don't know what they do; I've never had one. Mum is an only child and so is Dad. But I'm sure they don't usually swap notes with their nieces about hot men.'

'Does that mean I'm leading you astray?'

Posy laughed. 'You might not be the best influence.'

'Good,' he said. 'For a minute there I thought I might be getting old and boring.'

'I'm sure you could never be that.'

'I can be old – I can't help that.'

'Never boring then.'

'Coming from you I'll take that as high praise.'

'I mean it – I can't imagine you being boring for one second.'

'Perhaps not me, but perhaps my life at Oleander could be. And perhaps that might make me boring to some people…' Asa said, the comment loaded with subtext that suddenly charged the air of the car.

Posy suppressed a frown. She might not have known him well but she was beginning to see a trend. Whenever she got close to something like personal information he went all cryptic on her and drifted into an unfathomable mood that she didn't know how to react to. One minute it was laughter and jokes, the next pained looks into the middle distance.

'Well, here we are…' he exclaimed, so completely nonchalant again that Posy had to wonder whether the mood change she thought she'd seen had really happened at all. 'Home sweet home.'

Posy saw the gates of Oleander ahead, the house sitting proud and beautiful behind them, and she felt a little kick of excitement. She wasn't just visiting this time – for a few weeks at least, this was home.

As Asa pulled onto the gravel of the driveway and brought the car to a stop, Posy got out to see Giles striding back from the orchard. He gave them a cheery wave. Despite Asa's reassurances that they really didn't mind her staying, Posy had been anxious about how Giles and Sandra might feel about it. But seeing his broad smile now made her realise she needn't have worried. He was as welcoming as ever.

'Good trip?' he asked Posy as he approached the car.

'As good as it can be on the train,' Posy said. 'It was late, of course, and then there was a delay for a cow or something on the line…'

Giles laughed. 'That sounds about right. You're here now at least. What's your plan of action? Time to come and say hello to Sandra before Asa starts cracking the whip? He has warned you what a pedantic little slave driver he is, I take it?'

'Funny,' Asa shot back, and Posy smiled.

'I'm sure I've had worse clients. I'd love to come and see Sandra.'

'She's grafting some young trees in the orchard,' Giles replied. 'Come down with me if you like – we can go and fetch her together while Asa takes your cases to his place.'

Asa looked as if he might argue with this plan but then seemed to think better of it. Giles gave him a stern look and Posy could just imagine what the dynamic would have been like between the brothers when they were children.

'I'd say it's the least you can do,' Giles added.

'I'll see you back at the big house,' Asa replied, going round to the boot of his car to pop it open.

'Come on,' Giles said to Posy. 'This way; Sandra will be so pleased to see you…'

Posy opened her eyes as the light through a crack in the curtains heralded the first morning of her stay at Oleander House. Asa's study had been converted into a spare bedroom for the duration of her stay. He'd said he didn't even know why he had a study anyway, because he didn't study. It was a strange thing to install in your house if you didn't need one, but Posy had let it pass. It was just another of those unanswered questions that Asa kept posing.

She'd probably have to decamp to the main house when it came to the redecorating stage of Asa's refit, and Giles and Sandra had said they were only too happy to accommodate that. They'd also offered her Philomena's old place to live in if she wanted some privacy. It was empty and doing nothing and it wouldn't hurt to breathe a bit of life into the place, but that felt too weird to Posy, not to mention how dowdy and uninviting it was. If she had to stay there for any length of time, it might just have her pining for home again very quickly.

Her first coherent thought as she took in the unfamiliar surroundings was that she was in Somerset. It almost felt like the first day of a new life. It wasn't, she had to keep reminding herself, but it felt like it, or at least, it felt like something bigger than it realistically was.

From the way the sun was coming in it seemed to be early, but something had woken her. Perhaps it was the excitement. But then she heard a noise and realised that was probably it – the sound of a van door slamming and voices outside. Putting on a dressing gown she went to the window, but it was in the wrong position to see anything so she went through to Asa's silent living space and peered through the blinds there.

'That's the trouble with living in what is effectively a working farm.'

Posy turned to see Asa standing at his bedroom door, eyes gummed with sleep, hair sticking up.

'Everything starts so bloody early,' he continued.

'Workers?' Posy asked, looking out of the window again. She could see the van now.

'When I say workers… I mean worker, singular. Our brewery manager – Saul.'

'I thought Giles did that.'

'It's too much for him to do alone. We'll also be getting a few more seasonal workers as the chores build up towards harvest. I know the orchard isn't huge, but the apples really need to be pressed straight away so we like to have all hands on deck so we don't lose any of the crop. Saul's amazing – what he doesn't know about cider isn't worth knowing, but he does like his early starts.'

'Weirdo.'

Asa grinned. 'Finally, someone on my wavelength. Giles thinks we all ought to be up that early, but being up won't make the apples grow any faster so what's the point?'

'I'd say that makes sense,' Posy agreed with a smile. 'I'm guessing Giles doesn't agree.'

'Nope.' He stretched and yawned. 'I might as well stay up now; I won't be able to get back to sleep and there's no point in lying around in bed.'

'Me neither. I'm too excited to go back to bed now.'

Asa raised disbelieving eyebrows.

Posy laughed. 'I know! I just feel like a kid on a new adventure all of a sudden.'

'I'm glad somebody's excited to be here. So… do you want coffee? I have a potent Columbian blend I got at the farm shop. It's like a rocket up your bum – guaranteed to wake you.'

'Sounds good.'

Asa shuffled off to the kitchen as Posy let the blinds snap shut again and followed him.

'What time do you usually start work then?' she asked.

'Not this early.' Asa reached into the cupboard for two mugs. 'I don't have a set time as such; my work is more on the social media, PR for the orchard side of things, so I can suit myself largely. But Giles likes to get his hands dirty so he tends to be up with the lark, messing around in the orchard or in the cider house.'

'So were you the one who put the website together?'

'I was.'

'It looks brilliant. I spent ages looking at it before we came the first time.'

'Thank you. I'm not exactly a whiz – self-taught mostly – but I don't think I do too badly and it serves our needs well enough.'

'Do you ever do tours of the production facilities – like for visitors and stuff?'

'We've thought about it a lot over the years but we don't at the moment.'

'Why didn't you start? Lots of places like yours do, don't they?'

'Mother dearest didn't want strangers here. She was funny like that – liked everything to be very private. She wasn't even fond of visits from our own friends and family. I had such a fight on my hands when I wanted—' He looked in the fridge and sighed. 'Out of milk. Looks like a trek to the big house to see if I can steal some from under Sandra's nose. I knew I should have gone to get some last night but I totally forgot.'

'Want me to go?'

'No, it's fine. I'll do it.'

'Well then, maybe I could go and get some supplies later? I will be staying here, after all, and I ought to help with the grocery costs.'

'I couldn't—'

'I want to. I'd feel guilty expecting you to feed me all the time. I want to contribute so please don't argue because I won't listen.'

'In that case it would be most welcome. I could come with you.'

'No, you'll be sneakily trying to pay.'

'Where are you going to go? Into Astercombe? I'll warn you, there's no supermarket there. Any big shop we do we have to do online and get it delivered; failing that it's a twenty-mile trip to the hypermarket. Astercombe is alright if you want the farm shop or the little local, but that's about it.'

'That's OK – I can get a few things from there and maybe we can drive out for a supermarket another day. I'd like a good nosey round anyway.'

'That's alright; I'm sure you would. I was going to book some tradesmen later if that's OK with you, so I could do with us getting our heads together to decide what we need to do first.'

'No problem,' Posy said. 'Let me know when you want to do that and I'll make sure I'm back from the village. I am here to be at your service, after all.'

'Oh, I do like the sound of that – my own personal assistant. But Giles is already convinced I was Louis XVI in a previous life; perhaps we'd better not give him any more reasons to think so!'

Chapter Fifteen

It was grey and muggy as Posy walked the road that led to the village of Astercombe. That didn't bother her one bit; in fact, it would be a blessing if she had anything larger than a tub of butter to carry back. Asa had offered to drive her, but she'd told him that sort of defeated the point of her trying to make herself useful, and then he'd said she could take his car, but she'd said she would have been nervous driving it because she'd never driven it before. Besides, she wouldn't be able to buy all that much in Astercombe anyway if the shopping was as limited as he'd said it was, so it probably wouldn't be such a hardship to get it back on foot.

Occasionally, as she walked, a damp, useless sort of breeze would do its best to lift her hair, but it was hardly anything to speak of. For the most part, the humidity did nothing but somehow intensify the smells of the wildflowers growing alongside the road and various other farming aromas which made her nose wrinkle and reminded her that the countryside didn't always smell sweet.

She stopped at a field of cows and laughed as one poked its head through the hedgerow to get a better look at her. She cooed at the calves she could see on the grassland beyond through the gaps in the shrubbery, and then she walked on. Another field contained a handful of sheep, but most were vast and empty, until she noted the neat strips of green on the hills further away that marked out Lachlan's vineyard. Seeing them got her thinking of him, though as soon as she did she had to wonder why she was donating any brainpower to such an undeserving cause.

Astercombe was picture-postcard perfect. Posy hit the first houses and was instantly bowled over by a vision of thatched roofs, climbing roses and pristine white picket fences. Some were built from neutral stone, some rendered cream or pink or white. One was a beautiful sky blue with honeysuckle embracing the frame of a tiny front door and old bullseye windows, and Posy found herself staring at it for a moment, until she realised what she was doing and moved on quickly in case the owners came out. A stream separated the two sides of the high street, a single stone bridge linking the opposite parts of the village together.

Perhaps high street was a little generous as descriptions went, however, Posy mused as she smiled at a family of ducks paddling in the brook; it was little more than a loose collection of small shops operating from inside repurposed cottages. As she took in the view, she couldn't help but wonder which house John Palmer had lived in. Perhaps, if she felt brave enough and it still bothered her, she'd ask Asa later…

About half a dozen people passed by as she made her way – most of them wearing hiking boots and backpacks, some with walking sticks and some taking photos. They were almost certainly tourists, and Posy had to wonder how many months of the year the locals here spent outnumbered by visitors. She supposed it was what they'd come to expect, a necessary trade-off for living in such a beautiful place. She bid one or two of the tourists a good morning and then turned her attention to scanning the shopfronts to figure out where she needed to be.

*

The farm shop had a cute little bell that tinkled above the door like something from a black-and-white TV drama. The rest of the shop would have fitted that era well too – scrubbed wooden floors with the smell of sawdust, bullseye window panes and low beamed ceilings.

While the convenience store a little further up the road had everything Posy needed on a practical level it hadn't been very inspiring and, after a brief glimpse inside, she'd decided to try the farm shop first and go back there for anything they didn't have.

As she walked in to see wooden shelves groaning with baskets of produce, jars full of jams and preserves sealed with gingham cloth and boxes of home-made bread and cakes, this, she thought, was more like it. This was what she'd come to Astercombe for.

A girl who couldn't have been older than eighteen was behind the counter, a tortoiseshell cat lounging across the surface in front of her. The girl was running an absent hand down its back while holding a book to her nose with the other. At the sound of the bell she hurriedly dropped a bookmark onto her page and closed it.

'Hello.'

She was taller than average with a delicate, almost nervy type of grace and about the brightest shade of ginger hair Posy had ever seen. She also had an abundance of freckles and Posy would have bet a good deal of her shopping budget that the poor girl didn't often make the most of the summer sun because she'd probably burn to a crisp just looking out of the window for too long. She did, however, have the sort of quirky beauty that made her stand out. If ever she decided to take a walk down Oxford Street, some talent scout would be on her like a shot, desperate to sign her as the next big catwalk star. Perhaps

Posy ought to sow the seed. But, then again, perhaps not. Perhaps life here would be a lot more wholesome and a lot less stressful, and Posy wasn't sure she fancied being the architect of a ruined life.

'Do you want something in particular or would you just like to look?' the girl asked.

'I'll have a mooch if that's alright. I do want things, I just don't know what they are until I see them. I'm one of those sorts of shoppers, I'm afraid.'

'That's OK. Call me if you need anything.'

Posy smiled and the girl went back to her book.

Everything looked so good Posy hardly knew where to start. She picked up a hand basket and began to wander.

The food was displayed with a sort of rustic honesty. No waxed lemons or polished apples here, no shrink-wrapped asparagus, spotless balls of lettuce or poker-straight carrots, but vegetables and fruit as nature intended and probably as nutritious too.

Posy deliberated over a punnet of strawberries before popping them into her basket. She had no idea if anyone at Oleander House liked strawberries but decided it would be no hardship to eat them herself if they didn't. Gooseberries followed. She had no idea if she liked gooseberries because she'd never eaten them but thought she'd give them a go.

Next she dropped in a handful of peas still in their pods and some oranges that doubtlessly hadn't been grown locally but looked tasty all the same. She picked up a pack of butter churned on a farm less than five miles away and some eggs. Maybe she'd bake. Giles did a lot of baking and, though Posy was no expert, perhaps he'd give her some tips.

She was checking out some home-made flapjacks when the little bell over the shop door rang and she turned to see Lachlan walk in.

Great! Just what I need!

'Come to pick up your pork?' the girl said brightly. 'Butcher only dropped it off half an hour ago.'

'Thanks, Amber,' he said gruffly.

So, Posy thought, there is a shred of humanity in there after all; at least he could be bothered to recall someone's name.

The girl went into a room behind the counter and Lachlan stood and waited silently. Posy's gaze was somehow stuck to the back of his head as if magnetised. But then he seemed to sense it, and he turned to look.

In a violent (and later, she'd think, silly) reaction, she ducked behind a shelving unit and pretended to be fascinated by a bag of blanched almonds.

'So you're back…'

Posy stood up. Lachlan had to be talking to her because there was currently no one else in the shop. And he was looking directly at her. Not with any warmth, she noted, but with the expectation of someone who was used to getting immediate answers to his questions.

'Um, yes.'

'Holiday?'

'Sort of. I'm staying at Oleander House for a few weeks.'

'Hmm…' He nodded, but his features hardly softened at all. 'I hope they've explained how things work around here.'

'How things work?' Posy repeated.

'I don't go wandering around their orchards and they don't walk on my vineyard unless it's agreed in advance.'

Posy stared at him. Her mouth opened and then closed again.

'I didn't walk on your vineyard!' she finally managed to splutter. 'And I have it on good authority that the land I did walk on is a public right of way!'

'Who told you that?'

'It's none of your business who told me!'

Posy was aware that she was beginning to screech – at least she felt she sounded a little hysterical – but Lachlan was infuriatingly unruffled by it.

'The information you were given is wrong,' he said. 'Let me make it absolutely clear that—'

He stopped, mid-sentence, as Amber came back through to the shop with a large parcel wrapped in greaseproof paper and tied with rough brown string.

'It's fifteen pounds,' she said in a quavering voice, clearly aware that she'd walked into the middle of some kind of animosity between the two customers in her shop.

Lachlan thrust the exact money at her. 'Thanks,' he said stiffly. Amber handed the parcel over and he turned to leave, Posy still staring at him, smarting that he was prepared to walk out on what she felt was very unfinished business without another word. She half thought about chasing him to continue the argument, but, with a final glower her way, he was gone before she'd decided what to do.

Posy watched the door slam, the cheery little bell tinkling with some irony as he swept out. Then she took her basket to the counter, still reeling from whatever the hell had just happened.

'Do you have a bag I could buy for all this?'

Her enthusiasm for shopping had suddenly evaporated; all she wanted to do now was pay and get back to Oleander House.

'Of course,' Amber said, producing one from beneath the counter. She began to ring Posy's items through the till. 'You're staying with Giles and Sandra then?' she asked.

'Yes. Well, with Asa, technically.'

'Don't pay any mind to Lachlan,' Amber continued. 'He looks scarier than he is.'

'Really?'

'Yes.' Amber laughed at Posy's look of disbelief. 'He's actually quite kind; he's just not a people person, you know?'

'Well, I can definitely vouch for the last bit, though I haven't seen much evidence of the first.'

'His vineyard is very precious to him. We have some of his wine here if you want to try a bottle…'

Posy waved away the offer. 'I think Sandra has some – or at least, she says she usually has. But thanks.'

She paused, recalling suddenly that Sandra had once said Lachlan needed every penny of profit. It was hard to know what made her do it, but she thought about how Amber had just defended him and said he was a different man once you got to know him, and something changed her mind. 'Do you know what? I think I will take a bottle of that wine.'

'We've just got the sparkling. Will that be OK?'

'Yes; it all goes down the same,' Posy said with a smile. She watched as Amber took some from the shelving and put it in the bag before she continued to add the other items to her bill. 'If you don't mind me asking, do you know him well?'

'Lachlan?'

Posy nodded.

'Not really. But when Mum fell off a ladder trying to rescue the cat from the extension roof last spring and Dad was away for the day, Lachlan was passing. He jumped out of the car straight away to help. He drove us all the way to the hospital in Yeovil and that's miles away. And he stayed while they put her arm in a cast.'

'He did?' Posy gave a wry smile. 'I think I'd have taken my chances with the broken arm.'

'He's just quiet. And very serious. Some people are just like that, aren't they?'

'I suppose they are. I just don't know anyone who's quite *that* serious. Well, now I know what I'm dealing with I'll do my best to stay out of his way; then I can't fall foul of his spurious rules again.'

Amber gave a slight frown, as if she might try to defend Lachlan again, but then she seemed to think better of it and her expression cleared.

'He's fine with anyone if they respect his privacy,' she said.

She rang the last item through the till and announced the total. Posy was used to high prices in London, but even she had to ask Amber to repeat it, certain that her tiny bag of goods couldn't have come to that much. She very nearly asked Amber to put the bottle of wine from Lachlan's vineyard back after all, but decided to swallow the hit instead and handed over the money. Maybe next time the convenience store would be a better bet – for staples at least. Her savings would be gone in no time if she shopped here for everything, and no amount of pasture-fed milk or locally grown sparkling white was worth that.

Chapter Sixteen

Giles and Sandra had gone to the theatre in Bristol. Somehow, Posy couldn't imagine them being theatre-goers when outwardly they both seemed the sort of practical farming folk who wouldn't have the time or inclination to watch Ibsen's existential outpourings, but it just went to show that you never could tell. Their absence left her and Asa sharing a bottle of wine on the patio of the big house (as her uncle called it). Asa said he didn't want to drink cider as he was sick of the sight of it and they didn't have any of Lachlan's wine left, so they'd raided the cellar and settled for a good, reliable Chardonnay.

Asa waved an agitated hand. He wasn't quite drunk, but he was certainly on his way. 'The man acts like he owns the place! If he wasn't so good-looking I'm sure there'd be a petition to have him burned at the stake in the square in Astercombe. I'd get tickets too...' He shook his head as he filled Posy's glass. 'The only reason he doesn't come to the orchard is because that would mean the miserable toad would have to talk to actual real live human beings. Imagine how difficult that must be for someone who spends his evenings talking to rocks or something...'

'He had no trouble talking to me today.' Posy reached for the fresh glass of wine. She'd been taking it slower than Asa, but even she was on her way to pleasant tipsiness. They were getting on so well that the question she'd wanted to ask about John Palmer's house had been filed away; Posy worried that it might cause awkwardness if she aired it now. Instead, the conversation had turned to her run-in with Lachlan at the farm shop. 'He told me exactly what he thought of me – absolutely no communication problems whatsoever.'

'Don't even give it a second's thought – you've done nothing wrong.'

'I still feel as if I have. I bet he's told everyone in the village that I'm trouble.'

'I doubt it. Again, that would involve social interaction. If he talks to more than ten people in a day he probably explodes or something.'

'He complained to Karen.'

'Hmm…'

Asa took a large gulp of his wine and gave Posy a telling look.

'What does *hmm* mean?'

'He seems to turn to Karen a lot.'

'So?'

'The witch doesn't share a bit of it with anyone.'

'I suppose he just finds her easy to confide in. I can see why because she is. Although, she didn't seem very pleased to see him at the guest house the other day.'

'She doesn't take any bullshit from him; I know that much.'

'Maybe that's what he likes about her – that she's straight with him and gives as good as she gets.'

Asa stretched lazily. 'I have no idea but it's weird.'

'Not really. There's no accounting for things like that, is there? It's probably no more than Karen being really approachable,' Posy said. 'He probably goes to her because she makes him feel he can, where others aren't so welcoming.'

'It's not like nobody tried when he first arrived – it's not our fault he didn't want to know.'

'You don't think there's anything else to it, do you?'

'Why?' Asa asked with a wicked glint in his eye. 'Because you're hoping he's available for you? There's no shame in admitting that – we've all been there.'

'God no! Imagine how miserable life would be with a man like that.'

'But you must think he's handsome.'

'I'd be mad to think anything else – nobody can deny he's built like Adonis.'

'And you've already been up close and personal…'

'Not deliberately, I can assure you.'

'But it must have got you imagining all sorts…'

Posy grinned. 'I wouldn't tell you if it had.'

'Ah! So you admit it has!'

'Asa…' she said, trying not to laugh again. 'Is this an entirely appropriate conversation for an uncle to be having with his niece?'

'I think we established early on I was never going to be a good influence.'

Posy grinned again.

'But,' he continued, 'in answer to your question, it's more likely to be something going on between Lachlan and Pavla than Lachlan and Karen.'

'You think so? I suppose she's very attractive. Seems a bit high-maintenance for him, though.'

Asa shrugged. 'Who knows?'

Posy was thoughtful as she reached for her wine again.

Why did it matter what Lachlan did or who he might be seeing? Was it because Asa was right? Despite what ought to be, was Posy attracted to a dour, uncommunicative, misanthropic Scotsman who had no right occupying any of her thoughts at all? She reminded herself sternly that she had a new and very lovely boyfriend waiting back at home – refreshingly fun and honest and not hung up on any weird, self-absorbed, tortured-soul nonsense. Jackson was far better suited to her than a man like Lachlan could ever be – she just had to remember that.

The next two weeks were busy – various tradesmen came and went, gradually transforming Asa's house into the Scandinavian-inspired retreat he'd settled on. At times it was frustrating to live amongst the dust, clutter, debris and constant noise, but still Posy couldn't recall the last time she'd felt so content, so generally at peace with the world. They'd initially agreed that she'd move into the spare room of the big house when the work began, but she and Asa had got so comfortable around each other that she decided she'd rather stay in the annexe despite the chaos, and everyone was happy to agree.

She was proud of the way the project was taking shape too, and even more so whenever Asa expressed delight at some new feature or other finally appearing in his home. Days were spent overseeing the work, evenings scouring job sites or sitting with Asa, Giles and Sandra, and she explored her new home in the gaps in between.

Carmel phoned often, but she was in the middle of a huge commission for a stately home garden so didn't have time to visit. Posy wouldn't really have had much time to see her anyway, though Giles and Sandra would probably have liked it.

Marella called too for the odd chat, and so did Jackson, mostly to complain that he was missing her and to ask if she thought she might come home any earlier than planned. If anything, projects like this always overran, so it was more likely to be the opposite way round, but she didn't have the heart to tell him that. Instead, she thought, when a suitable moment arose she might ask if Jackson could come and visit them in Somerset. It might be fun to show him around – though she'd probably arrange for him to stay at Sunnyfields with Karen rather than at Oleander House, which, she decided, might be a request too far. They were family, but only just, and she didn't really know them well enough to take advantage of them in that way.

On the second Friday of the first fortnight she'd been there, Posy found herself at a loose end. The plasterers were hard at work in Asa's living room and didn't really need her to be there. Asa was helping Giles with some accounts and Sandra had gone to Wells to see a client who owned a bar there. Marella would be at work back in London, as would Jackson and Carmel. Posy didn't want to disturb any of them and her call wouldn't be welcome anyway if they were very busy. She could have taken a walk into Astercombe or simply around the nearby fields and meadows, and the weather was perfect for it, but she was in the mood for conversation and she wouldn't get much from the birds and bees out there.

Maybe Karen would be free for an hour in between her guest duties? Posy called Sunnyfields only for Pavla to answer and tell her that Karen was on her way back from the wholesaler's. She was sure, however, that if Posy walked over anyway Karen would probably be back by the time she got there; if Posy didn't mind hanging around in the kitchen while Karen put the supplies away then it would probably be OK to come over for a chat.

*

Posy arrived to find Pavla on reception duty. She was polishing the glossy wood of the desk, humming to herself, and looked up with a bright smile as she saw Posy walk in.

'Good morning!'

'Hi, Pavla… Is she—'

'One second…' Pavla interrupted, her gaze going to a spot behind Posy, who turned to see a white-haired gentleman in linen trousers and a golf shirt making his way to the counter. He looked agitated and Posy could see why Pavla felt the need to attend to him immediately.

'Do you need some help?' she asked.

'I've done something very silly,' he said. 'I was taking photos with my mobile phone through the window… lovely views from up there, you know… and of course I managed to drop it. I think it's gone into some flower beds at the back of the hotel but I can't quite tell where and I can't see it.'

'You want me to come and look with you?'

'Would you? I'm having a devil of a time working out which bit of garden sits below my window and my eyesight isn't what it used to be.'

'Of course…'

Pavla gave an apologetic grimace to Posy as she went outside with the guest. She had to tend to that first, of course, but now it left Posy standing alone in the silent reception not knowing what to do. Wait, she supposed, so she did.

She waited.

And waited some more.

At least ten minutes passed, maybe more, and no Pavla. Perhaps Karen had come in through the back way and was already in the kitchen right now, in which case it was silly for Posy to stand around here. Perhaps it was a tad cheeky, but Karen knew Posy well enough by now, didn't she? Surely she wouldn't mind Posy wandering through to find her? As Pavla knew she was coming, perhaps she'd told Karen to expect her anyway.

It took only another twenty seconds for Posy to make her choice, and she followed the corridor that she guessed led to the kitchens. She'd never actually been in there, but she'd seen Karen and Pavla rush in and out around mealtimes and the door had a sort of kitchen-y look about it – one of those swing-both-ways ones that you saw in restaurants. She gingerly gave it a push and peered round it.

'Karen…?'

There was no reply but a sudden horrible thought occurred to her. What if Ray was in there? Posy had never actually met Ray – Asa joked that he didn't think Ray existed because barely anyone ever saw him – but if he was and Karen wasn't that could be very awkward and more than a little embarrassing for them both. Posy had no issue talking to a stranger – she wasn't as shy as Karen said Ray was – but she would have to explain why she'd decided to wander into their kitchen uninvited. After the incident with Lachlan and then this, she might well get a reputation in Astercombe as a serial trespasser.

Thankfully, however, there was no Ray. No Karen either, which was slightly more disappointing. Posy could still smell the remains of one of Ray's legendary fried breakfasts on the air, and was attacked by the smallest pang of envy that she wasn't a guest being treated to the morning feast. The dishwasher hummed and sloshed in the corner and recently cleaned worktops gleamed in the sun from the windows.

'Hmm…'

She hesitated for a moment, uncertain if she should sit and wait or go back out to find Pavla, but then a voice from behind made her twist to look with a start. Karen was standing in the doorway.

'Hello, you,' she said, breezing in. 'Pavla said you might come over; you must have been running to get here so quickly.'

Posy grinned. 'You scared the life out of me!'

'Did I? Sorry about that. I try to be as non-threatening as possible but I can understand how this wrinkly face and mop of insane hair looming towards you might be a bit unnerving.'

Posy laughed. 'It was just so silent in here. Then you spoke and I nearly peed myself!'

'Oh dear!' Karen said with a grin of her own. 'Well, it's lovely to see you anyway. Did you come for something specific or did you just fancy a chat?'

'A chat mostly. If you're not too busy, that is.'

'I'm never too busy for you, my love. I've got some things to put away, but if you don't mind chatting while I do it, I don't mind either.'

'Pavla said you'd say that.'

Karen smiled. 'Sometimes I think Pavla knows my habits better than I do. Let me get these things out of the car and I'll be with you.'

'Is there a lot? Want some help bringing it all in?'

'I'd appreciate that.'

Posy followed Karen out to the battered old Land Rover parked on the driveway at the front of the guest house and between them they brought Karen's supplies in. It took four trips, even with them both going at it, and by the time they'd finished Posy had worked up a sweat. Karen rewarded them both with a cold glass of fresh orange juice and Posy sat at the countertop on a high stool while Karen (who insisted it would be quicker to do it alone because she knew where everything went) put her supplies away.

'How are you finding it at Oleander now that you're a permanent resident?'

'Not quite permanent,' Posy reminded her. 'Although I must admit it's starting to feel like home. There's the odd time I still feel a bit as if I'm imposing myself on them but that's more often when I'm at the big house. Even then it's mostly when Giles and Sandra have other things I know they need to attend to but they're helping me instead. They don't ever say I'm in the way – it's just me being paranoid, I suppose. Asa's a lot of fun, though.'

'I think Giles and Sandra let him get away with a lot too,' Karen said briskly as she stowed a large box of washing powder in a pantry cut into the kitchen wall. 'They treat him more like their child than Giles's younger brother – and not much younger at that.'

'What do you mean? He works just the same as they do… just different jobs.'

'They don't give him anything too taxing, though. And if he wants to go off and do other things that day, they let him. You must have noticed it.'

Posy hadn't really. But now that Karen mentioned it, perhaps she could recall occasions where Asa had more or less pleased himself how and when he made his contributions to the family business.

'I suppose they think he's still a bit fragile,' Karen continued mildly.

Posy frowned. 'Fragile?'

'Asa was always Philomena's favourite – there was no denying that. It hit him harder than anyone when she died, though he tries to pretend it's not true. He got especially attached to her once his father died so it hit him just as hard when she struggled to accept his coming out.'

Posy sipped at her juice. 'When was that?'

'Let's see… Asa would have been in his early twenties. His mother was never prejudiced, of course, but I think she struggled with the idea. And then there was the thing with Drew…'

The wrinkles on Posy's forehead deepened. 'Drew?'

Karen turned to her, suddenly looking mortified. 'Oh… you didn't know? I thought…'

'I know there's a reason Asa wants to gut his house and make it totally different, and I know it's not just that he fancied a bit of a change. Does it have something to do with this Drew character?'

Karen shook her head. 'I'm sorry, my love, but if Asa hasn't told you any of this then it's not my place to. Please don't take offence—'

'Of course not,' Posy said. 'I completely understand.' Although, truth be told, she didn't. She found it frustrating to get half a story and then for Karen to clam up, but pushing it probably wasn't going to help.

She paused for a moment, deep in thought.

'I know you can't tell me any more but when did Drew leave? Was it recently?'

'Just before Philomena died earlier this year – which is pretty bad timing by anyone's reckoning.'

'And I suppose it's common knowledge in the village?'

'People know Drew has gone,' Karen said. 'It would be hard for anyone to miss his exit. As for who knows what about the circumstances of his leaving…' She shrugged.

'So Drew lived at Oleander House? With Asa?'

'That's partly why they had the annexe refurbished, so that Asa and Drew could live there together and Asa wouldn't have to leave Oleander House.'

'So Asa was in love with Drew?'

'You don't need me to tell you all this – I'm sure you can work it all out for yourself. In fact, I'd say you're doing a pretty good job.'

'Still, it's only guesswork. You could say yes or no to my questions and then you wouldn't technically have told me anything at all.'

'*Technically* I'd still be gossiping.'

'You'd be helping me out by arming me with the information I need so I don't put my foot in it or upset Asa by saying the wrong thing.'

Karen stopped what she was doing for a moment. She folded her arms and grinned at Posy. 'You're a cunning little madam, aren't you? You'd get military secrets out of James Bond himself—'

She was interrupted by a tap at the back door.

'Karen…?'

Before she'd had the chance to reply the door opened and Lachlan walked in. For a moment he stared at Posy. Clearly, he hadn't expected to find her there. *However*, Posy surmised quickly, he *had* expected the back door to be open, was fairly confident he'd find Karen in the kitchen, and was very used to letting himself in. What did all that mean? Did it mean he visited in this way a lot?

'Now's not a good time?' he asked, his gaze tracked on Posy as if on a wire. Karen looked at her too, and suddenly Posy felt uncomfortably conspicuous.

'Not really,' Karen said. 'Was it something urgent?'

'Quite urgent.'

'So urgent I need to speak to you about it immediately?'

'Well,' he began, but Karen spoke again.

'Could I phone you about it later?'

'Um…' His gaze flicked to Posy again, mistrusting, doubtful… and something else, though she couldn't quite tell what. She only wished he would stop looking at her that way because it was making her feel hot and uncomfortable. Right now she was wishing that invisibility was a thing people could actually achieve. 'It's actually… a quick word is all I'm after…'

'About what, Lachlan?'

Another hesitation, another searching look at Posy before turning back to Karen and realising that he needed to spit out whatever it was. 'About Pavla…'

Karen frowned. 'What about her?'

He plunged his hands into his pockets.

'It's… work-related,' he said.

'She doesn't work for you anymore.'

'I know, but…'

He looked at Posy again, and at this point she was about ready to tell him to stop. But, she supposed, judging by his next careful statement, that he was perhaps wondering how much he could say in front of her.

'I'd like to talk to her anyway; I'd only take a minute,' he said.

'Does this mean I have to go back on duty myself now, since you're so determined to distract my staff when they're supposed to be working for me?'

Posy detected a faint smile on Karen's face, but still Lachlan looked flustered – not a state that Posy would ever have associated with the granite-featured Scot. He glanced uneasily at Posy again. If any portable object had been within her grasp, this time she might have thrown it at his head.

'Oh... I see...' he began. 'You're... this is a social visit?'

'Yes,' Karen said. 'Would you care to join us for a glass of orange juice and a chat?'

'Maybe I'll come to find Pavla later then... Sorry...'

Posy resisted the urge to raise her eyebrows in disbelief. Not that she knew him well, but in the space of about ten minutes she'd seen many emotions in Lachlan's face that she would never have expected: humility, uncertainty, almost desperation. And an apology – certainly the first one she'd ever heard fall from his lips.

It was weird but Karen, at least, had some sort of influence over him that nobody else had; or it certainly looked that way from what Posy had seen today. And he wanted to see Pavla but he was pretty cagey about it. That was intriguing too. What did he want her for? He'd said it was work-related but perhaps it was personal, or maybe it was to do with the fact she'd once worked for him? Was he looking to line up that seasonal help Sandra had said he'd need once the harvest began? But hadn't Sandra also said she didn't think there was much money to pay seasonal workers?

As these thoughts ran through Posy's head, Lachlan ducked out through the back door and was gone.

'Try around one thirty – she has a break!' Karen called after him, but whether he heard her or not was anyone's guess.

There was a beat of silence in the kitchen, during which the sound of the back door closing died away, and then Posy turned to Karen.

'Is he alright?' she asked, convinced that he wasn't and the notion of it unnerving her. Whatever had passed between them before now, she wouldn't want to think of him in some kind of trouble.

'Depends on your definition of alright.'

'Does he want Pavla to work for him again?'

'She'd never do that.'

'Does he know that, though?' Posy asked, wondering if this was Karen the boss talking, or Karen the woman who was very fond of Pavla and might be terribly hurt at the idea that the employee she'd come to rely on so heavily might even think about leaving her.

Karen went back to storing her groceries. 'I'd say so.'

Posy frowned slightly. It was a mystery, but one she ought to have left alone because it was really none of her business. Instead, she found herself wanting to track down Pavla too, if only so she could ask her about it. She looked up at Karen.

'Does Lachlan have serious money troubles?'

'Some,' Karen said. 'I expect Giles and Sandra have told you that.'

'A little. They said he's only been here for two years and that he was once an airline pilot. Where did he move from?'

'I'm not entirely sure.'

'He lives alone now at the vineyard,' Posy continued, 'but has he got anyone anywhere? A wife… husband? Kids? He can't just have dropped from the sky,' she added, repeating what Sandra had said. 'He must have a past.'

'I expect so,' Karen said simply, and then gave a smile that said she had no intention of saying anything more on the matter.

'All these secrets I can't be in on,' Posy continued with a mock pout of disappointment. 'It's hardly fair – I tell you all my gossip.'

'Do you?'

'Yes,' Posy said, knowing full well that she didn't but deciding that she wasn't ready to share the story of her real parents with Karen or anyone else in the village just yet.

'Well, that's *your* gossip to tell,' Karen said airily. 'You can have as much of mine as you like when it's about me, but some things aren't mine to gossip about.'

Posy smiled, but beneath it her mind was working overtime. Karen might be keeping secrets, but Posy was determined she would get to the bottom of it all eventually.

Chapter Seventeen

Good morning gorgeous!

Posy rolled over and grabbed her phone, the ping of an incoming text waking her far earlier than she'd intended, but the frown she was wearing, annoyed at herself for forgetting to silence her phone overnight, turned to a smile as she read Jackson's message.

You're up early.

Got a breakfast meeting at work. Woke up thinking of you… it's gonna make me late.

Gross!

I'm only human – I make no apologies.

Was I good?

Amazing!

Posy's sleepy smile turned into a grin. Ordinarily she'd find that kind of chat with a man a huge turn-off, especially as their relationship was so new, but for some reason she didn't mind it from Jackson this morning. Maybe there was a simple explanation. Maybe Jackson was that rare thing – a relationship that might last a while; at least, one she wanted to last.

You'll be even later if you're texting me instead of getting ready for work.

I know. When are you coming back to London? I've got nothing to do this weekend.

Oh, so I'm just something to occupy your time?

In the best possible way, yes.

I can't come back yet; I'm not finished here.

You can come for a visit? They don't have you locked up, do they?

Actually yes. I'm texting you from the cellar right now. Sometimes they bring me cold gruel and let me look at the sky through a crack in the wall, but I don't think they'll let me out to see real people.

I'll have to come and rescue you.

In your stormtrooper costume?

Could do. If I did would it float your boat?

Quite possibly… you could come to visit me here? I could ask if you could stay over.

I'd find it weird tbh. More to do in London too.

I guess… I'll see what I can do.

The conversation finished with more flirting and then virtual kisses, then Posy returned her phone to the bedside cabinet and rolled onto her back with a sigh. She wasn't sure she was all that bothered about rushing back to London just yet, but she did want to see Jackson.

Then again, perhaps the fact that she didn't want to go ought to tell her something about her state of mind. Maybe she was getting too comfortable here in Somerset in a life that was borrowed, not really hers. She'd have to go home sooner or later, and it was silly to allow herself to feel so settled at Oleander House like this. Not only that, but Marella would say Posy was getting staid and boring and she'd be right. London was where she belonged and where all the opportunities were; she'd be mad not to go back as soon as possible. Not to mention that, sooner or later, Giles, Sandra and even Asa would decide she'd outstayed her welcome and want her to leave.

It was Posy's turn to get supplies. Again. The amount of coffee and milk she and Asa managed to get through on a weekly basis was astonishing – it was a wonder they weren't permanently wired, and if it were a harder drug they'd certainly be bankrupt. They'd had to borrow from the big house again this morning for their first coffee of the day, and Giles had gently ribbed Posy about what exactly they were doing with their weekly supply.

While Giles had always been open and friendly with Posy, he was so different from his brother. She got along with him and was glad to be welcomed into his home, but she and Giles simply didn't 'click' the way she and Asa had, which was funny when Posy recalled that Asa had been the more reserved sibling in the beginning. The way things were with Giles felt more like a father–daughter (or perhaps uncle–niece, as it ought to be) situation than friends. Perhaps that was down to the bigger age gap, or perhaps it was just that he was married and settled and took life a lot more seriously than Asa did. In the end it didn't really matter, Posy supposed – she only knew that she liked him a lot and she felt he liked her too, which was confirmed by his generous offer that morning.

'We've been thinking,' he began, glancing at Sandra who was buttering toast for their 'after-breakfast breakfast' – the meal they ate almost three hours after they'd got up, after they'd been to inspect the grounds together and seen that all was well. 'Perhaps, as you're spending so much time here helping out, we ought to put you on the insurance for our little van.'

'That's really kind of you,' Posy said. 'Although Asa has already said I can use his car whenever I need.'

'True, but when you've got to pick up things from the hardware store – as you undoubtedly will need to once the structural work on Asa's annexe is finished and you come to decorate – you're going to need something bigger and tougher than his car.'

'Doesn't Asa drive the van?' Posy asked. When she thought about it, they could probably place online orders too, but maybe they would want a few on-the-spot things from time to time that they wouldn't want to wait for and perhaps Giles was thinking of those occasions.

'Well, yes. We just wondered if you might find it useful to be able to use the van too.'

'The thing is… I'm a little nervous driving, to be honest. I mean, I can drive, but I don't need to very often in London so I hardly ever bother and I think… well, I know it's made me a bit rusty.'

'Maybe now's the time to get better again,' Sandra said. 'The roads are quiet here so you wouldn't have to be nervous.'

Posy smiled gratefully. While it was true she rarely used her driving skills she also loved any excuse to walk around the orchard and the area around Astercombe. But, she supposed, Giles had a point about picking up hardware and the weather wouldn't always be kind enough for walking. Maybe she could even offer to help them with cider deliveries if she became more confident behind the wheel of their van – and it was only a small one anyway so it wouldn't be as intimidating as it could have been if they'd owned a transit or something much more unwieldy. It would be one way of repaying them for the kindness they'd shown her since she'd come to stay with them.

'OK,' she said finally, 'that sounds good. Thank you. If I can drive the van then I can run errands for you too.'

'Oh, we have plenty of people to do that,' Sandra put in. 'No need for you to worry.'

'But they're not here all the time and I am… well, I am at the moment.'

Sandra smiled. 'You'd really want to?'

'Of course!' Posy replied. 'I mean, I am taking huge advantage of your hospitality already.'

'Also helping Asa for free,' Giles reminded her.

'Oh, I'd enjoy doing that anyway – any excuse to redesign a room and I'm there.'

Sandra placed the plate of toast in front of Giles and turned to Posy. 'I'll give the insurance company a call later, get it all sorted – no point in messing around. Then you'll be able to start taking it out straight away.'

'Thank you.' Posy held up the jar of coffee Giles had furnished her with. 'And thanks for the coffee too. I'll walk to Astercombe straight after breakfast to get you a replacement.'

'Wait until the van insurance is sorted and go in that,' Giles said mildly. 'That way it's a great excuse for a trial run and you don't have to worry about how much shopping you might want to bring back.'

Posy didn't think she'd buy that much but having the van would enable her to drive to a bigger town for provisions if she was minded to, where she'd get a better choice and cheaper prices. Perhaps she'd ask Asa to come so she'd have a little moral support and someone to navigate while she concentrated on getting used to an unfamiliar vehicle. She nodded. 'That sounds like a good idea actually.'

'I'll let you know when it's all gone through,' Sandra said. 'There's nothing I ought to know about, is there? Motoring convictions, speeding tickets…? Anything the insurers might not like?'

Posy had to grin. 'If only my life was that exciting. I'm afraid there's nothing – no naughty things in my past at all!'

Later that afternoon it was raining heavily, and though she would have walked in it to get supplies regardless, it seemed the perfect time to take the newly insured and currently not in use van instead. Asa was needed by Giles, however, something about amending advertising copy, and so Posy decided to forfeit the longer drive out to a bigger town for more shopping and pop into Astercombe instead. The convenience store had a little car park and would do for now, and she might just call into the nearby (everything was nearby in tiny Astercombe) farm shop to see what treats they had. If something looked nice enough she'd take it and cook for everyone that evening.

Sandra and Giles insisted that Posy and Asa join them at the big house for supper almost every evening where they would cook, and Posy figured it was about time she took her turn, even if Asa kept telling her not to worry because they both loved cooking and always wanted to do it anyway.

The van was surprisingly light and easy to drive. Posy had expected some cumbersome, tank-like experience, but it wasn't all that different to the estate car her mum had back at home. Once she got used to it, she could see herself zipping up and down with deliveries and shopping in no time. In fact, she was glad she hadn't waited and given her anxieties time to get the better of her, otherwise it might have been ages before she'd plucked up the courage to take the van out.

With access to this and to Asa's car, she quickly began to realise, she also had the freedom to see a lot more of the surrounding area if people at Oleander House were too busy to drive out with her, and she really did want to see a lot more of it, from mystical Glastonbury Tor to the majesty of Cheddar Gorge. She wanted to go to the coast, to villages and towns like the quaintly named Street, Axminster, Wells... so many places she'd heard of and read about and she wanted to see them all.

There was years for all that, Asa had told her when she'd mentioned it to him, plenty of visits to Oleander House in the future when she could do all that – but if she had the means to travel then why wait?

No sooner had these thoughts entered and left her mind than she saw the roof of Sunnyfields Guest House behind a row of trees. She considered popping in to say hello but quickly decided that perhaps visiting unannounced wasn't the best idea. Besides, they'd probably seen enough of her this week anyway.

A moment later the sign informing her Astercombe was now less than two miles away appeared and made up Posy's mind for her on that score.

And no sooner had she seen that sign than she heard a loud pop, and then the van suddenly swerved on the road, forcing her to slam the brakes on. Shaking, Posy manoeuvred it onto a grass verge as best she could, out of the way of the road, and killed the engine.

After a moment of deep breathing to calm herself, she got out to see if she could find some explanation for why the van would behave like that. It didn't take her long to spot the blown-out tyre at the front. She was no great expert, but either the air pressure had been wrong or something very sharp had been on the road to cause it, although looking now she couldn't see anything that might be the culprit.

To add to her woes, no sooner had she stepped out of the vehicle than the rain became torrential. She glanced back at the rooftop of Sunnyfields. Could she get help there? It was certainly closer than Oleander House but, again, she didn't want to impose on Karen and Ray, who would have enough of their own to be getting on with.

Hurrying back to the driver's door and getting in, Posy grabbed her phone. So much for independence, she mused as she dialled Asa's number.

There was no answer. Rather than leave a message on his service she decided to call Giles – they were working together this morning, as far as she knew, so he ought to be close by. But there was no reply from him either and she had to assume that they were working together but didn't want to be interrupted and had both put their phones out of the way. Posy didn't have Sandra's number – she'd never needed it – but she did have the number for the house phone stored in her contacts. She quickly tried that, only to get no reply there either.

Silently cursing her luck, she decided there was nothing else to be done but to walk back for help. She didn't have the first clue how to change a tyre – a fact that would have been lamented by any twenty-first-century feminist worth her salt, but a fact just the same. Posy had never needed to change a tyre – just like she'd never needed to moonwalk – so why would she have learned? Although, she reflected ruefully as she climbed out of the van and zipped her coat up, if any situation was going to persuade her to rectify that, it would be one very much like this.

She'd barely taken ten steps when she checked herself. What was the good of making a nuisance of herself at the orchard when they were all busy?

Come on! Are you really that useless, Posy?

She turned back to the van and got her key out to open it. There had to be a manual or something in the glove box with instructions on how to change a tyre, and surely it couldn't be that difficult to follow them?

As she'd suspected, there was a booklet detailing where the spare and the jack could be found. It didn't tell her how to replace the tyre, but she took another look and it sort of made sense. There were a few tools in the back, including something that would take the wheel nuts off (though she had absolutely no idea what it was called and found it almost laughable that she'd survived twenty-seven years on the planet knowing very little about these things). It all looked heavy and grimy but still… if everyone at the orchard was working they really wouldn't thank her for making them come out for this.

Steeling herself, she decided to give it a go. What was the worst that could happen? She wouldn't be able to do it and she'd have to walk back for help. But if she could do it…? How proud and pleased she'd be, and how much less of a burden she'd be to everyone. The last thing she wanted was to be a burden, especially as Giles and Sandra had been kind enough to trust her with the van in the first place.

Firstly, she dragged the jack out and positioned it as best she could. She couldn't see instructions on where, exactly, to place it, but it looked fairly straightforward. Then she began to work it up so that the van would lift enough for her to get the damaged tyre off.

That was when she recognised her first mistake. The verge she'd parked on was soft and, instead of lifting the van, the jack simply began to sink into the soil. By the time she'd realised, however, it was well and truly stuck and no amount of pulling would get it out. So she resorted to yanking at clumps of grass and earth to try and free it, becoming so frustrated and increasingly annoyed at herself, and absorbed in her task to the point of near obsession, that she never even heard the car pull up alongside. At least, if she heard, she didn't register anything until she heard the voice.

'Alright there?'

She spun around and, as he recognised her, Lachlan's look of polite concern transformed into one of almost comical exasperation.

'Why is it always you?' he asked wearily.

Posy gave an audible groan, which probably didn't help the situation. 'I could say the same thing to you,' she said, unable to hide the vexation in her tone. She had enough on her plate without running into Groundskeeper Willie.

'In that case I'll leave you to… whatever it is you're doing.' He paused and frowned slightly. 'What are you doing?'

'Changing a tyre.'

She wanted to add something deeply sarcastic to her reply because what she was doing was obvious to anyone, but she was wet, getting wetter by the second, tired and fed up, and she didn't have the energy. She simply turned her attention back to the jack, which seemed to be sinking further into the ground in front of her very eyes, despite her efforts to free it.

'Is that what you're calling it?'

She looked up again, and if he didn't already have form that told her the man possessed no sense of humour whatsoever, she'd have sworn he was finding her predicament funny. Not that he smiled or displayed any of the normal clues to suggest amusement, but his tone was ever so slightly less aggressive than usual and his eyes were almost warm.

'You want some help?' he added.

'I can do it – thank you,' she said stiffly, blowing a lock of wet hair from her face, only for it to glue itself to her forehead.

'And a fine job you're doing,' he said. 'I can see my services would be wasted.'

She waited for more sarcasm but none came.

'It might be a bit heavy—' he began.

'For a little girl like me?' Posy fired back.

'For anyone. Easier with two pairs of hands.'

Posy stared up at him. Was this the same man she'd encountered before?

'Here,' Lachlan continued without waiting for her reply. He bent down to grab the jack, and with one swift pull he'd managed to free it. He turned to her. 'Get in and let the handbrake off so we can push it to level ground.'

Posy, caught somewhere between feeling slightly bewildered and annoyed, did as she was told anyway.

'Put it in neutral,' he called.

She did that too and a moment later felt the van start to move. She glanced at the wing mirror but she couldn't see where Lachlan was. He'd be behind the van, out of sight, she supposed. She couldn't quite believe he was pushing it all by himself, though he must have been because there was no other way the vehicle could be moving.

'Steer!' he shouted, with something more like his old impatience. Now here was a Lachlan she knew how to deal with.

'I *am* steering!' she shouted back. *Because I'm not that dim, despite what you think.*

The van bumped off the verge and onto the tarmac.

'That'll do!' he called.

Posy put the handbrake back on and got out.

'Will it be alright here?' she asked doubtfully. 'Isn't it on the road?'

'Where else do you suggest we put it?'

'But isn't it in the way?'

'There's room to drive around,' he said. 'You'd have to be an idiot to miss it standing here.'

Posy didn't know what to say to that so she said nothing. He went to the back of the van and hauled out the spare tyre, hurling it to the nearby grass. She stared at him, but then found herself with an inexplicable urge to laugh out loud. She held it in, certain he wouldn't appreciate a joke about tossing the caber – she wondered if it might even be a little bit xenophobic. Still, all she could think of right now was the image of him dressed in a kilt looking like the guy from the porridge oats box. It was probably best not to mention that to him either.

'What can I do?' she asked as he bent down to the jack and began to lift the van.

'Come grab these as I get them off,' he said, working at the first wheel nut. 'Won't get far if we lose them.'

Posy knelt down next to him. The wet of the tarmac soaked through her jeans instantly, but although it was hardly the most comfortable she'd been, it was probably the least of her worries.

She watched, fascinated, a little awestruck, and more irritated than ever by Lachlan's capability as he removed the wheel nuts with ease – far more ease than she'd have done. He handed each one to her with a vague grunt, his eyes always firmly on his task. Posy took them silently. She was grateful for the assistance of course, but did it have to be from him of all people? The current situation was so mortifying that she half wondered whether being stranded in a downpour wasn't preferable to help from her dour knight in not-quite-so-shiny armour.

'Thank you,' she said after a silent couple of minutes, because she knew she had to, even though it came out in a grudging tone that her mum would have disapproved of. *I brought you up better than that*, Posy could hear her saying, and she'd have been right.

But Lachlan simply gave a different, faintly more expressive grunt and yanked the damaged tyre off, flinging it to one side with ease, just as he had done the spare moments before. Then they were silent again as he inspected the new one – to check it was roadworthy, Posy supposed – which was good of him really because he could have stuck it on and sent her on her way without another thought. He probably had better things to do than worry if her spare tyre was going to stay on or not.

'Did you manage to track down Pavla the other day?' she asked finally, if only to break the oppressive silence. 'I mean, of course you don't have to say, it's none of my business but I just wondered—'

'You're right,' he said.

'Right... About what?'

'It's none of your business.'

Posy frowned. 'I was only trying to make conversation.'

'You could make it about anything – why that?'

'I don't know... I just thought of it. OK, what do you want to talk about?'

'I want to get this tyre changed before dark,' he said gruffly. 'Less talk makes quicker work.'

Posy's frown deepened. 'Don't you ever just want to make small talk? Just to be polite?'

'Don't see the point. What does small talk achieve? Doesn't tell you anything important, does it?'

'It achieves friendship.'

'Mindless chit-chat about the weather doesn't achieve friendship.'

'It can be the beginning. It breaks the ice so you can talk about other things – you've got to start somewhere.'

'You're saying you want to be my friend?' he grunted as he lifted the new tyre into place.

'Why not? Does that seem so strange?'

He held out his hand and Posy placed one of the wheel nuts she'd been saving into his palm. 'You still haven't forgiven me, have you?'

'What's to forgive?'

'If you don't know I'm not going to tell you because I know you do know and you're just pretending you don't care even though you do.'

'Sounds a bit counterintuitive to me – all that knowing and not knowing and pretending. But if that's the way you want it.'

Posy's frown turned into a scowl. 'Do you deliberately go out of your way to make people dislike you?'

'They can like me or not – it's no business of mine and I don't let it worry me.'

'Why not? Don't you care if people like you or not?'

'Why should I care?'

'I don't know… but you could try being a bit nicer—'

He turned to her. 'Oh, I could, could I?'

Posy flushed and was furious at herself for being unable to control it. In the circumstances, she understood immediately that perhaps her statement had been a little tone-deaf, but she was damned if she was going to let him see that she felt bad about it.

'Any other advice you want to offer?' he asked coldly as he returned to his task.

'I only meant you could be less abrupt with people,' she said lamely.

'A man is what he is. Like it or don't like it. I don't see why I should pretend to be someone I'm not to make you or anyone else comfortable.'

He gestured for the next wheel nut and Posy handed it over, feeling more flustered and ineffectual by the minute. Why did she have to be so helpless and hopeless? She could probably add tactless to that list too, now that she thought about it. Maybe she was lecturing Lachlan when she ought to have been looking at how she projected herself to others. She certainly wasn't doing a great job of looking like a well-rounded individual right now. Of all the men who could have driven by at this precise moment, it had to be him, didn't it? Even then, why did he choose to stop and help?

Try as she might to think otherwise, the fact remained that he had chosen to stop and help when he could have left her to it, so maybe he wasn't the cold-hearted tyrant he'd have people believe. He was still playing that role even now, here with Posy, but the more she thought about it the more she wondered if it was just that – a role, a performance to keep people at arm's length. The girl at the farm shop had said it too – Lachlan had taken her mum to hospital and stayed with her when he could have found an easier way to offer assistance.

Posy looked at him again, trying to throw off the prism of their first meeting, trying to see who he really was. So many theories and opinions jostled for her attention and she had to conclude that she simply didn't know how to feel about him. She only knew that the more she learned of him the more intrigued she was. He'd been a handsome but aloof, unlikeable and downright rude character, but, slowly, he was becoming something else – at least in Posy's eyes. More and more he was becoming a challenge, a riddle she found herself wanting to solve.

He had to ask for the last nut twice. Well, *ask* was perhaps the wrong word. The first request was a beckoning gesture and the second more of a monosyllabic utterance: 'Nut.' Posy had been distracted by her thoughts as she'd watched him work, his large, strong hands no stranger to physical labour and yet oddly sensual-looking. She flushed again, this time with weary acceptance that she had no control over it, and handed it over.

A couple of minutes later the spare was on and Lachlan was hauling the damaged tyre round to the back of the van.

'You can put the jack away?' he asked as he tossed in the offending tyre. It was hardly a question, more of a recognition that he'd done enough for one day and had no intentions of doing any more for her.

'Yes…'

'Right.'

'Um…'

Posy stalled. She suddenly wanted to say something to keep him there longer yet she didn't know why and she couldn't think of anything. By the time she'd managed to say thank you again Lachlan was already at the door of his own car. He didn't look back, and the only acknowledgement that he'd heard at all was a brief raise of his hand in the air before he got in and drove away.

Chapter Eighteen

Posy had tumbled over the threshold of Asa's little house, bursting with her news. Asa would want to know everything, full of his own questions about the ones Lachlan had refused to answer for Posy. On a more practical note, she also needed to find Giles or Sandra to let them know the van was currently running on the spare tyre so that they could do something about it. In the end she'd been to pick up the milk and coffee and foregone the mooch at the farm shop so that she could get back to the orchard quickly to do all that, but when she arrived at the annexe she found only a solo plasterer skimming a new partition wall. He had no clue where Asa had got to and didn't show much sign of caring.

Walking across the grounds to the big house, she supposed Asa must still be in with Giles working on the advertising, and while she couldn't disturb them with idle gossip she did need to tell them as soon as possible about the van in case someone else needed it later.

During the day the door to the big house was always unlocked. Posy had been shocked to discover this when she'd first arrived because she didn't know anyone in London who'd dare to leave their doors unlocked, even when they were home, but when she'd said as much to Sandra, her host had just shrugged. Who was going to travel out to the middle of nowhere to see what they had to steal? They could trust all their neighbours and their staff, and for the most part there was usually someone milling around who would soon spot a would-be burglar anyway.

Posy wasn't quite convinced by Sandra's argument, but today she was glad the door was open as she let herself in. It was likely she'd find Giles and Asa in the office, so she made her way through the ground floor to the front of the house where the study they used for administration was situated. Knocking gently, she waited a moment, but when she was greeted by only suspicious silence, she pushed the door open to see that the room was empty. With a vague frown she closed the door again and paused, her hand still clutching the doorknob as she thought.

Perhaps they were all in the orchard. Or in the cider house? Giles had mentioned at dinner the previous night some vats that were ready to bottle, hadn't he?

She was about to investigate both of those locations when she became aware of low voices coming from somewhere in the house. It was hard to tell where in a place this big, but it sounded like it might be the kitchen. Whether she was right or wrong, it was as good a place as any to look first.

As she made her way back through the voices grew louder – though the words were indistinct and she couldn't tell what they were saying.

'Hello…?'

She pushed open the kitchen door.

As soon as she had she wished she hadn't. It was clear she'd walked into something intense as both Asa and Sandra stopped talking and turned sharply at her entrance. Posy had never seen Asa look so distressed, and although he quickly tried to smooth his expression for her, she wasn't fooled. Something big was going down here – she could see it in both their faces. Typical that she should walk into the middle of it – it was that sort of a day.

'I'm sorry,' she began, 'this is a bad time…?'

'No, no…' Sandra forced a tight smile. 'Of course not. What can we do for you?'

'I can come back,' Posy said. 'It's not important. Well… it is important… sort of… but it could wait, you know… if you were busy…'

'We're not,' Asa said, more sharply than Posy had ever heard him say anything before, but at her involuntary look of shock he repeated himself in a more restrained tone. 'We're not busy, honey. What did you need?'

Posy glanced from him to Sandra and back again. Despite the new kindness in his voice there was still a tension in the air so thick she could grab hold and plait it.

'It's just… the tyre on the van blew.'

Sandra looked aghast. 'OH! Are you alright?'

'Yes, I managed to get it off the road and get the spare on… well, I didn't get the spare on, exactly… but it *is* on. That's what I came to tell you. I guess you'll want to get a new tyre as soon as possible.'

'Of course,' Sandra said. 'Thank you so much for letting us know. But what a shame for your first time out. I hope you weren't too traumatised by it.'

'Oh, no…' Posy said as brightly as she could manage, when even she was succumbing to the strange atmosphere in the room. 'It was fine.'

'You did well to get the spare on by yourself; you should have called us.'

'I just thought I ought to let you know,' Posy added. 'I've left it on the drive.'

'Thank you.' Sandra glanced at Asa, who simply looked dolefully at Posy.

'So… I'll just check the plasterer is OK… getting on with everything…' Posy continued, flailing now for something to say that would avoid addressing the very obvious issue in the room. She knew perfectly well that the plasterer was getting on just fine and that he didn't need any input from her at all.

At this point, Asa would usually make a quip, or at least reassure her cheerfully that he'd be over to join her just as soon as he was able, but not this time. It pained and puzzled Posy in equal measure.

'We'll see you later for supper?' Sandra asked.

Posy nodded, but then remembered that she'd meant to pick something up to cook for them as a surprise supper so that Sandra or Giles wouldn't have to do it. While she was vaguely annoyed at herself for forgetting, it didn't seem important now.

She left the kitchen wondering what the hell had just happened, both Asa and Sandra watching her go. She'd thought the day had already been eventful enough, but, apparently, it hadn't finished with her yet.

The rest of the afternoon was dull. Asa didn't make an appearance, the plasterer (as she'd suspected) didn't need her at all and it continued to rain so hard there was no joy in going out. Once again she was left grappling for something to keep her occupied. She decided against visiting Karen – there were only so many afternoons she could be expected to spare for idle gossip – and everyone else was busy. She phoned her mum for a quick chat, tried her dad but his phone was switched off, then she found Marella in a meeting that she couldn't leave. So she called Jackson.

'Hey! I was just thinking about you,' he said.

'Good. And what in particular were you thinking about?'

'Ah, now… that would be telling.'

Posy giggled. 'Aren't you at work right now? Whatever it was couldn't be *that* distracting.'

'You'd be surprised what I can still get done, even when I'm distracted.' He let out a chuckle. 'It's a pretty slow day, actually. I was just wondering if you were planning to come home any time soon?'

'I might. I was thinking I might put it to my uncles later at supper.'

'Can't you do what you want to?'

'Of course I can, but I'd rather run it by them.'

'Why would you need to?'

Posy shrugged. She didn't really know why she needed to and she couldn't imagine there'd be any objection. 'It just seems courteous to mention it up front. And I said I'd help at the orchard any time they wanted so I'd rather let them know in case they were planning anything that involves me. They've never actually taken me up on my offer, but I wouldn't want them working out a schedule and then not being there for it after all.'

'I'd say you're beginning to like it there.'

'I do like it. You'll like it too when you visit.'

'I mean, really like it. As in, you want to stay for good.'

'No…' Posy hesitated. 'I mean, it's lovely and there's nothing to dislike, but there wouldn't be much real work here for me. I'm just enjoying the break from my usual routine, I suppose. And it's weird, but I feel as if I belong here already. But I'd never leave my mum and dad, no matter how much I feel at home here in Somerset.'

'Well that's good, because once you're back in London I get to see a lot more of you. At least, I hope so.'

'As often as you like once I'm back.'

'Be careful saying things like that, I might just take you up on it and then you'll be sorry.'

Posy smiled. 'I won't be sorry at all.' The fact was, she was beginning to like Jackson. A lot. It had certainly been some time since she'd enjoyed talking to a boyfriend quite so much. Often she was bored by this point in a budding relationship, so this was a good sign.

Maybe, she thought with an unfamiliar sense of anticipation, he could even turn out to be The One. It seemed so unlikely, especially when she thought back to her initial impressions at the fancy dress party (although, even then, he must have done something to make her agree to the first date). But he was funny, cheery company, easy on the eye and totally on her wavelength. Speaking to him this afternoon had reinforced for her what he'd said via text that morning – it was about time they got together in person.

'So… this weekend, maybe?'

'Maybe. I'll let you know.'

'I'll be waiting by the phone for your call.'

Posy's smile spread a little wider. She liked the sound of that.

It wasn't long after Posy had finished her call to Jackson and the plasterer had packed up and left for the day that Asa came back to the annexe. He looked brighter than he had when she'd seen him with Sandra earlier (by brighter she meant not totally bereft), but he still wasn't his usual self.

'Has everything been OK?' he asked in a dull voice as he inspected the new plasterwork.

'Of course,' Posy replied, trying to keep her tone light. 'Not a problem.'

'Good… I'm sorry I haven't been here—'

'Honestly, it's fine; please don't worry about it. You have other things to do, and that's what you have a project manager for – right?'

His answering smile was so empty it almost broke her heart to see it. If he found it so hard to raise, and if he was making that much effort just for her, she wanted to tell him that he really didn't need to.

'I was going to wipe down the surfaces actually,' she said. 'Plastering… you know… leaves that fine dust everywhere.'

'Let me do it – you've been here working all afternoon and I've been…'

His sentence hung in the air, unfinished. Posy didn't feel she'd been working exactly, but now didn't seem the time to go into that.

'Let's do it between us – quicker that way and then we can have a drink before supper.'

Asa nodded. Posy went to the kitchen to get an extra cloth to go with the bucket of sudsy water she'd already prepared, her brain working furiously. This was horrible. She simply didn't know what to do with this new and strange Asa. She had to find a way to snap him out of it, but something told her that asking him about his problems wasn't going to help because she didn't think he'd want to talk about it. If he wanted to, surely he'd have put her straight by now.

'I should have asked if you were alright after your van trouble,' he said as she came back through to the living room.

Posy handed him the spare cloth. 'Oh, that… I'm fine. It was just a flat tyre, after all.'

'I don't know how you managed to change it; even I'd have struggled on my own.'

'Well…' Posy began sheepishly, 'I actually had some help. Lachlan changed the tyre.'

Asa's reaction was a satisfying one as his eyebrows rose even further.

'Lachlan?' he repeated. 'As in *Lachlan*?'

Posy grinned. 'I know – nobody's more surprised than me by that turn of events.'

'How on earth…? How did this even happen?'

'I don't know. One minute I was struggling in the rain, the next he was there like a hero from the mists. And the man is a machine! Threw that old tyre off like it was an Olympic sport he'd been training for his whole life!'

'Well,' Asa said, the ghost of his old smile showing now, 'those muscles had to be good for something. So he's not just form over function then?'

'Far from it. They really work – it's like watching Hercules in action.'

'Hmm… I always miss the fun. So he changed your tyre. And then what?'

'He just drove off.'

Asa folded his arms. 'That's it? He drove off? You didn't try to seduce him?'

Posy laughed. 'Oh, yeah, like that would happen! I don't think he's the seducible type, is he?'

'True, but having that heavenly physique at such close quarters, you must have been a little bit tempted to try.'

'I've also got a boyfriend,' Posy reminded him. 'I'm sure Jackson wouldn't be happy at the thought of me trying to seduce some random man who stopped to help with my tyre.'

'Honestly, if your boyfriend had been there he might have been tempted too. You'd have to be straighter than straight not to at least think about it.'

'Jackson is – I'm fairly sure of that,' Posy said with a grin, happy to see Asa more like his old self again. 'Which, apparently, is very lucky for me. Anyway, it's difficult enough to get Lachlan talking, let alone anything else.'

'He is the strong, silent type,' Asa agreed. 'I bet he's riveting at dinner parties.'

'Designed to be seen and not heard?'

'Couldn't have put it better myself.'

Asa began to wipe down a windowsill. Posy wanted to ask if he was OK now, if he wanted to talk yet about whatever had been going on earlier, but she didn't want to jeopardise the progress they were making here. He was already on his way to a happier mood and perhaps it just needed time. Torn, in the end she decided it could wait. Perhaps he'd tell her when he was ready without her prompting, and perhaps that was better.

'I was thinking I might go home this weekend,' she said instead. She'd been planning to mention it at supper, but now suddenly seemed like a good time. 'If you can spare me, that is.'

Asa turned to her. 'Not for good?'

Posy smiled. 'Of course not! I just feel like I haven't seen anyone back home for a few weeks and it's probably time I showed my face. Don't want them all forgetting who I am.'

'Oh,' he said, looking faintly relieved. 'You must go if you feel that way.'

Posy glanced across as he wiped down the TV cabinet. His expression gave nothing away, but something in his tone suggested his mood had slipped back again to the melancholy she'd seen earlier.

'Why don't you come?' she asked.

The idea struck her in a sudden flash. Asa had said on many occasions he wanted to visit London again and she'd thought before about inviting him – so why not now? Yes, she'd have to dedicate some time to Jackson, and she'd have to try to see Marella too – not to mention quality time with her mum, of course. But maybe she could take Asa out for a few hours and, when she couldn't be with him Carmel might enjoy the opportunity to get to know him better.

'That's sweet but I'm sure you have lots of people you need to see – you don't want to be dragging your dull old uncle around.'

'Asa – you're like nobody's dull old uncle. My friends will love you; they'll think you're more exciting than me!'

He looked round with a small smile. 'You think?'

'Are you kidding? Marella will go nuts for you!'

'It does sound fun – it's been ages since I had a wild night out.'

'I'm not sure it'll be wild,' Posy replied with a smile. 'But it's usually fun, especially if Marella is there.'

'Will Marella and Jackson be there at the same time?'

Posy frowned. Asa had spotted a situation that she hadn't even considered in her enthusiasm for the plan. Marella and Jackson had met, of course, at the same party where Posy and Jackson first hit it off. But being at the same party wasn't like being at a party together. They'd never all hung out as a single unit before – there'd barely been time for Posy and Jackson to go out as a couple before Posy had left for Somerset, let alone for Posy, Jackson and Marella to all go out together.

'I think,' she said slowly, 'with you there too it could be good. The more the merrier, like they say. More people to interact with, less room for awkwardness…'

'Hmm,' he said. 'I see what you mean. As long as they're not embarrassed to be out with me.'

'Of course they won't be!'

'I'm a bit of a bumpkin – I know that. Not to mention old.'

'You're not old and you're certainly not a bumpkin! You're cool and funny and they're going to love you!'

Asa grinned, and Posy knew she'd won the battle.

London wasn't going to know what had hit it.

Posy had never heard Jackson whine before. He'd have denied he was doing anything of the sort, of course, but if it wasn't whining then it sounded very close and it was irritating the hell out of her. She was beginning to wish she'd never phoned him with her news and now she wanted to end the call as quickly as possible – which was a novelty in itself. Usually she'd spend hours on the phone to him – schedule allowing – happy to chat. Thank God Asa was out of the way so he couldn't hear that the main topic of conversation and the reason for Jackson's complaints was him.

'I thought it would be just us, spending time together,' he said.

'It will be… at some point. I just wanted to bring Asa along; he needs cheering up. We can still fit in some time for each other over the weekend.'

'Can't he stay in with your mum when we go out?'

'No! Asa hasn't had a good night out in ages and he needs one. He's been desperate to go out in London and I promised—'

'But he's so old! Where are we going to take him?'

Posy glared at the phone; it didn't matter that Jackson couldn't see it. 'He's not on a walking frame yet! I'm taking him to a decent bar or club – wherever he wants to go. He's been putting me up for weeks – it's the least I can do. Marella's happy enough with it.'

'Yeah, but Marella… why can't Marella take him out then?'

'Because she doesn't know him!'

'Neither do I!'

Posy let out a sharp breath. 'But I'll be there, won't I?' she said through gritted teeth, trying very hard not to shout. 'You'd be asking Marella to take him out solo if you had your way; that's not fair to her or my uncle.'

'See, that's just weird too. He's your uncle and he's coming out with us.'

'It's not weird.'

'Of course it is! Who goes out clubbing with their uncle?'

'He's not like a normal uncle. And he's hardly older than us really.'

'You said he was about ten years older than you.'

'That's no big deal. He's fun. Jackson, please… when you get to know him you'll love him.'

The line was quiet for a moment. Finally Jackson spoke again.

'You're dead set on this?'

'Yes.'

'Will there be any time for just the two of us at all?'

'If you're free Sunday I could come over and Asa could go out sightseeing with my mum. How does that sound?'

'I don't suppose I've got much of a choice if I want to see you.'

'You *will* be seeing me on Saturday night.'

'You know it's not what I mean. Don't give me a hard time – I'm only complaining because I like you.'

'There's no need to complain; we have all the time in the world to see each other once I'm back in London for good.'

'I know but…'

The line was quiet again and Posy, though vaguely irritated by the conversation, couldn't help but smile to herself. It was nice to be wanted like this, even though it felt like Jackson's demands were a little unreasonable. If he liked her as much as he said then she supposed she couldn't blame him for wanting them to spend time together where it would be just the two of them. If she hadn't promised Asa a night out then perhaps she would have liked that too.

'So I can tell Asa it's all on?' she asked.

'I suppose you were going to anyway.'

'Honestly – yes. But I'd rather do it with you fully onboard.'

There was another pause. 'Fine. If there's no other option then you'll have to consider me totally onboard.'

Chapter Nineteen

They'd all agreed that the first wine bar – though it was perfectly trendy, situated in the very coolest part of Soho – lacked atmosphere. Marella had been annoyed – someone at work had gushed about an evening they'd spent there – and after half an hour announced that she'd been in livelier crypts and they'd decided to move on to a place she and Posy had been to before and knew was more fun. It was in a dingier street and it wasn't quite as trendy, but they'd always had a good time in there.

Jackson reached for Posy's hand as they walked to it. It wasn't far so there was no need for a cab and, besides, Asa had said if he was in London he wanted to see it all first hand, not through the window of a taxi.

'I missed you,' Jackson said in a low voice.

Posy gave him a brief smile. 'I missed you too,' she said.

'Honestly?'

'Of course.'

'Do you have to go back to his place again after this weekend?' Jackson asked, angling his head at Asa who was currently walking a few paces ahead chatting to Marella. Posy could tell they'd already clicked and were getting along famously. She'd known they would, but she was glad to see it just the same.

'You mean Asa?' Posy asked, knowing full well who Jackson meant but disliking the way he refused to use her uncle's name. 'Yes, I do. I haven't finished there yet.'

'But it's just workers there now, isn't it? Surely you've done your bit?'

'I said I'd project manage.'

'For free. You don't owe them – you can come back whenever you want; they can hardly complain.'

'They're not complaining and they've been very kind to me and my mum. They're family.'

Posy had never told Jackson the full story of how Asa, Giles and Sandra had come to be in her life. As far as he was concerned, distance meant they didn't see each other often but were a family just like any other. She'd meant to tell him – it was no secret – but the right moment had simply never presented itself. Now, she didn't feel much like telling him at all.

'So when are you coming back?' he asked.

Posy looked up at him. 'In a few weeks maybe. I don't know... when everything is done. It's hard to tell with these things; work gets delayed. It's not like I've got anything to come home for right now... I mean, jobwise,' she added quickly, seeing the expression of hurt cross his face. 'I mean, we can see each other whenever, can't we? I can come back for a weekend or you could even come to stay at Oleander House. I'll talk to Asa – now that he's met you I'm sure he won't mind if you bunk down at his place for a couple of nights. In fact he'd probably like it.'

Jackson threw a look at Asa's back, and Posy could have sworn it was one of distrust. Why, was another matter... Was he actually jealous of Asa? She couldn't think why, but neither could she think of a reason Jackson might have to dislike him.

'I guess,' was all he said.

She gave his hand a squeeze to rally his mood. She didn't want to be at odds with him – not tonight.

'You'll love Astercombe,' she said brightly.

'Where?'

'The village I'm staying at, silly.'

'Oh, yeah… that place.'

'I'll let you try all the cider they make,' she continued. She dropped her voice. 'Maybe even in the barn behind the hay bales when everyone has gone to bed…'

At this he grinned and she was glad to see his mood lift.

'That sounds good. Cider in the hay bales with you; like that book… Cider with Posy.'

She laughed. 'It's *Cider with Rosie*, but I think your version works for us.'

'Yeah, it works for me.'

'So you'll come?'

'I thought you had to clear it with your family?'

'I do, but I'm almost certain they won't mind. You're going to love them, you know, and you'll love Oleander Orchard.'

'I think I'll love the barn…'

Posy grinned. 'About that… we might have to share it with rather a lot of brewing equipment. And maybe a few hundred crates of apples…'

'We won't get hungry then.'

'That's for sure!'

Marella turned and called to them.

'Come on you two; we're wasting valuable clubbing time while you dawdle along like an old married couple!'

'Don't you worry, we're right behind you,' Posy called back. 'Go in and we'll follow.'

'And I thought I was the old man of the group,' Asa chipped in. Posy smiled, but when she glanced to her side she saw that Jackson wasn't smiling. Inwardly she gave a sigh. Hadn't she just sorted this out? How could he still be annoyed about this? If he'd only give Asa a chance and forget he was Posy's uncle he'd enjoy his company. Yes, he was a little older than them, but it was hardly a chasm of an age difference. They could all listen to the same music and laugh at the same jokes for one evening, surely?

Posy looked ahead once more to see Marella leading Asa into a bar called The Pin. It was a tiny place specialising in just about any gin you could care to name and transforming them into the most incredible cocktails. Its size was a large part of its atmosphere, but at the same time it was often full very early on. Tonight was no exception and the clientele were spilling out onto the street with their drinks, while it looked like anyone who had plans to get to the bar to order had a serious battle on their hands. Having sampled The Pin's wares before, Posy knew it was a battle worth undertaking and she was ready for it.

They squeezed in, Asa's face lighting up as he noticed the old teak shelves above the bar that had once contained chunky bottles of ancient remedies, back when the building had belonged to a thriving apothecary. These days the shelves were lined with a dizzying array of gin bottles of all shapes and colours.

'Not a cider in sight!' he exclaimed. 'I love it here already!'

Posy laughed. 'It's a good job we don't all feel like that about cider. Better not let Giles hear you say that.'

'Oh, just because we make cider doesn't mean I have to drink it day and night. You can get sick of something, you know.'

'The rhubarb and ginger is good,' Marella said. 'That's my fave. They do a nice pine-needle gin—'

'Pine needle?' Asa pulled a face.

Marella smiled. 'It's better than it sounds! They do this really incredible watermelon one too – you liked that, didn't you, Posy?'

Posy nodded. 'And the lime and orange… Was that what it was or was it lemon and orange…?'

Jackson looked at the shelves with almost as much distrust as he'd looked at Asa's back as they'd walked here. 'Don't they do anything other than gin?'

A man pushed past Posy, causing her to stumble and reach out for Jackson's arm to steady herself.

'It's a gin bar,' Marella said before Posy could reply. 'Gin is kind of its *raison d'être*.'

'Yeah, but not everyone likes gin.'

'Then they ought to go to a place that's not a gin bar,' Marella returned carelessly.

'I'll bet I can find one you'll like,' Posy said to him. 'Amongst all that there's got to be something to tickle your taste buds.'

Marella had indulged in pre-drinks or whatever it was she called them – drinks she had before she went out so that she was suitably 'warmed up' before they even got to the bars. Often she'd have had too many before they'd set foot in their first pub and tonight looked as if it might be one of those nights, otherwise she might have read the room better. So far Jackson was clearly not enjoying his night out as much as Marella and Asa were. And Jackson being less than enthusiastic meant that Posy wasn't enjoying her night out as much as she'd hoped she would either. All this seemed to have escaped Marella, though Posy saw her link arms with Asa, heads close as they giggled at a private joke. At least something was going well.

'You're alright, you are,' Posy heard her say to him.

'So are you,' Asa replied. 'Say that again, though – your accent is making me feel all warm and fuzzy. Why do northern accents sound so nice?'

'I think yours sounds nice,' Marella said. 'Makes me think of tractors and apples.'

'Oh God no!' Asa laughed and Marella collapsed into fits of giggles too.

'You both have nice accents,' Posy cut in. 'You both sound friendly and approachable; not like us lot in London, so bland and toneless we could be conveying any number of complicated emotions but so boringly nobody would realise.'

'Speak for yourself!' Jackson said. 'You can't beat a good cockney accent!'

Posy laughed. 'You're not a cockney! Have you heard yourself? Less East End and more Eton!'

'I never went to Eton!' he protested, but he was grinning now.

'You can't deny it,' Posy said. 'We do sound boring next to those two.'

As they discussed the virtues of their various accents they shuffled forward, continuing to chat and exchange banter and shuffle over the next few minutes as they made painstaking progress towards the bar. People pushed in the queue (such as it was) and got a tongue-lashing from Asa, but even that had no real malice in it. Posy could tell he was having too much fun to be seriously annoyed, and after seeing him so low the week before she was glad of it.

'Let's see if we can't make something up,' he said as they finally got close enough to inspect the contents of the bar properly.

Marella blinked. 'Make what up?'

'Well, I do work in the drinks industry... sort of. I'm sure we could invent our own brand-new gin cocktail. Maybe I'll patent it and make my fortune.'

'Can you even patent cocktails?' Posy asked doubtfully. 'Aren't they sort of like recipes?'

'I've no idea, but I bet we can still create one. What do you fancy? Sweet, spicy? Soothing or tonsil-stripping?'

Posy giggled. 'How about ear-blocking so I can shut out your rubbish?'

'Oh, I am mortally offended!' he cried dramatically. 'Go to your room at once!'

Posy stuck her tongue out. 'Shan't!'

'Then I shall be forced to tell your mother about this and it will break her heart!'

Posy's laughter grew louder. 'She won't care, I promise you; she brought me up feral, she did!'

Asa grinned broadly at Posy, and then at Marella and Jackson. 'Come on then,' he said. 'This round's on me – what are we all having?'

'Nothing that you've made up,' Posy said.

'I'd try something new,' Marella said. 'I'm always game for a new experience.'

Asa clapped his hands once. 'That's more like it! Now then, I wonder...' He gazed at the shelves, giving the impression of intense concentration. 'I see they have pear gin. Hmm... ginger ale and pear? A kick of apple sour to round it up? Or how about that lovely-looking cherry blossom gin... what would that go with?'

'Almonds go with cherries,' Marella said.

Asa clicked his fingers like a mad inventor. 'Amaretto! Maybe some lemonade to mix…'

'That sounds disgusting,' Jackson said. 'They must have a beer of some description.'

'Probably,' Posy agreed. 'We could ask if you really don't want to try anything else.'

Asa rolled his eyes and although it was in fun, Posy wished he hadn't because she caught the tiniest shift in Jackson's demeanour that told her he didn't like it and she'd been struggling enough with him tonight as it was. She'd never imagined anyone could dislike Asa once they got to know him and so she'd felt reasonably confident introducing him to Jackson and Marella, but right now Jackson was doing a pretty good job of proving her wrong. She still failed to see what Asa had done to cause such dislike, but perhaps there didn't need to be a reason. Sometimes people just didn't like other people and that was all there was to it.

'It doesn't matter,' Jackson said. 'I'm sure I can sink a gin if there's nothing else. Just none of that fancy crap – something normal will do.'

'G&T then?' Marella asked. Jackson nodded.

As Marella and Asa were closer to the bar and had managed to catch the attention of a bartender, they set about ordering for everyone and Asa paid the bill.

'Bloody hell!' he choked as the final amount was relayed to him. 'I know I'm in London now! You could buy our whole cider press for that much!'

Marella laughed. 'That's what I used to say when I first moved down here. You get used to it – when I go home now I feel like I've stepped back in time to 1970s' prices.' She paused as she handed Posy one of Asa's concoctions. 'You ought to come and visit Yorkshire with me one day, Asa; some cracking pubs where I come from and you don't get ripped off.'

'That does sound like fun,' Asa said. 'Name the date and I'll be there – haven't got anything better to do.'

'Oi!' Posy exclaimed. 'What about me?'

'Oh, but you'll be leaving me soon, won't you? Back to the glitz and glamour of life in the capital with your fabulous new job and I'll be bored again.'

'I'll come to visit.'

'Yes, I know, but I'll still have lots of time to spare. Besides, I've never been up north and I'd like to go.'

Posy laughed. 'Of course you have! How have you never been up north? It's not Mars!'

'Well, I'm quite sure I've never been to Marella's bit.'

'Come up together,' Marella put in. 'And you too, of course,' she added, looking at Jackson, though nobody could fail to see he'd been an afterthought.

In a bid to shift the focus, Posy held up her glass.

'This looks amazing!'

'It does a bit, doesn't it?' Asa agreed. He took a sip of his own. 'Not bad, though I do say it myself. I hope that bartender has kept a note of the ingredients because I'm definitely going to want another one of these.'

Jackson was looking so fed up that Posy realised she was going to have to do something drastic to rescue this situation. She'd promised him some time for just the two of them and perhaps, as Asa and Marella were clearly getting on so well, they wouldn't mind splitting the foursome up, allowing her and Jackson to go somewhere he'd like better. She pulled Marella to one side and put the question to her as discreetly as she could, though that wasn't easy when you could barely hear yourself think.

'You want what?' Marella asked.

'Do you mind staying with Asa for a few hours while I take Jackson somewhere else?'

Marella giggled. 'Oh, you dirty little minx! Can't you wait until the night's over?'

'Not that!' Posy frowned. She glanced at Jackson and Marella followed her gaze.

'I suppose he does look a bit miserable,' Marella said. 'I don't think we're really his sort of people, are we?'

'I don't know about that. Maybe these are just not his sort of pubs.'

'Don't you think Asa might have something to say about me whisking him off?'

'He likes you. You're getting on well, aren't you?'

'Oh, yes, he's a blast but it's still you he's supposed to be spending time with.'

'He's seen enough of me the last few weeks. I don't think he'll mind all that much. I'll have a word with him too, but I just wanted to clear it with you first before I did.'

'I don't mind at all. I'll take him to the gay clubs and get him a man.'

'Maybe not. Both of you drunk and in charge of matchmaking – there's no telling what might happen!'

Chapter Twenty

They'd parted company only half an hour before but already Posy found herself wondering if Marella and Asa were having a better time than she was. The answer was probably. Marella had received a text message from one of her colleagues to say a few of her workmates were out having a drink and did she want to join them, and as they were all funny and interesting people she'd insisted that Asa would have the most amazing time if they all met up.

Jackson had taken full advantage of their departure and currently had his arm draped around Posy's shoulder as they sat in the snug of a pub that had once been an old bank but was now filled with quiz machines and jukeboxes and jeering youths playing pool. At least they served good uncomplicated beer, which had cheered Jackson up no end, and their lucky find of a rare Saturday night vacant seat meant they could get up close and personal, which was making him even happier than the beer.

Posy, on the other hand, wished he'd stop trying to kiss her all the time; at least long enough for her to finish a sentence. She'd certainly begun enough of them, and surely the law of averages said that eventually one complete utterance would slip through the net.

'You look good tonight,' he said. 'I wanted to say it earlier but... you know... Got a tan since I last saw you.'

She smiled. 'It's all that time spent—'

His mouth was on hers again. She held in a squeak of frustration and reminded herself that it was nice to be desired like this – it had to be better than indifference. So she let him kiss her again and when he'd had enough she continued.

'… outside. It's so much easier to spend time outdoors when—'

Another snog. It was like dancing with an overzealous, tipsy-from-lager-shandy sixth former at the school disco. She pushed him off.

'Can't we just talk for a bit?'

'I thought we were talking. What else are we doing here?'

'Well, one of us is trying to talk. You're mostly trying to gag me with extreme suction.'

'What?'

Posy sighed. 'I'm sorry; that was mean, ignore me. I'm just tired… and a bit anxious.'

'Why would you be anxious?'

'Well, I'm wondering if Asa is OK with Marella for a start.'

'Of course he is – they got on like a house on fire.'

'Yes, I suppose they did. I'm sure there's nothing to worry about really.'

There wasn't – Posy knew that. So why couldn't she settle and enjoy herself here?

'Do you want to go somewhere else?' Jackson asked.

She let her gaze run over the room.

Sticky bar: check.

Loud music: check.

Cackling girls being ogled by spotty youths: check.

Disturbing smell coming from the toilet area: check.

'Maybe,' she said. 'At the risk of sounding like an old lady, it's a bit... *lively* in here. Maybe we could go somewhere a bit more intimate – you know?'

He waggled his eyebrows and grinned. 'Intimate? How intimate?'

She laughed. 'Not that intimate! Somewhere a bit more... *selective.*'

'You mean posh?'

'It doesn't have to be expensive. I'm out of work right now, don't forget; I'm happy to do cheap and cheerful. But cheap and cheerful can still have a nice atmosphere and be a bit classier than this.'

'You think this place is a dive?'

'No, I didn't mean it like that – maybe classy is the wrong word. Maybe the word I want is exclusive. Just a bit more interesting.'

The brief expression of offence was gone again and Jackson brightened. 'How about that place that does all the Belgian beers? It's quieter in there. Is that interesting enough for you?'

Posy had no idea – she'd never been in there. It sounded a little bit like where they were but it was worth a go. He was trying, after all. She nodded. 'That sounds nice.'

He downed the rest of his pint and offered his hand to help her out of her seat. She smiled as she took it, happy to be getting out of here, but somewhere in her head still sat the little thought that she'd rather be with Asa and Marella right now and, as she couldn't do that without upsetting Jackson, she dearly wished that little thought would bugger off and leave her alone.

Jackson was looking distinctly sulky. Posy had been feeling more and more irritated as the night wore on, though it was hard to pinpoint why. It was more of a general feeling, but she put it down to a long day and hoped it was no more than that.

'Please don't be annoyed,' she said as they left the bar at closing time and discussed where they were (or were not) going next. 'I'm just really tired.'

'I have a bed at my place.'

Yes, Posy thought, and you'd be in it too. Besides being tired and wanting her own bed, spending the night at his flat would very likely mean them sleeping together, and she really didn't feel they were at that point yet. It was probably better not to put herself in an awkward situation where she might have to refuse him in the first place.

'I know,' she said. 'But it just means me having to get up early tomorrow to go home.'

'Why do you need to go home early?'

'Well, because Asa is there and I can't very well leave him all day with my mum.'

Jackson pouted, and Posy could tell what he was thinking. He was thinking what he'd more or less been complaining about all night – that Asa was getting more attention than he was.

'He's my guest,' she added. 'He's come all the way from Somerset to visit and it would be rude of me to leave him. We already ditched him tonight and left him with Marella.'

'They got on.'

'Yes, and it's lucky.'

'I'll pay for a cab tomorrow morning, as early as you like.'

'Honestly,' Posy said, feeling slightly irked by his continuing demands, 'I've had a long day and I'm exhausted. I just want to go home.'

'Fine,' Jackson said, offering her a stiff kiss on the cheek. 'I guess I'll see you next time you're in London… whenever that is.'

Posy arrived home just after midnight to find Carmel still up. Asa and Marella turned up two hours after that, making enough noise to wake her, Carmel, and probably the rest of the street. So she got up and so did her mum and in some respects it was like old times for Posy – Carmel happily cooking bacon for sandwiches to feed a drunkenly ravenous Marella when she really ought to have been in bed, only this time they'd all aged a few years and there was a new addition to the gang in the form of Asa.

Posy decided she might as well have a sandwich with them as the bacon was cooked anyway, while Carmel sipped camomile tea and reassured everyone that she'd catch up on her sleep by staying in bed later.

As they all settled, Marella and Asa recounted the night's adventures. Posy was glad to hear they'd had a great time, though she was a little envious. Then Marella started to yawn and Carmel made up a bed for her on the sofa while Asa was happy to make do with a mound of cushions on the floor and wouldn't hear of any fuss. Posy went to her own bed having had the offer to give it up refused by both of them, and was secretly very glad as she slipped under the covers, sleeping soundly almost as soon as she hit the pillow.

It was gone eleven the next morning when Posy woke again. She went downstairs to find Marella, Asa and Carmel already drinking coffee, despite all having had a heavier night than her.

'Why didn't you wake me?' she asked, pulling out the last empty chair at the table to join them.

'You looked out for the count when I put my head in,' Carmel said. 'I didn't have the heart to.'

'But I've slept half the day. I bet you've been waiting for me to get up so we could go out sightseeing.'

'I thought you were meeting Jackson today…' Carmel returned mildly as she pushed a coffee across the table towards her daughter.

Posy gave a vague shrug as she took it and wrapped her fingers gratefully around the mug. The truth of the previous night was that she'd been finding Jackson hard work and she didn't feel she had the energy for him today, even though she knew that would probably make him sulky again. 'I thought maybe I'd come with you. I'd said to him we were going to spend time together today only because I didn't think we'd get to do it last night. But as we did get to do that last night…'

'Won't he be disappointed?'

'Oh,' Posy said airily, 'I don't think so. I'll text him; I'm sure it will be fine.'

Carmel and Asa exchanged a brief look of confusion, but Marella gave Posy a shrewder one.

'I'd love to come with you all,' she said, 'but I've got a scheme to finish for a meeting with a client tomorrow so…'

'Of course,' Carmel said. 'You must do that if you need to. It's been such a treat to see you again, though – seems like ages since we had a proper chat like this.'

'God, at least eighteen months,' Marella agreed. 'I don't know how that even happened.'

'We get busy and time seems to slip through our fingers,' Carmel replied, a faint note of melancholy in her voice. 'Still, that's how life is and really that's how life is meant to be.'

'The sign of a life well lived, eh?' Marella nodded and drained her cup. 'I'll have to freshen up and dash if you don't mind. Thank you so much for putting me up, Carmel; a cab back to mine would have cost an arm and a leg at that time of night.'

'And you had to get me back safe and sound anyway,' Asa put in with a grin.

'It's always a pleasure to have you,' Carmel said. 'Both of you.'

Marella turned to Posy. 'I don't suppose I could borrow a pair of jeans and a top? Don't fancy doing the Tube in my tiny red dress this morning.'

'I think you'd get a few looks,' Posy agreed. 'Come on, I'll sort you out.'

In her bedroom Posy closed the door and set about finding something that would fit Marella. Her friend was already standing in a pair of Posy's pyjamas and they were a little on the baggy side, so whatever she sourced would have to be a bit forgiving.

'So you and Asa had a good time?' she asked as she shook out a pair of black leggings and handed them to Marella with a silent question. Marella looked satisfied as she took them.

'God, yes. He's hilarious! The folks at work loved him.'

Posy held out a grey marl sweatshirt and Marella took that from her too. 'I'm glad you got along.'

'I can't imagine how anyone could fail to get along with him. And he's had such a tough time over the last few months, the poor bloke deserves some fun… What with his mum dying and Drew leaving him for that other man…'

Posy looked up sharply from her sock drawer. 'He told you that?'

'Yes. I didn't think it was a secret – at least he didn't say so when we talked about it last night.'

'No, I suppose it isn't then. It's just that…'

Posy had suspected something like that had happened to Asa, but he hadn't told her about it, despite all the time they'd been sharing his house. Yet here he was, one night out with Marella and it all came out. What did her friend have that Posy didn't? How was it her uncle had felt comfortable enough to share his past with Marella – who he'd just met – and not with Posy, who was family? Recently acquainted family, sure, but family all the same, and she'd felt they'd grown close quickly. She couldn't help being slightly offended by it and a little hurt too.

'Imagine being engaged, the wedding just around the corner, and then that. And they'd waited for so long, keeping it all under the radar because his mum… old trout… Sorry, I guess, because she's your gran really but… you know, she sounds quite stuck in the Dark Ages and a bit homophobic by all accounts… Well, Asa didn't want to upset her by rubbing her nose in it and a big gay wedding would have done that, I suppose. But they let Drew move in with him and everything, and he really shouldn't have moved in if he was in love with someone else – even if he only suspected in a teeny way he might be in love with someone else. Poor Asa. So all that sneaking about was for nothing in the end, and then your granny went and died anyway…'

Posy listened in silence. She wondered about the timeline of all this. Karen had mentioned Drew leaving just before Philomena's death so it was still quite new for Asa really, no more than a few months ago.

'And now he's messing Asa around terribly,' Marella continued, hardly pausing for breath. 'Wanting to get back together after all that…'

'What?'

'I'd tell him to sling his hook, as they say round here. I said that to Asa last night – delete the cheeky pig's number from your phone, I told him. He says he will but I bet he doesn't. I've seen it all before…'

'I'll talk to him later,' Posy said. 'Make sure he's done it.'

'Good idea.' Marella turned to her. 'How do I look?'

'Like me only much, much better,' Posy said, admiring how Marella had managed to keep her dark hair sleek and shiny and her eyes bag-less despite the late hour they'd all gone to bed. She certainly hadn't thought her hair shiny or her eyes bag-less when she'd looked in the bathroom mirror that morning.

'Don't be daft! I never asked, did you have a good night with Jackson?'

'Yes,' Posy said vaguely, though her mind was barely on Jackson at all. She'd have to find the right moment to ask Asa about all that he'd told Marella, but choosing it wasn't as simple as it might seem. Neither was the question of whether she even should. If he'd never volunteered the information before, did that mean he didn't want her to know? It seemed strange in light of everything else, but she couldn't think of any other explanation.

'Oh God, I nearly forgot the most important thing that happened last night!' Marella said suddenly.

'What's that?'

'Well… don't shout… but you know how you said you didn't want any favours helping you to find a job and I wasn't to ask my boss…?'

'Oh, Marella—'

'I didn't ask, I swear! I was only telling him about you being at Asa's, and Asa told Kier how amazing you were and how he hadn't a clue about his decor but you totally sorted him out with virtually nothing to go on, and then he showed him before and after photos from his phone of the bits you'd completed and my boss said he'd like to meet you. He said he couldn't promise anything but he might be able to find you a job.' Marella beamed. 'And wouldn't it be amazing if we worked together? You can't pretend it wouldn't be.'

'I suppose not. And you definitely didn't set this up?'

Marella frowned. 'Would I lie to you?'

Posy suspected that a little white lie wouldn't count in her friend's book, but she let it slide.

'If I was going to set it up I'd have done it weeks ago, wouldn't I? Kier isn't like that anyway – it would have to be his idea because he doesn't do favours. He wanted to meet you because he liked what you'd done for Asa and he thought, as you'd done it for free, it showed passion for design and commitment and that you were generally the sort of person he'd like to have around.'

Posy gave a small, bemused smile. 'In that case...'

Marella helped herself to a hair tie from Posy's dresser and fastened her hair into a ponytail. 'So you can pop in to see him tomorrow morning?'

'Tomorrow?'

'I know you're supposed to be heading back to Somerset tonight but Asa said he could hang on so you could meet Kier before you leave. You really ought to, you know, I don't know how long he'd be willing to keep this offer open and he's got graduates practically begging for work almost every day.'

Posy nodded. Put like that she'd be crazy not to go, despite a niggling, inexplicable misgiving that she couldn't quite name. That vague feeling of disquiet about one thing or another seemed to be a recurring theme in her life at the moment.

'You're right; of course I'll go. What time?'

'Around ten. Give him a chance to get coffee – he's an animal until he's had his first one. I'll let him know first thing you'll be there. You'll hang on afterwards to grab lunch before you go, won't you? I want to hear all about how it went.'

'As long as Asa is happy to.'

'Brilliant! Right, I'd better get going – if I don't finish that scheme today Kier will be giving you my job!'

Chapter Twenty-One

It was hard to get excited about sights that were so commonplace to Posy, but as Asa gasped his way around the landmarks of London, Posy was reminded of how she'd reacted the first time she'd explored Oleander Orchard and the countryside around it and supposed it wasn't so different. The locations couldn't have been more contrasting, of course, but the thrill of the new and the novelty of the unknown were the same wherever you went.

Carmel had wanted to take him to see lesser-known attractions and spots off the beaten track, and it was good to see her engaging with him because Posy had worried, on more than one occasion, whether things might be awkward between them, given their respective relations to her. But Asa had been more interested in the usual tourist fare, even though some of it he'd seen before on previous visits. In the end he'd seemed happy enough just to be amongst the noise and bustle, and although Posy was tired and still a little hurt that he'd chosen to share his past with Drew with Marella rather than her, she was content to see him enjoying himself.

They'd arrived back at home pooped, and after a spot of supper had gone to bed early so that Posy could be fresh for her interview with Marella's boss the following day. Informal chat, Marella had called it, but Posy still felt the pressure to make it count. Marella would have bigged Posy up, stuck her neck out to get Kier interested, and Posy felt she had to deliver – if only to repay her friend's kindness and not let her down.

The design company Marella was employed at wasn't housed in a swanky glass-walled building like the one Posy had worked for. It sat on the top floor of a grand, Regency-style three-storey town house on a leafy street in the north of the city. Asa and Carmel were waiting at home while Posy had got into unfamiliar-feeling formal wear and taken herself out of the house and onto the Tube to meet Kier. After being buzzed in and greeted by a super-friendly intern, who was manning a reception that looked more like someone's living room than it did a business entrance, Posy found herself and the portfolio she'd thrown together at the last minute being ushered into the boss's office.

Kier was tall and broad, with a booming laugh that he employed often and an accent that Posy couldn't place. As he went through the photos and drawings she'd brought in he asked questions about every one:

What was the inspiration for this?

How did you get such good lighting here?

Was this theme deliberate or a happy accident?

Did this stray far from the client's brief?

Where did you train?

What made you choose interior design rather than a more traditional art route?

Posy answered as honestly as she could – she wanted the job but she didn't see the point in pretending to be more than she was. Sell yourself, she'd always been told by college lecturers and careers advisors, but she'd never really put much stock in that approach. Selling yourself often meant overselling yourself, and it wouldn't take long for the failings you'd hidden to be revealed; far better to be straight from the start and avoid nasty surprises for them both.

'I love what I've seen here,' Kier said finally, handing the folder back to Posy.

'Um… thank you.'

Posy gave an uncertain smile. She'd never had a reaction like that at interview before. Usually her interviewers were cagey about her work, either staying tight-lipped about their opinion or even pretending to be completely disinterested (as her last boss, Joanna, had been before phoning hours later to offer her the job).

'You have commitments at the moment, I believe?' he continued.

'Oh, you mean my uncle's place? Yes, but I shouldn't think I'll be there much longer.'

'How much longer is not much?'

Posy blew out a breath. 'Well, I haven't been that strict over the timescales, not having to work at the moment, so I haven't really got a schedule mapped out as such. I suppose we could have it all done in two or three weeks if we pushed.'

'Would you be free by, say, September?'

'I could be.'

'Would you like to start working for me when you are?'

Posy blinked. 'You're giving me a job?'

'It certainly sounds like it,' he replied with that booming laugh again. 'Of course, we'd have to agree terms but we have plenty of time to do that before you start. For now, a word of agreement from you would be enough to get the ball rolling.'

'God, I'd love to work for you!'

'I'm glad to hear it. And you don't need to call me God – Kier will do.'

Posy smiled. 'I could… I mean, I'm sure my uncle would understand if I have to leave his project… I mean, if you need me earlier than September then—'

'Autumn is fine – it suits me too. I'll get my secretary to send you a copy of our usual employment contract and if you're amenable then I'll get your offer drawn up.'

'You don't want to see me again first? I mean, for a proper interview?'

He burst into laughter once more. 'What do you think just happened? Didn't you think that was a proper interview? Would you like me to do it again and make it tougher?'

'Well, it's just… I thought it was just an informal chat… I mean, Marella said—'

'I find the best way to get the measure of someone is to see them informally. Your guard is down and you haven't spent the week trying to figure out what I might want to hear from you. In my opinion, formal interviews are a waste of time.'

'Oh…'

'I hope you don't mind if I throw you out now, but I have a client due to arrive in the next ten minutes or so.'

'Oh, of course not.' Posy hastily gathered her things and headed for the door.

'Stay in touch,' Kier said as she was going, 'and if your timetable shifts or you change your mind let me know.'

'Yes, I will. And thank you!'

'No, thank you. I'm very much looking forward to welcoming you to the team.'

*

Posy was on her way out through the reception, scrabbling in her handbag to find her phone to text Marella, when her friend appeared in person, saving her the job.

'Listen, I know we were supposed to do lunch but I really don't think I'll have time. You don't mind if we give it a miss, do you? I'm really sorry but I'm absolutely snowed under…'

'God, no, if you're busy I totally understand. I should probably get back. Asa will be waiting and we have a long trip to Somerset later.'

'I knew you'd understand.' Marella pulled her into a brief hug. 'You'll call me later, let me know you got back OK?'

'Of course.'

'I've had a fab weekend.'

'Me too. And thank you so much for today; I know it must have—'

'Don't mention it.' Marella lowered her voice. The girl on reception didn't appear to be listening but it seemed Posy's friend didn't want to take any chances. 'How did it go? Kier liked you?'

'I don't know about that.' Posy broke into a slow smile. 'But I do appear to have been offered a job!'

'That's amazing!' Marella squeaked. 'Soon you'll be with me all the time – imagine how fabulous that will be!'

'Yes,' Posy said with a wry smile. 'Lucky me.'

Marella punched her playfully on the arm. 'Don't deny it, you love me.'

'It's true,' Posy replied, her smile fond now. 'I do – I bloody love you to bits.'

*

The interview had meant Posy hadn't had time to see Jackson in person again before she left, so she'd sent him a message. The problem with messages was it was hard to tell the tone of them, and that was exactly how she felt as she read his rather terse reply. The way they'd left things on Saturday night had planted the seed of doubt in Posy but, for now, it felt like something she didn't have the time or energy to tackle. She hoped that in no time she'd have the Jackson who'd been so much fun at the fancy dress party back. Maybe if she just let things breathe, that would happen, so she decided to do nothing at all for now except say she'd call him when she was back in Somerset.

She and Asa were just settling down on the train to go home when Posy saw someone she thought she recognised.

'Pavla?'

The woman had been making her way down the carriage dragging a wheeled suitcase behind her. She whipped around to see who'd called her name, and sure enough it was Karen's assistant at Sunnyfields.

'Oh, hello!'

'Are you travelling back to Astercombe too?' Posy asked.

'I am.'

Asa and Posy were currently occupying two of a set of four seats and, sensing that Asa wouldn't mind, Posy made the offer.

'Are you travelling alone?'

'Yes. I could sit with you?'

'Of course!' Posy glanced at Asa, who nodded his agreement.

'It's miserable sitting on your own,' he said. 'And you don't know what kind of weirdo might plonk themselves next to you.'

Pavla laughed as she hauled her suitcase onto the luggage rack and then sat down next to Posy.

'How lucky to meet you here,' she said. 'Have you been to visit your mama?'

'Yes,' Posy said. 'What have you been up to?'

'My brother has just arrived in the UK and is living in Finchley. Sometimes I have to see him, even though his miserable face gives me a headache.'

Asa laughed. 'That's brothers for you.'

Posy smiled. 'I bet you love him really.'

'Spoken like someone who doesn't have a brother,' Asa said, and Pavla grinned as Posy poked his leg with the toe of her boot and told him to behave.

As the train began to fill they made pleasant small talk in this vein. Then their departure was announced and things went quiet. They'd barely left the station when Posy looked at Asa to say something and saw that he'd dozed off, his cheek squashed against the window. He looked so uncomfortable that she couldn't imagine how he was sleeping, but the awkward position didn't seem to be bothering him at all.

'Did you wear him out?' Pavla asked, following Posy's gaze.

'Must have done. Although he did the same thing on the train here so maybe he's just one of those fortunate people who can sleep anywhere. At least I'm lucky enough to have you to chat to this time… Unless you fancy a power nap too, in which case don't let me stop you.'

'I'm perfectly awake,' Pavla said. 'I don't sleep on trains.'

'Me neither,' Posy replied. 'Terrified of missing my stop for a start.'

'If you want to sleep I would wake you.'

'Thank you but no. It's habit now – I see a train and I'm conditioned to suddenly feel wide awake no matter how tired I might be.'

'Did you like to be home?' Pavla asked.

'You mean this weekend? Yes, it was good to see my mum.'

'How is she? She misses you?'

'Probably, but she keeps busy and I know she'd never say so – wouldn't want to make me feel guilty about being away. And like she says, one day I'll be moving out for good so it's as well to get used to it. Did you enjoy your visit to your brother?'

'Perhaps not as much as you, but it's good to get a rest from working.'

'I'll bet Karen's missed you.'

'She is very good to me.'

'I imagine she's good to everyone. I mean, I haven't met anyone she won't try to help… even grumpy Lachlan.'

Pavla laughed. 'Yes. He is very grumpy. A very difficult man – sometimes kind, sometimes angry. You never know.'

'I don't know how you managed to work for him.'

'I felt sorry for him.'

'You did?'

'He was always sad.'

'He was? Why?'

'I don't know why, I just know he is.'

Posy regarded her thoughtfully. Had there ever been anything between Pavla and Lachlan? Pavla seemed rather well acquainted with what Lachlan did and didn't feel. Posy shook the thought – what did it matter anyway? It certainly oughtn't to matter to her. 'If he is sad he hides it well. He just seems annoyed at everyone all the time to me.'

'It wasn't always bad.'

'So if he could afford to pay you now you'd go back to him? I mean, I got the impression he was going to ask you the last time I was at Sunnyfields and he came looking for you… so he has money to pay you now?'

'No. I like Karen, and her job is nicer than being rained on all day in Lachlan's fields.'

'That's true. So you don't miss working for him?'

'Sometimes I liked how interesting it was. Every day different – in the spring tending, keeping a lookout for bugs, in the summer watching the grapes grow, in the autumn all the excitement of harvest and pressing the grapes…' She shrugged. 'But working for Karen is interesting too – I like to talk to the visitors.'

'Didn't he get anyone to replace you?'

'Sometimes he has money to pay, sometimes he doesn't.'

'Was it like that when you worked for him?'

'Not as bad, but last year was difficult and he didn't grow enough so I think things are worse now. Workers want to know they'll be paid.'

'Surely he doesn't plan to run that place alone – it's huge!'

'Harvest time will be hard.'

'He has to get someone in to help! Surely trying to do it himself to save money is counterintuitive? I don't know much about it, but wouldn't he just lose another harvest and go under anyway?'

Pavla gave a slight shrug. 'If he pays them and doesn't sell the wine he'll have no money left.'

'I don't understand… what does that mean?'

'No money, no more vineyard.'

'He'll sell his wine, though? I've tried it; it's good stuff. There must be a market for it.'

'Yes, but there are many wines out there just as good.'

Posy was thoughtful for a moment. 'I'm surprised he doesn't join forces with the orchard – surely they could tap the same markets and supply both wine and cider.'

'Perhaps they never thought of it. I think Lachlan would be too proud; he likes to do things alone.'

'It's all very well to be proud and isolated in your personal life, but as a business plan it stinks.'

'I don't think he cares too much for that,' Pavla said.

Posy paused again. 'I think I'll mention it to Giles and Sandra anyway,' she said after a moment of consideration. Even as she did, she was aware that maybe it was none of her business and that she might be overstepping the mark where both parties were concerned, but it made so much sense to her she was amazed it had never occurred to anyone before. Though they made different products they were practically in the same business, and many of the customers for one would be customers for both.

'I think it would be too late for this harvest, even if he said yes.' Pavla broke into her thoughts. 'And I think he would say no.'

'So how serious is this harvest problem? How many people does he need to get it in?'

'Last year he had six but that was still hard.'

'Six?' Posy gazed out of the window. The train had already left the grimy, jostling backs of London's apartment blocks behind and was whizzing through the airier suburbs.

'Yes.'

'The vineyard is good for people...' Posy began slowly. 'I mean, it's important to the village? There's a long history of it being there, so everyone keeps saying.'

'I don't know,' Pavla replied, looking slightly puzzled. 'Perhaps.'

'It could be important economically too,' Posy pressed. 'Like the orchard is. It brings money and visitors to the area and gives the place a reputation for good produce – at least it could. And that would carry to other producers – anyone who grows around there.'

'We don't have too many in Astercombe.'

'But there are some.'

'Yes.'

'And even Karen might benefit if it brings in buyers or visitors who need somewhere to stay?'

'Yes, perhaps.'

'So the people who'd potentially benefit have a vested interest in saving the vineyard no matter how they might feel about Lachlan personally…'

Pavla raised her eyebrows. 'What does this mean? You're worried for him?'

'Not worried… I just don't like to see anyone struggle.'

'Why bother? Lachlan means nothing to you.'

Posy was silent for a moment. 'I know,' she said finally. 'I suppose it sounds strange that I would be this bothered. He's rude, surly, pig-headed and arrogant…' She shook her head slightly. 'God knows why I'm bothered, now that you come to mention it,' she said, laughing. 'Perhaps it's because I've come to love Astercombe already and the vineyard is part of that.'

Pavla shook her head as if she couldn't quite believe what she was hearing, and Posy wondered if she might just have a point.

'Pavla,' Posy began, serious again. 'Why is he like that? Why does he shut everyone out and lock the door to his house? He can't be happy to live like that – nobody can.'

'Why not? You say that because you would not be happy, but everyone is not like you.'

'I know that, but I don't believe that of him. When he fixed my tyre that day I felt like I saw something, another side to him that he tries to hide.'

Pavla frowned, but then smiled slowly. 'He is handsome, you think?'

'That's got nothing to do with it.'

'So you don't—?'

'No!' Posy hissed, perhaps a little too hotly. 'No,' she repeated. 'I can take an interest in a fellow human being without it being… you know…'

'Yes, of course you can.'

Posy looked at Pavla, who had conceded the point but still looked smugger than she should had she actually believed it for one minute.

'I only said he's handsome,' Pavla said. 'And that is true.'

'Undeniably,' Posy replied primly. 'But there are plenty of handsome men in the world and we don't go round falling in love with them just because they exist.'

'No, we don't,' Pavla agreed, but the smug smile was still in place, and Posy had to bite her lip and keep her thoughts about it to herself.

Chapter Twenty-Two

Giles looked over his glass at Sandra. The remains of supper were still out on the table, uncollected and forgotten as the conversation had taken a more serious tone. The sun was still hot, though summer was undoubtedly breathing its last and autumn was fast approaching. Asa swatted at a wasp that was nosing round the rim of his wine glass. It showed the usual waspy persistence, until a breeze rolling over the patio finally took it off to the orchards beyond the garden.

'I don't know about this... cooperative arrangement you're talking about,' he said, turning his gaze to Posy, who'd just mooted the proposal of a joint effort between the orchard and Lachlan's vineyard that she'd discussed with Pavla on the train. 'I doubt Lachlan would be amenable to that. And if the vineyard is really in as much trouble as Pavla says – and I'm not convinced it's not just idle gossip on her part – then getting involved might just pull the orchard under with it. Rather than helping, both businesses might suffer. Oleander Orchard has ticked along since your great-grandfather's time and I'm certainly not going to throw away all his hard work and all his years of struggle to get established trying to save Lachlan's tenuous business.'

'But there must be something we can do?' Posy insisted, unable to deny the logic in what Giles was saying but stubbornly clinging to the idea of helping in some way.

'Hmm.' Her uncle nodded slowly. 'I know of one or two vineyards who get round the harvest issue by opening their doors to visitors who come and pick the grapes as a sort of day out. They get an experience and are sent away with a crate of wine and everyone's happy. One would presume Lachlan is perfectly aware of this easy fix and has chosen to snub it, which leaves me to conclude that he doesn't want help – at least he doesn't want the sort of help that might indebt him to anyone.'

'But he needs it; Pavla said—'

'That may well be, but even without the risks to our business I still don't see that he would accept it from us.'

Posy stared at her half-full wine glass, deep in thought. She didn't know much about running a business, but she couldn't believe that anyone who did would sacrifice its success just because it meant being civil to a few people for a day or two. And if saving a harvest meant being in the debt of a few well-meaning souls, Posy was quite sure she'd accept that and take the help – anyone who didn't must be mad.

'I'm afraid this is Lachlan's mess to clear up for himself,' Sandra said. 'And if he's too stubborn to reach out for help and take advantage of offers that exist then it's down to him if his business fails.'

Posy clamped her mouth shut. It wasn't something she wanted to let go of, but what else could she do? Sandra was right, though she hated admitting it.

'Bear in mind it'll be short notice too,' Giles said.

'What will?'

'As far as I know – and I'm no great expert – there's a small window for grapes just as there is for apples. There'll be a peak time and you won't know when that is until they're just about there, and then maybe you'll only have a few days to get them in and processed. You'd have to have your pickers on standby, and that's hard if you're asking people who've got other things to do.'

'Well, how do the places that let visitors in to pick do it?'

'That I don't know,' Giles said.

'I expect if that's something you rely on you'd invent some kind of notification system,' Sandra said. 'I suppose you could contact one of them to ask.'

'Though I wouldn't waste your time,' Asa put in. 'Lachlan will only say no to the idea anyway.'

Posy shook her head. 'I can't believe he'd sacrifice his harvest to protect his privacy.'

'I don't think he'll go that far,' Giles said. 'I wouldn't be surprised if he simply gave up sleep for a week and tried to power through it all himself.'

'But that's ridiculous!' Posy cried. 'Nobody could get all that in alone!'

'Well,' Sandra said with a wry smile, 'he is a rather ridiculous man.'

'We couldn't spare anyone at all?' Posy pressed. 'You have staff here…'

Giles let out a long, loud sigh, and Posy sensed he might be at the end of his patience with this conversation. She supposed she could see why that might be – she was probably asking a lot for something that didn't really affect them.

'While I admire your intentions and your generous spirit,' he said, 'I think you have to let this go. Autumn is a crucial time for us as much as it is Lachlan and we simply can't worry about his harvest when we need to secure our own. I'm sorry if it sounds selfish but that's just the way it is. Lachlan would understand this very well, and he would probably do the same if the tables were turned.'

Posy was finding it hard to let go of the argument, but what was the point in pushing it any further? Even she could see the sense in what Giles had said. The mood around the table was tenser than she'd like it to be, and when all was said and done she was still a guest in their home – perhaps it was best not to make herself an unwelcome one.

'Maybe if his harvest doesn't overlap too much with ours we could lend a hand for the odd hour here and there?' Asa asked, seeming to sense Posy's disappointment.

Sandra shook her head. 'That's not very likely to happen. He'll have more than one variety, and we have to assume that means his grapes will be ready at different times and he'll have to bring them in stages, just like we do. There might be a day or two overlap, but you know well that there's more to harvesting than just picking the fruit. We could do with you here, Asa, even on days when we're not in the orchard.'

He nodded and threw Posy a slightly apologetic look, and she suddenly felt incredibly guilty for not being more supportive of Oleander Orchard's own harvest. They probably hadn't asked her to get involved with theirs because she'd told them about her job offer in London and that she'd be leaving soon; at least, before they began bringing in their apples. But now she was fighting to get help for someone else's harvest when they'd perhaps have been grateful for her help with theirs. What must they think of her now? She sounded ungrateful and unreasonable and not like someone who wanted to be accepted as part of their family.

She hadn't even broached the question of having Jackson to stay and that suddenly didn't seem like such a good idea. If the next few weeks were going to be busy for them, they might not appreciate a stranger on site.

So that was that, she mused as she reached for her wine. Lachlan was on his own.

Pavla was manning the reception at Sunnyfields when Posy walked in the following day.

'Hello!' she said cheerfully. 'Have you finished designing your plan yet?'

Posy gave a rueful smile. 'I think so, although it didn't get a very warm reception at the orchard. They don't seem to think it'll get very far and I have to say, now that I've had time to think about it, they might be right.'

'Perhaps it is for the best,' Pavla said. 'Lachlan would not have wanted it.'

Posy didn't know how to take that statement. She guessed, of course, that Pavla didn't mean to offend her, but she couldn't help but feel a little offence. Of course, there were a million good reasons why she ought to keep her nose out – not least that she ought to be thinking about her imminent move back to London and the new job that was waiting for her, not hanging around here for some grapes to ripen, especially if Giles was right and there was no way to tell exactly when that would happen.

So, if she thought all that, why was she here to talk to Karen now? Maybe it wasn't such a good idea after all.

'Karen said she was expecting you this morning,' Pavla added. 'She's in the garden.'

'Which bit?' Posy asked.

'Weeding by the guest terrace while it's quiet,' Pavla said. 'Go through; it's perfectly alright.'

'Thanks, Pavla.'

Posy made her way down the corridor that led away from the lobby and down to the day room, where large French doors opened out to the guest terrace where she and her mum had shared a drink with Karen at the start of the summer. Those weeks had flown by so fast, and yet it seemed like a lifetime ago. Astercombe had been strange and new to her then, not like now when she felt almost more at home here than she did in London. She didn't know how to feel about that or what she was meant to do about it, but she did know one thing – she was going to miss this place terribly when she finally went back. But she had a new job waiting, exciting possibilities, and she supposed she'd get used to that way of living again soon enough.

Karen straightened up as Posy approached. She was wearing a floppy-brimmed straw hat, her usual flowing skirt and sandals, and a large crystal on a chain around her neck.

'That's lovely,' Posy said, pointing at the pendant. 'I don't think I've seen it before.'

'Ah, yes… picked it up on my most recent outing to Glastonbury. It gives the wearer wisdom, apparently. Thought I could do with a bit of that.'

'Could I borrow it then?' Posy asked. 'I could do with some wisdom right now too… although I think it might take more than a crystal to sort that out.'

Karen peeled off her gardening gloves. 'Really? Pavla told me about your chat on the train…' She stroked a thoughtful hand along the length of her gardening gloves as she studied Posy in silence. She looked torn, as if deciding whether to entrust a huge secret to her.

In the end, she simply asked if Posy wanted a glass of lemonade.

'You're busy,' Posy said. 'I don't want you waiting on me when you have so much to do.'

'Alright,' Karen said slowly, 'if you don't want to keep me then perhaps you want to tell me what you're here for. Not that I mind you popping in at all, but I get the feeling there's something you want to ask?'

'Sort of,' Posy said. 'I know you can't really say anything, but I suppose I just want to understand.'

Karen chuckled. 'Well, that makes two of us because I'm afraid I don't have a clue what you mean!'

'Well, for a start, why is he so angry all the time?'

'Who – Lachlan?'

Posy nodded.

'He's not angry all the time, he's just…' Karen paused.

'He's just what?'

'I'm sorry, Posy, but I can't have this conversation with you no matter how much I'd like to. He's entrusted me with this and I don't think he has anyone else in the village to confide in. If I broke that trust it would leave him with no one to turn to, and God knows the poor man needs someone.'

'See – that's what I mean! I know there's something going on with him and you've just confirmed it. If I knew what it was—'

'You'd do what?'

'I could help him. Like you help him.'

Karen smiled sadly. 'You couldn't. I don't mean to insult you but that's just the way things are. He's asked me to keep this to myself, and unless things change I intend to.'

'I wouldn't tell anyone – he wouldn't have to know I know; but at least I'd understand him.'

Karen regarded Posy carefully. 'Why do you need to understand him?'

'Because I…'

Posy stalled. Why? That was a very good question and she didn't have the answer to it herself. Why did it matter so much?

'All I can tell you is that he's rebuilding his life and he needs time and space to do that,' Karen said. 'Stay out of his way, Posy; it's the best thing you can do for him. He has a lot going on; please don't give him another thing to worry about.'

Posy could see that Karen was deadly serious, but as well as the question of why Posy cared so much about his welfare, she had to ask why Karen cared so much that Posy stayed out of his way.

'You mean with the vineyard? Money troubles?'

'Posy…' Karen said, more of a warning tone now. 'He'll deal with that.'

'But he has nobody to help—'

'You don't know that; you're only assuming. He's not a total pig-headed idiot. When he needs it, he'll ask for it.'

'I'm sorry,' Posy said finally. 'You're right – everyone's right; it's none of my business really. I just thought I could help.'

'I know that. Maybe if you'd arrived a year from now with the same offer things might have been different, but I fear the timing is just so off that this is not what the universe means for the two of you.'

Posy held back a frown. *The two of them*? That one odd phrase was enough to start firing a whole raft of new questions. It was such a strange thing for Karen to say – what on earth could it mean? She wanted to ask, but something told her she'd only get more cryptic answers.

'I should let you get on,' Posy said.

'Are you sure you won't stay for that drink? If you don't want lemonade I can get tea…'

'I won't stay – I'm pretty busy to be honest; I've got to get Asa's place finished because I've had a job offer from a design agency in London.'

'Oh, that's marvellous news!' Karen said.

Posy smiled. 'It is. As soon as I'm done here I'll be heading back to take up my post.'

'I'm so happy for you, but I'll miss your little visits. We all will – people have become fond of you.'

But not Lachlan, apparently, Posy thought, and wondered why the notion pained her so much.

'Posy…' Karen said suddenly, breaking in on these thoughts. 'Remember when you first came here and you asked me about John Palmer…? I don't want to pry, but I couldn't help but wonder… You have family at Oleander House and so you must know… I'm presuming you know…'

'That he had an affair with Angelica?' Posy asked. 'It's OK – I think we're good enough friends now that you can say it. Yes. I don't want it spread around – partly because I'm still dealing with it myself – but I know I can trust you because you've never given away anything I've asked you about anyone else…' She took a deep breath. After all, it might be a relief to finally say it to someone outside her family, almost as if saying it was accepting it. 'I think he might be my father.'

Karen didn't look shocked as Posy might have expected her to. She simply nodded slowly. 'So Angelica would be…'

'My mum. That much I do know.'

'I didn't even know she'd had a baby.'

'You and practically everyone else,' Posy said ruefully. 'Angelica gave me up for adoption, and Philomena was apparently so furious or ashamed or goodness knows what about the whole thing that she didn't tell anyone about me.'

'So how did you find out?'

'She must have relented at the end, because she named me in her will.'

'Ah.' Karen smiled briefly. 'For what it's worth, I think you're dealing with all that remarkably well.'

'Do you think?' Posy said. 'Maybe I'm just ignoring it all.'

'If you're still interested, John was a nice man. He was quiet and he worked hard and he loved his family – he just made a mistake.'

'A pretty big one.'

'Yes, but he would have been devastated to know that it had caused so much pain to so many people. He never really got over the guilt of what happened with your grandfather – that's why he and Debra moved away.'

'Did he know about me?'

'I don't know. I'd say no, to be honest, because I don't think he was the sort of man who would have ignored your existence.'

'What about my mum? You must have known her too then.'

'Oh, I did. Everyone did. She was lively – I think that was part of her charm. Full of energy, always looking for the next bit of excitement. I liked her a lot but I can see how she might have been a handful for her parents.'

Posy gave a strained smile. This information wasn't the best she could hope for, but she was glad to hear that her parents hadn't been the terrible people she'd feared they had been.

'If you need to talk more…' Karen said.

'Not right now,' Posy said. 'I suppose I'll think of other things to ask you and… I don't know… somehow it seems easier to ask you than Giles or Asa.'

'I can imagine,' Karen replied. 'When those questions do occur to you, you know where I am. Call any time you need.'

'Thank you,' Posy said gratefully. 'That means a lot to me.'

Chapter Twenty-Three

The evidence of autumn was everywhere. The branches of the apple trees were heavy, often guarded by a cloud of sugar-hungry wasps waiting for the odd one to fall, and even though the orchard was busy most times, activity had stepped up a notch now with the arrival of hired machinery and returning hired hands in readiness for the first of the crop being stripped from the groaning trees. Giles seemed to spend every hour of every day walking the rows of trees and inspecting the fruit, searching the grass where the early ones had fallen, sometimes picking them up and cutting them open to look inside. Every day he announced not yet, but soon, and Posy wondered how on earth he could know with such conviction.

Asa seemed increasingly impatient too, and Posy guessed he wanted (or needed) his renovations done before the distractions of harvest began. He snapped at workmen and hovered over them like a DIY-obsessed vampire as they toiled, annoying the hell out of them and causing more than one complaint to Posy. She was used to smoothing things over with tradesmen, but it didn't make her life any easier and she had plenty of reasons to be as impatient as Asa about the work. He had a harvest approaching and she had a job in London waiting. Marella's boss, Kier (*her* new boss, she had to keep reminding herself), had been gracious enough to give her time to finish up here, but he wouldn't wait forever.

Posy hadn't managed to see Karen or Pavla since the last time she'd been up to Sunnyfields either, and she'd barely had time to chat to Marella. There had been a few awkward conversations with Jackson, but something had changed there and neither of them seemed desperate to talk to the other when they did manage to find time. Now that she thought about it, she'd started to go off him last time she'd been in London on their night out, but she'd ignored the signs back then.

Almost with a heavy heart, she phoned him today – not because she necessarily looked forward to it, but because she felt she ought to. He'd asked on a few occasions about the visit to Astercombe she'd promised, and she'd had to keep putting him off. Now, as autumn and a busy harvest barrelled towards them and Posy's time at Oleander House was coming to an end, she decided she ought to tell him that the visit probably wasn't going to happen at all.

'Why would you say it if I can't come?' he asked, sounding more like a petulant child than ever.

'I honestly thought it was going to happen.'

'So it wasn't just to keep putting me off?'

'Why would I want to do that?'

'I don't know… because you like it too much there and didn't want to come to London to see me?'

'We've been busy – I told you that. I didn't realise how busy things would get here, and I didn't think it was right to ask if you could visit because it would be another thing for everyone to worry about.'

'They wouldn't have to entertain me – I'd be coming to see you, not them.'

'But you'd still be on site and they'd have to consider that.'

'Sounds like an excuse to me.'

'It's not.' Posy let out a sigh. 'Look, I'll be home for good soon and we'll be able to spend loads of time together. So much time you'll be sick of me.'

'Maybe you're already sick of me.'

'Of course I'm not.'

'I just want to see you – is that too much to ask?'

What used to be endearing – him being so desperate for her to like him – now felt like hard work. Part of her, even as she tried to reassure him now, wondered why she was bothering. She wondered if he felt the same, and that they only continued to limp along in this way because they were both too polite (or maybe spineless) to be the one to call it off.

'It's not too much at all; I get it. Things have just got away from me lately. I'm sorry, but it's not for much longer. So… are we OK?'

'Yeah,' Jackson said. 'We're OK.'

But he didn't sound very convincing, and Posy had to wonder if she even cared.

It was shortly after she'd finished her call to Jackson that Sandra found Posy in the orchard crying. She didn't even know why she was crying, only that the whole affair made her feel so wretched and helpless that it had been the only reaction she'd been able to muster.

'Something you want to talk about?' Sandra asked.

Posy looked up from her seat on the roots of a tree heavy with fruit.

'And you might want to move from your spot,' Sandra added in a more practical tone. 'Unless you want your Isaac Newton moment – and believe me, an apple falling on your head is a lot more painful than the history books might suggest.'

Posy gave her a watery smile and got up.

'I'm sorry—'

'No need to be sorry,' Sandra said briskly. 'You're welcome to sit where you like, but I feel it's only fair to warn you.' She went to the nearest tree and began to inspect the lowest-hanging apples. 'Some of these will be ready in the next week or so. I expect you'll be back in London by then. It's a shame – we could have done with you.'

'Oh. Well, I could put them off—'

'No, of course you couldn't; we wouldn't hear of you jeopardising such a big opportunity. I only say it because you've been lovely to have around – I've certainly appreciated another woman to talk to – and your help would have been most welcome. Harvesting is hard work but it can be fun too; I think you would have enjoyed it.'

Posy gave a small smile. 'I think I would have done too. If it wasn't for this job…'

'Of course… There will be lots of years to get involved if you wanted to.'

'I thought – well, Mum thought she might come to pick me up when it's time to leave so she could say hello at the same time. Unless you're too busy, of course…'

'That sounds lovely. Of course we'd put an hour aside for Carmel. Let me know the exact plans and I'll arrange something with Giles and Asa so they're free to see her too.'

'I'll miss this place,' Posy said.

'This place will miss you.' Sandra pulled an apple from the tree and pocketed it. 'You've been a breath of fresh air, especially for Asa. Things haven't been easy for him and having you around has helped him forget his woes for a while. Not to mention his annexe looks fabulous too, of course. It's a shame we can't hire you to do something with the empty one.'

'Philomena's?'

'Yes, although it would be difficult to do as we haven't really decided what we're going to use it for yet. I'm inclined towards a holiday let but Giles isn't convinced. I suppose it has more sentimental value to him, having belonged to his mother and not mine.'

'Holiday let sounds like a good idea to me; I bet it would be a welcome bit of extra income.'

'Yes, it would; I don't know how Karen would feel about the competition, though.'

'I think she'd understand. Anyway, I would imagine it's a different kind of client so it might not be competition at all.'

'I suppose so,' Sandra said. 'I hope you won't be too much of a stranger. I know you'll be busy but you mustn't forget about us.'

'I could never do that! I love it here; it feels like my second home now. If anything, I worry that I've been too much of an imposition to you.'

'You're welcome any time you like – our house is always open for you and Carmel.'

'Thank you,' Posy said, tears springing to her eyes again.

'Goodness!' Sandra exclaimed with a chuckle. 'I had no idea my offer would be so upsetting!'

Posy gave her a wet smile and dried her eyes on a sleeve. 'It's just… the thought of leaving… It's silly, I know, but it feels so like home these days…'

'I'm glad you've enjoyed your time here so much.'

'I have.'

'Why don't we have a barbeque when Carmel arrives – a sort of going-away party?'

'But I thought… the harvest…?'

Sandra wafted her hand. 'We'll fit it in somehow.'

'That does sound lovely.'

'Good, then I'll organise something. Perhaps see if your father can get time off to come. And if you want to invite that boyfriend in London…'

'Jackson? It's a bit far for him really,' Posy said. Even if it wasn't, she didn't think she'd be inviting him now anyway.

A few days later the annexe was all but finished. At least, the need for tradesmen was over, apart from a few final flourishes that Asa could probably do himself.

'I don't know what we do with our coffee…' Asa called from the kitchen as Posy sat in the living room staring at her phone. She'd barely woken up yet, despite having been up for an hour already, and was supposed to be reading her emails, though not much information from the ones she'd read so far had sunk in.

'You'll use a lot less when I'm gone, I expect,' she called back.

'It explains why you're so perky all the time,' Asa replied, bringing two mugs through. 'There was just about enough for these but we'll have to get some later.'

Posy took a mug from him and put her phone to one side. 'I'll go. It's a nice day and I could do with a walk.'

'Take the van if it's free.'

'Unless we have loads of other things to pick up I'd rather get the exercise.'

Asa sipped his coffee. 'Whatever you want. Taking a last look around, eh?'

'Something like that. Although you make it sound like I'm leaving forever.'

'You'd better not.'

'You'd be lucky to get rid of me that easily.'

Asa grinned. 'It won't be the same without you – this little house will feel very big.'

'You'll learn to love it. Bathroom to yourself, no hair in the plughole, no more tripping over the cord to my straightening irons… You must have got a bit fed up of me over the last couple of months.'

'Not at all. Although, stretching across the sofa and not having to fight over the TV remote does sound nice. Do you want me to come to the shops with you?'

'Don't you have things to do here?'

'Don't remind me…'

Posy laughed lightly. 'I'd better not take you away from your chores – Giles would never forgive me.'

'Spoilsport.'

Posy got up and stretched. 'I'll take my coffee into the bedroom and get dressed. If I'm going I'd rather go sooner than later – lots of packing to start on and I don't want to be doing it when Mum gets here.'

Asa nodded. 'I suppose so. It's a shame Marella isn't coming to the barbeque.'

'Too much work. That'll be me in a few weeks, I expect.'

'Then you'll never call me.'

'Of course I will.'

'No, you'll be at work or out with Marella or Jackson. Lucky Marella and Jackson, that's what I say.'

'I don't know about that. Maybe Marella but…'

Asa raised a questioning eyebrow and Posy shrugged slightly.

'Nobody's said it yet but I think we're unofficially fizzled out.'

'Oh,' Asa said. 'If that's the case, don't you think one of you ought to say so and make it official?'

'It's that tricky business of who goes first, isn't it?'

'Oh, Posy, please blink first, for your sake if nobody else's. I can't tell you how miserable it is clinging on when there's no hope.'

Posy stared at him, but he said no more. He didn't need to. He spoke from bitter experience, of that she was sure, and perhaps it was a warning she'd do well to heed.

This path had become so familiar to Posy she hardly needed to think about it. Instead, as she walked into Astercombe she turned her attention to the trees, showing the first gold and orange leaves of the season, still heavy with foliage and fruit but not for much longer, and the insects, the sun making their wings glow as they circled the fields and hedges so that it was easy to imagine how people might have once thought fairies existed. Squirrels were busy, darting in and out of the undergrowth and scampering up trees, the hedgerows were dewy and heavy with a sweet, green scent, and the sun shone down on it all with the friendliest warmth.

Ahead, Lachlan's vineyard striped the hills. And as she looked up towards it, she caught sight of a lone figure, too far away to see properly, though she could only think of one man it might be. He was walking the path between two rows of vines, stopping every now and again to inspect one. Seeing him so distant, so alone, pulled at her in a way she couldn't explain. He'd gone out of his way to make it so, after all, and yet she felt he didn't really deserve to be that lonely. Nobody deserved that, and Karen's words at their last meeting came back to her now – surely his self-imposed exile wasn't really what he wanted? She'd seen as much, she'd swear it, the day they'd changed the tyre together in the rain, in the way he'd looked at her when he thought she hadn't noticed…

Instinct took over, and before she'd even realised it she'd left the road to take the next turning and the path that led up the hill.

Everyone had told her to leave it but she couldn't. The idea had come to her, sudden and irresistible, and she could no more ignore it than stop breathing. And she was going home soon so what did it matter if he rejected her, told her to leave – he could be as rude as he liked because she was hardly likely to see him again, but at least she would know she'd done all she could to reach him.

The lane was hidden by thick branches of low-hanging foliage so she was at the gate before her progress could be noted by anyone on the hill beyond. She rattled at the gate to find it locked and Lachlan was probably too far away to hear if she shouted for him to come and open it. But the obstacle in question was only a low farm gate (it looked new and Posy wondered if he'd had it installed to secure his land from the walkers he so often complained about), and she was damned if she'd come this far to let a gate stop her. In a moment she'd stepped onto the lowest bar, swung her legs over and dropped down on the other side. Then she marched off in pursuit of the man she could see striding through the rows of grapes.

'Lachlan!' she called as she moved into range of his hearing. He turned sharply.

'What are you doing up here?'

'Good morning to you too,' she returned dryly.

'How did you get up here?'

'It wasn't hard. I have these appendages called legs – marvellous things, they get me to all sorts of places.'

He didn't show a flicker of emotion to say whether he found her sarcasm funny or annoying. 'The gate is locked.'

'But also very low.'

'A locked gate isn't there to test your climbing skills. It means keep out – even you must know that. What is it about my land that compels you to break and enter whenever you walk past it?'

Posy rested her hands on her hips. 'I'm not sure you can break and enter a field. I mean, you can enter… doesn't the breaking bit have to involve a house?'

He looked as if he might fire back another reply but then shook his head and turned back to his vines, lifting up a bunch of grapes and peering closely at it. 'What do you want? I presume you've broken in to talk to me about something.'

'I…'

Now that Posy was here, about to say it, she realised how insensitive it might sound. Would her offer of help damage his pride? Would it look as if Pavla and Karen – the only two people he really confided in – had been gossiping about him? Was it fair to drop them in it?

'It's nearly harvest time, isn't it?' she said.

'And?'

'Well, some vineyards… I read about it… allow members of the public to help pick the grapes. I wondered if you were going to do that.'

'Why would I do that?'

'I just thought you might. You know, because some do.'

'That's their business.'

'But it does everyone a favour, surely? Visitors get a day out in the countryside, some wine to take home, and you get help. I bet people would love it. I mean, the idea is quite romantic, isn't it?'

'And I suppose you're going to tell me how a load of your city mates fancy a day out.' He turned back to his grapes. 'Not on my land.'

'I haven't got a load of *city mates*,' she said, trying to bite back a note of irritation. 'And if I did I expect there are things they'd rather be doing than get moaned at by you. I just thought… well, isn't this vineyard kind of important…? To the area, I mean. Didn't I once hear that there's been a vineyard on this site since the Dark Ages or something?'

'And?'

'Then historically it's important. To the area, I mean.'

'I had no idea you were so invested in the history of the area.'

'Of course I am! I have—'

For a moment she thought about telling him her own history, about her connection to Astercombe, but looking at him now, she wondered if he'd even care and how that would make her feel, so she didn't.

'Damn it, Lachlan! Don't you ever want anyone's help?'

He faced her again and narrowed his eyes. 'You mean *your* help? Have you been talking to Pavla…?'

'No… Alright, yes! And what's wrong with my help?'

'Do you know anything about grape-picking?'

'No, but you could teach me, couldn't you? It can't be that hard to pull some fruit off a tree.'

'I won't be in anyone's debt—'

'I'm in your debt – remember? You helped me fix the tyre on the van.'

'That was an hour of my time – it's hardly the same.'

Posy folded her arms tight across her chest. 'Who have you got to bring your grapes in?'

'It's none of your concern.'

'Indulge me – pretend that it is. Who? How many people?'

'Why don't you ask Pavla, as you're so pally with her?'

'Tell me you've got enough and I'll leave you alone.'

He spun around, hurling a pair of cutters to the ground. 'What's wrong with you? Why do you have to keep pushing? Why do you care so much what happens here? You're like a wee terrier, yap, yap, yapping away, wearing me down till you get what you want! You're worse than—'

He stopped dead. His shoulders sagged and the fire dimmed in his eyes.

'Worse than what?' Posy asked, confused by the sudden shift in mood, ready for the fight but now left bewildered and desperately sorry for the man who looked as if the bottom had fallen out of his world. Worse than what?

Or maybe it was not *what*, but a *who*…

'You need to leave,' he said in a dull voice.

'But—'

'Please leave me alone. I can't help you.'

'I don't want you to help me; I want to help you!'

'I don't need it! Go back to London and get on with your life – don't keep bothering me!'

Posy stared at him. 'Has anyone told you you're a pain in the arse?'

'Aye, more than once,' he said, and if Posy hadn't seen overwhelming evidence of a man who was pathologically incapable of expressing any emotion apart from contempt, she'd have sworn he was about to burst into tears.

'I'm not trying to make your life difficult,' she said carefully.

He went back to his grapes.

'I just want to do a good thing for someone who looks like they might need it. I'm thinking of more than just you; I'm thinking of the area too… I care about this place and the vineyard is a part of it… Lachlan! Are you going to say anything?'

He didn't look up.

'For God's sake! Fine, be that way…'

She turned and began to make her way back to the gate. A second later the sound of his voice made her look round.

'Posy…'

Lachlan retrieved his cutters and straightened up to hold her in a frank gaze. 'You really want to help?'

'I wouldn't have come here if I didn't.'

He nodded slowly. 'You're right – I could do with an extra pair of hands. For the sake of the village, mind, for all that history you seem so fond of…'

'When? Don't you have to wait until the grapes are just right?'

'Someone's been doing their homework. I'd say they're about there. I'll be making a start tomorrow.'

'Tomorrow? I can come then.'

Sadness was still etched into every shadow of his face, but his features were more composed now. 'Eight a.m.,' he said. 'Bring a water bottle – it's going to be hot. I'll leave the gate open for you.'

'Eight. Water bottle. Open gate. Got it.' She began to jog down the path for the gate, eager to make some distance before he changed his mind. 'See you tomorrow!'

Chapter Twenty-Four

Posy had been so excited to tell Asa about her morning that she almost ran back to Oleander House without the coffee. A few steps in the wrong direction had reminded her and she retraced them to continue to the village.

As she looked up the hill she could see Lachlan still walking the rows, stopping every so often to inspect a vine. She'd gone up there with the intention of getting this result but she'd never expected it to actually happen. Lachlan had only agreed to her going up there, of course, and the two of them wasn't really enough, but she'd work on that tomorrow. Her mum would be coming soon and maybe she could help if he'd allow it – Posy had no doubt that Carmel wouldn't object to lending a hand. And once Lachlan saw how much they could get done with extra help he'd have to agree to more. Harvesting at the orchard wasn't happening yet so maybe Asa could come too – even if it was only for an hour or so. Who else? Marella had said she had to work, but maybe there was a way she could get out of it? Oh, and Posy would have to call Karen to let her know. And she supposed Pavla could maybe pop in to lend a hand…

Posy's mind was a whirl of chaotic thoughts – no sooner had one taken hold than it blew away again to leave room for something new. She was helping someone in need, but she couldn't deny that the idea of grape-picking sounded heavenly; idyllic and romantic, like the sort of thing you saw on travel programmes or in soft-focus films. Perhaps she'd learn all about Lachlan's grapes, how the wine was made, what happened when it was finally bottled…

If she closed her eyes she could still see his face, sad and desperate. She pushed the image out of her mind. He'd relented, he'd let her in, and she had a feeling she'd made more progress in that regard than anyone else in Astercombe (aside from Karen, perhaps) and the idea lifted her spirits. She was going to do more, so much more than just save his vineyard. This was her new mission. She was going to save *him*.

'No, no… I'm very impressed.'

Asa stopped typing and looked up from his laptop. Posy caught a glimpse of the open webpage. It looked as if he was tweaking the orchard website now that the builders were no longer hammering and whistling all day and he was able to work in his own house once more. Posy had just placed a mug of freshly purchased coffee next to him and had begun to tell him about her surprising morning coup.

'I just don't know why you'd want to go to so much trouble,' he added.

'It's no trouble really.'

He raised his eyebrows and then turned back to his laptop.

'It's not,' Posy insisted. 'There's not much to do here now and your apples aren't ready yet. I might as well make myself useful up there.'

'I thought you had to pack.'

'I can do that quickly enough.'

'That's not what you said this morning. This morning it was like Hannibal equipping his elephants for a trek up the Alps.'

'Maybe I made it sound like more work than it is. I just thought I might as well offer help at Lachlan's place because I'm at a bit of a loose end right now.'

'And the only way you could think to tie it up is to break your back on Mr Grumpy's vineyard?'

'It'll be fine… fun, in fact. It'll be an experience.'

'It'll be that alright.'

'I'm not that much of a delicate flower! You weren't complaining when I was taking a sledgehammer to your walls!'

'I don't think you're that at all but… Well, have you ever harvested a crop of any kind?'

'No, but—'

'I'm just saying it's harder than you might imagine – certainly harder than collecting a few peas from your mum's garden.'

'I know that!'

'Good. That's alright then.'

Asa was silent again, eyes locked onto the screen of the laptop. Posy felt like she'd been dismissed, but she also felt like he was trying to tell her she was foolish and misguided.

'I still can't believe he agreed to it,' she said, choosing to ignore his obvious jibes about her expectations and suitability to the task she'd set herself.

'Neither can I,' he said vaguely. 'It'll be a shock to everyone once word gets round. Whatever you've got you ought to bottle it – might make your fortune.'

She took a seat on the sofa. Her uncle was obviously busy but she wasn't ready to leave him to it – she needed to talk. He looked up.

'You want to know what I think?' he asked.

'What?' she said, suddenly deciding that maybe she didn't want to talk after all. His tone suggested she was about to be lectured.

'I think you ought to be careful.'

And there it was.

'He looks like a romantic hero,' Asa continued, 'but I doubt the reality lives up to the promise.'

'You've changed your tune.'

'No I haven't. I've always said he was ridiculously handsome, but I never said he was a nice man.'

'Neither did I.'

'You're not expecting some about-face, then? That you'll suddenly discover he's got a heart of gold when you spend a little time with him?'

'Of course not.'

'You're absolutely sure you're not a teensy bit interested?'

'Interested?'

'Don't play coy – you know exactly what I'm talking about.'

'I have a boyfriend.'

'I thought you were going to give Jackson the elbow.'

'No, you said I ought to but I didn't say I would. I haven't decided yet if I ought to give him another chance.'

'And they say romance isn't dead…'

'Oi!'

'Well, I don't know why you'd want to continue seeing a man you're only mildly interested in. I think that the lady doth protest too much…'

'I'm more than mildly interested.'

'No you're not.'

Posy frowned. Asa had called her out, but she was feeling suddenly stubborn about being told what to do. 'Well, I don't know how you're any great expert on it.'

Asa's tone was sharp now. 'What's that supposed to mean?'

'Nothing…'

He went back to his laptop. Posy sighed. She'd succeeded in getting an enemy onside today but she didn't want to negate that achievement by alienating a friend, and she could tell that she'd annoyed Asa.

'I'm sorry,' she said.

'It's fine.'

'No, it's not. But… why didn't you ever tell me about Drew?'

He looked up again, but this time Posy could tell she'd caught him off-guard.

'How come you felt able to tell Marella about Drew but not me?' she asked. 'I thought we got on well.'

'We do. I suppose that's why. Posy – we're friends but I'm still your uncle.'

'What does that matter? I tell you things.'

'I'm sure there are things you wouldn't want to share with me and things I'd be glad not to hear.'

Posy couldn't help a small smile. 'I suppose so. But now you know what I know… I mean, Marella told me some of it. I wouldn't judge, but if I had the full story I'd know how to avoid putting my foot in it.'

'What did Marella tell you?'

'That you were engaged, that Drew had moved in here and the wedding date was set, but then he cheated on you.'

'Hmm, in a nutshell that's pretty much it.'

'But you still miss him?'

'Marella told you that?'

'No, your face did. I'm right, aren't I?'

'Did anyone ever tell you you're an insufferable know-it-all?'

'More times than I can count.'

'I suppose,' he said, 'it would be all the more bearable if he'd leave me alone to get over him.'

Posy had guessed as much but she asked the question anyway. 'You're still in contact?'

'Not for want of trying on my part. The stupid boy refuses to stop calling.'

'Let me guess... the cheater got cheated on? Now he's sorry and he realises what he's put you through and that his grass was already green enough without wandering off to look for a new pasture? It wasn't like him and if you take him back he'll never take you for granted again?'

'God, you're good.'

'I know. So what are you going to do? Surely you're not going to let him back into your life?'

'That's what all this was about...' He waved a hand at the room. 'The refurbishment. I thought if I was going to move on I had to get rid of all reminders of him; start afresh.' He gave her a fond smile. 'And then I got you into the bargain, so it wasn't all bad. Now that you know about it, I feel safe in saying that having you here has made me so much stronger in moments when I felt weak.'

'Really?'

'Really. You filled the space, made my house feel less empty, stopped me getting lonely and caving in. You've been amazing.'

'I didn't do anything special.'

'You didn't have to; you were just here, great company and lovely to have around. It was enough.'

Posy was silent for a moment. While she was pleased he'd felt that way about having her around she now felt less than happy about the fact she'd be leaving soon. What would happen then? Would he be able to cope when he was alone again? He had Giles and Sandra, of course, but he'd had them before and it didn't seem to have helped.

'So Drew wants to come back?'

'Don't worry,' he said with a rueful smile. 'I won't cave in the moment you've gone.'

'That's not what I thought,' she lied. 'But it can't be easy. Isn't there a way to block him from contacting you?'

'I could change my number I suppose.'

'Then why haven't you?'

'I couldn't see the point. If he really wants to contact me he'll find a way.'

'But you'd be stronger if you didn't have to see his messages.'

'Maybe.'

'You need a new man!' Posy said suddenly.

Asa burst out laughing. 'Steady on! I'll find my own man when I'm good and ready so don't even think about it!'

'You don't want to be alone forever.'

'I'm not alone. As long as I have my family, I never will be.'

His smile was bright and brave – if only Posy could believe that it was genuine.

Chapter Twenty-Five

Posy woke at six the next morning. Common sense told her to skip the make-up and hair-curling and to wear clothes that she didn't care about ruining, but she ignored common sense. She did the hair and the make-up and, grateful that the forecast was for unseasonably warm weather, donned a pair of cut-off denim shorts and an embroidered smock top in a light cotton. In a teeny concession to common sense she did pull on a pair of stout boots, though only because she really couldn't get away with the tiny gold sandals she would have worn, and because she had a feeling it would have confirmed everything Lachlan probably thought about her – that she was a pathetic city girl playing at farming.

She'd made toast but couldn't eat it, so she grabbed an apple to take with her from the bowl that was always full of them and filled her water bottle as Lachlan had told her to. Then she headed out.

She'd never walked the lane this early before. There was a different smell than there would be later in the day; fresher, greener. There was a sharp chill in the air while the sun was still a low hazy orb, struggling to crest the hills, and a blanket of mist sat in the hollows of the fields. The hedgerows were festooned with dewy cobwebs and pearly berries and birdsong filled the air. It was like the countryside she knew, only magical, as if some wizard had cast an enchantment over it.

As she walked and marvelled, it felt like the start of something, like a promise she could snatch from the air and make real, though she couldn't say what or why she felt that way.

When she got to the vineyard gate it was unlocked, as Lachlan had said it would be, but he was nowhere to be seen. She checked her watch, and as it was only 7.45 a.m. she figured he was on his way and took a seat in a clearing to wait. She'd worked up a little heat walking up, but now as she sat and waited she cooled down and had to put on the cardigan she'd had tied around her waist. The weather would be good later, but it was September and the dawns were chilly.

The vines stretched out ahead of her, lit by the hazy sunlight, row upon row with grapes of all hues. Looking at them now, picking them all by hand seemed an impossible task, even more so with just the two of them and limited time. Posy didn't know much about it, but even she could guess that if they took too long some of the crop would spoil and be lost. She wondered, in that case, why Lachlan hadn't decided to start earlier – if it had been her place she'd have been up with the sunrise.

For ten minutes she sat and daydreamed, losing herself in the sounds of birds, the breeze whispering through the vines, even a plane blazing a trail across the dawn sky. The sunlight was warming where it touched now, but the air was still crisp and sharp. Then her eyes picked out a figure dragging a sort of truck slowly along the path and focused to see it was Lachlan. She got up and made her way over, noticing as she did that the truck was already heaving with fruit.

'You started already?' she asked, looking at it.

'Five thirty,' he said.

'But you told me eight.'

'I wasn't going to ask you to come at five thirty – it's far too early.'

Posy planted her hands on her hips. 'For a city girl like me, you mean?'

'No,' he said, 'because you're good enough to do me a favour and I'm not about to push it.'

'Oh,' Posy said, the wind gone from her sails. 'You wouldn't have been; I'd have come as early as you needed. There's a lot to do for just the two of us.'

'Pavla has said she's coming this afternoon,' he said, handing her a pair of cutters. She looked at them and then at him.

'So I just cut the grapes off?'

'There's a way to cut and trim,' he said. 'I'll show you. You might be slow at first but it won't take you long to speed up.'

'Wouldn't it be faster with a machine?' she asked as she followed him to a vine and he began to demonstrate. 'There must be machines that can do this – the orchard has machines.'

'I like to do it the traditional way. Gentler... better quality wine.'

'Will you also be squashing these grapes later with your feet?'

'Why – would you want to join in if I was?'

He didn't smile but Posy laughed anyway. The image of them both tramping around in a huge vat of grapes invaded her thoughts and she couldn't help it.

'Probably,' she said.

'Maybe I'll fill a bucket later and you can get in as a reward for helping me.'

'I'd only get in if you did.'

Posy blushed. The sentence had slipped out before she'd had time to stop it. She hadn't meant to, but nobody could have heard it and failed to conclude anything other than that she was flirting with him.

He gave her a curious look and then guided her hand to a spot on the stalk connecting the grapes to the vine.

'About here,' he said. 'See that bulge on the stalk? Cut there; it's a lot less tough… you leave this much and you don't damage the fruit or the plant. If you see anything rotten like this' – he indicated a shrivelled bit of mush – 'see if you can trim it away. Some of it will be a bit of drying out rather than rot and you can probably keep that. You'll know it's rot because it will smell a bit like vinegar and there'll probably be flies. Basically, if you wouldn't eat it, don't keep it. You won't get all of it first go, but the more waste we can keep out of the crop the better and easier it will be when we come to process it later.'

'How do you know if they're ready to cut or not? Is this whole lot ready?'

'This section is…' He swept a hand over the hillside, but Posy was none the wiser as to which area he meant. 'I've checked.'

'How did you do that?'

'You don't need to worry about that.'

'I know, I'm just curious.'

'Yes,' he said, 'I've noticed.'

'So how? Is there a gadget or something? A colour chart? A smell? What?'

'Some people use fancy gadgets but I taste them – nothing wrong with a bit of human judgement.'

'And what are they supposed to taste like?'

'If the brix—'

Posy frowned.

'The sugar,' he continued in answer to her silent question. 'If it's right you can taste it. Here… try one for yourself so you see what I mean.'

Posy pulled off a grape. 'Shouldn't I wash it?'

'If you can find a tap up here be my guest.'

There was something like a subtle mocking humour in his eyes now. He was making fun of her, and while she shouldn't like it, somehow she did. But she scowled anyway, just for show, and put the grape into her mouth with a defiant jut of her chin.

But where she'd expected the plump sweetness of her usual supermarket fruit, this one was so tart her mouth instantly puckered into a grimace.

'God, that's foul!'

'At least you won't be eating them as we go,' Lachlan said. 'That's one less thing to worry about.'

'*That* makes a nice wine?'

'It makes a *good* wine. If you want sweet go and get yourself a carton of grape juice. If you want a quality vintage – there's your perfect fruit.'

'I can't believe anyone ever tasted that and thought, I know, I'll make a lovely drink out of that.'

'Like many things we eat and drink, it's not immediately apparent why anyone thought it was a good idea.'

'That's true. Jellied eels for a start – who looked at eels and thought, *Yum, they look tasty; even better if I cover them in slime.*'

'Haggis,' he agreed solemnly.

'You're Scottish! Are you telling me you don't like haggis?'

'I can imagine how that might come as a shock to an English girl. I don't like haggis and I've never eaten a deep-fried Mars Bar.'

'You're a traitor to your nation.'

'I'm sure they'll get over it.'

Posy smiled up at him.

'So let's have a look at you cutting one of your own,' he said, scattering her thoughts.

'Right.'

Posy scooped what looked like a natural bunch in one hand and located the place to cut like he'd just shown her. Bunches on the vine didn't look as tidy and obvious as the ones she'd seen in supermarkets either, but she supposed they were made to look appealing for the shelves. Here, there were stragglers and spots on the grapes, and shrivelled bits and curling tendrils snaking out all over the place.

'Snip it in that direction,' Lachlan said, and she followed his hand gesture to separate the bunch from the plant. 'Good.'

'That's it?'

'That's it. Ready to crack on?'

Posy glanced along the row, and then to the next and the next, and then the row after that. 'I think we better had if we're going to get this all done today.'

'We won't be done today, not by a long shot,' he said, starting to cut at a vine next to the one he'd set her to work on. 'I'll be lucky to finish this week, though I need to. But you don't need to worry about that.'

'I could come again tomorrow.'

He shook his head slightly but didn't look up from his task. 'We'll see.'

They worked in relative silence for the next couple of hours. Posy didn't mind it, which was strange because ordinarily she liked chat, no matter how mundane it was. But the sun climbed higher and warmed her back, and as she became absorbed in the comforting repetition of snipping and trimming she was at peace with the world.

Lachlan never strayed far from where she was, and if her pace ever slowed his seemed to slow too. Posy sensed perhaps he was keeping a close eye on her work, making sure she was OK, and she didn't mind that either, though she worried a little she was holding him up rather than helping him.

'You haven't had a break yet,' he said after one of these long, easy silences.

Posy turned to him and dragged the back of her hand across her brow as she took a sip of water.

'Neither have you.'

'I don't need one.'

'Neither do I.'

She held his gaze, and then he shrugged.

'I don't want you getting heat exhaustion, that's all.'

'It's England… in September. That's hardly going to happen.'

He could have pointed out her sweaty forehead and obviously damp clothes, but perhaps he was far too much of a gentleman because he didn't. Or perhaps he simply couldn't be bothered to argue.

'Yes,' he replied patiently. 'But this is very hard manual work.'

It was true that it was more strenuous than Posy had imagined, even though everyone had told her to expect that, but there was no way she was going to admit it now. 'I have my water,' she said. 'I'll be fine.'

'And if you get too hot, I'm sure you know where to find a pool you can cool off in…'

Posy stared at him now. He wasn't laughing or even smiling, but undoubtedly he'd made a joke. He simply continued to pull and cut at the vines in a motion so practised and fluid he was like a machine. She smiled uncertainly. How was she meant to react? Why did he make himself so hard to read? Clearly there was a human being in there somewhere, so why couldn't he let anyone see that?

She was about to say something along those lines when she felt a tickling sensation at the nape of her neck. Absently, she reached to scratch it.

Instantly there was a sharp, needlepoint prick followed by a burning sensation. 'Ow!' she cried, and as she reached for the spot there was another strike further down on her shoulder.

She could only assume she'd been stung, and as she felt another fire-hot pinprick it seemed as if whatever was stinging her was trapped in her clothing. With a panicked squeal she tipped herself over and shook at her top, only to be stung again. This time she ripped her top off and the wasp flew free. She stood in her bra now, her skin burning and tears filling her eyes. It bloody hurt.

Lachlan stared at her. Maybe he was shocked to see her half-naked in front of him and not giving a damn but she didn't care.

'You've been stung?'

Stating the obvious, she thought savagely, but she nodded and fetched her top from the ground now to hold over her chest. She didn't put it on – her shoulder and neck were far too sore.

'Are you allergic?' he asked urgently.

'I don't know.'

'What do you mean you don't know?'

'I don't know! I've never been stung before!'

'You've never been… Where the hell have you been living?'

'I'm just careful!' Posy yelled. She was in considerable pain now and he wasn't exactly helping.

He threw down his tools and strode over to have a look. 'They're nasty.'

'You don't say – they feel nasty!'

Without another word he swept her into his arms and began to march up the hill with her.

'What the hell are you doing?' she cried.

'Quad bike,' he panted.

'What?'

'EpiPen. Quad bike. Just in case.'

'In case of what?'

'Reaction.'

'I don't need it. If I was going to react I would have done by now.'

'You just said you don't know. Better to be safe. There's one in the first aid kit anyway…'

What the hell was going on here? It was like she'd just stepped onto the set of an action film and he was carrying her away from an exploding bomb, not working on a peaceful English hillside. But he was clearly determined about this and she didn't see that arguing would change his mind.

'I can walk to the bike if I must,' she said, despite having no idea how far away he'd parked it. She couldn't see a quad bike anywhere but perhaps it was obscured by the vines.

'Quicker this way,' he grunted, an unflattering sound which showed how he was labouring under her weight.

'You'll do your back in – I'm too heavy to carry.'

He shook his head and carried on.

'I'm hardly going to die from a wasp sting,' she continued, though right now her skin was burning so much she wondered if she might. But saying this only set Lachlan's jaw tighter and his strides longer, and a moment later she saw that there was a quad bike parked in a clearing at the end of a row. He set her down on the grass and opened a metal box stored at the back.

'Sit down,' he ordered.

She did so, knowing it was pointless to do anything else. 'Why have you even got an EpiPen? Are you allergic?'

'No, but I used to have one on hand in case any of the workers were and it's still in the box. Stop your yammering and let me take a proper look.'

'You're not going to use the pen on me, are you?'

'Not unless your throat starts to close up. I have some ointment, though – should help to ease the pain.'

'So we came all this way for ointment?'

'We came all this way to be close to supplies if things took a turn for the worse. How do you feel?'

'Stupid.'

He grunted something that she didn't catch and took a small tube out of the box.

'I can do it,' Posy said, holding her hand out for the ointment.

'Let me take a look first,' he said, holding it back.

Without waiting for permission he walked behind her. She could feel his breath on her neck as he moved closer. Her head swam with the pain and a sudden rush of excitement as he moved closer still so that she could feel the heat of his body.

'What are you looking for?' she asked, fighting to keep her voice level.

'Making sure there's no sting in there.'

'I thought wasps didn't leave a sting behind.'

'They don't, but I want to be certain.'

Then he touched her lightly, and even though it was directly onto a sting as he applied the ointment, a sudden wave crashed through her. She closed her eyes, heart thumping as he moved from one wound to the next. No man's touch had ever done this to her and she couldn't think about her stings at all, only that she wanted more. She wanted him to touch her everywhere.

When he was done he sat next to her, peering intently into her face as he handed her a water bottle. 'How do you feel? Not struggling to breathe? Throat OK?'

She nodded weakly. She was struggling to breathe alright but it was nothing to do with anaphylactic shock. 'I'm fine… that lotion's done the trick. Thank you.'

Everything happened quickly after that. They both moved together and met in the middle and somehow they were kissing. Nobody had needed permission and neither had asked. Later, Posy wouldn't be able to say what had made her do it, only that she had and that he'd reciprocated.

Kissing Lachlan was like breathing, effortless and necessary, and she almost felt the moment they stopped she might die. His hands moved to caress her lower back, rough from outdoor work but sexier for it. She tugged at his shirt to release it from his trousers and lifted it to feel his chest pressing against hers. He fell backward and took her with him so that she was now astride him, frantically working to unfasten his buttons. This moment, this primal, feral desire, was the most exciting, the most wildly sexy thing she'd ever experienced. Their kisses settled into a rhythm, still deep and feverish but less chaotic.

Then her hands began to work at his belt, flicking it undone, and just as she was about to free the button of his jeans he grabbed her hand.

'Please…' he whispered, almost a cry for mercy. 'Don't…'

Posy stopped and pulled away. There was lust in his eyes – she could see he wanted this as much as she did. Yet something else told her there was a problem.

'You want to stop?'

'We *have* to stop.'

'I don't understand…'

'It's madness – we hardly know each other.'

'We can fix that,' she said, moving to kiss him again, but this time, even though she wanted it, something felt off. She hesitated.

'It's not that you're not beautiful,' he said, 'and God knows I want to but…'

'Oh. God…' She sat back, suddenly plagued by doubts. 'I'm not usually forward like this; I don't know what happened—'

She never got to finish. She never got to explain herself, to tell him that he had this crazy, unexpected effect on her, because a shout echoed up the hillside and stole her chance.

'Lachlan! Where are you?'

'Pavla!' he muttered, scrambling from beneath Posy and grabbing his shirt.

Posy cast around for the top she'd thrown to one side, hastily slipping it over her head despite the wasp stings, recognising in a new and cold reality how bad this situation would look if Pavla saw it. But even then, her hair was a mess, her top covered in grass stains and she was quite sure she had lust written all over her face. She did her best to smooth her hair and her expression and stood up.

Lachlan began to march down the hill to meet Pavla, but then he turned briefly.

'You're sure you're alright?' he asked.

'Lachlan... I don't... I don't want you to get the wrong idea. I don't do that sort of thing normally, it's just...'

'Your stings,' he said, choosing not to address her bumbled explanations for what had just happened. 'You don't feel ill?'

She shook her head miserably. She didn't do what she'd just done – not with any man ever – but now she was beginning to wish she hadn't done it with this man. *Seriously*, she chided herself. With Lachlan? What the hell had possessed her? Rude, judgemental, conceited Lachlan.

But she had, whatever the reason, and she couldn't deny she'd loved it. It wasn't just lust; it had meant something to her. Had it meant anything to him? Would she ever know or would he simply close up again now that the moment had passed?

Pavla certainly made it difficult to get a moment alone with Lachlan. Not for kissing, although Posy still felt his lips on hers every time she looked at him, but to explain herself. She was increasingly worried that her impulsive display of desire might not actually have been welcome. He had, after all, put the brakes on things, and the more she thought about that the more thankful she was that he had. She was only glad that he wasn't the sort of man to tell anyone else about it, because that was one bit of gossip she wouldn't welcome getting out.

As Posy tried to work out how she actually felt about all this and how she might broach the subject with Lachlan if she got the chance, Pavla talked incessantly as she worked alongside them. Usually Posy would be happy to listen, but today it was irritating her. Then Lachlan announced he was going to start on another row and that Pavla and Posy could manage to finish that one by themselves, and his departure only added a new worry to the mix. Had he gone because he didn't want to be near Posy or because he'd had enough of Pavla's talking too? To think it might be the former made Posy want to cry, and if it was the latter then, secretly, she didn't blame him. Much as she liked Pavla, she dearly wished she'd shut up.

They stopped for a quick break but Lachlan didn't sit with them. Instead, he spent the time wandering the vines of a different grape variety further up the hill, checking them to see how ripe they might be, which left Pavla and Posy together eating the plain cheese sandwiches he'd supplied for them.

'He never stops, does he?' Posy asked. She bit into a sandwich, her eyes trained on his figure as he walked.

'His life is all work,' Pavla said carelessly.

'Did you live at the vineyard when you worked for him?'

Pavla shook her head.

'So you didn't see much of him outside work hours?'

'No.'

'You wouldn't have known much about his private life then?'

'I don't think he has one of those. All he talks about is grapes.'

'But he comes to see Karen – surely he talks about other things with her?'

Pavla shrugged and reached for another sandwich.

'You and Lachlan…' Posy began slowly. It was a risk to ask this question, but now more than ever she needed the answer. 'You never… there's no… you know…?'

At this, Pavla burst out laughing. 'Is that what you think?'

Posy blushed. Now that she thought about it, she probably sounded stupid to ask such a question. 'Sorry… I just wondered.'

'Is that because you like him?'

'No…' Posy said with a little too much heat. 'Lachlan seems to trust Karen,' she said in a bid to change the subject. 'More than anyone else in Astercombe. How come?'

'Perhaps,' Pavla said, 'he feels comfortable with her because she's like him.'

'How so?'

'He is not from the village and neither is Karen.'

'You're not from the village either but he doesn't come to see you all the time.'

'But I worked for him. I think that makes him look at me differently.'

'I suppose so,' Posy said thoughtfully, though she still wasn't convinced there wasn't more to it than that. Maybe it was just that Karen had this special something, a kindness that shone from her, a quality that couldn't fail to draw people in. Everyone who met her ended up loving her – maybe not even stone-cold Lachlan was immune?

Pavla looked squarely at Posy now. 'Did something happen this morning?'

'Apart from being attacked by the world's grumpiest wasp?' Posy asked, forcing a carefree laugh. 'No. Why?'

'He keeps looking at you. And you keep looking at him.'

'He's probably checking to make sure I don't die. He did threaten me with an EpiPen. And I'm watching to make sure he doesn't come after me with it and try to get me when I'm not looking.'

Pavla nodded but she didn't look convinced. Posy had told her some of what had happened that morning – she didn't see the point in keeping it from her – but she'd obviously kept the very delicate details to herself. She'd never tell anyone about those, she'd decided, not for as long as she lived.

'Will you come back tomorrow?' Pavla asked.

'I've said I can. Will you?'

'Karen needs me tomorrow. Perhaps the day after.'

Posy's gaze swept the hillside. 'He's going to need more people; there's still so much to do.'

'I've already told him that.'

'I'll mention it again later.'

'You will be wasting your breath.'

'I know. But he agreed to me being here today and I didn't expect that. Maybe he's starting to realise he can't do it alone and it's silly to try. Eventually he has to be practical.'

'You could be right.'

Pavla didn't look convinced of this either, and Posy had to concede that she probably knew better. It didn't mean she wasn't going to try, though. She'd already thought about asking her mum when she arrived. Pavla had just said she was busy so that was out, but Oleander's harvest hadn't yet begun so perhaps Asa might be able to spare at least an hour, which had to be better than nothing.

The big problem was that it was probably going to take longer than she had left in Astercombe. After all, she was meant to be leaving in a couple of days. She didn't like the thought of doing that knowing that Lachlan still needed help, but if her new job was waiting then she didn't really have a choice. And what about her and Lachlan? Something huge had happened between them, no matter how they might both deny it, but where did that leave them? Were they a thing? Were they even a possibility of a thing? Was there any kind of future to be had or was today it? It seemed crazy to think anything could come of it but the question wouldn't leave her.

One thing she knew with absolute certainty was that she needed to break things off with Jackson. It was one thing to feel it was over, quite another to make it official, and they couldn't continue in light of what had happened here today. Though she wasn't looking forward to it, it was the first phone call she needed to make when she got back to Oleander House.

Chapter Twenty-Six

The sun was low when Lachlan finally came back to them.

'I can't keep you any longer,' he said. 'It's getting late and it'll be dark soon.'

Posy looked up from a vine she'd been working on. It was true that her shoulders and neck ached and they were still sore from the stings, and that her hands now had blisters on blisters, but she still had some work left in her if he needed it.

'What about you?' she asked. 'I don't mind staying while there's still daylight.'

'Sundown isn't far off,' he said. 'It's really not worth it. I'll be going home too – dinner is waiting.'

Posy and Pavla both nodded, though Posy didn't believe for a minute that Lachlan had dinner waiting, or that he intended to stop working. She had a hunch Pavla suspected the same.

'What time shall I be here tomorrow?' Posy asked, straightening up and stretching her tired arms.

'About that…' he began, his gaze flicking uneasily from her to Pavla and then back again. 'You've done so much for me today and I'm grateful. I'll work something out from here.'

'I can come; it's no trouble.'

'I know, but I owe you so much already.'

'I don't want paying.'

'I meant another kind of debt. I know you don't want money, but as I can't offer anything much in return for your work I don't feel right to keep taking advantage of it.'

'Will you be here if I come at seven?'

He let out a sigh.

'Seven it is then,' she said.

He didn't contradict her, though he looked as if he wanted to. She wouldn't tell him of her plans to bring more people because he'd definitely kick up a stink about that – she'd simply ask them to come, and once they were here he couldn't very well complain without looking like a totally ungrateful arse. He might not care about the arse bit but maybe looking ungrateful would bother him enough to let it slide.

The phone call to Jackson had been every bit as horrible as she'd feared, but now it was over Posy felt lighter than she had in ages, and strangely hopeful too. Hopeful for what – that was a question she couldn't yet answer. All she knew was a strange optimism had swept over her and it had to do with Lachlan.

Tomorrow they could start again. No weird, primal sexual tension, no moments of crazy indiscretion, just getting to know each other in a way that was far more natural. Safer too, with other people there to filter their interactions, and maybe this kind of contact would lead to something more wholesome.

She and Asa ate a quiet supper together while Giles and Sandra were busy doing health and safety training with the seasonal workers for their own imminent harvest. Posy was bursting to tell him about her day, but it didn't seem wise to share it all. She'd told him some general stuff, of course, about how she'd found the work, and she'd even proudly showed off the wasp stings she was now claiming as battle scars, but she was desperate to share more, if only to get it off her chest. She didn't want to divulge particulars, but she wanted his help to pick apart how she felt about the kiss she and Lachlan had shared, help her work out what it might mean.

But, in the end, she didn't. When it came down to it, she didn't know who she *could* tell. The most likely candidate was Karen, who knew Lachlan well enough to perhaps shine some light on where it was likely to go (if anywhere at all), or Marella, who wouldn't have a clue about that but would at least be a tried and trusted confidante to offload on.

There was one other option: she could go and talk to Lachlan himself. She could ask him straight out why he'd stopped her before they'd gone too far, how it had left him feeling about her, whether he saw it as a foolish moment of weakness or the start of something more. But knowing what she knew of him, would she get an answer? He was always so closed, so unwilling to communicate, she didn't see that a visit to him would be any more fruitful than a chat to someone else. But surely he'd have to talk about this if she confronted him? Wasn't this too big to ignore? Was he thinking about it right now, as she was, trying to work it out, wondering if he ought to come and talk to her?

'I'm going for a walk,' she announced as Asa loaded the last of the plates into the dishwasher.

He turned to her with a look of faint surprise. 'Now?'

'I won't be long.'

'Where are you going?'

'To get some air.'

'Didn't you get enough of that at the vineyard today?'

'Yes, but it's a nice evening and I won't get many more opportunities for country walks after this weekend.'

Asa looked doubtful but he shrugged. 'Don't be out after dark, will you?'

'I won't get far then – it's pretty much dark now.'

'There are no lights on the lanes here – where on earth are you planning to go?'

'Towards Astercombe.'

'Nothing will be open now.'

'The pub will.'

Asa's eyes widened. 'You're going to the pub? You've never shown an interest in the pub the whole time you've been here.'

'Well, I'm leaving soon so maybe this is the time to try it out.'

'Hmm… want me to come with you?'

'No,' Posy said hastily. If Asa came along her plan was sunk. 'I probably won't end up going to the pub and then you've had a wasted journey.'

'Make up your mind!'

Posy couldn't help but smile. 'I'll take a torch with me if you're worried – it'll be fine and I won't be long.'

'I can't say I'm happy to let you go.'

'What can possibly happen to me out here? I'm perfectly safe.'

'If you're not back in an hour I'm coming out to get you.'

'OK, fine, but you're worrying for nothing.'

Posy didn't hear his reply, too busy rushing to get her coat before he had time to change his mind and try to go out with her after all.

*

Posy had never been to the house attached to Lachlan's vineyard, but she guessed she wouldn't have to now. At least, she was banking on that because she wasn't altogether sure how to find it; so she was gratified to see the pinpoint of light moving across the darkness of the slopes where his vines grew that she could only assume was him, continuing to work into the night. Of course, it did mean that she had to somehow find her way up there in the dark and that wasn't going to be easy. She had the torch she'd promised Asa she'd take, but it wasn't that bright and allowed for just a few inches of illumination at any one time. Not only was there a very real danger of a broken ankle, but who knew what manner of nocturnal creatures she might disturb, some of them even less friendly than the wasp she'd encountered earlier that day.

After a moment of procrastination that saw her torn between going up there or heading back to grab a nice, safe nightcap with Asa, she steeled herself and left the road to make her way up. As she'd feared, the path (hardly a path and more a line of slightly flatter vegetation) was far more difficult to negotiate in the dark, and it hadn't been all that easy in daylight. By the time she got to the gate her legs were covered in scratches, she'd managed to turn her ankles a couple of times on uneven ground and she'd almost lost her footing entirely and been in danger of rolling all the way back down the hill. The gate was locked, as she'd fully expected it to be, but she'd come this far and she wasn't going to let a locked gate stop her now.

She scaled it, dropped down at the other side and then paused, scanning the darkness. The sun had sunk behind the hills but the sky was still starless, washed in a turquoise blue. At first it seemed the light that had shown her Lachlan was there had now disappeared, but then she spotted it winking back into existence as he moved from behind a vine and she headed for it.

When she got close enough she could see that Lachlan was waiting for her.

'I saw the torch,' he said, and though she expected him to show some surprise to see her there he didn't.

'Oh, of course. So you're still working then?'

'I was.'

'I thought you were going to call it a day.'

'You wouldn't have left if I'd said otherwise. I've got to get this lot in somehow.'

'I said I'd help.'

'I know.'

They were silent for a moment as Posy tried to fathom his mood. Why did he have to be so infuriating and yet so bloody attractive? *Just say it*, Posy chided herself. *Just say it, you stupid cow!*

'Lachlan…' she began, 'about today…'

She waited, and getting no response carried on.

'What happened after I got stung—'

'I'm sorry,' he said.

'I'm not. I'm not sorry at all. I let it go too far, but the rest of it… I loved it.'

'Posy, I can't—'

'Why not?' she demanded. 'What's stopping you?'

'For a start you're going back to London.'

'I don't have to.'

'Of course you do. Secondly' – his tone darkened – 'you can do better.'

Talk about your clichés… 'Don't you think I ought to decide that?'

'I'm not good to be around.'

'You're a miserable pig, I'll give you that.'

The glow of his lantern cast his face into an odd pattern of shadows. She stepped into the circle of light and moved towards him. He gave a pained smile but didn't step back. She'd barely seen him smile at all since she'd met him, but somehow it hadn't seemed to matter. She'd assumed he would when he found something funny. Now, seeing the pain in this one, she wished he'd go back to being dour again.

He held his hand out. 'Best to be friends, eh?'

She looked down at his gesture. It looked like they were meeting to discuss a bank loan. 'I can't do that.'

'And I can't do anything more.'

'You like me – you must have done to kiss me today…' she said. She sounded needy; she was probably a bit whiny, but something about him made her powerless to stop.

'Of course I do! That's the problem!'

'I don't understand… how can it be a problem?'

'Please… I'm asking you for the last time – offer me friendship but don't give me anything else.'

A few days ago she'd have seen friendship as a triumph. Not now. She couldn't get their kiss out of her head. How could a kiss that had burned like that mean nothing to him? How could he pretend it had never happened? She couldn't. She'd never be able to look at him without thinking of it.

Her voice was thick with emotion when she spoke again, but she did her best to contain it. 'Do you still want my help tomorrow?' They'd already agreed it, but she didn't know what else to say.

'I'll understand if you don't want to come.'

'I said I would.'

'Still, it's a promise I wouldn't hold you to.'

She shook her head, still fighting to keep a grip on tears that even she didn't understand. She was only glad it was dark so he wouldn't notice her struggle. It wasn't the rejection that hurt, but frustration that he was so willing to discard something she felt could be amazing. It didn't make any sense. 'I said I'd come and I will.'

'Thank you. So I'll see you first thing? I'll leave the gate open.'

She nodded silently, now afraid that if she spoke her voice would betray her.

'Goodnight, Posy,' he said.

She turned and started the walk back down the hill, feeling more foolish than she ever had in her life.

Chapter Twenty-Seven

Asa was already up when Posy went through to the kitchen at six the next morning.

'Wow,' she said. 'What happened to your bed?'

He gave a slight smile. 'Couldn't sleep.'

'Anything you want to talk about or just too much coffee before you turned in?'

'Neither,' he said. 'Speaking of coffee…'

He held up the jar and Posy nodded. 'It's not Drew, is it?'

'Well, he is still messaging but you don't need to worry about that – I'm staying strong.'

'Good.'

'You're going up to the vineyard today?'

'Yes.'

'I never heard you come in last night.'

'You were snoring on the sofa so I went to bed. That's probably why you couldn't sleep in this morning.'

'Probably,' Asa agreed.

'So much for your hour and then you're sending out a search party,' Posy added dryly.

'I'm a terrible uncle.'

'Yes, you're rubbish. Good job you never had to babysit me when I was a kid. But you do make a great friend.'

'So do you,' he said, and then turned away to mess around at the sink, washing mugs that Posy was pretty sure were already clean, having been just fetched from the cupboard.

'Asa…' She put a tentative hand on his shoulder.

He sniffed hard but he didn't look round. 'I'm just… they looked a bit dusty.'

Posy left it. She didn't have to ask – she understood. In a couple of days she'd be on her way back to London and this wonderful summer would be over. She was going to miss Astercombe but, more than that, she was going to miss all the people in it. She'd be able to visit, of course, but it wasn't ever going to be like this again. Oleander House had felt like home and everyone here had become family – and not just by blood – so quickly it was like they'd always been in her life.

'I thought I might lend a hand today,' Asa said, turning to face her now and seemingly composed once more.

'At the vineyard?'

'You said how much there was to do and things haven't really got going here with our harvest yet. I've just sent a text and cleared it with Giles.'

Posy had hoped for this, even thought about asking, but after last night's conversation with Lachlan she was no longer certain that she wanted to go to the vineyard today, let alone take anyone else, though she'd still woken early with the intention of going.

'I thought about asking Mum to come and help when she gets here later, but I suppose she'll be tired; it's a long drive. Although Lachlan could certainly do with as many pairs of hands as he can get.'

'Is that him talking or you?'

'Me,' Posy said with a smile. 'He'd never admit it. He doesn't even have Pavla there today so if we don't go he's on his own…' She hesitated, but then wondered why she was hiding things from Asa. 'I saw him last night and he was still out working.'

'In the dark?'

'Yes. He had a lantern but…'

'You do what you have to do to get a crop in.'

'You say that, but he doesn't. He pushes everyone away who wants to help.'

Asa appeared to weigh her up for a moment. 'By everyone do you mean *you* specifically?'

'No, I mean everyone.'

'Hmm.' Asa turned back to making their coffee while Posy took a seat at the table, yawning. 'No regrets about Jackson this morning?' he asked after a brief silence. His tone was casual but the question felt loaded.

'Did you think I would have?'

'No, but you came to a very swift decision after you'd dithered for so long. I wondered if something might have prompted you to change your mind like that.'

'Why does everyone think everything I do is because I fancy Lachlan?' Posy snapped.

Asa's eyebrows shot up his forehead. 'Nobody's saying that.'

'I'm sorry…' Posy traced a finger along the grain of the wood on the table. 'The truth is I do like him. OK? Happy now that I've admitted it?'

'You don't owe me an explanation.'

'No, but I want to get it off my chest. He drives me mad. There's no reason on earth I ought to feel the way I do about him – he certainly doesn't provide any. He's rude, he's stand-offish, he's antisocial, arrogant, opinionated, uncommunicative, stubborn…'

'Kind, principled, determined and very, very hot. He's your classic tortured, misunderstood soul, and there's nothing more attractive than that.'

Posy looked up with a half-smile. 'Pathetic, isn't it?'

'What are you going to do about it?'

'Nothing. I'm going back to London after this weekend – what's the point in doing anything?'

'So it hasn't crossed your mind to tell him how you feel before you go?'

'It wouldn't change anything.'

'Hmm.'

'I mean, it might change the way we thought about each other but I'd still have to leave.'

'I suppose I was hoping if you two got together you'd stay after all.'

'And live here? I couldn't live here forever.'

'There's an empty building, don't forget.'

'I thought Sandra wanted to turn that into a holiday let?'

He shrugged. 'Plans can change. I think Giles and Sandra would agree to you renting it if you wanted to, so it would be your own place.'

'What would I do for work?'

Posy was throwing out obstacle after obstacle, but even as she did new and fantastic possibilities occurred to her, snapshots of an alternative fantasy life in which she stayed in Astercombe for good, able to live and work in this glorious place at a pace and manner of her choosing, in which she had the independence she could barely afford in London and yet caring family on the doorstep. She'd have to leave her mum, of course, but hadn't that always been the plan? Carmel would worry far less about her if she was living with Sandra, Giles and Asa close by. And hadn't Carmel said she'd begun to dream of a life outside London one day? Maybe eventually she could relocate to Astercombe too? As for Posy's dad, he'd be happy with anywhere as his base, and her friends could come and visit as often as they wanted to.

But was any of this a realistic prospect? It wasn't as simple as upping sticks and moving her stuff in, was it?

'You said one day you'd set up in business for yourself,' Asa said. 'Screw the job in London and do it from here.'

'I can't.'

'Why not?'

'Well, it's miles from everything.'

Asa frowned. 'It's miles from London…' He slapped his forehead. 'I'm so sorry; I forgot that London is, in fact, *everything*! What does that make the rest of the country – Scotch mist?'

'You know what I mean.'

'No, I don't.'

'I thought you liked London.'

'I do, but I don't think it's the centre of the universe.'

'Neither do I.'

'Then why can't you find a way to work from here?'

'Asa…' Posy said, tempering the tone of frustration that was beginning to creep in, 'I love that you want me to stay and a bit of me wants to stay too, but I'm too young to settle into a life out here. I need to build my career first and the best place for that to happen is in London. This job – it's too good an opportunity to throw away.'

'I think you're making excuses because you're scared to take the risk.'

Posy sipped at her coffee but she didn't reply. Maybe Asa was right, but this morning she felt as if she'd taken all the risks she wanted to and they hadn't exactly turned out well for her. Risk-taking was overrated and if she got through the next ten years without having to do it again she'd be very happy.

'I'll think about it,' she said, which was all she could say without offending her uncle with a flat-out refusal of his idea. 'It's a kind offer, but I think you'd make more money renting that place out to holidaymakers than you would to me.'

'If you decide you need to we can talk it through with Giles and Sandra,' he said, seeming satisfied with her answer for now. 'Do you want some breakfast before we go out?'

'It's a bit early for me. Maybe I'll take something for later.'

'Me too,' Asa said. 'I thought my days of early starts were over when Giles put me in charge of the publicity for the orchard – I must be mad volunteering for this.'

'Won't you be getting up early when it's the orchard's turn to harvest?'

'Not quite this early. After all, I can roll out of bed and walk across the courtyard, ready to go.'

'Well,' Posy said, downing the last of her coffee and realising, with a wince, that it had probably been too hot to drink that quickly, 'we'd better get dressed and get to the vineyard if we're going to be any use to Lachlan at all.'

'Oh…'

If Lachlan had been surprised to see Posy he looked even more surprised to see Asa with her.

'He wanted to lend a hand today,' Posy said firmly as she saw his uncertain expression. He looked set to protest but she wasn't going to stand for it. Besides, it was deeply ungrateful to do that with Asa standing there ready to go, and if one word along those lines came out of Lachlan's mouth she was going to say so.

'I know I look like I'd snap in a headwind,' Asa said, cannily reading the situation and defusing it, 'but I'm stronger than I look. I do work at the orchard, after all.'

'Of course,' Lachlan said. 'I'm just… I wasn't expecting you.'

'I know, but I'm here now, so use me.'

Lachlan might not have recognised Asa's cheeky innuendo for what it was but Posy did, and on a different day she might have laughed out loud. Today she was too tense. Things that had been said and done the day before were still fresh in her mind and emotions still raw. She wondered if they troubled Lachlan the way they troubled her, but it was hard to tell with him.

Asa shielded his eyes from the sun with an outstretched hand and gazed up at the hillside climbing away from them, row after row of vines heavy with fruit. 'Think you can get all this in on time?'

'I don't know,' Lachlan said, throwing Posy with his candour. Perhaps he felt his white lies and bravado would be wasted on Asa, who knew enough about fruit farming to see right through them. 'Depends if the weather holds and how many hours a day I can stand up for.'

Asa grinned. 'Spoken like a true farmer.'

Posy was more than a little surprised to hear this from Asa too. He'd always seemed so at odds with his life in the countryside that she'd assumed he wasn't attuned to it at all. But, she supposed, you didn't grow up surrounded by apple trees and not learn a little about growing them.

'I've only got two trucks,' Lachlan said.

'Have you got spare cutters?'

'Yes; I'll have to go and get them from the quad bike.'

He strode off and Asa fired a grin at Posy. 'Well, that was easier than I thought it would be.'

'Maybe he's not as stubborn as people think.'

'Or maybe he's just that desperate.'

Whatever the reason, Posy was glad she'd decided to come after all. If only she could lock her feelings away for the next few hours she might just get through this and do a good thing in the process. And at least she had the arrival of her mum to look forward to. If anything could make her feel better it was that.

Asa began to inspect the nearest vine. He pulled off a grape, rubbed it between his thumb and forefinger and then popped it into his mouth.

'Not bad.'

'I take it you're saying that with your alcohol-brewing head on because I ate one yesterday and it was disgusting.'

Asa laughed. 'I wouldn't want to live on them but they're not that bad – a little on the dry side maybe. I would imagine they'd make a good wine.'

'That's what Lachlan said.'

A movement at the corner of her eye made her look to see him returning. He handed a pair of cutters to each of them.

'That set's a little rusty, I'm afraid,' he said to Asa. 'Will you manage?'

'I expect so,' Asa said cheerfully. 'Show me where to get started and I'll soon find out.'

*

Asa was telling Lachlan that the forecast was for rain by the close of the weekend. Actually, as Lachlan was half a dozen vines up, Asa was shouting this information to him. He snipped away as he did, barely even looking at his work. He'd picked up the technique quickly, far quicker than Posy, who still took great care with hers, and he was now whipping through the harvesting. As for the weather forecast, Posy was sure Lachlan would have checked this for himself and would be well aware, and she wondered whether Asa was simply trying to break the unbearable tension.

Even when she wasn't looking she could feel Lachlan's eyes on her, and whenever she did glance up he turned quickly away. He'd barely spoken to her, apart from giving directions for their work and to inquire early on how her wasp stings were healing, but even that question seemed to have a sting of its own because recalling the wasp stings also forced Posy to recall what had happened after that, and she guessed it would do the same for Lachlan. She'd never been in a situation like this before and she didn't know how to deal with it.

Asa's packing for the day was far more comprehensive too. The weather was mellow, hot and humid again as it had been the day before, but whereas Posy had come armed only with water, Asa had brought a Thermos flask full of iced pomegranate juice and a cool bag containing fruit, crudités and other nibbles for lunch. Lachlan had apologised that he'd only been expecting Posy and had made only enough cheese sandwiches for the two of them, and although Posy appreciated the gesture they looked a bit rubbish compared to Asa's feast. Whatever talents Lachlan might have, catering wasn't one of them.

They'd stopped to eat when there were voices from the gate. Posy twisted on her blanket to see Carmel, Giles and Sandra walking up the hill.

'Mum!' she squealed, quite forgetting that she'd ever been in a weird mood and leaping up to go and meet her. Carmel threw her arms around her daughter and held on tight.

'Look at you!' she said as they let go, running her eye over Posy. 'Like a regular country-dweller now, aren't you?'

Posy glanced down at her denim shorts and walking boots, her tanned legs bearing the scratches she'd earned walking up the hill in the dark the night before, her knees grass-stained and her top all crumpled. Carmel reached to pull a twig from her hair and held it out for Posy to see. 'You don't get that walking around Knightsbridge!'

Posy laughed. 'No. When I'm here I feel like I'm in one of those Famous Five stories you used to read to me. I keep expecting some mad old uncle to tell me not to go snooping around mysterious caves.'

Giles grinned. 'I hope I'm not the mad old uncle!'

'That'd be me!' Asa called over.

'Who's got the ginger beer?' Carmel asked.

Asa wandered over. 'I don't have ginger beer but I do have pomegranate juice.' He reached to give Carmel a peck on the cheek. Lachlan came over a second later looking vaguely alarmed at the sight of so many newcomers.

'Giles, Sandra…' He looked at Carmel. 'Forgive me if I don't remember your name.'

'This is my mum,' Posy said.

Lachlan nodded. 'We've met before, haven't we?'

'Oh, of course you have…' Posy said, recalling now an awkward moment in the lobby of Karen's guest house. It seemed like such a long time ago that she'd almost forgotten it.

'I don't think we were ever formally introduced though,' Posy's mum said. 'I'm Carmel.'

'Carmel…' Lachlan stuck his hands in his pockets. 'Right.'

No '*Pleased to meet you*', no shaking hands, just 'Right.' Posy was right – Lachlan was rude and he really didn't care who knew it. And yet, there was still a part of her that looked at him with a pang of regret. How obnoxious did this man have to be to cure her of such unwelcome feelings?

'Mum's up from London for the weekend,' she said, although she didn't know why she was bothering to explain anything to him; it wasn't like he cared.

'So you'll be wanting to call it a day now,' Lachlan said, looking at Posy and Asa in turn.

'Actually, we thought we might lend a hand this afternoon if you needed more help,' Sandra said.

Lachlan stared at her. 'All of you?'

'Well, Carmel had intended to come over to see Posy anyway and we decided we'd come with her. Now that we're here we might as well stay.'

'Don't you have your own work at the orchard?'

'Yes, but neighbours are neighbours and one good turn deserves another, and we managed to jiggle the schedule so that we had an afternoon to spare.'

Posy didn't know whether Lachlan was going to fly into a rage or burst into tears. Every conceivable emotion seemed to cross his face at once.

'I couldn't ask you—' he began, but Giles cut in.

'Of course you could. As Sandra says, neighbours are neighbours. Life is tough enough for growers; we have to help each other where we can.'

'I don't have enough equipment here with me.'

'I thought you might not.' Giles showed him a metal carry box. 'So we've brought our own. It might not be just what you'd use but I think they'll do the job.'

Giles walked off without giving Lachlan the chance to reply. With the same critical eye that Asa had used earlier he walked the rows, looking at the vines.

Sandra and Carmel turned to Lachlan.

'Once he's made up his mind there's no unmaking it,' Sandra said. 'Might as well give in and let us help.'

Lachlan still wore the expression of someone who really didn't know how he was feeling.

'Aye,' was all he said before walking off to join Giles. Posy watched as they began to discuss the work, Lachlan pointing at different parts of the nearest plant and Giles nodding every so often.

'That man… he really is a one-off, isn't he?' Carmel said.

'Yes,' Sandra agreed. 'You have to wonder how he came to be that way.'

The mood was very much lighter by the time they finished lunch and began to work again. Carmel was like a little kid on a school trip, marvelling at the novelty of her situation, while Giles kept Lachlan company for most of it as they swapped wisdom and opinions on farming, the current market and the reliability of the weather.

Strangely, out of every interaction Posy had ever witnessed Lachlan involved in, it seemed Giles got through better than anyone else. With him he was open and almost friendly. Maybe it was because the things they were discussing were practical things that didn't require an emotional response, conversations where Lachlan could control the direction – and that was always a safe place. Posy even witnessed a brief chortle, and the only thing that would have been more shocking was if one of the vines had started to talk to her. Although, she was so sick of seeing them right now that at least it would have livened things up.

In a strange way, though, seeing Lachlan get along with Giles made her envious and a little sad. She would never get him to open up like that. Maybe she ought to try talking about things that didn't matter, like weather and soil acidity and natural pesticides.

Asa and Carmel had become something of a double act too. They weren't discussing farming but had somehow got to playing *Snog, Marry, Avoid*, passing judgement on male celebrities, and some of Asa's replies had Carmel in fits of giggles, her own getting more and more daring in response until Posy wasn't sure she wanted to hear any more and was considering asking if anyone had earplugs.

Sandra glanced across and smiled at them. 'You and your mum certainly know how to cheer him up,' she said to Posy in a low voice. 'Sometimes I feel Giles and I have failed him.' Posy looked at her with a silent question. 'He's told you about Drew?'

'Yes,' Posy said.

'When he left we simply didn't know what to do for Asa. We couldn't give him what he needed and Philomena certainly never could – she didn't even try to understand him and yet he worshipped her. He was devastated when she died, you know, even though she'd never really accepted his sexuality and made him feel guilty about it for as long as she lived.'

'She sounds horrible.'

Sandra turned and stared at Posy.

'Sorry,' Posy said. 'But she does. She gave up on my mum and never tried to find her, denied my existence and she made Asa miserable because she didn't like him being gay. I'm glad I never knew her.'

Sandra was silent, and for a moment Posy thought she'd offended her. Perhaps her assessment had been rash and out of line, but she'd answered instinctively and from the heart and it was too late to take it back now.

'She was a complicated woman,' Sandra said finally.

'And yet for all that she had Asa and Giles, who are lovely people,' Posy said.

'Yes. One has to wonder how they turned out so well.'

'I wish I'd known my mum a little…'

Sandra gave a small smile. 'She was long gone by the time I met Giles so I never knew her either. She sounds like a character though, a real wild child. I don't know where she got it from because it's not a trait I see in Giles at all. Maybe Asa a little sometimes, but nowhere near in that league.'

'It's funny, I don't imagine I'm much like her at all either,' Posy said. 'I think I've got more of my adopted mother in me than my birth one.'

'I wouldn't necessarily say that's a bad thing,' Sandra said. 'Carmel is a wonderful woman – you could be a lot worse than like her.'

'I was a bit worried that she might be hurt at the idea I'd want to spend time getting to know you all here, but she's been brilliant. I know it must scare her a little, the idea that I might grow to like life here better than I do with her in London, but I also know she'd never put those feelings before what I might want. I'm so lucky to have her as my mum.'

'You are,' Sandra agreed. 'We didn't want or need another addition to the family and we were terrified of where it might lead when we were forced to seek you out, but I'm so glad we did. Giles and I couldn't have children but, if we had, I would have hoped they'd be like you.'

Posy's hand rested over a bunch of grapes and Sandra covered it briefly with hers and gave Posy a warm smile.

'Of course,' she added, 'I would expect Carmel to put up a fight if we wanted to steal you away, but we'd never do that to her. That said, if you should decide you want to spend a little longer here in Astercombe…'

'Sandra…' Posy began. 'I don't suppose… well, one day you could take me to the village and show me the house where my dad lived?'

'John's old place?' She was thoughtful for a moment, and then she gave a small smile.

'I suppose it makes perfect sense that you'd want to see it. Of course I can, though you could probably find it yourself easily enough if you wanted to – it's right next to the stream, the little blue house with the bullseye windows—'

'Sandra!' Giles shouted. 'Come and see this!'

Sandra rolled her eyes and gave Posy an apologetic smile. Whatever else she was about to say would have to wait now, though it struck Posy that the house Sandra had described was the one she'd stared at during her first visit to Astercombe.

'I'll bet he's found a two-headed earthworm or something – he's not usually this excited about anything else.'

Posy watched her walk the slope to join her husband and Lachlan looked up, momentarily catching Posy's eye. He held her gaze and then seemed to realise what he was doing and looked away.

In some ways, having so many people here made it easier for them, but in other ways it made things more difficult than ever. Lots of people meant they didn't have time or privacy for an awkward conversation, but that same fact prevented conversations that they really needed to have, awkward or not. With all hands on deck the pace of work was much faster, and Posy wondered if Lachlan would even ask anyone to come back to the vineyard to help after today. She would, even though she really needed to pack for her departure. It was doubtful he'd ask anyway.

As she watched him, deep in thought, she suddenly felt another pair of eyes on her and looked to see Asa studying her now. He made his way over.

'You know he keeps looking at you,' he said, his voice low. Posy didn't react. 'You must have noticed,' Asa continued. 'Considering how many times you've looked at him.'

'He's here in the field – I can't not look at him from time to time.'

'You know exactly what's going on here as well as I do,' Asa said.

Posy stopped cutting at a vine and looked him square in the eye. 'Well,' she said, 'even if I did, it doesn't make a blind bit of difference. I don't think he even knows how to be nice or show affection or any kind of humanity whatsoever, so I don't know why he's looking at me and I'm only looking at him because he's so bloody annoying I'm dreaming about punching him in the face.'

Asa chuckled. 'So that told me! I didn't expect you to get quite so riled. And for the record, the way he's looking at you, I'd say that's pretty damn human.'

Posy snatched at the bunch of grapes she'd just cut free and left Asa to go back to his own vine.

Everyone had an opinion about her and Lachlan but none of them really knew anything about it. And as she had no intentions of enlightening anyone, it would be better if they kept their opinions to themselves because they weren't helpful at all.

Chapter Twenty-Eight

Sandra had invited Lachlan to Posy's farewell barbeque but none of them actually thought he'd come. Sandra thought that was a pity because she was warming to him, and Giles agreed that his ways might be brusque but he was a salt-of-the-earth, no-nonsense kind of fella that he could get on with.

Posy could think of plenty of nonsense that he was, while Asa bemoaned that if only he'd make an appearance at their get-together it would give him something nice to look at.

Lachlan didn't show, of course, just as everyone had predicted.

In the garden now as Giles filled the air with the glorious smells of chargrilled vegetables and meats stood Carmel, Asa, Sandra and Karen – who'd allowed herself an hour off to come and say goodbye to Posy and then would head back to Sunnyfields so that Pavla could have an hour to come over and do the same. Ray would stay on duty, as he always did, but as Posy had barely said two words to him the whole time she'd been in Astercombe she really didn't think they needed any kind of goodbye anyway.

Sandra had dragged over a vat of cider from the press that hadn't yet been bottled, while Lachlan, as a thank you for their help in the vineyard, had dropped a crate of wine by the gates of Oleander House that morning before anyone had woken (another clue he hadn't intended to come to the party). The guests were making steady progress through it all now.

'So you start your new job on Monday?' Karen said.

Posy nodded.

'How do you feel about it? Nervous?'

'A bit,' Posy admitted. 'Mostly I don't want to mess up because my friend put in a word for me.'

'You'd have got the job on your own merit,' Carmel said. 'Marella might have brought you to her boss's attention but he wouldn't have taken you on unless he thought you were a good fit for his business.'

'In that case,' Posy said, 'I need to prove he was right. Either way it's a bit nerve-wracking.'

'I wouldn't like to be in the job market again,' Karen said. 'Too stressful by far. Give me a busy day at the B&B any time.'

'Stress is different when you work for yourself, isn't it?' Carmel agreed. 'It can be terrifying but the rewards are far greater.'

'Burgers!' Giles yelled across the patio. Posy grinned.

'Do you think he might be trying to tell us the burgers are ready?'

Carmel laughed. 'Whatever led you to that conclusion?'

They went over to get some food from the first batch. Posy had been saving herself all day and she was starving. Asa came up close behind and pretended to try and trip her up so he could be first in the queue and she giggled.

'Out of the way, tin ribs,' she said. 'I've seen you hoover up food – there'll be nothing left for us if you get in first.'

'Cheeky cow!'

It was a measure of just how far their relationship had come that they could share this banter. When Posy had first met Asa she hadn't been able to work him out at all and she wasn't even sure she liked him. Now she couldn't imagine her life without him in it.

Carmel gave them both an indulgent smile. Asa really was more like an older brother to Posy than an uncle, and perhaps Carmel saw it that way too.

Burgers were accompanied by salad from Oleander's garden, grilled halloumi, home-made coleslaw, guacamole and salsa. Even as everyone was groaning from the amount they'd eaten Giles added some hickory-smoked chicken wings to the grill, though it was unclear who was going to manage them. Even Asa had said he was full, and that was probably the litmus test for everyone else. Still, Posy went over and helped herself to one and forced it down, and even though she might regret it later she was glad she had because it was delicious.

The flow of food from the grill had started to calm a little and Asa took the opportunity of a lull to crack open one of Lachlan's bottles. He held it aloft to call for attention. Once everyone was quiet he began to speak.

'I just want to say a few words about my lovely niece,' he began.

'Oh God…' Posy groaned. 'Please don't.'

Everyone laughed and Asa – who was now very visibly drunk – took a swig from the wine bottle. 'No, no… I have to talk and you have to listen. If you're buggering off back to London it's the least you can do.'

Everyone laughed again and Asa, buoyed by the appreciation of his performance, continued.

'Carmel,' he said. 'I'll get to you shortly, love.'

'I can wait, darling,' Carmel said dryly, making everyone laugh again.

'So,' Asa carried on, 'we all know that we'd never even heard of Posy before this summer,' he slurred, 'and boy, was it a shock when we did—'

'Asa!' Sandra hissed. Perhaps she was worried he was about to give away something entirely inappropriate that they'd really rather keep secret. He waved away her admonishment and carried on unperturbed, and Sandra looked even more nervous than she had a moment before.

'None of that matters anyway.' Asa swayed slightly before taking another swig of his wine. 'Because even if we thought she'd be a hideous gold-digger we were wrong.'

There was an audible, horrified gasp from Sandra. Posy didn't know where to look. While she appreciated Asa's sentiment the situation was starting to feel distinctly uncomfortable. She glanced across to see a similar set of emotions playing across her mum's face.

'The fact is,' Asa continued, 'I love—'

He stopped mid-sentence and the smile slipped from his face to be replaced by a sudden expression of shock. He stared at a spot beyond the patio and everyone turned to look.

'The gate was open,' the man said apologetically. 'I couldn't get any answer at the house. I hope I'm not interrupting anything…'

Posy looked at Sandra, but before she could ask what on earth was going on Giles was striding across the garden towards the newcomer.

'You've got a nerve showing up here!'

And then, all at once, Posy worked it out. The man currently gate-crashing their party was Drew.

*

As Giles tried to herd Drew away, Posy craned for a good look. She needed to see what kind of man had managed to so utterly destroy her uncle. Whatever she'd been expecting, the reality didn't really live up to it. Perhaps she'd been expecting someone like Lachlan – proud, haughty, impossibly handsome. Drew – if this was Drew – was soft-featured, sandy-haired, blue-eyed, slight of build and probably around her own age – certainly younger than Asa – and he looked almost ordinary. He didn't arrive like a whirlwind of destructive emotional menace; he came with a soothing, gentle, polite presence that was instantly likeable. Or it might have been, had there not been such a complicated history.

'Who's that?' Carmel whispered in Posy's ear.

'I think it's the man who broke Asa's heart.'

Carmel knew something of Drew as Posy had mentioned his existence briefly in conversation, but Posy hadn't told her just how much damage he'd done, so she looked slightly bemused now but didn't ask anything else. Posy watched as Asa seemed to come to his senses. She'd never seen a man sober up so quickly. He dashed after Giles, who was ushering Drew into the house.

'So… what do we do now?' Karen asked. She didn't seem all that surprised to see any of this drama unfold, and like all the other supposedly secret business going on in Astercombe, she probably knew a good deal more about it than anyone else.

'They'll be back shortly,' Sandra said as she came over with a plastic rubbish bag that Posy hadn't seen her go and fetch. She forced a brighter tone as she began to clear away discarded napkins. 'I'm sure we can all keep the party going while the men are missing.'

Posy and Carmel exchanged an anxious glance.

'I'll help you clear up,' Karen said, following Sandra.

'God, I hope he's alright,' Posy said quietly once Karen and Sandra were out of earshot.

'Why do you think he came here?' Carmel asked. 'Asa didn't look very happy – to be expected – but Giles looked furious.'

'I can only imagine,' Posy said, and she was saved further speculation by the return of Giles, marching back to the garden trying to look relaxed, though his body language said he was anything but.

'Sorry about that,' he said, taking his spot at the grill again.

'I really don't think we need any more food,' Sandra called over. Giles glanced at the barbeque and then gave a short nod of agreement.

'I've probably been here too long actually,' Karen said. 'I ought to get back and relieve Pavla of her duties so she can pop over.'

She gave Posy and Carmel a hug and bid Giles and Sandra goodbye and then left. Now there were only four of them in the garden, struggling to make any kind of genial conversation. Posy wondered what was going on in the house. What were Asa and Drew discussing? Was Asa OK? Would he be able to stay strong?

It was obvious why Drew was here – at least it was to her. What other reason could there be other than him trying to win Asa back? He'd been trying for weeks as far as she could tell, but to come here like this he must really mean business this time. A bit of her had to grudgingly admire his bravery – to walk into totally expected hostility took some nerve. Perhaps he really was sorry; perhaps he'd come to realise just what he'd lost, what a mistake he'd made letting Asa down like that.

But could Asa trust him again, and would it do his already fragile emotional state any good to try?

'Would you excuse us for a minute?' Sandra asked, breaking into Posy's thoughts. 'Giles and I just need to attend to something.'

Carmel smiled tightly. 'Of course.' She looked at Posy as Giles and Sandra went into the house. Were they going to give Asa backup? Or stop him making a terrible mistake? Or were they having a separate discussion of their own?

Posy and Carmel waited in the garden. Ten more minutes passed and nobody came back.

'Is Asa terribly in love with this man?' Carmel asked after a long pause, during which the only sounds had been the hissing and cracking of the coals as they cooled on the barbeque and leaves being lifted from their branches by the breeze in the orchard.

'It looks like it, doesn't it?'

'I thought so too. What do you think he'll do?'

'Goodness only knows. He's been struggling, I know that much.'

'I wonder why Drew's come here.'

'I expect he wants to try again.'

'I expect you're right.'

'I don't think that's a very good idea, though.'

'But if there's love there—'

'Mum, this man utterly destroyed Asa. He can't be good for him, no matter how much love there is.'

'Are you sure about that?'

'Yes.'

'Well, just remember that things aren't always as clear-cut as they seem. You've heard one version of events but there are always others, and if you heard them you might think differently.'

Posy mused on Carmel's words. Would she? What could she hear that would change her mind on this? It would have to be persuasive, whatever it was.

Carmel's phone bleeped faintly and she took it from her handbag to read a message from Karen.

'Pavla can't make it,' she said. 'She sends her apologies and says she'll come to say goodbye just before we leave if that's alright.'

'Karen's told her it's not a good idea to come.'

'Probably. She always reads a situation perfectly, doesn't she? And I'm quite sure Pavla wouldn't want to walk into all this anyway.'

'I wouldn't,' Posy agreed.

As Carmel put her phone away, Asa, Giles and Sandra came back into the garden, but Drew wasn't with them.

'I'm so sorry about all that,' Asa said.

'God, don't even think about apologising!' Posy said. 'Was that…?'

'Yes,' he said. 'That was Drew. He's gone now. He didn't mean to interrupt our evening; he obviously didn't know we had guests…'

Posy wanted to ask what had happened but wondered if maybe Asa didn't want to discuss it right now, especially not in front of Carmel either, someone he still hardly knew, so she didn't. She guessed that he'd share some of it with her when he was ready, and she had to be content with that.

'I suppose…' Asa let out a long breath. What he'd been about to say Posy would never know because his phone started to ring and he teared up as he checked the display. 'Drew…' he said tensely as he took the call to a quiet corner. 'Don't cry…'

Posy felt the blood drain from her face.

'He's only just left here,' she said to her mum. 'Where on earth is he calling from already?'

'He can't have got far,' Carmel agreed. 'I'm guessing he's been sent away and is making a fuss about going.'

Giles and Sandra had begun to pack up the food that hadn't been eaten.

'I'll go and help them,' Carmel said.

'I'd better hang back for a few minutes to see if Asa needs me.'

Pavla was no longer planning to come over, and as it had gone eight thirty from a 6 p.m. start, it didn't look as if Lachlan was going to show either. Posy hadn't really expected him to, though she was unreasonably disappointed all the same. Though, in light of what had happened here in the last hour, perhaps it was for the best. As for that, could they rescue this evening, and was it even worth trying?

When a couple of minutes had passed and Asa still hadn't returned, Posy, feeling useless and dejected, decided to go and help with the clean-up. It was better than standing around in the garden by herself.

'We're all but finished really,' Sandra said when Posy offered her services. 'We thought we might wind down and have some quiet drinks on the patio – would you mind? I know it's not the going-away we'd promised—'

'It sounds lovely,' Posy said.

Giles twisted the tie on a bag of bread rolls and gave her a pained smile. 'Thank you for being so understanding.'

'Honestly, please don't worry. I've had such an amazing time with you this summer and that was enough – I wasn't expecting a fuss when I left, but this has been the cherry on the cake.'

'It's just a shame it had to be cut short,' he said.

Posy gave him an encouraging smile. 'It hasn't been cut short; it's just calming down. All parties do that eventually but they're still as nice, only in a less rowdy way.'

'That's the one thing we've noticed you take everywhere you go,' Sandra said. 'Optimism and positivity. You see the best in every situation and every person.' She looked at Carmel. 'You must be so proud of her.'

'Of course I am,' Carmel said fondly, and while Posy felt an embarrassed appreciation of the compliment, she also wondered if Sandra would still think that if she knew half the cock-ups and pessimistic thoughts that had characterised her last few days in Astercombe.

They were settled round the table on the patio in low, easy conversation when Asa returned. Posy had a blanket over her knees and there was a heater glowing nearby so, although the temperature had dropped, she'd be happy to stay out there all night if everyone else wanted to. Asa sat down to join them with a strained smile.

'I suppose I owe you an explanation,' he said to Posy and Carmel.

'You don't,' Carmel said. 'Unless it would help to talk about it.'

'Not especially.'

'Then it doesn't matter.'

'Just…' Posy said, 'are you alright? You don't have to tell us anything else.'

He nodded. 'I'm more worried about Drew. He's in a state.'

'Do you feel as if he might do something silly?'

Posy glanced at Sandra, who now had real concern in her voice.

'I don't think it's that bad,' Asa said. 'But I am going to stay in contact over the next few days to be certain. And no' – he looked at his brother and sister-in-law firmly – 'in case you're wondering, we haven't got back together and I've no intention of it.'

Was he just saying that but thinking something different? Posy wondered. What had Carmel said about taking a risk if they had real love?

Asa poured himself a glass of Lachlan's wine. Posy watched him. Though he looked troubled, he was composed and very sober considering he'd been legless not more than an hour before. Would she get a chance to really talk to him before she left? And even if she did, what could she do to help? Maybe very little, but the idea that he might have to face this alone when she was gone made her sad. He had Giles and Sandra, of course, but she had the feeling they saw things in a very much more black-and-white way, and sometimes black and white wasn't enough. Sometimes you needed the whole spectrum to see the truth of something, to find your real answer. Sometimes it was the mess in the colours that made you happy even if it didn't make sense. Asa had turned Drew away and that had made sense, but would it make him truly happy?

Chapter Twenty-Nine

It was just after midnight when they'd turned in. Asa had been subdued, though he'd tried his best to be cheerful, and most of the quiet conversation had focused on the orchard, Posy's new job and Carmel's latest commissions. Lachlan had cropped up too, but he was almost as tough for Posy to talk about as Asa's dilemma was for him. Sandra and Giles had said they were planning to keep an eye on how things were going at the vineyard when they could spare the time. Asa had said Lachlan was likely to tell them to bog off and mind their own business, which Posy agreed was probably true, but she was nonetheless glad to hear someone would be looking out for him. She had a feeling that even though he didn't let people close enough to care, he needed it.

It took another hour to fall asleep. Carmel was spending the night in the spare room at the big house while Posy took her usual bed in Asa's annexe. As she got up for the third time that hour, restless and unable to figure out why, she looked across to see the lights finally go out in the main building. She wished she was in there, just so she could talk to her mum for a while.

Eventually, though, her mind a mess of open-ended questions and unformed thoughts, she drifted off.

*

It was hard to say how long she'd been asleep when something woke her. A sort of roaring, whooshing noise. Posy lay still, listening for a moment, groggy and unable to pull herself together. What the hell was that? And then she noticed the light outside – it looked so strange, so different to any she'd seen before.

She leapt out of bed and yanked up the blinds to be greeted by a sight that froze her blood.

Oleander House was on fire.

Chapter Thirty

Asa almost knocked her flying as she ran into him at her bedroom door.

'Call for help!'

Posy was already dialling for the emergency services; the first thing she'd done was grab her phone. As she gave the address and nature of the emergency to the operator Asa raced outside into the courtyard.

'Giles! Sandra!'

Posy finished her call and rushed out to him.

'Why aren't they out here?' he cried. 'Why haven't they woken up?'

'Must be the smoke!' Posy stared helplessly at the building. 'Mum's in there too!'

In the courtyard the air was getting thick. Vast, soupy clouds rose up to blot out the stars, but the changing direction of the wind was forcing it to billow back down to engulf the grounds too. It was in Posy's throat and nose already, acrid and bitter, and she couldn't even begin to imagine what it was like inside the house. The idea filled her with suffocating panic. There was so much smoke it was hard to see how widespread the actual fire was. The epicentre had to be somewhere inside, but where? Why hadn't anyone come out yet? There was nothing else to be done and they couldn't wait for help – somehow she and Asa had to get in.

Posy ran to the back door and pushed against it, but it was stuck fast. The one time Sandra bothered to lock up, it had to be now. She'd probably imagined she was making Carmel feel safe, but instead it had put her in greater danger. Posy swept the building, looking for an alternative entrance, but she couldn't see anything that looked accessible. She was about to run off and search for something that would smash the kitchen window when she saw Asa race back into his house. Had he thought of that too? But he returned a second later with a key.

'Spares,' he said tersely. 'Never thought I'd need them.'

Posy was glad he had them, though.

They opened the door and ran in together, immediately hitting a thicker wall of smoke. Posy pulled her pyjama top over her nose and mouth.

'I can't see a thing!' Asa shouted.

Posy could just about hear him over the din of the fire raging somewhere within, but she couldn't see him despite the fact they'd just walked in. How much worse was the rest of the house going to be? She was filled with dread once again, her insides churning. The effects of the smoke were already biting at her too; it was no wonder anyone inside hadn't come out yet. Did that mean she and Asa were already too late to save anyone?

She had to push the idea from her head or she'd sink with the hopelessness of it. Instead, she steeled herself and began to feel her way through the kitchen, eyes streaming, lungs burning, her skin itching.

'Are you there?' Asa called, coughing out his words.

'Here.'

His hand brushed against hers, and though she was as terrified for him and for herself as she was for everyone else she was glad to have him with her.

'You should go back outside,' he said as she lost his hand again.

'No chance.'

He didn't waste breath on a reply but yelled into the house.

'Giles!'

He started to cough again. It was all Posy could focus on, knowing that every spasm would force him to draw in a bigger breath and more smoke. It wouldn't take long for both of them to be overcome. They had to find the others fast and get out or they were all going to die.

'Asa…?'

'Here,' he croaked. 'I'm OK.'

They were moving painfully slowly, but their surroundings were so disorientating that she barely knew where they were. The house was in darkness and that was bad enough, but the smoke and the noise made everything a hundred times worse.

Then she thought she heard a sort of dragging, muffled thump. A second later Posy could make out a shape, moving in the smoke.

'Asa…?'

'Posy!' It was Giles. 'What are you doing in here?'

'Giles! We thought…'

'I've got Sandra. We're alright.'

'My mum?'

'I'll go back for her. Take Sandra outside.'

'But—'

Posy's sentence was cut short by a violent coughing fit. Before she'd managed to catch her breath a hand closed around her wrist and she was yanked backward. A moment later she could see the shape of the back door and could tell that the air was a tiny bit clearer and colder. Asa pulled her through it and out into the courtyard. Giles followed with Sandra in his arms. She was unconscious and he laid her gently down onto the ground before racing back into the house, coughing constantly and violently as he did.

'I have to go back in; I have to help find Mum!' Posy cried.

Asa shook his head firmly. 'It's not safe,' he panted. 'Giles will find her.'

'It's not safe for *him*!'

'Posy! Let him find her! He knows the house better than you – it makes sense!'

He knelt down and placed Sandra's head onto his lap as he began to talk softly to her, trying to get a response. She was still breathing, but it was shallow and laboured.

Posy stared miserably down at her, and then back up at the house. She could see flames now, licking at a front downstairs window. She tried desperately to work out where they might be coming from, where the worst of the blaze might be. Asa was still talking to Sandra but she didn't open her eyes.

A minute passed that felt like a year and then a figure emerged from the house.

It was Giles, but he was alone. Bent double, he dragged at the air, coughing so hard he could barely get any.

'Mum?' Posy shrieked.

He shook his head.

'Where is she?'

'Can't... find...'

Posy broke into a run. Dimly aware of a hand reaching out for her, she shook it off.

'Posy – no!'

She ran into the kitchen, everywhere sharp corners of furniture hitting her arms and legs, her hands outstretched to feel for walls and doorways, the sounds of the growing fire now almost overwhelming. She had no clue where she was going but she couldn't stand outside and do nothing while her mum choked to death in here.

'Mum!'

The only reply was the cracking and breaking of the house as it burned and dim voices from somewhere outside. She hoped that nobody would be stupid enough to follow her in. She had to save her mum, whatever it took, but she didn't want to put anyone else in danger.

'Mum!'

Her breath came shorter and shorter and every one with a cough. She tried to cover her face with her pyjama top again, but this time it did nothing to help. The realisation was beginning to hit her – she couldn't do this. It didn't make her turn back, but she was certain now that she was going to die in here and Carmel was going to die because she'd failed, and tears rolled down her face and her sobs made her breathing harder than ever.

There was a crash from somewhere in the house, but she couldn't pinpoint the source. Her mum, trying to get out? But it sounded like *something*, rather than someone, and she wondered if it was sections of the building collapsing. The thought gripped her with a new terror. She picked up the pace, abandoning her cautious navigation of whatever room she was in and ignoring the sharp knocks from unseen furniture, but then her foot caught on something and sent her sprawling across the floor. It knocked what little breath she'd had from her. Now, as she tried to draw something, anything into her lungs, it felt as if her head would explode. She began to cry harder, dry, painful, gasping sobs.

It was strange but, as she closed her eyes, things began to calm. She was scared but resigned, and her biggest regret was not being here staring death in the face but being unable to reach Carmel before it came.

I'm sorry, Mum. I'm so sorry.

Chapter Thirty-One

All hope was lost. Posy's body would simply take her no further. Every movement, every tiny breath was like trying to climb a mountain. She could only hope that somehow Carmel had made it out because she would not be the one to rescue her – she couldn't even rescue herself.

When a pair of arms wrapped around her and lifted her up, she could barely comprehend it. She tried to open her eyes but she couldn't. She tried to speak but she couldn't do that either. In the end she allowed herself to be carried and a moment later sensed the smoke beginning to thin and the air around her getting colder. She was laid onto the ground and something soft was tucked beneath her head.

'Posy… Posy!'

Asa… good old Asa… you'd think he'd snap in a headwind but he's stronger than he looks.

Then there was a second voice. 'She needs oxygen! Where the hell is that fire service?'

That wasn't Asa. It wasn't Giles. It was… but how did he get here?

She forced her eyes to open. Her head thumped and she could barely drag a breath to fill her lungs, but at least the fact she was trying meant she was alive.

'Mum…?' she croaked.

'Don't worry,' Asa said. 'Lachlan got her out.'

'I thought she was you,' Lachlan said, and in any other circumstances it might have sounded just a little ungracious and resentful.

Posy stared up at him. She couldn't quite believe he was here.

'How could you be so stupid?' he growled. 'What the hell were you thinking – you could have got yourself killed!'

'Lachlan,' Asa said quietly, 'it's what we all would have done in her shoes.'

Posy wasn't listening. She was confused. If Lachlan had brought Carmel out, then who had rescued her?

'She should have waited for help, she's not strong—'

His voice cracked. Posy looked at his face but nothing she saw made sense. He'd looked scared, but now there was only fury there.

'I might not have been able to save you!' he shouted.

He got up and strode off. Posy didn't know where and she was too weak and tired to care; she only saw Asa's gaze follow him for a moment.

For now, there were more important things to think about than Lachlan's mood.

'Mum?'

Asa turned back to her. 'She's alright, she's safe. Giles is with her.'

'Sandra?'

'She's alright too. I mean, they've both taken in a lot of smoke like you but—'

His sentence was cut short by the wailing of a siren. By now, Posy could see the flames beginning to break through the roof and into the night sky.

That beautiful house – it was almost as much a part of this family as the people who lived in it. How would they survive if it burned down? She couldn't imagine a world in which Oleander House didn't exist. And what if the blaze spread to the orchards? It was an entirely feasible and heart-breaking thought. All those years of nurturing, all that love and care destroyed in a single night. If she had any tears left in her she'd cry again.

Her thoughts were pulled back to the present by the sounds of heavy boots on the ground and Giles's clipped tones responding to voices she didn't recognise. Then a firefighter came to Posy and Asa and put an oxygen mask over her face.

'Better?' he asked.

She gave a tiny nod.

'Ambulance is on its way,' the firefighter said to Asa. 'Stay with her and try to keep her comfortable until it gets here.'

'I've no intention of doing anything else,' Asa said.

Posy closed her eyes. Her head was filled with the roaring and cracking of the fire and the footsteps echoing on the cobbles of the courtyard and voices tumbling over one another to issue and acknowledge instructions.

Everyone was safe. She hoped the firefighters would be able to save the house too.

She just wanted to sleep now.

Chapter Thirty-Two

Posy was still in Somerset. She'd spoken to her new boss on the phone and he'd advised without hesitation that she ought to take as long as she needed to recover from her ordeal and get well. Giles had wanted to drive Posy and Carmel back to London to recuperate, but there was so much to do at Oleander House and Carmel had refused his offer, telling him that she and Posy had agreed they would stay for a while because he needed all the help he could get. With the main house unusable and Asa's barn already full with him and Posy, Giles and Sandra were moving into Philomena's old place for now.

At first appraisal, it looked as though the fire had been caused by faulty wiring. Giles hadn't seemed surprised, but ashamed and sad. He'd known, he admitted, that the electrics of Oleander House had needed fixing for some time – some of it had been installed in the sixties. As well as the structural repairs, they now had to rewire the place from top to bottom to make sure nothing like this ever happened again before they could move back in. The insurance wouldn't cover that aspect of the repairs either, so that was a whole heap of extra money they would have to find, though Giles seemed fairly confident they'd manage somehow.

On top of all that, harvest was still fast approaching, though by now half the village had heard of their plight and had promised help.

Carmel, understandably, hadn't wanted to stay in Philomena's old place with Giles and Sandra, but she did want to stay close by with Posy, to offer any support she could. So Karen had provided a room free of charge – her own way of lending a hand. Posy's dad had raced back from his latest installation and was staying there with her for as long as she needed him. Carmel seemed to be struggling more with her recovery than Posy, and when Posy voiced concerns about this, her mum reminded her of the age difference and that her taking longer was no reason to worry. She was on the mend, and it would take as long as it took.

Even Posy was struggling. She'd forced herself to walk to Sunnyfields this grey morning in a bid to make her lungs strong again, but it had taken twice the time it normally would. It had been only three days since the fire, though, and perhaps she was expecting too much so soon – after all, she'd spent two of those in hospital.

As she passed Lachlan's vineyard she looked up to the hill. She hadn't seen him since the night he'd saved her and her mum, though she'd wanted to, if only to thank him for that, but Karen had been to see her in hospital and warned her to wait. As usual, she seemed to know things nobody else did. He needed time, she'd said, and then no more, as was also usual, and so Posy was left with a cryptic half story and had had to try to guess the rest.

What she had learned was that Lachlan had gone to tend his vines just before dawn and as a result had seen the fire from his hillside. He'd jumped onto his quad bike and sped over to make sure everyone was safe. He'd been horrified to arrive just in time to see Posy run into the burning building. He'd gone in after her, as he'd stated himself, and it was pure blind luck that he'd come across Carmel first, in the confusion mistaking her for Posy and bringing her out, because nobody had had time to tell him there was anyone else in there.

'He was like a man possessed,' Asa had told Posy afterwards. 'As soon as he realised he hadn't got you but your mum he went straight back in and we couldn't stop him.'

Posy had wanted to believe that it meant something special, but, really, any decent person would have done what they could to help. It wouldn't always be running into a burning house, but still...

There was no sign of Lachlan on the hill now. She didn't know how he'd managed to get the rest of his crop in but the vegetation definitely looked sparser – from this distance at least – and she guessed from that fact a good deal of it had been saved. She was glad of that, at least, because she was in no state to go and help but she still would have worried about it. In light of recent events she would have felt honour-bound to somehow repay him for saving her and her mother too.

By the time she arrived at Sunnyfields to find Karen manning a quiet reception, she felt as if she'd run a marathon.

'You never walked here!' Karen rushed over to lead Posy to a seat. 'Honestly, what does it take to slow you down?'

'It seemed like a good idea at the time.' Posy let her head rest against the wall behind her chair and closed her eyes as she caught her breath. 'Don't worry... won't catch me doing it again...'

'Your mum and dad are out on the guest terrace,' Karen said briskly. 'At least Carmel has the good sense to be resting.'

Posy nodded. Maybe her mum was resting but it was nothing to do with common sense. She was as eager to get back on her feet as Posy, and it was only because Anthony was around, able to keep a closer eye on her, that she wasn't. He'd wanted them both home;

he'd said that was the place where he could look after them both best. But Carmel had refused; she wanted to stay a while to help at Oleander House and Posy had backed her up. They were, Anthony said, both cut from the same frustrating cloth, unable to see when they ought to step away from a situation for their own good. Posy had eventually won him round with the argument that the air in Astercombe was so much cleaner and better than in London that they'd recover much more quickly here. He didn't like it, but he could hardly dispute it.

'I'll go out to her in a minute.'

'And no walking back either,' Karen said.

'I expect Dad will give me a lift.'

'Do you want anything to drink?'

'Some water would be good please.'

Karen headed off and left Posy alone, listening to the sound of her own chest heave and struggle. Despite this, the lobby was now quiet and peaceful, with the tourist season winding down and fewer visitors, and she savoured the moment. There had been too much noise for her over the last few days, a constant flow of people treating her, fussing over her, worrying and checking on her. While it was appreciated and she understood it was only because they cared, she was glad of the break from it.

'I thought it was you...'

Posy opened her eyes. Lachlan was framed by the light of the doorway.

'I saw you from up the hill – I'd know that stride anywhere.'

'I'm not sure whether to take that as a compliment or not. Are you saying I've got a funny walk?'

'How are you?'

'I'm OK. I should say thank you, because that's down to you. And my mum…'

Posy squeezed her eyes tight again to shut out the memory, the ghost of fear that still plagued her. If he hadn't been there, if he hadn't found Carmel first…

'There are no words,' she continued. 'You'll never know what it means to me that you saved her.'

'I'm glad you're both alright,' he said, and he didn't repeat what Asa had told her about only finding Carmel by mistake. It didn't make any difference – Posy was certain that if he'd known Carmel was in there he'd have gone after her too. The intention was what really mattered, not the deed. He'd intended to save lives and he had.

'How are you?' she asked.

He raised his eyebrows slightly. 'I'm fine. Shouldn't I be?'

'I mean, did you get your grapes in?'

'We're almost there.'

'We?'

'Karen has given Pavla a few days to help. She says the hotel is quiet right now.'

'She's a good friend, isn't she?'

'They both are,' he said. 'And I realise I don't always deserve friends.'

Posy blinked. Was he being humble? Was he actually recognising what a pain in the arse he could be? Was this really happening or was she hallucinating from sheer exhaustion?

At this moment Karen came back. She stopped at the scene with a look that Posy could have sworn was a little too knowing.

'Lachlan…' she said. 'Come to talk?'

'Yes, I… Could I borrow Posy? It would only take a few minutes.'

Karen handed Posy the glass of water. 'Alright with you? I need to see Ray in the kitchen about something anyway.' She turned to Lachlan. 'If you want some privacy the bar's free.'

She left them and went back to the kitchen. Lachlan, like some Regency dandy, offered Posy his arm. Feeling vaguely bewildered, she stood and took it.

'I still tire easily,' she said apologetically.

'I'm hardly surprised at that. How's your mother doing?'

'She's much the same but she's alright. She's in the garden with my dad right now – you could go and see her; they'd both like to thank you in person.'

Lachlan looked desperately uncomfortable at this, but then, he'd hardly looked at ease since he'd arrived. As they walked slowly to the bar, Posy wondered whether being so nice was actually a huge effort for him. If it was, why bother? It wasn't like anyone ever expected it from him.

In the bar she took a seat, and before he joined her he went to the optics to pour himself a neat whisky. Aside from the blatant familiarity with Karen's alcohol supply, Posy resisted the urge to express any kind of surprise that he needed it, especially at this time of the morning. He downed it in one and slammed the glass onto the counter before coming to join her.

'I've been inexcusably rude to you over the weeks you've been in Astercombe and yet you've still been kind to me.'

'You haven't been that rude,' Posy said. She was feeling generous towards him right now, but he had been rude by anyone's standards.

'I owe you an explanation,' he said.

'You don't have to—'

'I do. If only because Karen will skin me alive if I don't.' He paused, seeming to steel himself. 'It all became clear the day you kissed me. I'd been denying it; I thought that if I kept you at arm's length…'

Posy frowned but she didn't interrupt.

'When I first saw you I couldn't believe my eyes,' he continued. 'You were so like her and it was a shock…' He glanced towards the bar. 'Do you mind if I…?'

'Be my guest.'

'Would you like one?'

'No… thanks.'

She was getting more and more confused by the minute. She watched him pour another drink and this time he brought it back to the table.

'I was like who?' she asked.

'My wife,' he said, and the words seemed to sting him as they came out. 'She died. About three years ago now.'

'Oh, Lachlan… I'm so sorry—'

He held up a hand. 'I don't want to dwell on that now; it's not why I'm here.'

Posy understood. It wasn't that his wife's death meant nothing, but that it still meant everything to him. He was still hurting, and she could only imagine how that felt. He looked at her now and she wondered if he was seeing his wife, whether simply seeing Posy caused him pain. The thought of it made her want to cry. She didn't want to be the cause of that even if she wasn't doing it deliberately.

'I'm not here for sympathy,' he said. 'I just want to tell you why…' He took a sip of his whisky. 'Why…'

Posy gave a slight smile. 'Why you were the rudest man alive?'

'I was that bad?'

'That's why you're here – didn't you just say that?'

'That day by the pool when we first met I was shocked, but I thought you were a passing tourist and I'd never see you again. I was shaken but I could have coped with that. But then we kept running into each other and it got harder and harder. I couldn't understand why you were so patient, why you kept trying with me, but you were so kind and it only made things worse. The day you got stung I forgot myself.'

'I don't understand.'

'I had feelings for you. But what if it wasn't you really? What if my feelings for you were just a way of bringing back Diana?'

It sounded a bit morbid and Posy tried hard to understand. 'But I'm not her.'

'I know that. When I look now you're not so much like her at all, but perhaps that's because I'm beginning to know you better and to see in you all the things that make you different from her. At first I thought I was falling for Diana all over again, that I only thought of you at night because I wanted you to be her. It was all too weird, even for me, and it was very unfair to get into a relationship based on that. I wanted to stay away from you, get you out of my head because it wasn't right. But now I know that's not it. I think about you because you're you. It's you I have these feelings for. And I understand, after the way I've treated you, if your feelings for me have changed.'

She paused, watching him wait for an answer. She didn't know what she ought to say, but she knew what she wanted to do. She needed a chance to think about all he'd told her but she didn't need any time at all to acknowledge that her feelings for him were still real and present. She kissed him.

'Does that answer your question?'

'I suppose it does,' he said, and for the first time since they'd met she saw a real smile. It was there and gone in just a second, chased away by his next thought. 'When I saw you go into the fire—'

Posy shook her head. 'It doesn't matter.'

'No, it does. I have to say it. I thought I was going to lose you too. I lost Diana because I was too weak; I couldn't save her and I thought I wasn't going to be able to save you.'

Posy took his hand. 'You don't have to tell me, but I feel it might help if you do. How did she... how did she die?'

He took a deep breath. 'We were cave diving in Thailand and she got lost. She couldn't find her way back. I tried to reach her but... It took two days for the rescue team to find her. They said there was no way I'd have been able to get in where she was...'

Posy felt an involuntary shudder take her. 'Cave diving?' Of all the ways she could have imagined Lachlan's wife dying, this wasn't one of them.

'She'd always wanted to do it; she was such an adrenaline junkie, an adventurous streak a mile wide. Parachuting, gliding, safaris... you name it, she wanted to do it. I was happy enough with a quieter life, but I loved seeing her light up at the thought of a new trip and I was always too willing to go along with her schemes, even when I had doubts.'

'Sounds as if she was pretty amazing.'

'She was reckless too. If someone told her not to do something it would be like nectar to a bee. The trainer beforehand had warned us to stick to the route, not to lose sight of the guide rope, but as usual

Diana couldn't help herself. She wanted to see how far she could push it – she always did. I often said it would be her undoing. There's some irony in that, I suppose.'

'It must be hard to talk about.'

'It is… though not so much with you. Funny, eh?'

'I'm sorry I look like her.'

'You're the same build, same hair, similar features, but your eyes… now that I look at you, your eyes are not the same at all. Kinder, softer, less… Diana was selfish. It was being selfish that took her away from me. She did what she wanted without considering the consequences for her or for me. She destroyed my life for the sake of a stupid rebellion, because she didn't want to do as the guides had told her. I'd always loved her wild side, especially when we first met; it was exciting. But now I see it for what it was. If she'd cared more she'd have tried harder not to die.'

'I'm sure she couldn't have foreseen that.'

'When you went into the fire I was so angry. I'd hoped you'd be different but at that moment you were just like her. But now I know you just wanted to save your mum and it makes you as selfless as Diana was selfish.'

Posy took a sip of her water. She ought to have been elated to hear all this and to find out that Lachlan had real feelings for her as she did for him, but it wasn't that simple. There was a lot of past to wade through, not to mention that she wasn't sure she could live with the idea of him looking at her and seeing his dead wife. He'd said he didn't do that now, but how could she ever be certain? How could she be sure that when he kissed her he wasn't really kissing Diana? How could she know it was her he was loving and not a stubborn memory? Was she prepared to be that?

'When are you going back to London?' he asked.

'I can take as much time as I need. Technically I'm not on the payroll at my new company yet so everything will simply be on hold until I join them.'

'So you might be in Astercombe for a while yet?'

'I'm not sure. I suppose I might. I'd like to help Giles and Sandra if I can too – at least until they have somewhere to live.'

'What are they going to do about that?'

'They have the spare building where... where my grandmother lived. I think they're planning to use that until the main house is repaired. But there's a lot to do clearing it out first and there's a lot to do at the big house trying to salvage what didn't get destroyed in the fire.'

'And when all that's done? Will you come back to Astercombe?'

'I'll be visiting all the time, I expect.'

'Oh.'

'You mean for more than visits? But my life... I have a great job waiting for me in London and I'd be mad not to take it.'

'Of course,' he said stiffly. 'I completely understand.'

'I don't have to go yet. We could spend some time together before that.'

'I don't think I can, not knowing you'll leave.'

'Right. Well, I suppose I can understand that.' She forced a bright smile. 'I'm glad we're friends now at least.'

'Yes, friends,' he said with a sombre nod. 'Perhaps that's for the best after all.'

Lachlan had left, making excuses about being busy. Posy suspected the reality was that he hadn't wanted to face Carmel and Anthony for another outpouring of thanks, and the fact was that if their heart-to-heart had left him half as emotionally washed-out as it had her then she was hardly surprised he was looking for a way to make his escape. For her part, she was desperate for some time alone to make sense of it all, but her mum and dad were expecting her and it would just have to wait.

Chapter Thirty-Three

'What about this?' Posy pointed to an old teak wardrobe.

'Ugh!' Sandra scowled at it. 'I've always hated that monstrosity.'

'I think it's nice,' Posy said. 'In a kitsch sort of way.'

'Well, if you can get it back to London you're welcome to have it.'

'I don't like it *that* much,' Posy replied with a smile.

Giles strolled over and looked at it. 'I can't imagine it's worth much to anyone. I don't think it's a quality piece or anything.'

'Might get a couple of quid at auction?' Posy suggested.

Giles opened it and peered inside. 'Doesn't look terribly sturdy either. I think the vibrations from the auctioneer's gavel would shake it apart.'

It was true that any kind of pressure would probably send the wardrobe rocking, but Posy still thought a few nails and a bit of glue to secure it would sort that out. But they had so much stuff to get rid of before they could make Philomena's flat habitable for Giles and Sandra while the big house was being repaired and she could see why they wouldn't want to waste their time on things like this.

'So it's going?' Posy asked.

'One hundred per cent,' Sandra said. 'I rather think it's a hotel for woodworm too. Even if I liked the hideous thing I wouldn't want to risk it infecting all our good furniture.'

'Right then!' Giles nodded at Lachlan, who was silently following the conversation. He'd come down to offer his services an hour earlier and was helping to move the heavy items. Posy knew there were probably a ton of things to be done at his place, but she also realised that this was his way of repaying them for their help with his harvest. For her part, she felt that he'd repaid that a million times over simply by being there on the terrible night of the fire, but he'd never acknowledge that, even if she said it to him. Not to mention that, despite what they'd agreed a few days before as they'd sat in Karen's bar, he seemed to be awfully keen to be where Posy was. He tried extra hard to be pleasant whenever she caught his eye (smiling, she was learning, was not an expression that came naturally to him and she wondered whether it ever had, even before his wife's death), and even Carmel had commented in passing on how often he seemed to be at Oleander House these days, though she put it down to neighbourly concern for a family who had almost lost everything. It could be that too, Posy reasoned, but secretly she hoped not. She and Lachlan had said they would be friends, but the idea that they might become more than that wouldn't leave her.

Posy's dad wandered in from another room. He had pieces of splintered wood in his hands and a guilty look on his face.

'I'm afraid we might have broken that old bureau,' he said.

Giles grimaced. 'You mean Asa did?'

'I think,' Anthony said ruefully, 'it might have been a joint effort. There was almost certainly a failure of communication on both our parts. I'm not sure if you were planning on keeping it, and I might be able to repair it if you want to, but I'm afraid that secret drawer is damaged and I don't know if that will repair.'

Giles looked at Sandra. 'Secret drawer?'

Sandra shrugged. 'How should I know?'

A moment later Asa ran in. 'Look at what just fell out of that secret compartment in the old bureau!'

'You mean the one you just broke?' Giles asked.

'Yes, but…' Asa held out an envelope. 'Isn't that… doesn't it look like Angelica's writing? It's addressed to Mother. Should we open it?'

Giles took it from him. It was sealed and mildew-stained, with the subtle bulk of a folded page inside. 'I think you're right about it being Angelica's handwriting. I don't know who else's it might be; it's certainly not Mother's…'

'Are you going to open it?' Posy asked.

Giles slid his thumb beneath the flap. It flicked open easily, the old adhesive rotten and barely sticky at all.

Posy watched with something like trepidation. Sandra looked more concerned, while Lachlan was observing with interest more than anything else. Posy couldn't say why, but she had the strangest feeling that what was in the envelope was going to concern her. Giles took two pages out and separated them, his eyes running over the first sheet. There were folds embedded into the paper and a small, grainy photo fell from the crease of the second. Sandra bent to pick it up and handed it to Giles with a silent question. Posy could see, even from her vantage point, that it was a photograph of a tiny baby.

'That looks like…' Carmel began, her mouth falling open as she stared at the picture. She looked at Posy. 'I have that same photo… it was the first photograph ever taken of you and it was given to us when we adopted you.'

Posy felt the earth shift beneath her as she stared at everyone in turn.

'It's me?' she croaked.

'The first page is a note from Angelica to Mother,' Giles said. 'It's dated just after you were born, Posy. She's telling her about having a child and giving her up for adoption and asking her to keep a letter to that child safe.'

'Do you think Mother ever replied?' Asa asked.

Giles shrugged, his eyes still fixed to the page. 'If she did, then I certainly didn't hear about it. I didn't even know this letter had ever arrived.'

'She must have hidden it deliberately,' Asa said. 'Why hide it? Why not just throw it away if it meant nothing to her?'

'I suppose it must have meant something to her,' Giles said. 'She made the request for us to find Posy as she was dying – perhaps she'd meant for this letter to be given to her too and something happened to prevent that.'

'You mean she forgot where she hid it or that she even had it?' Asa asked doubtfully.

Giles looked up. 'I suppose we'll never know now.' He turned to Posy and gave her the photo, along with the second letter. 'Perhaps you ought to have this,' he said. 'It's for you, after all.'

Posy took it and began to read.

Dear Baby,

I'm sorry I haven't named you, but it didn't seem like a good idea. I'm sure in time I would have come to love you, but as we're to part today, it doesn't seem like a good idea to let that happen either, and naming you wouldn't help. I'm sure your new mummy will be able to think of the perfect name for you, far nicer than I would.

I'm writing this letter and leaving it in the care of my own family in the hope that one day you'll be reunited with us. I'm not the woman to raise you, and if you knew me you'd understand why, but perhaps when we're both older we can have a relationship of sorts. For now, your grandma will take care of this and keep it safe for you, and when you come looking, perhaps she'll have it in her heart to forgive me for the terrible things I've done and we can all be together again. By then, you won't need me quite so much and the thought of being responsible for you won't be quite so terrifying. It sounds cruel and selfish, I know, and it probably is, but I do believe you'll have a happier life with someone far better equipped than me taking care of you. Giving you up is my way of loving you, and it's the best I can offer.

Your mother,
Angelica

Things had escalated in such a strange and rapid way that Posy suddenly felt as uncertain and afraid as she had that very first day when she'd arrived at Oleander House to meet her new family.

'Those are the words of someone very scared and confused,' Carmel said quietly to Posy. 'I believe there was a part of her that wanted to keep you.'

'We failed her,' Giles said. He turned to Posy. 'We failed both of you.'

'You didn't,' Sandra said. 'Philomena did. You must stop feeling guilty about things you had no control over. How could you have done anything about it? You were so young at sixteen – barely a man yourself – and Philomena chose to keep this from you. Everyone has had their lives changed and their beliefs challenged, but nobody in this room is to blame for a single thing that has happened.'

As Sandra spoke, Posy glanced to her side to see Lachlan regarding her with a curious look on his face. Did that go for him too? Had his beliefs been challenged? His life had been changed by the death of his wife, but now? He was here with them – something that had been unimaginable only a few weeks ago. How did he feel about that? Did he feel anything had changed?

Posy looked at the photo again. 'I still don't really know why she gave me away, why she never tried to contact me when she was alive, why she thought Philomena would forgive her eventually when she'd been so stubborn up to that point, why she entrusted this to her of all people when they weren't speaking. This letter doesn't really say anything. In a way it poses more questions than it answers.'

'But you're alright?' Giles asked. 'This hasn't changed anything with us?'

'Has it changed for you?' Posy asked quietly.

'Regardless of Mother's actions, we're still glad she relented at the end so that you could come into our lives – you and your wonderful family have made ours so much richer. I hope that doesn't change.'

Carmel wiped away a fresh tear. Posy saw Sandra do the same. She didn't know how to feel; there was only a numb kind of shock and a million questions racing around her head.

Posy took a deep breath. 'I'll take this rubbish bag out to the skip,' she announced in a dazed voice.

She grabbed the sack and hauled it outside. There was too much to think about, and in a strange way she didn't want to think about any of it. She was afraid she might not like the conclusions she'd come to. Over the last few months she'd fallen in love with Astercombe and Oleander House and with the family who had welcomed her. She almost wished they'd never found the damned letter.

With this running through her head, she hurled the rubbish sack into the skip they'd hired.

'You're strong for a city girl, aren't you?'

She spun around.

'Lachlan! You made me jump!'

'Sorry. I can't pretend to understand what just happened in there but I'm guessing it's something to do with why you're here at Oleander House.'

'It's a long story, but Asa and Giles are my uncles. Their sister, Angelica, is my mother. She gave me up for adoption.'

'That bit I guessed. I didn't even know they had a sister.'

'Older than Giles by four years and has been gone from Astercombe since before I was born. She's dead now. My grandmother – Philomena – had apparently been refusing to acknowledge my mother for many years… for lots of reasons that are just too painful and would take too long to go into right now…'

He nodded. 'You don't have to tell me anything you don't want to.'

'It's not that I don't want to, it's…'

'I understand. When you're ready. And how do you feel about all this in light of the letter?'

'Honestly?' Posy ran a hand through her fringe. 'I don't really know. I don't know how I'm supposed to feel about something like this – it's almost too huge to feel anything.'

'Aye, I know how that is. You know, if you ever want to talk to an impartial observer, I have a good ear.'

'Thank you. You're a good friend.'

'I don't know about that. I try…'

They were silent for a moment and Lachlan stared at her, seemingly labouring suddenly under the weight of something he wanted to say.

'Not that I don't appreciate you coming out to see if I was OK,' Posy began slowly, 'but is there something else you wanted?'

'Aye. Though I don't know how you'll feel when I tell you what it is, and given what we've just talked about I'm not sure this is the right time to say it.'

Posy frowned slightly. 'Lachlan… you can say anything to me – you must know that by now.'

'Anything? Are you sure of that?'

'Of course.'

He stepped forward and took her face in his hands.

'OK then… I want you.'

'Lachlan—'

'Please… let me finish. You just told me I can say anything; you can't change your mind now. Forget friends, forget that you'll be in London most of the time – I don't care. I want you and I'll do whatever it takes, whatever you ask and however we have to make it work. I know you feel the same so don't say it's not so.'

'You know I do, but—'

He kissed her, and she could feel the truth of his words in the passion that burned from his lips.

'No buts,' he said as they broke apart. 'Life's too short and who knows which way it will take us. I've spent too long hiding from it.'

'What's changed your mind?'

'I never changed my mind. I was respecting your wishes to stay as friends but now I realise you ask too much of me. I'm selfish; I can't stop thinking about you and it's driving me mad, but at least if I can think of you and have hope for something more then I can bear it better.'

'Lachlan… you know how I feel about you.'

'Then what's in our way?'

'Distance.'

'I'd come to London, as often as you want.'

Posy raised her eyebrows. 'All those people, all that noise – you'd hate it.'

'I'd do it for you.'

There was no doubt in her mind that she felt the same but could they make it work? They were different people, with different life paths and different ambitions, and they lived in different parts of the country. Was love enough, because even as the word popped into her head she realised it was true – she loved him. She'd loved him for some time, though she struggled to pick out the moment it had happened. Perhaps it had been when she'd opened her eyes as she'd lain on the cobbles of the courtyard of Oleander House as the fire burned and seen him above her, angry and terrified, and learned just what she meant to him.

'I'd like it if you came to London sometimes,' she said. 'And I suppose it wouldn't be a huge hardship for me to come here some weekends too.'

He smiled. It was a shame he didn't smile more often because it changed his whole face, made him look like a man who could look forward to the future instead of being trapped in his past. She could get used to a smile like that, and maybe, just maybe, if things went well, she'd get to see it a lot more often.

Chapter Thirty-Four

Spring had come early and with some force. Just as it had done a year before, the sun burned down with a heat that was more like July than May, the countryside around Astercombe bursting violently into life. Those twelve months had gone by in a blur, with harvests to save and homes and lives to rebuild, but things were more tranquil these days. Asa had made peace with Drew and had stayed firm on their separation. He'd even been flirting online with someone he'd met on another visit to London. Posy and Lachlan's relationship had gone from strength to strength, though she'd kept her job in the capital and they had to be content with visits when they could manage.

Today was one of those visits, and Posy had remarked on her arrival that she couldn't have chosen a more perfect weekend. They'd walked the lanes together, birds flitting tirelessly from tree to tree, bees hunting the first flowers of the season, the grass in the meadows lush and new and the hedgerows bright with spring foliage.

Now, Posy unbuttoned her blouse with a sort of careless flourish, her eyes fixed on Lachlan. 'Do you realise what today is?' she asked.

'The day they're due to finish renovating Oleander House,' he said as he pulled off his belt. 'I saw Giles before you arrived. He's going to get the holiday let built now that's done.'

'That's true – but it's not what I meant. There's something else.'

'Oh, God – is there? Have I forgotten something important? It's not your birthday, is it?'

Posy laughed. 'No. You know it isn't – that was last month. We had extra-special birthday sex – remember?'

'Oh, of course,' he said solemnly. 'Now I'm worried.'

Lachlan still had the capacity to take things far too seriously, though it was something she'd grown used to and something she'd even learned to love about him. He took things seriously because he cared about them.

'It's exactly one year to the day since I first saw your naked butt.'

His worried frown turned into a smile as he kicked off his boots. 'So it is.'

'God, you were angry that day,' she said. 'I've never seen anyone so angry.'

'I wasn't that bad.'

'You terrified me!'

'I didn't mean to.'

She kissed him lightly and then set her own shoes down next to his. 'I know that now. I really shouldn't have been walking where I wasn't meant to be.'

'That's true.'

She slapped his arm playfully. 'You're not supposed to agree with me!'

'But I'm glad you did,' he added. He pulled his shirt over his head and dropped it to the grass. 'Seems only fitting that we should be here today then.'

'Yes,' Posy agreed, undoing the clasp of her bra. 'I suppose it does. I wondered if you'd remembered and that's why you'd suggested it.'

'If only I were that romantic.' His trousers followed his shirt, landing in a heap.

'And the rest,' Posy said, eyeing his boxers.

'You first.'

'Surely you're not shy? It's not like I haven't seen it all before.'

'Aye, and in this very spot too a year ago to the day.'

'I've seen it since then,' she replied coyly.

He laughed. 'Not in cold water you haven't.'

She loved his laugh. She'd waited so long to hear it, and she knew she'd never get sick of it.

'You might never look at me in the same way again.'

She rolled down her knickers and kicked them off, letting the warm breeze and the sunshine kiss her skin. The air was filled with the scents of the wildflowers that were scattered over the nearby meadows and blossoms bursting from trees. 'Oh, I don't think the cold water did you any disservice this time last year.'

'Thank you,' he said.

A moment later they were both naked, hand in hand.

'It suddenly looks a lot colder,' Posy said, eyeing the pool doubtfully.

'Man up.'

'Easy for you to say.'

'Don't think about it too much – it'll be fine once we're in.'

'Also easy for you to say – you do this all the time.'

'First time this year it's been warm enough.'

'Hmm. You know most blokes take their girlfriends out for lunch when they come to visit…'

'I'm not most blokes.'

'I know that.'

'It's why you love me.'

'I can't deny that either, even though it's galling to admit.'

'When are you going to stay in Astercombe for good?'

She looked up at him. 'When I have a good reason.'

'I'm not a good reason?'

'I haven't decided yet.'

He began to lead her to the old wooden jetty that stuck out over the water.

'How can I change your mind?' he asked.

'You can't change what isn't made up.'

'You're teasing me.'

'I'm glad you noticed.'

'I love you.'

'I love you too.'

'So marry me.'

They were at the water's edge. She turned to him and smiled, and she didn't miss a beat.

'OK,' she said. 'Why not?'

Then they leapt into the lake together.

A Letter from Tilly

I want to say a huge thank you for choosing to read *The Little Orchard on the Lane*. If you did enjoy it, and want to keep up to date with all my latest releases, just sign up at the following link. Your email address will never be shared and you can unsubscribe at any time.

www.bookouture.com/tilly-tennant

I'm so excited to share *The Little Orchard on the Lane* with you. I worked on it largely through the second half of 2020, a year that has sorely tried everyone's patience, but it proved to be a welcome distraction and a lovely escape from the miserable news reports. I hope it proves to be the same for my lovely readers. Let's face it, we all deserve an escape every now and again!

I hope you loved *The Little Orchard on the Lane* and if you did I would be very grateful if you could write a review. I'd love to hear what you think, and it makes such a difference helping new readers to discover one of my books for the first time.

I love hearing from my readers – you can get in touch on my Facebook page, through Twitter, Goodreads or my website.

Thanks,
Tilly

tillytennant
@TillyTenWriter
www.tillytennant.com

Acknowledgements

I say this every time I come to write an author acknowledgement for a new book, but it's true: the list of people who have offered help and encouragement on my writing journey so far really is endless and it would take a novel in itself to mention them all. I'd try to list everyone here regardless, but I know that I'd fail miserably and miss out someone who is really very important. I just want to say that my heartfelt gratitude goes out to each and every one of you, whose involvement, whether small or large, has been invaluable and appreciated more than I can express.

It goes without saying that my family bear the brunt of my authorly mood swings, but when the dust has settled I'll always appreciate their love, patience and support. Unless you've spent the last twelve months under a rock, you'll be aware that 2020 has been a strange and difficult year for pretty much everyone on the planet and I, like so many other people, have spent much of it struggling to keep working while in a small house surrounded twenty-four/seven by my family who all had their own things to do too. They've been truly amazing, however – as supportive and patient as ever, willing to give me space and time to do what I needed to, even when it meant they had to sacrifice space and time of their own.

I also want to mention the many good friends I have made and kept since Staffordshire University. It's been ten years since I graduated with a degree in English and creative writing but hardly a day goes by when I don't think fondly of my time there. I'd also like to shout out to Storm Constantine of Immanion Press, who gave me the opportunity to see my very first book in print. Nowadays, I have to thank the remarkable team at Bookouture for their continued support, patience and amazing publishing flair, particularly Lydia Vassar-Smith – my incredible and long-suffering editor – Kim Nash, Noelle Holten, Sarah Hardy, Peta Nightingale, Alexandra Holmes, Cara Chimirri and Jessie Botterill. I know I'll have forgotten someone else at Bookouture who I ought to be thanking, but I hope they'll forgive me. I hope 2021 is the year of people being able to cram into a bar once again to celebrate, so that our annual publisher bash can return and we can all enjoy a drink together! Their belief, able assistance and encouragement mean the world to me. I truly believe I have the best team an author could ask for.

My friend, Kath Hickton, always gets an honourable mention for putting up with me since primary school, and Louise Coquio deserves a medal for getting me through university and suffering me ever since – likewise her lovely family. I also have to thank Mel Sherratt, who is as generous with her time and advice as she is talented, someone who is always there to cheer on her fellow authors. She did so much to help me in the early days of my career that I don't think I'll ever be able to thank her as much as she deserves.

I'd also like to shout out to Holly Martin, Tracy Bloom, Emma Davies, Jack Croxall, Carol Wyer, Clare Davidson, Angie Marsons, Sue Watson and Jaimie Admans: not only brilliant authors in their own right but hugely supportive of others. My Bookouture colleagues are all incredible of course, unfailing and generous in their support of fellow authors – life would be a lot duller without the gang! I have to thank all the brilliant and dedicated book bloggers (there are so many of you, but you know who you are!) and readers, and anyone else who has championed my work, reviewed it, shared it or simply told me that they liked it. Every one of those actions is priceless and you are all very special people. Some of you I am even proud to call friends now – and I'm looking at you in particular, Kerry Ann Parsons and Steph Lawrence!

Last but not least, I'd like to give a special mention to my lovely agent, Madeleine Milburn, and the team at the Madeleine Milburn Literary, TV & Film Agency, who always have my back.